William Shakespeare

HENRY VI, PART II

Edited with a Commentary by Norman Sanders
Introduced by Michael Taylor
The Play in Performance by Rebecca Brown

PENGUIN BOOKS

PENGUIN BOOKS

Published by the Penguin Group
Penguin Books Ltd, 80 Strand, London WC2R ORL, England
Penguin Group (USA) Inc., 375 Hudson Street, New York, New York 10014, USA
Penguin Group (Canada), 10 Alcorn Avenue, Toronto, Ontario, Canada M4V 3B2
(a division of Pearson Penguin Canada Inc.)
Penguin Ireland, 25 St Stephen's Green, Dublin 2, Ireland (a division of Penguin Books Ltd)
Penguin Group (Australia), 250 Camberwell Road, Camberwell, Victoria 3124, Australia
(a division of Pearson Australia Group Pty Ltd)
Penguin Books India Pvt Ltd, 11 Community Centre, Panchsheel Park, New Delhi – 110 017, India
Penguin Group (NZ), cnr Airborne and Rosedale Roads, Albany, Auckland 1310, New Zealand
(a division of Pearson New Zealand Ltd)
Penguin Books (South Africa) (Pty) Ltd, 24 Sturdee Avenue, Rosebank 2196, South Africa

Penguin Books Ltd, Registered Offices: 80 Strand, London WC2R ORL, England

www.penguin.com

This edition first published in Penguin Books 1981
Reissued in the Penguin Shakespeare series 2005

2

Account of the Text and Commentary copyright © Norman Sanders, 1981
General Introduction and Chronology copyright © Stanley Wells, 2005
Introduction and Further Reading copyright © Michael Taylor, 2005
The Play in Performance copyright © Rebecca Brown, 2005

All rights reserved

The moral right of the editors has been asserted

Set in 11.5/12.5 PostScript Monotype Fournier
Typeset by Palimpsest Book Production Limited, Polmont, Stirlingshire
Printed in England by Clays Ltd, St Ives plc

Contents

General Introduction

Every play by Shakespeare is unique. This is part of his greatness. A restless and indefatigable experimenter, he moved with a rare amalgamation of artistic integrity and dedicated professionalism from one kind of drama to another. Never shackled by convention, he offered his actors the alternation between serious and comic modes from play to play, and often also within the plays themselves, that the repertory system within which he worked demanded, and which provided an invaluable stimulus to his imagination. Introductions to individual works in this series attempt to define their individuality. But there are common factors that underpin Shakespeare's career.

Nothing in his heredity offers clues to the origins of his genius. His upbringing in Stratford-upon-Avon, where he was born in 1564, was unexceptional. His mother, born Mary Arden, came from a prosperous farming family. Her father chose her as his executor over her eight sisters and his four stepchildren when she was only in her late teens, which suggests that she was of more than average practical ability. Her husband John, a glover, apparently unable to write, was nevertheless a capable businessman and loyal townsfellow, who seems to have fallen on relatively hard times in later life. He would have been brought up as a Catholic, and may have retained

Catholic sympathies, but his son subscribed publicly to Anglicanism throughout his life.

The most important formative influence on Shakespeare was his school. As the son of an alderman who became bailiff (or mayor) in 1568, he had the right to attend the town's grammar school. Here he would have received an education grounded in classical rhetoric and oratory, studying authors such as Ovid, Cicero and Quintilian, and would have been required to read, speak, write and even think in Latin from his early years. This classical education permeates Shakespeare's work from the beginning to the end of his career. It is apparent in the self-conscious classicism of plays of the early 1590s such as the tragedy of *Titus Andronicus*, *The Comedy of Errors*, and the narrative poems *Venus and Adonis* (1592–3) and *The Rape of Lucrece* (1593–4), and is still evident in his latest plays, informing the dream visions of *Pericles* and *Cymbeline* and the masque in *The Tempest*, written between 1607 and 1611. It inflects his literary style throughout his career. In his earliest writings the verse, based on the ten-syllabled, five-beat iambic pentameter, is highly patterned. Rhetorical devices deriving from classical literature, such as alliteration and antithesis, extended similes and elaborate wordplay, abound. Often, as in *Love's Labour's Lost* and *A Midsummer Night's Dream*, he uses rhyming patterns associated with lyric poetry, each line self-contained in sense, the prose as well as the verse employing elaborate figures of speech. Writing at a time of linguistic ferment, Shakespeare frequently imports Latinisms into English, coining words such as abstemious, addiction, incarnadine and adjunct. He was also heavily influenced by the eloquent translations of the Bible in both the Bishops' and the Geneva versions. As his experience grows, his verse and prose become more supple, the patterning less apparent, more ready to accommodate the rhythms of ordinary speech, more colloquial in diction, as in the speeches of the Nurse in *Romeo and Juliet*, the characterful prose of Falstaff and Hamlet's soliloquies. The effect is of increasing psychological realism, reaching its greatest heights in *Hamlet*, *Othello*, *King Lear*, *Macbeth* and *Antony and Cleopatra*. Gradually he discovered ways of adapting the regular beat of the pentameter to make it an infinitely flexible instrument for matching thought with feeling. Towards the end of his career, in plays such as *The Winter's Tale*, *Cymbeline* and *The Tempest*, he adopts a more highly mannered style, in keeping with the more overtly symbolical and emblematical mode in which he is writing.

So far as we know, Shakespeare lived in Stratford till after his marriage to Anne Hathaway, eight years his senior, in 1582. They had three children: a daughter, Susanna, born in 1583 within six months of their marriage, and twins, Hamnet and Judith, born in 1585. The next seven years of Shakespeare's life are virtually a blank. Theories that he may have been, for instance, a schoolmaster, or a lawyer, or a soldier, or a sailor, lack evidence to support them. The first reference to him in print, in Robert Greene's pamphlet *Greene's Groatsworth of Wit* of 1592, parodies a line from *Henry VI, Part III*, implying that Shakespeare was already an established playwright. It seems likely that at some unknown point after the birth of his twins he joined a theatre company and gained experience as both actor and writer in the provinces and London. The London theatres closed because of plague in 1593 and 1594; and during these years, perhaps recognizing the need for an alternative career, he wrote and published the narrative poems *Venus and Adonis* and *The Rape of Lucrece*. These are the only works we can be certain that Shakespeare himself was responsible for putting into print. Each bears the author's dedication to Henry Wriothesley, Earl of Southampton (1573–1624), the second in warmer terms than the first. Southampton, younger than Shakespeare by ten years, is the only person to whom he personally dedicated works. The Earl may have been a close friend, perhaps even the beautiful and adored young man whom Shakespeare celebrates in his *Sonnets*.

The resumption of playing after the plague years saw the founding of the Lord Chamberlain's Men, a company to which Shakespeare was to belong for the rest of his career, as actor, shareholder and playwright. No other dramatist of the period had so stable a relationship with a single company. Shakespeare knew the actors for whom he was writing and the conditions in which they performed. The permanent company was made up of around twelve to fourteen players, but one actor often played more than one role in a play and additional actors were hired as needed. Led by the tragedian Richard Burbage (1568–1619) and, initially, the comic actor Will Kemp (d. 1603), they rapidly achieved a high reputation, and when King James I succeeded Queen Elizabeth I in 1603 they were renamed as the King's Men. All the women's parts were played by boys; there is no evidence that any female role was ever played by a male actor over the age of about eighteen. Shakespeare had enough confidence in his boys to write for them long and demanding roles such as Rosalind (who, like other heroines of the romantic comedies, is disguised as a boy for much of the action) in *As You Like It*, Lady Macbeth and Cleopatra. But there are far more fathers than mothers, sons than daughters, in his plays, few if any of which require more than the company's normal complement of three or four boys.

The company played primarily in London's public playhouses – there were almost none that we know of in the rest of the country – initially in the Theatre, built in Shoreditch in 1576, and from 1599 in the Globe, on Bankside. These were wooden, more or less circular structures, open to the air, with a thrust stage surmounted by a canopy and jutting into the area where spectators who paid one penny stood, and surrounded by galleries where it was possible to be seated on payment of an additional penny. Though properties such as cauldrons, stocks, artificial trees or beds could indicate locality, there was no representational scenery. Sound effects such as flourishes of trumpets, music both martial and amorous, and accompaniments to songs were provided by the company's musicians. Actors entered through doors in the back wall of the stage. Above it was a balconied area that could represent the walls of a town (as in *King John*), or a castle (as in *Richard II*), and indeed a balcony (as in *Romeo and Juliet*). In 1609 the company also acquired the use of the Blackfriars, a smaller, indoor theatre to which admission was more expensive, and which permitted the use of more spectacular stage effects such as the descent of Jupiter on an eagle in *Cymbeline* and of goddesses in *The Tempest*. And they would frequently perform before the court in royal residences and, on their regular tours into the provinces, in non-theatrical spaces such as inns, guildhalls and the great halls of country houses.

Early in his career Shakespeare may have worked in collaboration, perhaps with Thomas Nashe (1567–c. 1601) in *Henry VI, Part I* and with George Peele (1556–96) in *Titus Andronicus*. And towards the end he collaborated with George Wilkins (*fl.* 1604–8) in *Pericles*, and with his younger colleagues Thomas Middleton (1580–1627), in *Timon of Athens*, and John Fletcher (1579–1625), in *Henry*

VIII, *The Two Noble Kinsmen* and the lost play *Cardenio*. Shakespeare's output dwindled in his last years, and he died in 1616 in Stratford, where he owned a fine house, New Place, and much land. His only son had died at the age of eleven, in 1596, and his last descendant died in 1670. New Place was destroyed in the eighteenth century but the other Stratford houses associated with his life are maintained and displayed to the public by the Shakespeare Birthplace Trust.

One of the most remarkable features of Shakespeare's plays is their intellectual and emotional scope. They span a great range from the lightest of comedies, such as *The Two Gentlemen of Verona* and *The Comedy of Errors*, to the profoundest of tragedies, such as *King Lear* and *Macbeth*. He maintained an output of around two plays a year, ringing the changes between comic and serious. All his comedies have serious elements: Shylock, in *The Merchant of Venice*, almost reaches tragic dimensions, and *Measure for Measure* is profoundly serious in its examination of moral problems. Equally, none of his tragedies is without humour: Hamlet is as witty as any of his comic heroes, *Macbeth* has its Porter, and *King Lear* its Fool. His greatest comic character, Falstaff, inhabits the history plays and *Henry V* ends with a marriage, while *Henry VI, Part III*, *Richard II* and *Richard III* culminate in the tragic deaths of their protagonists.

Although in performance Shakespeare's characters can give the impression of a superabundant reality, he is not a naturalistic dramatist. None of his plays is explicitly set in his own time. The action of few of them (except for the English histories) is set even partly in England (exceptions are *The Merry Wives of Windsor* and the Induction to *The Taming of the Shrew*). Italy is his favoured location. Most of his principal story-lines derive from printed writings; but the structuring and translation of these narratives into dramatic terms is Shakespeare's own, and he invents much additional material. Most of the plays contain elements of myth and legend, and many derive from ancient or more recent history or from romantic tales of ancient times and faraway places. All reflect his reading, often in close detail. Holinshed's *Chronicles* (1577, revised 1587), a great compendium of English, Scottish and Irish history, provided material for his English history plays. The *Lives of the Noble Grecians and Romans* by the Greek writer Plutarch, finely translated into English from the French by Sir Thomas North in 1579, provided much of the narrative material, and also a mass of verbal detail, for his plays about Roman history. Some plays are closely based on shorter individual works: *As You Like It*, for instance, on the novel *Rosalynde* (1590) by his near-contemporary Thomas Lodge (1558–1625), *The Winter's Tale* on *Pandosto* (1588) by his old rival Robert Greene (1558–92) and *Othello* on a story by the Italian Giraldi Cinthio (1504–73). And the language of his plays is permeated by the Bible, the Book of Common Prayer and the proverbial sayings of his day.

Shakespeare was popular with his contemporaries, but his commitment to the theatre and to the plays in performance is demonstrated by the fact that only about half of his plays appeared in print in his lifetime, in slim paperback volumes known as quartos, so called because they were made from printers' sheets folded twice to form four leaves (eight pages). None of them shows any sign that he was involved in their publication. For him, performance was the primary means of publication. The most frequently reprinted of his works were the non-dramatic poems – the erotic *Venus and Adonis* and the more moralistic *The Rape of Lucrece*. The *Sonnets*, which appeared in 1609, under his name but possibly without his consent, were less successful, perhaps because the vogue for sonnet sequences, which peaked in the 1590s, had passed by then. They were not reprinted until 1640, and then only in garbled form along with poems by other writers. Happily, in 1623, seven years after he died, his colleagues John Heminges (1556–1630) and Henry Condell (d. 1627) published his collected plays, including eighteen that had not previously appeared in print, in the first Folio, whose name derives from the fact that the printers' sheets were folded only once to produce two leaves (four pages). Some of the quarto editions are badly printed, and the fact that some plays exist in two, or even three, early versions creates problems for editors. These are discussed in the Account of the Text in each volume of this series.

Shakespeare's plays continued in the repertoire until the Puritans closed the theatres in 1642. When performances resumed after the Restoration of the monarchy in 1660 many of the plays were not to the taste of the times, especially because their mingling of genres and failure to meet the requirements of poetic justice offended against the dictates of neoclassicism. Some, such as *The Tempest* (changed by John Dryden and William Davenant in 1667 to suit contemporary taste), *King Lear* (to which Nahum Tate gave a happy ending in 1681) and *Richard III* (heavily adapted by Colley Cibber in 1700 as a vehicle for his own talents), were extensively rewritten; others fell into neglect. Slowly they regained their place in the repertoire, and they continued to be reprinted, but it was not until the great actor David Garrick (1717–79) organized a spectacular jubilee in Stratford in 1769 that Shakespeare began to be regarded as a transcendental genius. Garrick's idolatry prefigured the enthusiasm of critics such as Samuel Taylor Coleridge (1772–1834) and William Hazlitt (1778–1830). Gradually Shakespeare's reputation spread abroad, to Germany, America, France and to other European countries.

During the nineteenth century, though the plays were generally still performed in heavily adapted or abbreviated versions, a large body of scholarship and criticism began to amass. Partly as a result of a general swing in education away from the teaching of Greek and Roman texts and towards literature written in English, Shakespeare became the object of intensive study in schools and universities. In the theatre, important turning points were the work in England of two theatre directors, William Poel (1852–1934) and his disciple Harley Granville-Barker (1877–1946), who showed that the application of knowledge, some of it newly acquired, of early staging conditions to performance of the plays could render the original texts viable in terms of the modern theatre. During the twentieth century appreciation of Shakespeare's work, encouraged by the availability of audio, film and video versions of the plays, spread around the world to such an extent that he can now be claimed as a global author.

The influence of Shakespeare's works permeates the English language. Phrases from his plays and poems – 'a tower of strength', 'green-eyed jealousy', 'a foregone conclusion' – are on the lips of people who may never have read him. They have inspired composers of songs, orchestral music and operas; painters and sculptors; poets, novelists and film-makers. Allusions to him appear in pop songs, in advertisements and in television shows. Some of his characters – Romeo and Juliet, Falstaff, Shylock and Hamlet – have acquired mythic status. He is valued for his humanity, his psychological insight, his wit and humour, his lyricism, his mastery of language, his ability to excite, surprise, move and, in the widest sense of the word, entertain audiences. He is the greatest of poets, but he is essentially a dramatic poet. Though his plays have much to offer to readers, they exist fully only in performance. In these volumes we offer individual introductions, notes on language and on specific points of the text, suggestions for further reading and information about how each work has been edited. In addition we include accounts of the ways in which successive generations of interpreters and audiences have responded to challenges and rewards offered by the plays. The Penguin Shakespeare series aspires to remove obstacles to understanding and to make pleasurable the reading of the work of the man who has done more than most to make us understand what it is to be human.

Stanley Wells

The Chronology of
Shakespeare's Works

A few of Shakespeare's writings can be fairly precisely dated. An allusion to the Earl of Essex in the chorus to Act V of *Henry V*, for instance, could only have been written in 1599. But for many of the plays we have only vague information, such as the date of publication, which may have occurred long after composition, the date of a performance, which may not have been the first, or a list in Francis Meres's book *Palladis Tamia*, published in 1598, which tells us only that the plays listed there must have been written by that year. The chronology of the early plays is particularly difficult to establish. Not everyone would agree that the first part of *Henry VI* was written after the third, for instance, or *Romeo and Juliet* before *A Midsummer Night's Dream*. The following table is based on the 'Canon and Chronology' section in *William Shakespeare: A Textual Companion*, by Stanley Wells and Gary Taylor, with John Jowett and William Montgomery (1987), where more detailed information and discussion may be found.

The Two Gentlemen of Verona	1590–91
The Taming of the Shrew	1590–91
Henry VI, Part II	1591
Henry VI, Part III	1591

Introduction

There may be no better introduction to Shakespeare's genius as a writer of history plays than *Henry VI, Part II*. It is notably superior to *Part I* and is unmatched in literary and theatrical power until the culminating play of the series, *Richard III*. It is the second of four connected plays, a tetralogy, dealing ambitiously with two enormous subjects: the so-called Hundred Years War between the English and the French (1337–1453), and the civil war in England between the Houses of York and Lancaster, known popularly as the Wars of the Roses, which came to an end at the battle of Bosworth in 1485 with the death of Richard III. *Part I* deals largely with the wars in France, though we are never allowed to forget that the loss of France is due in the first place to the self-destructive rivalries in England among the English nobility, as the First Messenger tells us in the play's opening scene: 'here you maintain several factions; . . . whilst a field should be dispatched and fought' (I.1.71–2). *Part II* focuses on the beginnings of the civil war in England between these several factions, the enormity of whose complicated antagonisms frequently produces a kind of despairing personification such as Gloucester's:

> Virtue is choked with foul ambition,
> And charity chased hence by rancour's hand;
> Foul subornation is predominant,
> And equity exiled your highness' land. (III.1.143–6)

The signatories of rancour's hand, with the significant exception of Henry himself, are virtually all the major and minor characters of the play, operating in a mélange of mutual hatred.

BEGINNINGS

These are the opening lines of *Henry VI, Part II*:

> As by your high imperial majesty
> I had in charge at my depart for France,
> As procurator to your excellence,
> To marry Princess Margaret for your grace;
> So, in the famous ancient city Tours,
> In presence of the Kings of France and Sicil,
> The Dukes of Orleans, Calaber, Bretagne, and Alençon,
> Seven earls, twelve barons, and twenty reverend bishops,
> I have performed my task and was espoused . . . (I.1.1–9)

Spoken by Suffolk, the passage confirms the importance of *Part II* in the play's title by establishing a connecting link with the play that immediately preceded it, *Henry VI, Part I*. At the end of *Part I* we watched Suffolk in France woo Margaret, daughter of Reignier, Duke of Anjou, ostensibly on behalf of his king, the young and callow Henry VI, but really on behalf of his own sexual and political ambition as the play's last lines make chillingly

clear: 'Margaret shall now be Queen, and rule the King; |
But I will rule both her, the King, and realm' (V.5.107–8).
In similar fashion, the last line of *Part II* looks forward
just as chillingly to *Henry VI, Part III* with Warwick's
prediction: 'And more such days as these to us befall!'
(V.3.33). *Henry VI, Part II*, then, as its opening and closing
lines make clear, is one among a group of plays that seem
to have been composed in serial fashion with each play
looking before and after until the cathartic confrontation
between Richmond and Richard at the close of the fourth
and finest play of the series, *Richard III*.

Or so it would seem. In fact the situation is murkier
than the plays' sequence in the 1623 Folio would have us
believe. The consensus of critical opinion has long held
that for complicated reasons *Henry VI, Part I* was in all
likelihood written after *Henry VI, Part III* rather than
before *Henry VI, Part II*. Counter-intuitively, then, we
are asked to think of these opening nine lines as beginning not only *Henry VI, Part II* but also Shakespeare's
career as a writer of history plays, and, given the equally
murky situation with the dating of all of Shakespeare's
early work, as probably the first lines of drama that
Shakespeare ever wrote. The case for those still convinced
of the Folio's authority in this matter, however, continues
to produce the occasional advocate: in *Shakespeare's Serial
History Plays* (2002), for instance, Nicholas Grene
recharges his side of the debate with a sturdy defence of
Henry VI, Part I as the first to be written of a planned
tetralogy of plays, launching a hugely ambitious response
on Shakespeare's part to the success of Christopher
Marlowe's two-part play *Tamburlaine the Great* (1587–8).
But we have to remember that *Henry VI, Part II* first
appeared in print in a quarto version called *The First
Part of the Contention betwixt the Two Famous Houses*

of York and Lancaster in 1594, and that *Henry VI, Part III* first appeared in print in 1595 in an octavo version entitled *The True Tragedy of Richard Duke of York*. *Henry VI, Part I* didn't appear in print until the 1623 Folio, published seven years after Shakespeare's death. So at one time *Henry VI, Part II* was not the second part of anything but the *First Part* of what might have been designed originally as a two-part play, perhaps a more likely response to Marlowe's ground-breaking two-part *Tamburlaine*.

If we return for a moment to the opening lines of *Henry VI, Part II*, we might see them as contributing in their own way to the debate about the uncertainty of these beginnings. If these nine lines were the first ones penned by Shakespeare as a dramatist, would he have been proud of them? They certainly don't announce his arrival on the London stage as perhaps the greatest writer of history plays the world has ever seen with any degree of rhetorical splendour, despite the enumeration of all those dukes, barons, and reverend bishops who are reported as witnessing Suffolk's fatal success with Margaret. The best that might be said of them in their 'as by . . . as . . . so' sequence is that they do the job more or less competently of linking *Part II* with *Part I*. They do not sound like the beginning of a famous beginning. If we consider the Marlovian opening lines of *Henry VI, Part I*, on the other hand, a case can surely be made for their self-conscious sense of beginning something important:

> Hung be the heavens with black, yield day to night!
> Comets, importing change of times and states,
> Brandish your crystal tresses in the sky,
> And with them scourge the bad revolting stars
> That have consented unto Henry's death –
> King Henry the Fifth, too famous to live long! (I.i.1–6)

This is a passage brandishing its own crystal tresses, we might say, importing a change in the time and state of the history play as much as in this play's history, and suitably portentous and emphatic for the opening of such an epic endeavour. And so we have a strong verb in the imperative mood – 'Hung be' – to kickstart *Part I*, not a couple of commonplace adverbial conjunctions – *Part II*'s 'As by' – whose main verb is then delayed for another eight lines.

It is instructive to consider the case of the only other play in the canon to begin with an 'As', *As You Like It*, which is also the only play in the canon to have an 'as' clause as its title. The play begins with Orlando's exposition in prose: 'As I remember, Adam, it was upon this fashion bequeathed me by will, but poor a thousand crowns, and, as thou sayest, . . .' (I.i.1–3). The second and parenthetical 'as' clause, 'as thou sayest', tells us that Orlando and Adam have entered in mid conversation and it helps to maintain the suitably informal, conversational tone that the play's opening subordinate clause establishes. We are not in mid conversation at the opening of *Henry VI, Part II*, nor are we in prose, nothing so casual, although we might just conceivably be present at a clumsy early attempt at the gravity of an epic or extended simile in an anticipation of Milton in the famous opening lines of *Paradise Lost*: 'Of Man's First disobedience, and the Fruit | Of that Forbidden Tree'.

Be that as it may, the lameness of *Part II*'s opening lines is something of a wayward introduction to the intensity, ferocity and wit of the play that follows. But they do suggest how complicated the play's background is. To pick one's way through all the 'dire division' (*Richard III*, V.5.28) of the 'furious peers' (*Henry VI, Part II*, II.1.33), as Henry calls them, not to mention those of the

lesser characters, is almost as difficult as to follow the
genealogical justifications for the candidates to England's
throne, including the one for Henry VI himself, that
crop up in many of Shakespeare's history plays, most
notoriously in *Henry V* (I.2.33–95). Suffice it to say with
Gloucester that 'these days are dangerous' (III.1.142)
or to agree with Henry's lament, 'what mischiefs work
the wicked ones' (II.1.181), or to acknowledge with
Gloucester again that 'Rancour will out' (I.1.140). 'Ancient
bickerings' (I.1.142), and some not so ancient, dominate
the proceedings and draw into their squabbling discourse
the likes of Gloucester, 'the haughty Protector', as
Margaret calls him, Cardinal Beaufort, 'The imperious
churchman', and 'grumbling York' (I.3.66, 67, 68). Nearly
all the play's characters are at each other's throats verbally
and literally, and as the play continues words and action
become more extreme. The closer we get to the killing
fields of *Henry VI, Part III* the more dire the pronounce-
ments and the more cruel the action. There are six deaths
in *Henry VI, Part I*, thirteen in *Henry VI, Part II*, with
an emphasis on the gruesome and grotesque: decapi-
tated bodies fall, heads roll, sometimes to be picked up
and fondled or paraded on the ends of poles. By Act
V, scene 2 'dead [dying] men's cries do fill the empty
air' (V.2.4). All is 'Shame and confusion!' (31). For
Young Clifford war is the 'son of hell' (33), and he says
this before he sees his father's corpse who died in 'ruffian
battle' (49). He predicts that from now on hearts will
be 'stony' (51). As for himself, 'tears virginal | Shall
be to me even as the dew to fire' (52–3), beauty 'Shall
to my flaming wrath be oil and flax' (55); he will cut
infants into 'gobbets' (58). Like many others, particularly in *Part II*, 'In cruelty will I seek out my fame'
(60).

The play draws its verbal energy from the intensifying ferocity of its action. Its characters often speak of each other as though they were animals in some medieval bestiary. A powerful and cunning example of this is Act III, scene 1, one of the two longest in the play, which pits Gloucester against his accusers, who throughout the scene substitute invective for evidence against him. The talk is all of curs, lions, foxes, lambs, ravens, wolves and dogs. When Henry compares Gloucester to the 'sucking lamb or harmless dove' (III.1.71) Margaret immediately changes these benign creatures to the 'hateful raven' (76) and the ravenous wolf. For Suffolk, Gloucester is more fox than wolf, because he is as crafty as he is savage: 'The fox barks not when he would steal the lamb' (55); and later he says, 'were't not madness then | To make the fox surveyor of the fold?' (252–3). His mistress, Margaret, acknowledges that Gloucester may seem lamb-like, but 'Who cannot steal a shape that means deceit?' (79). York joins in the chorus comparing Gloucester to 'an empty [starving] eagle' guarding the 'chicken' (Henry) from 'a hungry kite' (248, 249). Even Gloucester cannot resist his accusers' language, thinking of himself, for instance, as an ill-treated dog: '"A staff is quickly found to beat a dog"' (171).

In this scene Shakespeare masterfully conveys his characters' frenzied surrender to the irrational. They are so caught up in the imaginary animal world they have constructed that all questions of legal procedure, of the reality of guilt and offence, of what really happened (if anything did), of rules of evidence (a notion to which Gloucester foolishly clings), drop away to be replaced by what seem to them self-evident laws of nature. And so for Suffolk it's a good idea to kill Gloucester not so much because he's done anything (although he might have) but because he is a fox: 'let him die, in that he is a fox, | By nature proved an enemy to the flock' (III.1.257–8). They should move against him 'Before his chaps be stained with crimson blood' (259; the crimson blood, that is, of the lamb-like Henry). The fox's disposition 'by nature proved' becomes in Gloucester's case 'proved by reasons' (260), though the 'reasons' are no more than the line of unproven, unprovable analogies with animal behaviour that dominate his opponents' thinking. Gloucester for them is an inherently vicious animal, and should be put down to prevent him from turning on them: 'So he be dead; for that is good deceit | Which mates him first that first intends deceit' (264–5). The hollowness of Suffolk's claim is made clear by his earlier admission that 'yet we have but trivial argument, | More than mistrust, that shows him worthy death' (241–2). Its absurdity is crowned by Suffolk's grandiose claim that 'the deed is meritorious' (270), a word that describes an action especially deserving of reward from God.

And so it goes. York in soliloquy speaks of himself as the 'starvèd snake' (III.1.343) who 'will sting your hearts' (344). When Henry comes out of his swoon he thinks York sings 'a raven's note' (III.2.40), his touch is 'as a serpent's sting' (47), his sight that of the 'basilisk' (52). For Margaret England is a 'scorpion's nest' (86) and her husband 'like the adder waxen deaf' (76). Warwick likens the commons – one of the play's terms for the populace – to 'an angry hive of bees' (125) who sting indiscriminately. The commons, through Salisbury, talk of 'fell serpents' (266) like Suffolk. Suffolk's curses in Act III, scene 2, invoke basilisks, lizards' stings, a serpent's hiss, and boding screech-owls. The climax of this dazzling

attempt by Shakespeare to set men's self-deluded actions
in the context of a transgressive nature is in the Lieutenant's
highly wrought scene-setting speech in the opening scene
of Act IV:

> The gaudy, blabbing, and remorseful day
> Is crept into the bosom of the sea;
> And now loud howling wolves arouse the jades
> That drag the tragic melancholy night;
> Who with their drowsy, slow, and flagging wings
> Clip dead men's graves, and from their misty jaws
> Breathe foul contagious darkness in the air. (IV.1.1–7)

PRE-BEGINNINGS

The Lieutenant's description of a sunset tells us if nothing
else that Shakespeare's early history plays do not come
out of the blue. Behind this passage we can hear the
cadences of Marlowe's *Tamburlaine the Great, Parts 1* and
2 (1587–8):

> Black is the beauty of the brightest day;
> The golden ball of heaven's eternal fire,
> That danced with glory on the silver waves,
> Now wants the fuel that inflamed his beams;
> And all with faintness, and for foul disgrace,
> He binds his temples with a frowning cloud,
> Ready to darken earth with endless night. (*Tamburlaine,
>   Part 2*, I.4.1–7)

Unlike Marlowe, however, Shakespeare was constrained
to a large extent by his adherence to the facts of English
history, though the Lieutenant's speech hardly suggests

this. And in contrast to Gloucester's accusers, Shakespeare does not play fast and loose with historical circumstance except in one important respect which I shall deal with later. Instead he weaves his play's patterns on the template of the story of England as conveyed by its principal chroniclers Edward Hall and Raphael Holinshed (with a nod to John Foxe's *Acts and Monuments* (first published in 1563) – also known as the *Book of Martyrs*). Hall's *Union of the Noble and Illustre Families of Lancaster and York* (1548) and Holinshed's *Chronicles of England, Scotland, and Ireland* (1577 and 1587) supply the plots for much of Shakespeare's history plays in both tetralogies, with colourful authorial inserts and embellishments, and, borrowing from Holinshed's title, they are often known as his chronicle history plays, in part to distinguish them from others of his plays that deal imaginatively with real events in real time past: *Macbeth*, for instance, or the Roman plays, *Julius Caesar*, *Coriolanus* and *Antony and Cleopatra*, or *Cymbeline*. *Henry VI, Part II*, in fact, cleaves closer to the chronicles than *Part I*, with the emphasis on Hall, though Shakespeare probably consulted the 1587 Holinshed which modified Hall by placing the blame for the breakdown in England principally on Henry's weakness of character, an emphasis with an obvious appeal for any playwright, especially for one who was at least indirectly influenced by the chroniclers' desire to please both Henry VIII and Elizabeth I and to justify the ways of the Tudor monarchs to men. We have to bear in mind that the chronicles were just one manifestation of a huge interest in English history on the part of the reading public in Shakespeare's England; many in Shakespeare's audience would come to the plays already knowledgeable about the events they dramatize, which would of course make

Shakespeare's deviations from his sources a provocative pleasure.

There are other influences on these plays. Perhaps the one that modern readers and playgoers find most appealing is the pressure of what we would now call popular culture – the demotic speech of London's streets, proverbial lore, the language of carnival. The aristocrats in this play drop into proverbial utterance almost as often as do the commons. Even more powerful an influence, however, is the tradition of classical grandiloquence – Marlovian of course, but it is also to be found in other playwrights of the time – Thomas Kyd, for instance, whose *Spanish Tragedy*, published in 1592, had been in the London theatres for a while and was a useful model for Shakespeare for his adaptation of a Senecan framework. Seneca, himself, the Roman playwright and philosopher (*c.* 4BC–AD 65), is an important influence on *Henry VI, Part II* (and on *Richard III*, *Titus Andronicus*, *Julius Caesar* and *Hamlet*). In the English tradition, behind Kyd and Marlowe loom the medieval pageant and the morality play, whose Vice figure, both sinister and comic, is an important predecessor for Jack Cade, not to mention Richard III or Iago in *Othello* (although Cade's energy is altogether different from that of Iago and Richard III). We can trace the roots of the history plays further back to John Bale's *King Johan* (written in the 1530s), or to *Gorboduc* (first acted in 1561, and warning England of the perils of division), or, closer to Shakespeare's time, the anonymous *Thomas of Woodstock* (1591–5), or the *True Tragedy of Richard III* (1588–94) or *The Famous Victories of Henry V* (before 1588). Nor should we forget the pressure of current events. The times were uneasy. The Spanish Armada in 1588, the Babington plot against the life of the Queen in 1586, the execution of Mary Queen of Scots in 1587, the factionalism at court throughout the 1590s (among and between the likes of Essex, Sussex, the Cecils, Norfolk, Leicester and Walsingham) all combined to spread alarm and dismay. A young writer hoping to make his mark with the London intelligentsia could do worse than select as the subject of his plays a time in history that had many parallels with the present. For the discerning theatregoer *Henry VI, Part II* was a highly topical play.

COMPLICATIONS

Just how different Shakespeare's *Henry VI, Part II* is from previous history plays (including *Henry VI, Part I* if we can think of it as 'previous') can best be gauged by considering the opportunities it offers its actors for the creative manipulation of language and situation. For possibly the first time in English drama, interpretative flexibility seems to be a principle of dramatic construction, part of the dramaturgy itself, perhaps because the writer was also an actor and especially sensitive to the desirability of writing suggestively rather than prescriptively. At one point in this play Shakespeare teases his characters and us with an equivocal prophecy, as he does in later plays, the ambiguity of which might stand as the articulation of a general guiding principle. York reads aloud Margery Jourdain's riddling prediction: '*The duke yet lives that Henry shall depose; | But him outlive and die a violent death*' (I.4.58–9). Understanding that '*shall depose*' and '*die a violent death*' could refer to either York or Henry, York glosses this traditionally unstable oracular prophecy with its unstable classical forebear from the Pythian Apollo, recorded by Cicero, when asked by

Pyrrhus if he would conquer Rome: '*Aio te, Aeacida, Romanos vincere posse*' (I.4.61). This can mean two contradictory things: (1) I proclaim that you, the descendant of Aeacus, can conquer the Romans, or (2) I proclaim that the Romans can conquer you, the descendant of Aeacus. Throughout his career Shakespeare seems to relish playing the role of the Pythian Apollo, or the god's later more vulgar manifestation, the witch Margery Jourdain: hence his fascination with the slipperiness of language, the way it can be turned inside out like a cheveril glove, as Feste says in *Twelfth Night*, as it is, for example, in this play, by Jack Cade's sardonic followers who in Act IV, scene 2 demolish their patron's every utterance protesting his aristocratic lineage with their puns and sarcastic put-downs. More importantly, perhaps, their amusing linguistic romp provides different opportunities for staging. Most editions, including this one, mark these impertinent comments by Cade's henchmen as asides. But there are virtually no asides marked as such in the quartos and Folio of Shakespeare's plays, however apparently intended. They are nearly always left to the discretion of the performer. So in Roger Warren's Oxford edition of this play he leaves these inflammatory remarks by Cade's supporters unchaperoned by any stage direction, as nakedly impudent utterances to be heard and relished by everybody, including Jack Cade himself, as was the case in Edward Hall's production of the play at the Watermill Theatre, Newbury, in 2001. To play the scene in this way mitigates the customary presentation of Cade as the fascistic self-deceiver (brought out best by the English Shakespeare Company's production in the 1980s of Cade as a National Front hooligan heading a reactionary rebellion). Neither interpretation, of course, is intrinsically superior to the other; both are perfectly viable; which one the director chooses will no doubt depend upon his or her interpretation of the play as a whole.

Henry VI, Part II offers numerous opportunities for these kinds of mitigations, equivocations, qualifications and improvisations. We might consider, for instance, the kiss that Henry bestows on Margaret in the play's opening scene. After the somewhat turgid transitional speech by Suffolk, Henry welcomes Margaret to England with a 'kind kiss' (I.1.19). Kind it may be, but what else is it? In performance it usually isn't given the intensity of Suffolk's kiss for Margaret in the penultimate scene of *Henry VI, Part I*, even though that kiss was supposed to be a proxy one from Henry, here to be replaced by the real thing. Directors, however, usually make it clear that Suffolk's kiss was the real thing, Henry's the pale substitute (often on the cheek, rather than on the lips). In mid-line, sometimes in mid-kiss in the theatre, Henry breaks off to express his thanks to God, often to the marked astonishment of the actress playing Margaret: 'O Lord that lends me life, | Lend me a heart replete with thankfulness!' (19–20). Margaret's bewilderment with Henry's unexpected appeal to the Lord is clearly a perfectly viable interpretation of the relationship between the three principals in the love triangle, Margaret, Henry and Suffolk. But if we move on to what Margaret says in her response to Henry's piety, another possible, if unfashionable, interpretation emerges, one that might mitigate or qualify her worldly incredulity. Like his, her vocabulary is simple, direct and idealistic; she talks of the 'mutual conference' that her 'mind' has had with Henry 'In courtly company or at my beads' (27), and her 'overjoy of heart' (31). She responds to him in kind, in other words, as though to his kind kiss, and it need not at this stage be a mere pretence, a piece of cynical play-acting on her part, as so many productions of the play insist that it is. I shall have occasion to revisit this moment in the play later.

The lines themselves are often open-ended. When Henry witnesses Margaret's hysterical grief over the death of her lover, Suffolk, he draws a wry moral: 'I fear me, love, if that I had been dead, | Thou wouldst not have mourned so much for me' (IV.4.23–4). Margaret replies: 'No, my love; I should not mourn, but die for thee' (25). It's a peculiarly opaque line, made peculiarly grotesque by the fact that Margaret is still clutching Suffolk's severed head to her bosom while she says it. Is it said contemptuously, or is it an expression of Margaret's still basically uncontaminated love for her husband, all appearances to the contrary? Or does she mean that she would avenge Henry's death whereas he would merely mourn hers? In Terry Hands's production at the Royal Shakespeare Theatre in Stratford-upon-Avon in 1977 it was clear that Margaret and Henry were deeply in love and the line was said with genuine passion. In the BBC TV production of 1983, directed by Jane Howell, on the other hand, Julia Foster as Margaret pronounced it with grim asperity. Again, how the line is spoken depends on how director and actors read the play as a whole. The same can be said for Gloucester's reply to Margaret's challenge to his authority: 'Madam, I am Protector of the realm, | And at his pleasure will resign my place' (I.3.118–19). Are these lines said angrily? Patiently? Patronizingly? In a similar situation, how does Warwick speak his rebuke to Margaret for her advocacy of Suffolk: 'Madam, be still, with reverence may I say, | For every word you speak in his behalf | Is slander to your royal dignity' (III.2.207–9)? Should the actor take 'with

reverence may I say' at face value or should he lace it
with sarcasm? A seemingly harmless statement frequently
offers the actor opportunity for suggestive inflection.
The actor playing Suffolk, for instance, often renders
his promise to aid Margaret in England with a subtle
suggestion of sexual menace: 'so will I | In England
work your grace's full content' (I.3.64–5). While
Gloucester's wife, Eleanor, another of the play's indefatigable women characters, conveys an equally elusive,
understated menace (often in Shakespeare the more
menacing, the more elusive): 'I will not be slack | To
play my part in Fortune's pageant' (I.2.66–7). In later
plays Shakespeare skilfully exploits this opacity, as with
Don John's threat in *Much Ado About Nothing*, 'if I had
my liberty, I would do my liking' (I.3.32–3). The most
sinister manipulator of this oblique use of language is
Iago: 'It is as sure as you are Roderigo, were I the Moor,
I would not be Iago' (*Othello*, I.1.57–8).

As we saw in the case of Henry's kiss, the play's
actions are often as susceptible as its language to different
interpretations in the theatre. Or scenarios may change
depending on whether the director keeps a non-speaking
character or a prop onstage or removes them. In this
respect we might consider the stage direction at III.2.148:
'Bed put forth with Gloucester's body in it'. The corpse's
bloated face, 'black and full of blood' (III.2.168), is then
exhaustively and horrifically described by Warwick,
perhaps in lieu of holding up the body for examination
by the theatre audience (though the one does not preclude
the other). What then happens to the body? Most editions,
including this one, follow the lead of the Quarto and
Folio and leave it onstage for the rest of the scene. The
Oxford, however, has it removed by attendants when
everybody exits the stage at line 299, except for Margaret

and Suffolk who then exchange lengthy passionate farewells until the scene ends a hundred or so lines later. In the theatre a director could make the corpse's baleful presence felt in a number of ways as Margaret and Suffolk circle round it in their passionate encounter. Its continual presence is a reminder, a literal memento mori, of the fates that await the lovers and their love for each other. A similar effect is achieved at the beginning of *Henry VI, Part I* if the coffin of Henry V is allowed to remain conspicuously present for the rest of that first scene in which a relay of Messengers bring in news to the quarrelling lords of the English debacle in France.

As for silent characters, should Alexander Iden in this play stay onstage in Act V, scene 1 after he has been knighted by Henry though he says nothing for the rest of the scene? Keeping him there, as this edition does, means that this morally authoritative representative of an emerging rural middle class gets to witness the beginnings of the Wars of the Roses. In Jane Howell's BBC production the camera lingers on his troubled face. A peculiarly pregnant silence is maintained by Margaret in Act IV, scene 9 – peculiar because she is normally such a torrential speaker – imperious, sarcastic, aggressive – but for these forty-nine lines she is ominously/self-pityingly/distractedly (it is impossible to say which for sure) wordless, even when addressed directly by Henry in a manner that at any other time would surely have provoked her to a scornful rejoinder: 'Come, wife, let's in and learn to govern better; | For yet may England curse my wretched reign' (IV.9.48–9). The play's refusal to give her anything to say here, despite Henry's offensive 'let's in and learn to govern better', seems to be a broad hint to the actress playing Margaret to make sense of her situation herself, in terms of the production she's in at the time: Shakespeare isn't telling her what to do. Nor does he earlier in the play when Margaret is again uncharacteristically silent when the peers turn on Gloucester. Her only line in over a hundred is the mysteriously proverbial one, 'But I can give the loser leave to chide' (III.1.182). How and why does she say this?

POLITICS

The questions of how and why take on greater potency when we consider the controversy swirling around the play's politics (see the sections on 'Background' and 'Jack Cade' in Further Reading). *Henry VI, Part II* has become something of a cause célèbre, especially in left-wing circles. The controversy centres on Shakespeare's presentation of Jack Cade, the rebel from Kent, who, like the play's aristocratic characters, was a real person in history. But he was so in a very different way from the way he is in Shakespeare's play, as any historian can tell us, and as both Hall and Holinshed, Shakespeare's principal sources, confirm. In them he and his cause are treated respectfully – Hall, for example, describing Cade as 'sober in communication and wise in disputing'. Cade's rebellion in 1450 resembled that of the Peasants' Revolt of 1381: on both occasions the rebellion took the form of men from the south-east of England riding to London to present petitions to the king; both risings were precipitated by the war against the French; both protested against misgovernment and failure of the judicial system; both produced murderous violence. In this matter Shakespeare flouts his sources and distorts history. He chooses to blacken the historical Cade's character and, to make matters worse (or better), to transform him into a comic figure unrecognizable as the serious-minded, idealistic, articulate and literate rebel of history, who in real life was much more like Shakespeare's Alexander Iden than his Jack Cade. A number of critics have responded uncertainly, as well they might, to the very success that Shakespeare has in making Cade funny. (He may well have been played originally by the company's famous clown, Will Kemp.) It is undeniable that for much of the time our enjoyment of him is disturbingly compromised. What we so often see on stage is a process whereby a Cade joke produces an horrific action (uncompromisingly displayed in most modern performances). So when one of Cade's soldiers comes running in calling out the name Jack Cade instead of Lord Mortimer, as Cade has just proclaimed that everyone must now do, Cade orders him to be knocked down and killed for calling a Cade a Cade, despite his not having been onstage to hear the proclamation in the first place. The comic sequence is completed by Smith's grim joke after the Soldier's death: 'If this fellow be wise, he'll never call ye Jack Cade more; I think he hath a very fair warning' (IV.6.9–10). After Cade has ordered the offstage beheading of Lord Say and his brother-in-law Sir James Cromer, the heads are brought back onstage for a macabre imitation of the play's lovemaking with Cade's order: 'Let them kiss one another; for they loved well when they were alive' (IV.7.122–3) and, as an afterthought, 'at every corner have them kiss' (128). Most productions are only too happy to oblige.

What can be said in mitigation of the play's Jack Cade, apart from this uneasy laughter he provokes? Does Shakespeare's blackening of his character also blacken Shakespeare's reputation as a man of the people, as an angry critic like Richard Wilson charges in his

essay 'A Mingled Yarn'? Does the play offer its actors
opportunities for a different take on Cade? Or at least a
different emphasis? Of course any production might well
highlight those brief moments when the play allows us
to catch a glimpse of the legitimacy of Cade's cause.
Behind the caperings of this 'wild Morisco' (III.1.365),
the machinations of this 'shag-haired crafty kern'
(III.1.367) – so some readings propose – gleams the pure
gold of justified rebellion. Despite the obvious corruption and depravity, we need to register the possible truth
to Cade's claim that he is 'the besom that must sweep the
court clean of such filth as thou art' (IV.7.27–9), or that
what he is doing ''tis for liberty' (IV.2.173). A partisan
reading of this nature helps us to understand the rebels'
obsession with literacy and the law. It is no wonder, in
this context, that Dick the Butcher's first thought is to
'kill all the lawyers' (IV.2.72), for they can undo a man
with 'parchment, being scribbled o'er' (75–6). It's not the
bee so much that stings but the bee's wax, as Dick goes
on to say. And what's 'monstrous' about the Clerk of
Chartham is that 'he can write and read and cast accompt'
(80–81) and can 'make obligations [i.e. legal bonds], and
write court-hand' (87). Dick and Jack's pointedly outrageous accusations against the Clerk might well remind
many in Shakespeare's audience of their own powerless-
ness in the face of the country's literate elite, of the truth
behind Cade's charge against Lord Say that because poor
men could not read 'thou hast hanged them' (IV.7.41). At
odd moments too Cade's personal brutality is also mitigated. Consider, for instance, his momentary hesitation
following Lord Say's eloquent plea: 'I feel remorse in
myself with his words; but I'll bridle it' (IV.7.98–9).
(Bridle it he does: 'He shall die, an it be but for pleading
so well for his life' (99–100).) And earlier in the play,

York mentions unironically Cade's loyalty and heroism: even if he's 'racked, and torturèd | I know no pain they can inflict upon him | Will make him say I moved him to those arms' (III.1.376–8).

The play does not insist that we see Cade exclusively in one way or another (although it allows us to), but it does, of course, insist that we see Cade as a character in a play. He is not first and foremost someone taken distortedly from history but a fictional character dreamed up in a writer's mind. Cade is not his own man – though he likes to think he is – on many levels. When York says that he moved Cade to those arms we might see him as not only a pawn in Shakespeare's game, but in York's too. As such this makes Cade an extension of a corrupt aristocracy rather than a rebel against them, and in so doing makes the charge against Shakespeare misguided. Shakespeare spells out this possible interpretation for us at some length with York's words:

> And, for a minister of my intent,
> I have seduced a headstrong Kentishman,
> John Cade of Ashford,
> To make commotion, as full well he can,
> Under the title of John Mortimer. (III.1.355–9)

As far as York is concerned Cade is his agent of commotion, one who will head up 'some black storm' (349), a 'fell tempest' (351), a 'mad-bred flaw' (354). York rams the point home: 'This devil here shall be my substitute' (371). His insistence is made doubly significant in that there is no historical basis for the collusion between York and Cade. It is entirely Shakespeare's invention.

Cade's cruelty, barbarism, even his comic sense, mirror those of his patrons. The strange and pathetic episodes

of Simpcox and his wife, and the 'duel' to the death
between Peter and his master, Horner, feature a compla-
cent, patronizing aristocracy entertained and amused by
the spectacle of the lower orders behaving self-
destructively. (It is not surprising that Shakespeare
replays the Peter–Horner episode in a comedy, *Twelfth
Night*, with Sir Andrew Aguecheek and Viola as the
reluctant duellists.) Margaret makes quite clear the
pleasure she expects to get from Peter and Horner's
confrontation (which ends with the drunken Horner's
death): 'for purposely therefore | Left I the court to see
this quarrel tried' (II.3.52–3). Her reaction to the un-
masking of Simpcox is the same as that of the theatre
audience: 'It made me laugh to see the villain run' (151).
Margaret's reaction to the Simpcox affair is made more
vivid by its difference from Henry's, who is first of all
naively convinced of the genuineness of the 'miracle'
of Simpcox's cure: 'Now God be praised, that to
believing souls | Gives light in darkness, comfort in
despair!' (64–5). (In Foxe's *Book of Martyrs*, Shakespeare's source for this episode, it is Gloucester, not
Henry, who at first believes in and is delighted by this
seemingly divine intervention.) Then, instead of being
amused by the spectacle of an allegedly blind and lame
man on the run, literally and figuratively, Henry can
only lament it as an instance of the depravity of the
human race: 'O God, seest thou this, and bearest so long?'
(150).

Any performance gives the actors opportunities to link
Jack Cade in our minds with the rebellious courtiers:
Cade, the rebel, and York, the rebel, are two sides of
the same coin. York's disdainful attitude towards the
populace is little different from Cade's and no different
from Suffolk's or Margaret's (or, for that matter, Sir

Humphrey Stafford's). Suffolk, in particular, knows no restraint in his contempt for those whom he calls 'rude unpolished hinds', 'a sort of tinkers' (III.2.271, 277). He's at his most obnoxiously imperial with the Lieutenant and Whitmore: he describes the Lieutenant as an 'obscure and lousy swain', 'a jaded groom' with an 'abortive pride' and a 'riotous tongue' (IV.1.50, 52, 60, 64). He talks of 'these paltry, servile, abject drudges' (105). He will not stoop, not he: 'True nobility is exempt from fear; | More can I bear than you dare execute' (131–2). This is the general position taken by the nobility in this play, and its disastrous political consequences will be dramatized later in *Coriolanus*. As with Coriolanus there's no stooping, tactical or otherwise, by most of these peers. Hence Sir Humphrey Stafford's address to the rebels in Act IV, scene 2: 'Rebellious hinds, the filth and scum of Kent, | Marked for the gallows, lay your weapons down' (IV.2.114–15). Are we not gratified, a mite perversely perhaps, by the fact that the Staffords and their army then fall before this 'ragged multitude | Of hinds and peasants, rude and merciless' (IV.4.32–3) 'like sheep and oxen' (IV.3.3)? And would not an audience in Shakespeare's day respond clamorously to Gloucester's wife's disgrace following her absurd and treasonous consultation with the witch, Margery Jourdain? Her contempt for the 'giddy multitude', the 'rabble', the 'envious people', throwing their 'hateful looks' (II.4.21, 32, 35, 23) on Gloucester as well as on her – 'The abject [low, common] people gazing on thy face' (11) – might well aggravate a substantial portion of the audience, especially if, as is now often the case, she speaks these lines looking out disdainfully into the auditorium. (Gloucester, on the other hand, may continue to be well received by the play's customers, as he refuses to join in her lament.) There may be something to be said, the play says, for John Holland's criticism: 'it was never merry world in England since gentlemen came up [became fashionable]' (IV.2.8–9), or in George Bevis's: 'Virtue is not regarded in handicraftsmen' (10–11).

A one-dimensional view of Cade is un-Shakespearian. And the same may be said of those whom Eleanor describes as the abject people. The play, in fact, carefully offers a number of different terms for the entity she so despises: commons, people, citizens, rebels. The Second Messenger distinguishes between London's citizens who 'fly and forsake their houses' and the 'rascal people, thirsting after prey' (IV.4.50, 51). The play never calls its citizens rascal citizens or abject, envious citizens; but the commons and the people seem to be neutral terms defined by a positive or a negative qualifier. Even though by definition the word 'rebels' can only be used negatively, someone like Henry can take a charitable view of them as 'so many simple souls' who 'know not what they do' (IV.4.10, 38). At the turning point of the play in Act III, Gloucester's murder, Salisbury acts as the commons' spokesman, their 'quaint . . . orator' (III.2.274) according to Suffolk – 'quaint' because they are demanding Suffolk's banishment:

> And mere instinct of love and loyalty,
> Free from a stubborn opposite intent,
> As being thought to contradict your liking,
> Makes them thus forward in his banishment. (III.2.250–53)

For once Henry is decisive:

> And therefore by His majesty I swear

Whose far unworthy deputy I am,
He shall not breathe infection in this air
But three days longer, on the pain of death. (III.2.285–8)

And for once he is masterful with Margaret: 'No more,
I say' (291).

The rebels' desperation mirrors the broader state of
affairs. Three of the four Petitioners, 'base cullions'
(I.3.38) in Margaret's view, have legitimate grievances
against the nobility: one of them, for instance, accuses
Suffolk of 'enclosing the commons of Melford' (20) –
that is, seizing the common grazing land from those
who depend on it for subsistence. Somerset talks of
Gloucester's 'sumptuous buildings' (128) and Eleanor
Cobham's wardrobe as costing 'a mass of public treasury'
(129), echoing Margaret's earlier accusation that Eleanor
'bears a duke's revenues on her back' (78). Although the
accusations against Gloucester are no doubt either untrue
or grossly overstated, they tell tales that would be familiar
to Shakespeare's audience: the 'sale of offices and towns
in France' (I.3.133); the levying of 'great sums of money
through the realm' (III.1.61) for the soldiers' pay in
France, which is never sent; cruelty to prisoners. The
play offers us glimpses of the consequences for ordinary
people of corruption among their masters. Simpcox's wife
has her moment of poignancy: 'Alas, sir, we did it for
pure need' (II.1.153). So too does the apprentice Peter,
who remembers his friends just before his encounter with
Horner: 'Here, Robin, an if I die, I give thee my apron;
and, Will, thou shalt have my hammer; and here, Tom,
take all the money that I have' (II.3.74–6). And
Shakespeare's Second Murderer, the first of a number of
conscience-stricken murderers in his plays, laments his
hand in Gloucester's death: 'O that it were to do! What

have we done? | Didst ever hear a man so penitent?'
(III.2.3–4).

EDENS

Cade is not then the only character in the play who
suggests a fugitive idealism. Although an actress may well
play Margaret primarily as a besotted shrew – clutching
Suffolk's severed head, boxing Eleanor Cobham's ears –
there is more to her than that. Shakespeare gives her the
play's longest speech (III.2.73–121) in its longest scene.
In it she rounds on Henry, passionately upbraiding him
for his lukewarm affection for her, retelling as an epic
journey her voyage to him across the Channel from
France, a Dido to Henry's Aeneas, with Suffolk playing
the role of Ascanius. (In Virgil's *Aeneid* Venus's son
Cupid takes the form of Aeneas's son Ascanius to
persuade Dido to fall in love with his father.) It's an
extraordinary bravura performance and has left many
critics puzzled. How can she talk this way, they wonder,
given the indefensibility of her association with Suffolk?
In his Oxford edition Roger Warren suggests a number
of possible explanations (including a miscalculation on
Shakespeare's part): in one Margaret is temporarily
unhinged, in another cynically insincere, in a third desper-
ately eager to divert Henry from mental illness (as in
Terry Hands's 1977 production). We get no help from
the other players on the stage as the play does not give
them an opportunity to speak. Margaret's last line is
followed by the urgent stage direction: '*Noise within. Enter
Warwick, Salisbury, and many Commons*'. How Henry
reacts while Margaret is speaking is left up to the director
of the production.

Perhaps we should see Margaret's passion in Act III as driven by the huge disappointment to her expectations that Henry has turned out to be. If we think back to the play's opening scene with its high-flown expressions of idyllic mutuality from Margaret and Henry, there is no reason to suppose that Margaret didn't contemplate England rapturously at that time as a demi-paradise, as this 'other Eden', in John of Gaunt's infatuated words about England in *Richard II* (II.1.42). She may well have seen England and Henry through Suffolk's eyes, and have expected to find in Henry's person the attractiveness of Suffolk. (She later says that she had thought that Henry would have been like Suffolk in 'courage, courtship, and proportion' (I.3.52)). In France Suffolk must have seemed to her a harbinger of things to come in her relationship with Henry. Henry's kind kiss on her arrival in England should have been the triumphant equivalent of Suffolk's passionate one in the penultimate scene of *Henry VI, Part I*. Their 'mutual conference' (I.1.25), as she imagined it, conveys the high-minded, 'pastoral', unrealizable intimacy that the idealistic Henry would doubtless have welcomed had not character and events made it impossible. Paradoxically enough, for the ideal to work, as she contemplates it in this opening scene, the actual partner would have to have been someone like the sexy Suffolk. Her quaint, archaic language – 'mine alderliefest sovereign' (I.1.28) – spoken perhaps with a strong French accent (as Peggy Ashcroft did in the Royal Shakespeare Company's 1963 *Wars of the Roses*) – lends her an aura of otherworldly romance. Henry's own excursion into archaism is nicely linked to Margaret's language: 'her grace in speech, | Her words y-clad with wisdom's majesty' (32–3).

Margaret's vision of England at the beginning of *Henry VI, Part II* and at the end of *Henry VI, Part I* is of an

Eden of knightly, erotic gallantry exemplified by the consummate courtier, Suffolk, who in *Henry VI, Part I* had represented for her an ideal court with an ideal king in the offing. (Had Shakespeare read, one wonders, Sir Thomas Malory's *Le Morte D'Arthur* (printed in 1485), with its depiction of the most famous and famously troubled love triangle, King Arthur, Guinevere and Lancelot?) Her strong feelings for this other Eden help us to understand the long, impassioned speech at the centre of *Henry VI, Part II*. Here Margaret sees England and Henry as one and the same: England's 'chalky cliffs' (III.2.101) are 'thy' chalky cliffs; it's 'thy' land, 'thy' shore. She throws the 'costly jewel' (106) in the shape of a heart more towards the land than into the sea: 'The sea received it, | And so I wished thy body might my heart' (108–9). It is at this point that she brings in the story of Dido:

> How often have I tempted Suffolk's tongue –
> The agent of thy foul inconstancy –
> To sit and witch me, as Ascanius did
> When he to madding Dido would unfold
> His father's acts, commenced in burning Troy! (III.2.114–18)

It isn't difficult to imagine Margaret as Dido, but Henry VI as Aeneas is another matter. Given Suffolk's eloquence – Henry had talked in *Henry VI, Part I* of the 'force of your report' (V.5.79) in persuading him to fall in love with Margaret – it isn't difficult either to think of him as witching Margaret into a maddening state of anticipation in that boat crossing the Channel. Shakespeare may be remembering here what happens in Marlowe and Nashe's *Dido, Queen of Carthage* (1587–91), when Dido succumbs to Cupid's incitement:

I'll make me bracelets of his golden hair;
His glistering eyes shall be my looking-glass,
His lips an altar, where I'll offer up
As many kisses as the sea hath sands. (III.1.83–6)

The contrast with Margaret's situation could hardly be greater. In Marlowe's story, Aeneas abandons Dido in order to found Rome, and memories of this famous account re-channelled through Marlowe's popular play may help to explain Margaret's exaggerated talk here of Henry's 'flinty heart' (III.2.99), harder than the 'splitting rocks' in the 'sinking sands' (97).

If Margaret's 'Eden' is the medieval world of chivalric romance, Gloucester's is the martial world of his brother, Henry V, who had already assumed Arthur's legendary status by the time of Henry VI. (Margaret would surely not have been disappointed had Henry V's body received her heart.) In the opening scene of *Henry VI, Part II* Gloucester '*stays all the rest*' after Margaret, Henry and Suffolk have left the stage, in order to lament with them the differences between the two reigns. He contrasts the decadence of the present reign with the simple physical realities of warfare and hard work – lodging in winter's cold and summer's heat, the receiving of scars, the toiling of wits – that distinguished the reign of England's warrior-king, Henry V. As in *Part I*, 'that ever-living man of memory' (*Henry VI, Part I*, IV.3.51), Henry V, continues in this play to function as the (impossible) standard of kingly excellence, to be magnificently celebrated later in Shakespeare's *Henry V* (1599). Gloucester's nostalgia is as Arthurian as Margaret's, minus the troubling story of Guinevere and Lancelot. And we experience at unexpected moments in the play brief ritualistic expressions of Gloucester's old-fashioned ideal of the bonded, masculine world of knighthood. York, for instance, pauses before engaging in another encounter with Clifford (each has already slain the other's horse) at the battle of St Alban's. Clifford asks: 'What seest thou in me, York? Why dost thou pause?' (V.2.19). And York, momentarily overcome by the martial beauty of his opponent, replies: 'With thy brave bearing should I be in love, | But that thou art so fast mine enemy' (20–21). Clifford reciprocates in kind. York then kills Clifford but not before Clifford gasps out some courtly French, 'La fin couronne les oeuvres [The end crowns the works]' (28). Even the future monster-king, Richard, has his moment of gallantry at the end of this play when he three times saves Salisbury from death. And at the point of death, Suffolk's nobility, his 'imperial tongue' (IV.1.123), is emphasized. 'True nobility is exempt from fear' (131), he says. Despite the Lieutenant's command, 'Hale him away, and let him talk no more' (133), Suffolk goes on for another seven lines of ostentatious Roman comparisons.

Henry V scores one notable triumph in *Henry VI, Part II*. In their dealings with the rebels, Buckingham and Old Clifford don't make the same mistake as Sir Humphrey Stafford, who had treated the rebels with such contempt. However much of a ruse it may have been, they follow the King's instructions and treat the rebels respectfully. Their eloquence wins the day: the rebels respond to their masters' verse at the expense of Cade's prose, gentrified by it for a moment, and we may see this sudden submission as evidence that could be used both for and against Cade's men, depending on our interpretation of it. In Cade's view, of course, their collapse proves them to be 'base peasants', 'recreants and dastards' (IV.8.20, 26). And we may have some sympathy for his argument that it is 'no want of resolution in me, but only my followers' base and ignominious treasons, makes me betake me to my heels' (61–3). At one point the crowd is momentarily swayed by Cade's question, 'Will you needs be hanged with your pardons about your necks?' (20–22). But Clifford produces the royal talisman in the nick of time: 'Is Cade the son of Henry the Fifth, | That thus you do exclaim you'll go with him?' (33–4). He then inspires them, as Henry V had done, with promise of foreign booty:

> To France! To France! And get what you have lost;
> Spare England, for it is your native coast.
> Henry hath money; you are strong and manly;
> God on our side, doubt not of victory. (IV.8.48–51)

Cade then blames Henry V for the collapse of his rebellion: 'Was ever feather so lightly blown to and fro as this multitude? The name of Henry the Fifth hales them to an hundred mischiefs and makes them leave me desolate' (54–7).

This is one of the few occasions in this play when characters are haled by the force of a past ideal to change a course of action. Most of the time beliefs in ideals are shown to be disastrously naive. Gloucester himself is a victim of his own ingenuousness. His view of England is distorted by an idealistic belief in the efficacy of English law. Many critics have pointed out how *Henry VI, Part II* showcases legal terminology, and how its structure depends upon a sequence of trials and mock trials. But it's clear that the law itself is on trial in this play, as the actual legal decisions are in most cases arbitrary and superstitious, including Gloucester's. (His judgment that Somerset should be given the regentship of France, and that Horner and Peter should fight, collapses the law into his own ego: 'This is the law, and this Duke Humphrey's doom' (I.3.208).) Nonetheless Gloucester clings to an idealization of English common law that proves to be just as illusional as Margaret's original misjudgement of the English court or Henry's stubborn belief in God's providence (Henry's last line in the play typically provokes Margaret's scorn: 'Can we outrun the heavens? Good Margaret, stay' (V.2.73)). Gloucester naively believes that 'I must offend before I be attainted' (II.4.59); there must be a 'breach of law' (66). To be 'loyal, true, and crimeless' (63) will inevitably carry the day. And yet he immediately reveals that he should know better when he learns that he has not been informed ahead of time about the parliament at Bury St Edmunds in Suffolk. 'This is close dealing [secret plotting]' (73), he says. The only other character in the play who proves to be even more credulous than Gloucester is Henry himself, who echoes his mentor's sentiments – just as unavailingly: 'What stronger breastplate than a heart untainted! | Thrice is he armed that hath his quarrel just' (III.2.232–3).

Henry's untainted heart turns him away from the tainted world. Margaret contemptuously describes Henry's transformation of his father's martial world into that of the canonized saint:

> But all his mind is bent to holiness,
> To number Ave-Maries on his beads;
> His champions are the prophets and apostles,
> His weapons holy saws of sacred writ;
> His study is his tilt-yard, and his loves
> Are brazen images of canonized saints. (I.3.53–8)

This is at one end of the play and the sentiment is repeated by York at the other: 'That head of thine doth not become a crown; | Thy hand is made to grasp a palmer's staff, | And not to grace an awful princely sceptre' (V.1.96–8). Henry's utopian vision of England comes closest to a literal version of Eden, despite all the occasions that the play supplies to prove to him that he is dealing with fallen angels. Like Gloucester, he believes in the transcendent power of the law. He gives Eleanor Cobham and her conspirators over to 'Justice' equal scales, | Whose beam stands sure, whose rightful cause prevails' (II.1.199–200). The only official representative of the Church in this play, Cardinal Beaufort, proves how difficult it would be for any rightful cause to prevail. His example brings on Gloucester's magisterial rebuke in Latin: '*Tantaene animis coelestibus irae?* [Is it possible for there to be so much wrath in the minds of heavenly creatures?]', which he then translates for the groundlings into the less magisterial but equally potent, 'Churchmen so hot?' (II.1.24, 25). Even Henry sees that the Cardinal's terror of his mysterious imminent death is a sign of an 'evil life' (III.3.5) and his judgement is echoed by Warwick: 'So bad a death argues a monstrous life' (III.3.30).

The monstrous lives that *Henry VI, Part II* parades for our fascinated disgust render the visions of England as these other Edens pathetically far-fetched, though not without a certain poignancy. But there is one vision of an unfallen state that the play seems to be offering with a more than sneaking admiration for its plausibility. It comes in the person – one might almost say the personification – of Alexander Iden (possibly pronounced Eden) who faces down and kills the fugitive Jack Cade. Everything about Iden, including the verse he speaks, sets him apart as more an emblem than a real character, although oddly enough, considering the patness of his name, he can be found in Shakespeare's sources. As he himself points out, he is physically Cade's superior (Cade calls him 'the burly-boned clown' (IV.10.55)):

> Set limb to limb, and thou art far the lesser;
> Thy hand is but a finger to my fist;
> Thy leg a stick comparèd with this truncheon. (IV.10.45–7)

The point of this confrontation, as the lines above illustrate, is not only to free the kingdom of a rebel but to do so as humiliatingly as possible and to establish Iden as a new breed of representative independent English gentleman, an esquire or landed proprietor, with a heart (and body) of oak and a well-stocked larder to provide hospitality for passing strangers. Iden is neither a disaffected aristocrat nor a threatening commoner; on the contrary, he is an industrious man apparently happy with his 'small inheritance' (17). Like the citizens of London he is a cut above the commons but below a knight (at least for the moment). He is a member of the 'middling sort' that was to become the bedrock of English society. Today we would call him 'middle England'.

He is also, like Jack Cade ironically enough, from Kent, 'an esquire of Kent' (IV.10.41) as he proudly tells Cade, or 'A poor esquire of Kent, that loves his king' (V.1.75), as he more modestly describes himself to Henry. (Historically Iden was a Kentish gentleman who married Lord Say's daughter when she became Sir James Cromer's widow.) The fact that Cade and his followers are also from Kent incites Lord Say's sour description of the county as '*bona terra, mala gens* [a good land, a bad people]' (IV.7.52). But Say then goes on to qualify this judgement, referring to Julius Caesar who in his

Commentaries thought it 'the civilest place of all this isle' (56). But more than merely civil, the county was traditionally idealized in popular literature as the land of liberty, climaxing in the seventeenth century with Michael Drayton's great topographical poem on England, *Poly-Olbion* (1612), and resurfacing in the nineteenth in Wordsworth's 'To the Men of Kent' (1803):

> Vanguard of Liberty, ye men of Kent,
> Ye children of a Soil that doth advance
> Her haughty brow against the coast of France,
> Now is the time to prove your hardiment!

In *Henry VI, Part II*, we remember, it is Clifford's appeal to this hardiment of Cade's men that tips the balance in favour of the King's forces: 'To France! To France! And get what you have lost; | Spare England, for it is your native coast' (IV.8.48–9). Iden represents the positive side of a libertarian Kent, and I think we are supposed to see him as Kent in the same way that Margaret saw the yet-to-her-unseen Henry VI as England. In Margaret's case dream and reality collide; in our case Iden lives up to his name and offers us a vision of Kent and by extension England free of the insurrectionary ambitions of both populace and nobility. It is an Eden/Iden of middle-class virtues.

But not quite. Although Iden claims, as part of his general immaculacy, 'not to wax great by others' waning' (IV.10.19), once he discovers who his intruder is, whom he has killed, his attitude and his language change:

> And as I thrust thy body in with my sword,
> So wish I I might thrust thy soul to hell.
> Hence will I drag thee headlong by the heels

> Unto a dunghill, which shall be thy grave,
> And there cut off thy most ungracious head;
> Which I will bear in triumph to the King,
> Leaving thy trunk for crows to feed upon. (IV.10.76–82)

We could be listening to Suffolk here, or to Margaret. The Oxford editor's addition of a bracketed stage direction after the first line, '*stabbing him again*', makes clear the remarkable distance Iden has travelled since his modest opening some sixty lines before. The quiet walks that he earlier celebrated have been replaced by a shambles and a dunghill; now a vindictive avenger he stabs Cade's dead body and joins the ranks of the play's other cruel decapitators; he forgets his previous enjoyment of 'the small inheritance my father left me' (IV.10.17) in anticipating the glory he'll earn when he bears in triumph Cade's head to the King.

Iden's new status is confirmed by Henry at the instigation of Buckingham, who argues that such yeoman service on Iden's part warrants a promotion. There and then Henry creates Iden a knight: 'Rise up a knight. | We give thee for reward a thousand marks, | And will that thou henceforth attend on us' (V.1.78–80). (Henry's last line helps to justify keeping Iden onstage until the scene's end.) We may perhaps see this action as an indication of a new alignment: not between the King and nobility, but between the King and a newly emerging propertied class; and we might see the knighting of Iden as a symbolic celebration of this new alliance, Henry's action anticipating the strategic creation of dozens of knights from the financial and commercial classes by England's new king, James I, in the early years of the seventeenth century. Iden's second introduction of himself as 'A poor esquire of Kent, that loves his king'

(V.1.75) is not then merely formulaic: in this play, in these times, loving the king has as much revolutionary potential as manning the barricades.

To see the play's characters as inhabiting in their dreams the landscapes of lost or impossible Edens, or to see them (or some of them anyway) as quasi-abstractions or morality figures, fails to do justice to the overwhelming sense we have of them as flesh-and-blood-and-language creations. We might argue that the attention given to Cade and his followers by readers and playgoers (and even by critics) has mostly to do with the comic genius of Shakespeare's presentation of them. More than in any previous history play the characters inhabit the stage with an almost Rabelaisian gusto. This is especially true of Jack Cade, and I want to return to him and his followers for a moment to suggest how forcefully the play makes us think of them (and the others) as individuals rather than types or abstractions. It has everything to do with the language they speak, with the entertaining intrusiveness of their prose with its comic puns and local references. Only after several readings does the modern reader enjoy the dialogue as it might have been enjoyed by the original audiences. So when Cade's henchmen are first introduced, instead of the stage direction '*Enter George Bevis and John Holland*' (IV.2.1), we might just as well have '*Enter a Plethora of Puns*'. But we need to pause over the stage direction we do have. Why are the characters given these names in the 1623 Folio? The Quarto doesn't have them. Oxford replaces them with 'two rebels with long staves' and gives them the speech-prefixes 'First Rebel' and 'Second Rebel'. Are they the names of actors? Are they authorial? Again, at IV.2.102 the Folio has '*Enter Michael*'; and again, Oxford replaces him with '*Enter a Rebel*'. At no time in the text itself are any of these characters addressed by their names.

I have no contribution to make as to the provenance of these names. But we might note that they occur in a play that is at some pains throughout to individualize its minor characters as well as its major ones, to give them, as we have seen, their moments of poignancy or absurdity, to dress them in a little brief authority before they fade into oblivion. George Bevis, John Holland and Michael join Thomas Horner, Peter Thump, Dick the Butcher and Smith the Weaver – to name but a few – in the roster of characters for whom the act of being named, as in *Henry IV, Part II* and *A Midsummer Night's Dream*, is of a piece with the individualizing words they speak and the actions they perform. To give characters their own names, if only typographically in the case of the first three, is one small but symbolic aspect of the concern Shakespeare has in his history plays to bring history to life. The process might be summed up by Cade's punning reply to Michael's question, 'Where's our general?' (IV.2.103): 'Here I am, thou particular fellow' (104). A particular fellow Jack Cade truly is, in more ways than one, and, to a greater or less degree, so too are all the others.

ENDINGS (AND BEGINNINGS)

But these are particular fellows caught up in the sweep of important national events. The last scenes of the play abandon the likes of Bevis, Holland, Horner and Thump; the names – with the short-lived exception of Alexander Iden – now have Duke, Earl, Lord or Sir before them. We are squarely in the aristocratic world, and with the end of the play's concern for the commons, the people

and the citizens, we, like Iden with his troubled countenance, witness the beginning of the actual fighting of the
Wars of the Roses, as the aristocratic Houses of York
and Lancaster confront each other in their savage struggle
over the *'sancta majestas'* (V.1.5) that culminates the events
of *Henry VI, Part II* and prepares us for the remorseless
carnage of *Henry VI, Part III*. There is no room now for
representatives of the populace, and one of the reasons
perhaps that theatregoers and readers have found the third
part of *Henry VI* less vital, less human, than its immediate predecessor, is in its relentless concentration on the
eddies and flows of its battle sequences as the 'ancient
bickerings' (*Henry VI, Part II*, I.1.142) of its corrupt aristocracy take the form of bouts of bloodletting.

A glance at the list of Characters in the Play for *Henry
VI, Part III* is instructive. All thirty-one named characters are from the nobility or royalty. The rest are unnamed
functionaries – bit parts – restricted to bringing messages,
guarding aristocratic prisoners, watching over noble
estates or the king's tent, their subsidiary roles exempli-
fied by the Second Watchman's rhetorical question,
'wherefore else guard we his royal tent, | But to defend
his person from night-foes?' (IV.3.21–2). In contrast to
Henry VI, Part II, Shakespeare seems intent on avoiding
naming his subsidiary characters. The most significant
omission, in the light of the preceding play, occurs in the
second act when, for once, minor characters from the
neglected commons have something important to say.
But they say it in the distant, sepulchral tones of emblem-
atic characters, those unnamed ones described in The
Characters in the Play as 'A SON that has killed his father'
and 'A FATHER that has killed his son'. It doesn't matter
who they are; they are there merely to record the vile-
ness of the times, the incestuous killings of a civil war.

No doubt in any production they may be affecting, but the kind of language the Father speaks is a world removed from Horner and Thump, or Simpcox and his Wife:

> O, pity, God, this miserable age!
> What stratagems, how fell, how butcherly,
> Erroneous, mutinous, and unnatural,
> This deadly quarrel daily doth beget! (II.5.88–91)

Yet every word he speaks more accurately depicts the world of *Henry VI, Part III* than those of Edward that end the play: 'Farewell, sour annoy! | For here, I hope, begins our lasting joy' (V.7.45–6). How wan a hope this is can best be seen when we remember that the next and final play in the series is *Richard III*.

Michael Taylor

The Play in Performance

In the opening scene of the play Humphrey, Duke of Gloucester, is fulfilling his duty as Lord Protector of the realm in the formal reading of the articles drawn up by Suffolk for the marriage of Margaret of Anjou to the English King. He begins, accordingly, to deliver the stately phrases but in the first printing of the play his speech breaks down halfway through the word 'father' and, following the stage direction, he lets the paper fall. That brief, broken syllable 'fa-' (I.1.51) and its accompanying, simple action illustrate much of the play's style and strength. Duke Humphrey's abrupt stop communicates to the audience the enormity of the loss of Anjou and Maine – a grievous loss that will be reiterated throughout the play with violent emphasis. How does Margaret react to the unconcealed dismay of the Lord Protector at this demeaning marriage? How does she respond to her new husband and these new surroundings? How does she behave towards Suffolk? Audiences will watch Margaret closely here to see what can be learnt from her expression and behaviour. Her relationship with Suffolk will immediately be under an audience's scrutiny and will remain so for as long as he lives.

In the most economical way, this 'fa-' establishes the play's concern with the gap between public and private actions and feelings. There will be other moments when the hot-tempered Duke Humphrey will fail to keep his anger under control and be forced to break off and break away from the stage. The orderly formality of courtly proceedings will, on other occasions, be disrupted by the unpredictable and spontaneous emotions and desires of other characters, not least the King himself. The Quarto and Folio stage directions tell us that King Henry's state entries and exits are always marked by a ceremonious flourish of trumpets, and he is also accompanied by a considerable number of mighty peers, jostling for positions of power. The lack of any flourish at his departure in Act III, scene 1 (at line 222), therefore, tells the audience that Henry's action at that point is unexpected and unfitting. He is in anguish at the persecution of Duke Humphrey by the other nobles and unable to contain his private feelings within the public proprieties of royal etiquette.

This play has one of the longest cast lists of any of Shakespeare's plays and any successful production has to help its audience easily identify each character. The dramatist himself acknowledges this in the opening scene, by having first King Henry and then Duke Humphrey address half a dozen or more of the lords by name. At the RSC's Swan Theatre in 2000 Henry's enumeration of the peers' titles, as he pointed to each in turn, was performed explicitly for the benefit of his newly arrived French bride. The lords' respective allegiances to the Houses of York or Lancaster are often indicated by the wearing of the white or red rose in their hats, belts or, in the case of the English Shakespeare Company's modern dress production in 1987, their buttonholes.

In a manner characteristic of *Henry VI, Part II*, the big public opening of the first scene yields to a more private affair as the stage gradually empties. Significantly, Suffolk exits with the new bride and the King and, equally significantly, Duke Humphrey is the first of the other lords to leave. Finally only York remains, taking advantage of his privacy to confide to the audience his ambition for the crown. Thus, in the space of the opening scene, the audience sees clearly the ground plan laid for the ensuing action – the fall of Humphrey and the rise of York.

At the centre of this maelstrom sits Henry. This role presents particular challenges to the actor – he is passive, ineffectual and pitifully unsuited to the demands of controlling his pack of ferocious peers. How does the actor make the King register onstage, so that it is the character and not the actor who is overwhelmed by such competition? The intimidating nature of Henry's aristocratic subjects was powerfully expressed in Michael Boyd's production, which made full use of the specially designed traverse stage at the Swan Theatre in 2000. For the opening of Act III, scene 1, the King and Queen stood together at one end of the stage, awaiting the entry of the peers through the huge double doors opposite. After a tense pause filled with an ominous drumbeat, the doors opened and four ranks of straight-backed, stern-faced men strode forward. The two parties faced each other. No sign of deference or submission was given by the peers, who looked more like a fighting squadron than obedient subjects. At last, Henry made a slight movement forward and the peers scattered, making brief bows. It was clearly never going to be easy for the gentle Henry to master this group's power and independence.

On the page Henry's silences can make the reader almost forget his presence in a scene, but in performance the effect is quite different. David Warner, in 1963 for the RSC, used his long, doleful face and frame to best advantage in communicating his distress. Henry's costume is usually designed to be much simpler and more self-effacing than that of his courtiers. This was strongly marked with Warner, whose rough cassock-like garment contrasted starkly with the richly jewelled and padded splendour of those around him. His only adornment was a simple cross about his neck, and, with his heavy boots and unkempt hair, he appeared as some kind of Dostoevskian holy fool, desiring only the rejection of earthly things and the mortification of the flesh.

Henry's silent presence is, perhaps, most telling in Act III, scene 1, during the peers' attack on Duke Humphrey. He finally speaks at length, not to prevent the arrest of his beloved Protector but to assert Humphrey's innocence and to punish himself with accusations of his own impotence. Ralph Fiennes's interpretation of the role, at the RSC, in 1988, was particularly powerful here, both in bitterly acknowledging responsibility for his failure to prevent Humphrey's fall and, in the following scene, in the proclamation of Suffolk's banishment. His grief, anger and thwarted moral strength registered fully with the audience. The small competence of Alan Howard's Henry, in 1977 for the RSC, was impaired to an even greater extent by his evident bouts of madness. His swoon on hearing the news of Duke Humphrey's death left him in a catatonic trance, from which Margaret strove to rouse him by means of her long, highly rhetorical speech.

In the course of the play both Duke Humphrey and Cardinal Beaufort are displayed to the audience dead in their beds. This repeated stage image underlines the truism that blood will have blood; having plotted Duke Humphrey's death, the Cardinal swiftly follows him to the grave. Likewise, Suffolk, the other man responsible for Duke Humphrey's death, soon meets his end. This sequence of retribution was powerfully played out in Michael Boyd's expressionistic production, in which Duke Humphrey's ghost escorted each of his murderers into a tormented afterlife. Having forcibly held down the dying Cardinal's hands so that he could give no sign to the King of any hope of heaven, in Act III, scene 3, Humphrey's ghost remained alone onstage to strip the bed and chain the body up to a pulley before hoisting it away. He exited, with his burden, through the huge double doors at the rear. The red light of hell flooded through these doors as the Cardinal (in fact, now his ghost) cried out in spiritual torment. Then the figures of Lord Talbot and his son, recognizable from *Part I* to the audiences in the Swan Theatre (who were able to see all three of the *Henry VI* plays, as well as *Richard III*, that season), entered through a hatch flung up in the wooden bed frame to play the roles of the Lieutenant and Walter Whitmore. This wooden frame now signified the ship on which Suffolk is killed, in Act IV, scene 1. It metamorphosed one stage further as Boyd presented it to the audience not as a literal ship but as the ferry that would waft Suffolk to his fate in the underworld.

The doubling of actors is a convention often used by directors to cast this most populous of plays and to delineate the patterning of the play's action and themes. Boyd pushed this convention one stage further in that he was not simply doubling the actors who had previously played the Talbots, but rather recasting those characters in these new roles. Talbot and his son are central to the action of *Henry VI, Part I*, where they represent the heroic self-sacrifice of the chivalric ideal in the wars in France. Their deaths in that play are the direct result of the nobles' selfish feuding at home. Their reappearance here, as characters who upbraid Suffolk for the losses in France, illustrates the director's imaginative response to the patterns that shape these plays, as he figured out the ways in which the present is permeated by the past throughout the trilogy. Boyd's presentation of the *Henry VI* plays thus anticipated *Richard III*, his final production that season, in which Margaret, as a still-living character, haunts the courts and battlefields of England, and the ghosts of Richard's victims return to take vengeance upon him.

With Suffolk's death, the play takes a new turn in direction and tone. The audience is brought face to face with the physical reality of violent death as Suffolk's body and head are brought on stage. The Folio text's wonderfully bold stage direction begins Act IV, scene 4: '*Enter the King with a supplication, and the Queen with Suffolk's head . . .*' Here is a disruption of the public by the private, with a vengeance! The moment offers the actress playing Queen Margaret a great opportunity to dig deep into her emotional resources and initiate the character's development from adulterous queen to pitiless avenger.

In his final scene, Act IV, scene 1, Suffolk's blank verse speeches of overweening pride, in which he glories in his aristocratic rank, serve only to make more extreme his utter humiliation at the hands of base-born men. Rebellious, prose-speaking commoners now take over the stage in the form of Jack Cade and his murderous crew. Although, by order of Cade, the heads of Say and Cromer are made to kiss at every street corner, directors have frequently found this too tame an expression of the anarchy unloosed by York's destabilizing stratagem. In *The Plantagenets*, the Royal Shakespeare Company's adaptation at Stratford in 1988, Adrian Noble created a nightmare vision as a dozen or so heads were stuck on

long poles and waved menacingly over the front stalls of
the auditorium in an image worthy of the worst excesses
of the French Revolution. These grisly poles were left
in the middle of the stage, sticking up in a circle from
which radiated long shadow-fingers, catching at the
envoys of the King. Edward Hall's production at
the Watermill Theatre in 2001 played in a set based on the
abattoir of Smithfield meat market, complete with tiled
floor (for easy blood cleansing) and metal spikes (useful
for the displaying of heads). Red cabbages were placed
on the execution block next to the actors' heads, and it
was these that were sliced and chopped by white-aproned
butchers. The inevitable mess of red matter provided a
suitably unpleasant pathway for York to tread upon as
he returned from Ireland and prepared for the battle of
St Albans.

In the 1987 production by the English Shakespeare
Company Cade was presented in the style of a brutal
leader of the British National Front in the late twentieth
century. Decked out in Union Jack flags, he sharpened
his followers' appetite for the avenging of personal griev-
ance under the cloak of patriotic fervour. This contemporary dress worked very well with the creation, in the
initial court scenes, of an early-twentieth-century period,
since the peers now coming to parley with Cade were
resplendent in ceremonial military uniform of scarlet and
black, with crested, golden helmets. This is still current
for state occasions in the early twenty-first century; it is
traditional and, therefore, timeless. Michael Pennington
exploited to the full his enjoyable double of Suffolk and
Cade, exchanging the persuasive suavity of the first for
the punk-rocker aggression of the second. The sheer
entertainment value of Cade's scenes was likewise recog-
nized by Michael Boyd and his designer, Tom Piper, at

the Swan in 2000. They released the topsy-turvy energy of the action with their dynamic use of vertical space, with Cade dominating the stage from a trapeze, while his followers nimbly shinned up and down ropes, suspended from the flies. Characteristically in this production, those ghostly revenants, Duke Humphrey, Cardinal Beaufort and the Talbots, helped Cade wreak havoc on the body politic.

Although there is plenty of violence in *Henry VI, Part II*, as the Cade scenes illustrate, there is only one battle, occurring in the closing stages of the play. Here, at last, York has his forward sons at his side. On their first appearance in Act V, scene 1, the original stage directions call only for Richard and Edward, but most modern directors have added the third son, Clarence, to strengthen the arrival of this new generation and introduce another of the Yorkists who will have an important role in *Henry VI, Part III*, when the battles will be more frequent and more bloody.

Richard is called by Clifford a 'foul indigested lump' (V.1.157). Directors must decide whether this insult is justified by Richard's appearance. Whatever deformity is chosen for him must not actually cripple him, since he fights very successfully at St Albans. Richard and his Lancastrian counterpart in cruelty, Young Clifford, are ominous harbingers of the pitiless violence that will characterize *Part III*. In the battles of that play there will be no room for the few chivalric words and deeds performed at St Albans. Jane Howell, in her production for BBC television in 1981, used Salisbury to draw attention to this. Salisbury is slow to follow his victorious fellow-Yorkists as they take their final exit, because he is gazing at the butchery around him. The camera follows his gaze and presents to the audience the slaughtered bodies of young men from both sides of the conflict, lying in bloody heaps. A few moments earlier, King Henry had likewise delayed his departure from the stage; he was transfixed by the sight of a dead youth, spread-eagled upon a cannon, his white and gold tabard soaked in blood. Salisbury's old, sorrowful face had given us similar pause in Act II, scene 2, when the camera had lingered on him as he silently listened to York's justification of his right to the English throne. Building on this thoughtful silence, the director clearly communicated the character's foreboding of the terrible bloodshed that must now ensue.

Rebecca Brown

Further Reading

EDITIONS

The complicated and controversial relationship between the 1594 Quarto and the 1623 Folio editions of *Henry VI, Part II* can best be pondered with the help of recent major editions of the play: Michael Hattaway's New Cambridge Shakespeare (1991), Andrew S. Cairncross's Arden Shakespeare (1962) and, especially, Ronald Knowles's Arden Shakespeare (third series; 1999) and Roger Warren's Oxford Shakespeare (2002). Warren's edition argues that the Quarto text is mainly illegitimate, but complicatedly so: 'Q and F show signs of two different kinds of revision of the play as originally written. Q seems to report changes to it made in rehearsal, F to reflect changes made in a later revision, probably for a revival.' Thus, as with most modern editions of *Henry VI, Part II* the Oxford text largely follows the Folio, since it represents in all probability, as Warren argues, Shakespeare's latest thoughts on the play.

The Introductions to these editions offer the reader a variety of helpful discourse: on sources, analogues, background, date of composition and first performance, theatrical and critical history (Knowles's Arden edition is quite exhaustive on this score, at the expense perhaps of a certain fluidity of exposition). Hattaway suggests a useful way to assess Shakespeare's originality in this play: look at other history plays written at this time or later, he urges – Thomas Heywood's *Edward IV*, for instance, or *Sir John Oldcastle*, a collaboration by Michael Drayton, Richard Hathway, Anthony Munday and Robert Wilson. (See also A. J. Hoenselaars' essay, 'Shakespeare and the Early Modern History Play', in *The Cambridge Companion to Shakespeare's History Plays* (2002).) All of these editors are in fact enthusiastic advocates of the distinction of *Henry VI, Part II* and their welcome partisanship is best caught by Knowles: he writes his Introduction, he says, 'in the conviction that had a barely known young Warwickshire playwright been carried off by the London plague of 1592, *Henry VI, Part II* would remain as the greatest history play in early modern drama and one of the most exciting and dynamic plays of the English Renaissance theatre.' Amen to that.

At the same time, the partisanship is not blinkered. Roger Warren, for instance, provides a number of moments of judicious reflection on the play's shortcomings. A thought-provoking one is his hesitancy over the play's longest speech, Margaret's, at III.2.73–121, roughly halfway through the play. For Warren it's a great puzzle, 'since its dramatic purpose is far from clear'. Is it sincere? Is it an indication of Margaret's insincerity? Or is it an attempt, as played in Terry Hands's 1977 production, to divert Henry from what may well be a bout of mental illness? If nothing else, it's a tribute to the play's stature that an editor should pause to brood in this way on one of its major speeches. The same might be said more generally of John W. Blanpied's book *Time and the Artist in Shakespeare's English Histories* (1983) which, while acknowledging the considerable art of *Henry VI, Part II* argues that the play is emotionally incoherent with a disappointing ending in which 'the play seems to have withdrawn from us'.

All editions of *Henry VI, Part II* necessarily take up and brood upon the question of its place in the first tetralogy. Is it Shakespeare's first history play – perhaps his first play ever – with *Henry VI, Part I* written out of sequence after *Henry VI, Part III* – a 'prequel' – as most critics, following John Dover Wilson in his 1952 Cambridge edition, now believe? Or was it written in real time where it comes in the 1623 Folio, namely after *Henry VI, Part I* and before *Henry VI, Part III*? Cairncross and Hattaway still think so. Reopening the debate, Nicholas Grene in *Shakespeare's Serial History Plays* (2002) defends the Folio's accuracy as to time as well as place. From the beginning, he says, the four plays of the tetralogy were serially intended in response to the success of Marlowe's two-part *Tamburlaine*: 'the chickens coming home to roost in *Richard III* have long been flying through the night skies of the *Henry VI* plays'. So *Henry VI, Part I* was necessarily written first, *Henry VI, Part II* second, and so on. Grene does not, however, succeed in demolishing the counter-arguments of those in the Dover Wilson camp. (Emrys Jones is a more convincing and thorough demolisher of the prequel theory in *The Origins of Shakespeare* (1977), though he too is not irresistible.) At the very least, the question remains moot.

BACKGROUND

Two succinct essays explore the background of Shakespeare's *Henry VI, Part II*. In 'Shakespeare and English History' in *The Cambridge Companion to Shakespeare*

(2001) David Scott Kastan sees Shakespeare's history plays as one symptom of a rabid general interest in history in Shakespeare's time; his plays 'experiment with different formal strategies as they seek a form for history: homiletic tragedy, saturnalian comedy, the prodigal son play, epic history, and these often in improbable mixtures that bring incompatible visions of history into contact and conflict'. In 'The Shakespearean History Play' in *The Cambridge Companion to Shakespeare's History Plays* (2002) Michael Hattaway entertainingly traverses the now familiar furrowed landscape of paradox and ambivalence in Shakespeare's flirtation with ideology, made familiar by such classic essays as A. P. Rossiter's 'Ambivalence: The Dialectic of the Histories' in *Angel with Horns* (1961). 'Handy-dandy, what is substantial, what is mere "shadow"?' Hattaway asks about the history plays, as does Wolfgang Iser in *Staging Politics: The Lasting Impact of Shakespeare's Histories* (1993), for whom the plays show 'human dislocation to be the hallmark of history'.

Human dislocation notwithstanding, the notion that Shakespeare's history plays subscribe to and propagandize for the Tudor myth of kingship refuses to disappear entirely, despite the battering it has taken in recent years. And so E. M. W. Tillyard, the propagator in the twentieth century of the theory of a providential teleology for the plays, is still widely read and his two books, *Shakespeare's History Plays* (1944) and *The Elizabethan World Picture: A Study of the Idea of Order in the Age of Shakespeare, Donne and Milton* (1943), remain stubbornly in print. Tillyard's books have spawned a number of often caustic rebuttals, the most thoroughgoing of which are D. L. Frey's *The First Tetralogy, Shakespeare's Scrutiny of the Tudor Myth: A Dramatic Exploration of Divine Providence* (1976) and H. A. Kelly's *Divine Providence in*

the England of Shakespeare's Histories (1970). But, as
Ronald Knowles acknowledged in his Arden edition of
Henry VI, Part II in 1999, the issues of providence,
sin and justice are paramount in the first tetralogy
even though we may reject the Tudor myth. Knowles
suggests that for the sceptic in Shakespeare's original audiences the second part of *Henry VI* might well have been
considered 'a burlesque on the idea of providence'. And
the trial between providentialism and Renaissance machia-
vellianism might well be considered the most important
of the numerous trials dramatized in this play. In his reveal-
ingly entitled *Shakespeare's Arguments with History* (2002)
Knowles feels reobliged to re-encounter Tillyard. For
Edward Berry in *Patterns of Decay: Shakespeare's Early
Histories* (1975), Henry's 'exaggerated belief in the active
intervention of divine judgment in human affairs' is not
entirely discredited by the play as a whole.

Rejection or qualification of Tillyard's position is
part of a more general recent acknowledgement of
Shakespeare's sophistication as a historian and histori-
ographer. Yet we should bear in mind Graham
Holderness's interesting take on Tillyard in *Shakespeare
Recycled: The Making of Historical Drama* (1992), where
he points out that originally Tillyard's method was radical
and controversial, 'unacceptable to critics committed to
a more traditional notion of art as free from the construc-
tions of ideology or the determinants of history' (such
as Irving Ribner, A. P. Rossiter and Robert Ornstein),
for whom Shakespeare becomes 'a free-thinking liberal
judiciously suspicious of all ideology'. Holderness's other
books, *Shakespeare: The Play of History* (1988, with Nick
Potter) and *Shakespeare: The Histories* (2002), ask us to
see Shakespeare's grasp of history 'as more akin to a new
historiography of the seventeenth century than to . . .

older perspectives'. Shakespeare is not only an interesting historian of the sixteenth and seventeenth centuries but also of the fifteenth. For Paola Pugliatti in her fine book, *Shakespeare the Historian* (1996), Shakespeare practised 'a problem-oriented, multivocal kind of historiography that probed into events in depth rather than in extension'. The plays' literary sophistication is explored by David Riggs in *Shakespeare's Heroical Histories: 'Henry VI' and Its Literary Tradition* (1971).

MARGARET

For the modern reader and playgoer the multivocality of *Henry VI, Part II* has been dominated by two voices, Margaret's and Jack Cade's. Both characters are marvellous parts for any actor. As Jean E. Howard and Phyllis Rackin argue in *Engendering a Nation: A Feminist Account of Shakespeare's English Histories* (1997), there is a huge difference between the presentation of women in the first tetralogy (*Henry VI, Part I* to *Richard III*) and the second (*Richard II* to *Henry V*). The first is arguably in thrall to its women characters; in the second they have virtually disappeared. Susan Bassnett in *Shakespeare: The Elizabethan Plays* (1993) notes that in the first tetralogy women represent 'disorder, animality, deceit, disloyalty, with the strongest criticism directed against women who fight and women who consort with witches and devils'.

In *Henry VI, Part II* Margaret (and Jack Cade) is made worse, morally speaking, than in Shakespeare's sources, and there is a heightened sexuality in her presentation. She is the only character who appears in all four of the plays, beginning as a winsome sex object in *Henry VI, Part I* and ending as a prophetic harpy in *Richard III*. But how are we to read her in the transitional *Henry VI, Part II*? Does she *really* love Henry? Or in the face of her love for Suffolk is her 'love' for Henry merely a cynical affectation? A measure of the play's sophistication lies in the capacity for its actors to push us in either direction (or, even, in both at the same time). Critics sometimes rush to judgement. Gwyn Williams, for instance, in 'Suffolk and Margaret: A Study of Some Sections of Shakespeare's *Henry VI*', *Shakespeare Quarterly* (1974), describes the love affair between Margaret and Suffolk as 'Shakespeare's first essay in tragic, destructive love, and there is something grand in this shameless affection between two passionate, ruthless and physically splendid lovers'. But for Joseph Candido (to go to the other extreme), in his 'Getting Loose in the *Henry VI* Plays', *Shakespeare Quarterly* (1984), the love affair is an example of debased idealism full of 'rhetorical posturing' and 'tortured Petrarchanism'. For more balanced interpretations, the reader should consult Marilyn L. Williamson, '"When Men Are Rul'd by Women": Shakespeare's First Tetralogy', *Shakespeare Studies* (1987), Phyllis Rackin, 'Foreign Country: The Place of Women and Sexuality in Shakespeare's Historical World', in *Enclosure Acts: Sexuality, Property, and Culture in Early Modern England* (1994) and Kathryn Schwarz, 'Fearful Simile: Stealing the Breech in Shakespeare's Chronicle Plays', *Shakespeare Quarterly* (1988).

JACK CADE

Shakespeare's presentation of Jack Cade, the Shylock of the first tetralogy, has provoked much controversy. We look at him askance; he arouses all kinds of anxiety – a

word often used of him and his effect in the critical literature, as in Edward I. Berry's remark in *Patterns of Decay:
Shakespeare's Early Histories* (1975) that Cade kindles 'a
peculiarly anxiety-ridden laughter'. (Compare Stephen
Greenblatt's 'a strange laughter . . . a taut, cruel laughter'
in his wonderful essay, 'Murdering Peasants: Status, Genre,
and the Representation of Rebellion', in *Representing the
English Renaissance* (1988).) Cade arouses not just anxiety
but anger. Richard Wilson in his trenchant essay, '"A
Mingled Yarn": Shakespeare and the Cloth Workers',
Literature & History 12 (1986), pp. 164–80, castigates
Shakespeare for the play's 'venomous fourth act' with its
'outraged version of Jack Cade's 1450 uprising'.
Shakespeare changes the historical Cade, Wilson charges,
'into a cruel, barbaric lout' in a 'travesty of evidence';
Shakespeare's Cade is 'a projection of the sexual and canni-
balistic terrors of the Renaissance rich' and is presented
in terms of a 'sneering impatience with the language of
peasants and artisans of the literate bourgeois'.

Much criticism treads nervously over this ground. Can
we save Shakespeare from Cade? Just how extensively
Shakespeare blackens Cade's character can be seen first
of all in the differences Shakespeare introduces from the
Cade of the sources (see the third volume of Geoffrey
Bullough's *Narrative and Dramatic Sources of Shakespeare*
(1960) for a convenient compilation). Secondly, a measured view of him in history can be found in I. M. W.
Harvey's *Jack Cade's Rebellion of 1450* (1991): 'Cade's
rebellion throws into sharp relief the society it criticized:
its debt-burdened monarch, its corrupt and greedy
courtiers, its dishonest and cynical local representatives,
and its disgraced troops. It is not a handsome picture.'
Shakespeare's is not, however, a measured view.

Many critics try to present a more measured view of

Shakespeare's lack of moderation. Cade is after all a character in a play and functions accordingly. The defence often seizes upon the fact that in the play Cade is York's idea; what Cade does and says therefore is a carnivalesque re-enactment of the corruption of his social superiors. This is the burden of Annabel Patterson's *Shakespeare and the Popular Voice* (1989), of E. W. Talbert's *Elizabethan Drama and Shakespeare's Early Plays: An Essay in Historical Criticism* (1963), and of Thomas Cartelli's fascinating essay, 'Jack Cade in the Garden: Class Consciousness and Class Conflict in *Henry VI, Part Two*', in *Enclosure Acts: Sexuality, Property, and Culture in Early Modern England* (1994). This view of things is best summed up in Knowles's edition (1999): 'The depiction of Cade and his followers . . . is not simply the expression of anti-egalitarianism, the anarchic many-headed monster run wild, but rather the recognition that such rebellions become a grotesque mimicry of the barbarism of feudal hierarchy.'

Or we simply have to acknowledge the fact that Shakespeare presents Cade's complaints in a manner that (somehow) retains their validity. Thus Cartelli, who argues that we are supposed to see what's behind Cade: 'But it is Cade's *impulse* to change radically the system by which goods and offices are distributed that might better occupy our attention.' Alexander Leggatt in *Shakespeare's Political Drama: The History Plays and the Roman Plays* (1988) argues that at times Cade is an articulate spokesman for the oppressed, and asks us not to dismiss out of hand Cade's dying words: 'Tell Kent from me she hath lost her best man' (IV.10.70–71).

However impassioned the defence of Jack Cade (and/or Shakespeare), perhaps we should leave the final word on him to Roger Warren's sober reflections on his meaning in the shadow of the events in Cambodia and

Serbia in the twentieth century, or of the riots in 2001 in the England of Bradford and Oldham: 'I draw these uncomfortable modern parallels because I think it important not to allow the savage cruelty of the Cade scenes to get lost in laughter, carnivalesque or otherwise.' We may be able to save Shakespeare from Cade but not Cade from himself.

Michael Taylor

THE PLAY IN PERFORMANCE

John Barton and Peter Hall, *The Wars of the Roses* (1970)

John Russell Brown, *Shakespeare's Plays in Performance* (1966)

Ralph Fiennes, 'King Henry VI' in Russell Jackson and Robert Smallwood (eds.), *Players of Shakespeare 3* (1993)

William Shakespeare, *Henry 6, Part 2* (BBC TV Shakespeare, 1983; with an introduction discussing the production choices)

William Shakespeare, *The Plantagenets* (1989; text of RSC's 1988 adaptation, with introduction by the director, Adrian Noble)

Robert Smallwood (ed.), *Players of Shakespeare 6* (2004)

A. C. Sprague, *Shakespeare's Histories* (1964)

Videos

The Wars of the Roses: Henry 6, Edward 4 (a recording of Peter Hall and John Barton's adaptation for the RSC, 1965)

The Wars of the Roses: Henry 6, House of Lancaster, Edward 4, House of York (a recording of the English Shakespeare Company's adaptation, directed by Michael Bogdanov, 1990)

BBC Shakespeare: Henry 6, Part 2, dir. Jane Howell (1983)

Rebecca Brown

THE FIRST PART OF THE CONTENTION BETWIXT THE TWO FAMOUS HOUSES OF YORK AND LANCASTER

The Characters in the Play

KING Henry the Sixth

Margaret, QUEEN of England, daughter of King Reignier

Duke of YORK, Richard Plantagenet

EDWARD ⎱ sons of the Duke of York
RICHARD ⎰

Duke of GLOUCESTER, Humphrey of Lancaster, Protector of England, uncle of the King

DUCHESS of Gloucester, Eleanor Cobham

CARDINAL Beaufort, Bishop of Winchester, great-uncle of the King

Duke of SUFFOLK, William de la Pole

Duke of SOMERSET, Edmund Beaufort

Duke of BUCKINGHAM, Humphrey Stafford

Earl of SALISBURY, Richard Nevil

Earl of WARWICK, Richard Nevil, son of the Earl of Salisbury

Lord CLIFFORD

YOUNG CLIFFORD, son of Lord Clifford

Lord SCALES

Lord SAY

Sir Humphrey STAFFORD

William Stafford, BROTHER of Sir Humphrey Stafford

Sir John STANLEY

VAUX

Alexander IDEN, a Kentish gentleman

John HUME, a priest
John SOUTHWELL, a priest
Roger BOLINGBROKE, a conjurer
Margery JOURDAIN, a witch
SPIRIT

Thomas HORNER, an armourer
PETER Thump, Horner's assistant
PETITIONERS
NEIGHBOURS
PRENTICES

Saunder SIMPCOX
WIFE of Simpcox
A MAN
MAYOR of Saint Albans
A BEADLE

Jack CADE
George BEVIS
John HOLLAND
DICK, a butcher   } followers of Jack Cade
SMITH, a weaver
MICHAEL

A LIEUTENANT
A MASTER
A master's MATE
Walter WHITMORE
Two GENTLEMEN, prisoners with Suffolk

MESSENGERS

SERVANTS
SHERIFF
A HERALD
A POST
TWO MURDERERS
COMMONS
CLERK of Chartham
FIRST CITIZEN
A SOLDIER

Guards, soldiers, servants, attendants, falconers, aldermen, neighbours, prentices, officers, a sawyer, rebels, citizens, Matthew Gough

Flourish of trumpets, then hautboys. Enter the King,
Gloucester, Salisbury, Warwick, and Cardinal
Beaufort on the one side; the Queen, Suffolk, York,
Somerset, and Buckingham on the other

SUFFOLK
As by your high imperial majesty
I had in charge at my depart for France,
As procurator to your excellence,
To marry Princess Margaret for your grace;
So, in the famous ancient city Tours,
In presence of the Kings of France and Sicil,
The Dukes of Orleans, Calaber, Bretagne, and Alençon,
Seven earls, twelve barons, and twenty reverend bishops,
I have performed my task and was espoused;
And humbly now upon my bended knee,   10
    (*he kneels*)
In sight of England and her lordly peers,
Deliver up my title in the Queen
To your most gracious hands, that are the substance
Of that great shadow I did represent –
The happiest gift that ever marquess gave,
The fairest queen that ever king received.
KING
Suffolk, arise. Welcome, Queen Margaret.

I can express no kinder sign of love
Than this kind kiss. O Lord that lends me life,
20   Lend me a heart replete with thankfulness!
For Thou hast given me in this beauteous face
A world of earthly blessings to my soul,
If sympathy of love unite our thoughts.

QUEEN

Great King of England and my gracious lord,
The mutual conference that my mind hath had
By day, by night, waking and in my dreams,
In courtly company or at my beads,
With you, mine alderliefest sovereign,
Makes me the bolder to salute my king
30   With ruder terms, such as my wit affords,
And overjoy of heart doth minister.

KING

Her sight did ravish, but her grace in speech,
Her words y-clad with wisdom's majesty,
Makes me from wondering fall to weeping joys,
Such is the fullness of my heart's content.
Lords, with one cheerful voice welcome my love.
    All kneel

ALL

Long live Queen Margaret, England's happiness!
    Flourish

QUEEN

We thank you all.

SUFFOLK

My Lord Protector, so it please your grace,
40   Here are the articles of contracted peace
Between our sovereign and the French King Charles,
For eighteen months concluded by consent.

GLOUCESTER (*reads*) *Imprimis, it is agreed between the
French King Charles and William de la Pole, Marquess of*

Suffolk, ambassador for Henry King of England, that the
said Henry shall espouse the Lady Margaret, daughter
unto Reignier King of Naples, Sicilia, and Jerusalem,
and crown her Queen of England ere the thirtieth of May
next ensuing. Item, it is further agreed between them that
the duchy of Anjou and the county of Maine shall be   50
released and delivered over to the King her father —
   (*Gloucester lets the contract fall*)

KING

  Uncle, how now?

GLOUCESTER   Pardon me, gracious lord.

  Some sudden qualm hath struck me at the heart
  And dimmed mine eyes, that I can read no further.

KING

  Uncle of Winchester, I pray read on.

CARDINAL (*reads*) *Item, it is further agreed between them*
  that the duchy of Anjou and the county of Maine shall
  be released and delivered over to the King her father,
  and she sent over of the King of England's own proper
  cost and charges, without having any dowry.   60

KING

  They please us well. Lord Marquess, kneel down.
  We here create thee the first Duke of Suffolk
  And girt thee with the sword. Cousin of York,
  We here discharge your grace from being Regent
  I'the parts of France, till term of eighteen months
  Be full expired. Thanks, uncle Winchester,
  Gloucester, York, Buckingham, Somerset,
  Salisbury, and Warwick.
  We thank you all for this great favour done
  In entertainment to my princely Queen.   70
  Come, let us in, and with all speed provide
  To see her coronation be performed.

                Exeunt King, Queen, and Suffolk

Gloucester stays all the rest

GLOUCESTER

Brave peers of England, pillars of the state,
To you Duke Humphrey must unload his grief,
Your grief, the common grief of all the land.
What? Did my brother Henry spend his youth,
His valour, coin, and people in the wars?
Did he so often lodge in open field,
In winter's cold and summer's parching heat,
To conquer France, his true inheritance?
And did my brother Bedford toil his wits
To keep by policy what Henry got?
Have you yourselves, Somerset, Buckingham,
Brave York, Salisbury, and victorious Warwick,
Received deep scars in France and Normandy?
Or hath mine uncle Beaufort and myself,
With all the learnèd Council of the realm,
Studied so long, sat in the Council House
Early and late, debating to and fro
How France and Frenchmen might be kept in awe?
And had his highness in his infancy
Crownèd in Paris in despite of foes?
And shall these labours and these honours die?
Shall Henry's conquest, Bedford's vigilance,
Your deeds of war, and all our counsel die?
O peers of England, shameful is this league,
Fatal this marriage, cancelling your fame,
Blotting your names from books of memory,
Razing the characters of your renown,
Defacing monuments of conquered France,
Undoing all, as all had never been!

CARDINAL

Nephew, what means this passionate discourse,
This peroration with such circumstance?

For France, 'tis ours; and we will keep it still.

GLOUCESTER

Ay, uncle, we will keep it, if we can;
But now it is impossible we should.
Suffolk, the new-made duke that rules the roast,
Hath given the duchy of Anjou and Maine
Unto the poor King Reignier, whose large style
Agrees not with the leanness of his purse.   110

SALISBURY

Now by the death of Him that died for all,
These counties were the keys of Normandy.
But wherefore weeps Warwick, my valiant son?

WARWICK

For grief that they are past recovery;
For, were there hope to conquer them again,
My sword should shed hot blood, mine eyes no tears.
Anjou and Maine? Myself did win them both;
Those provinces these arms of mine did conquer;
And are the cities that I got with wounds
Delivered up again with peaceful words?   120
Mort Dieu!

YORK

For Suffolk's duke, may he be suffocate,
That dims the honour of this warlike isle!
France should have torn and rent my very heart
Before I would have yielded to this league.
I never read but England's kings have had
Large sums of gold and dowries with their wives;
And our King Henry gives away his own,
To match with her that brings no vantages.

GLOUCESTER

A proper jest, and never heard before,   130
That Suffolk should demand a whole fifteenth
For costs and charges in transporting her!

She should have stayed in France, and starved in France,
Before —

CARDINAL

My lord of Gloucester, now ye grow too hot;
It was the pleasure of my lord the King.

GLOUCESTER

My lord of Winchester, I know your mind;
'Tis not my speeches that you do mislike,
But 'tis my presence that doth trouble ye.
140   Rancour will out; proud prelate, in thy face
I see thy fury. If I longer stay,
We shall begin our ancient bickerings.
Lordings, farewell; and say, when I am gone,
I prophesied France will be lost ere long.

Exit Gloucester

CARDINAL

So there goes our Protector in a rage.
'Tis known to you he is mine enemy;
Nay more, an enemy unto you all,
And no great friend, I fear me, to the King.
Consider, lords, he is the next of blood
150   And heir apparent to the English crown.
Had Henry got an empire by his marriage,
And all the wealthy kingdoms of the west,
There's reason he should be displeased at it.
Look to it, lords; let not his smoothing words
Bewitch your hearts. Be wise and circumspect.
What though the common people favour him,
Calling him 'Humphrey, the good Duke of Gloucester',
Clapping their hands and crying with loud voice
'Jesu maintain your royal excellence!'
160   With 'God preserve the good Duke Humphrey!',
I fear me, lords, for all this flattering gloss,
He will be found a dangerous Protector.

BUCKINGHAM

    Why should he then protect our sovereign,

    He being of age to govern of himself?

    Cousin of Somerset, join you with me,

    And all together, with the Duke of Suffolk,

    We'll quickly hoise Duke Humphrey from his seat.

CARDINAL

    This weighty business will not brook delay;

    I'll to the Duke of Suffolk presently.   *Exit*

SOMERSET

    Cousin of Buckingham, though Humphrey's pride   170

    And greatness of his place be grief to us,

    Yet let us watch the haughty Cardinal;

    His insolence is more intolerable

    Than all the princes' in the land beside.

    If Gloucester be displaced, he'll be Protector.

BUCKINGHAM

    Or thou or I, Somerset, will be Protector,

    Despite Duke Humphrey or the Cardinal.

              Exeunt Buckingham and Somerset

SALISBURY

    Pride went before; Ambition follows him.

    While these do labour for their own preferment,

    Behoves it us to labour for the realm.   180

    I never saw but Humphrey Duke of Gloucester

    Did bear him like a noble gentleman.

    Oft have I seen the haughty Cardinal,

    More like a soldier than a man o'th'church,

    As stout and proud as he were lord of all,

    Swear like a ruffian, and demean himself

    Unlike the ruler of a commonweal.

    Warwick, my son, the comfort of my age,

    Thy deeds, thy plainness, and thy house-keeping

    Hath won the greatest favour of the commons,   190

Excepting none but good Duke Humphrey;
And, brother York, thy acts in Ireland,
In bringing them to civil discipline,
Thy late exploits done in the heart of France,
When thou wert Regent for our sovereign,
Have made thee feared and honoured of the people.
Join we together for the public good,
In what we can to bridle and suppress
The pride of Suffolk and the Cardinal,
200   With Somerset's and Buckingham's ambition;
And, as we may, cherish Duke Humphrey's deeds
While they do tend the profit of the land.

WARWICK
So God help Warwick, as he loves the land
And common profit of his country!

YORK
And so says York – (aside) for he hath greatest cause.

SALISBURY
Then let's make haste away, and look unto the main.

WARWICK
Unto the main! O father, Maine is lost!
That Maine which by main force Warwick did win,
And would have kept so long as breath did last!
210   Main chance, father, you meant; but I meant Maine,
Which I will win from France or else be slain.
                              Exeunt Warwick and Salisbury

YORK
Anjou and Maine are given to the French;
Paris is lost; the state of Normandy
Stands on a tickle point now they are gone.
Suffolk concluded on the articles,
The peers agreed, and Henry was well pleased
To change two dukedoms for a duke's fair daughter.
I cannot blame them all; what is't to them?

'Tis thine they give away, and not their own.
Pirates may make cheap pennyworths of their pillage   220
And purchase friends and give to courtesans,
Still revelling like lords till all be gone;
While as the silly owner of the goods
Weeps over them, and wrings his hapless hands,
And shakes his head, and trembling stands aloof,
While all is shared and all is borne away,
Ready to starve, and dare not touch his own.
So York must sit and fret and bite his tongue,
While his own lands are bargained for and sold.
Methinks the realms of England, France, and Ireland   230
Bear that proportion to my flesh and blood
As did the fatal brand Althaea burnt
Unto the Prince's heart of Calydon.
Anjou and Maine both given unto the French!
Cold news for me; for I had hope of France,
Even as I have of fertile England's soil.
A day will come when York shall claim his own,
And therefore I will take the Nevils' parts
And make a show of love to proud Duke Humphrey,
And, when I spy advantage, claim the crown,   240
For that's the golden mark I seek to hit.
Nor shall proud Lancaster usurp my right,
Nor hold the sceptre in his childish fist,
Nor wear the diadem upon his head,
Whose church-like humours fits not for a crown.
Then, York, be still awhile till time do serve;
Watch thou, and wake when others be asleep,
To pry into the secrets of the state,
Till Henry, surfeiting in joys of love
With his new bride and England's dear-bought queen,   250
And Humphrey with the peers be fallen at jars.
Then will I raise aloft the milk-white rose,

With whose sweet smell the air shall be perfumed,
And in my standard bear the arms of York,
To grapple with the house of Lancaster;
And force perforce I'll make him yield the crown,
Whose bookish rule hath pulled fair England down.

Exit

I.2   *Enter the Duke of Gloucester and his wife the*
             Duchess

DUCHESS

Why droops my lord like over-ripened corn,
Hanging the head at Ceres' plenteous load?
Why doth the great Duke Humphrey knit his brows,
As frowning at the favours of the world?
Why are thine eyes fixed to the sullen earth,
Gazing on that which seems to dim thy sight?
What seest thou there? King Henry's diadem,
Enchased with all the honours of the world?
If so, gaze on, and grovel on thy face,
10   Until thy head be circled with the same.
Put forth thy hand, reach at the glorious gold.
What, is't too short? I'll lengthen it with mine;
And having both together heaved it up,
We'll both together lift our heads to heaven,
And never more abase our sight so low
As to vouchsafe one glance unto the ground.

GLOUCESTER

O Nell, sweet Nell, if thou dost love thy lord,
Banish the canker of ambitious thoughts!
And may that thought, when I imagine ill
20   Against my king and nephew, virtuous Henry,
Be my last breathing in this mortal world!
My troublous dreams this night doth make me sad.

DUCHESS
    What dreamed my lord? Tell me, and I'll requite it
    With sweet rehearsal of my morning's dream.
GLOUCESTER
    Methought this staff, mine office-badge in court,
    Was broke in twain – by whom I have forgot,
    But, as I think, it was by the Cardinal –
    And on the pieces of the broken wand
    Were placed the heads of Edmund Duke of Somerset
    And William de la Pole, first Duke of Suffolk.   30
    This was my dream; what it doth bode, God knows.
DUCHESS
    Tut, this was nothing but an argument
    That he that breaks a stick of Gloucester's grove
    Shall lose his head for his presumption.
    But list to me, my Humphrey, my sweet Duke:
    Methought I sat in seat of majesty
    In the cathedral church of Westminster,
    And in that chair where kings and queens were crowned,
    Where Henry and Dame Margaret kneeled to me,
    And on my head did set the diadem.   40
GLOUCESTER
    Nay, Eleanor, then must I chide outright:
    Presumptuous dame! Ill-nurtured Eleanor!
    Art thou not second woman in the realm,
    And the Protector's wife, beloved of him?
    Hast thou not worldly pleasure at command
    Above the reach or compass of thy thought?
    And wilt thou still be hammering treachery,
    To tumble down thy husband and thyself
    From top of honour to disgrace's feet?
    Away from me, and let me hear no more!   50
DUCHESS
    What, what, my lord? Are you so choleric

With Eleanor, for telling but her dream?
Next time I'll keep my dreams unto myself,
And not be checked.

GLOUCESTER
Nay, be not angry; I am pleased again.

Enter a Messenger

MESSENGER
My Lord Protector, 'tis his highness' pleasure
You do prepare to ride unto Saint Albans,
Where as the King and Queen do mean to hawk.

GLOUCESTER
I go. Come, Nell, thou wilt ride with us?

DUCHESS
60   Yes, my good lord, I'll follow presently.

Exeunt Gloucester and Messenger

Follow I must; I cannot go before
While Gloucester bears this base and humble mind.
Were I a man, a duke, and next of blood,
I would remove these tedious stumbling-blocks
And smooth my way upon their headless necks;
And, being a woman, I will not be slack
To play my part in Fortune's pageant.
Where are you there? Sir John! Nay, fear not, man.
We are alone; here's none but thee and I.

Enter John Hume

HUME
70   Jesus preserve your royal majesty!

DUCHESS
What sayst thou? 'Majesty'! I am but 'grace'.

HUME
But, by the grace of God and Hume's advice,
Your grace's title shall be multiplied.

DUCHESS
What sayst thou, man? Hast thou as yet conferred

With Margery Jourdain, the cunning witch,
With Roger Bolingbroke, the conjurer?
And will they undertake to do me good?

HUME

This they have promised: to show your highness
A spirit raised from depth of under ground,
That shall make answer to such questions   80
As by your grace shall be propounded him.

DUCHESS

It is enough; I'll think upon the questions.
When from Saint Albans we do make return,
We'll see these things effected to the full.
Here, Hume, take this reward. Make merry, man,
With thy confederates in this weighty cause.   *Exit*

HUME

Hume must make merry with the Duchess' gold;
Marry, and shall. But how now, Sir John Hume?
Seal up your lips and give no words but mum;
The business asketh silent secrecy.   90
Dame Eleanor gives gold to bring the witch;
Gold cannot come amiss, were she a devil.
Yet have I gold flies from another coast –
I dare not say from the rich Cardinal
And from the great and new-made Duke of Suffolk.
Yet I do find it so; for, to be plain,
They, knowing Dame Eleanor's aspiring humour,
Have hired me to undermine the Duchess,
And buzz these conjurations in her brain.
They say 'A crafty knave does need no broker';   100
Yet am I Suffolk and the Cardinal's broker.
Hume, if you take not heed, you shall go near
To call them both a pair of crafty knaves.
Well, so it stands; and thus, I fear, at last
Hume's knavery will be the Duchess' wrack.

And her attainture will be Humphrey's fall.
Sort how it will, I shall have gold for all.   *Exit*

I.3   *Enter four Petitioners, Peter, the armourer's man,*
             being one

FIRST PETITIONER My masters, let's stand close. My
Lord Protector will come this way by and by, and then
we may deliver our supplications in the quill.

SECOND PETITIONER Marry, the Lord protect him,
for he's a good man. Jesu bless him!

             Enter Suffolk and the Queen

PETER Here 'a comes, methinks, and the Queen with him.
I'll be the first, sure.

SECOND PETITIONER Come back, fool. This is the Duke
of Suffolk and not my Lord Protector.

10   SUFFOLK How now, fellow? Wouldst anything with me?

FIRST PETITIONER I pray, my lord, pardon me; I took ye
for my Lord Protector.

QUEEN (*reads*) 'To my Lord Protector'? Are your supplications to his lordship? Let me see them. What is thine?

FIRST PETITIONER Mine is, an't please your grace,
against John Goodman, my lord Cardinal's man, for
keeping my house, and lands, and wife, and all, from me.

SUFFOLK Thy wife too! That's some wrong indeed. —
What's yours? What's here? (*Reads*) 'Against the Duke
20   of Suffolk, for enclosing the commons of Melford.'
How now, sir knave!

SECOND PETITIONER Alas, sir, I am but a poor petitioner
of our whole township.

PETER (*offering his petition*) Against my master, Thomas
Horner, for saying that the Duke of York was rightful
heir to the crown.

QUEEN What sayst thou? Did the Duke of York say he was
    rightful heir to the crown?

PETER That my master was? No, forsooth; my master said
    that he was, and that the King was an usurper.   30

SUFFOLK Who is there?

    Enter a Servant

    Take this fellow in, and send for his master with a pur-
    suivant presently. We'll hear more of your matter be-
    fore the King.   *Exit Servant with Peter*

QUEEN

    And as for you that love to be protected
    Under the wings of our Protector's grace,
    Begin your suits anew and sue to him.

    She tears the supplications

    Away, base cullions! Suffolk, let them go.

ALL PETITIONERS Come, let's be gone.   *Exeunt*

QUEEN

    My lord of Suffolk, say, is this the guise,   40
    Is this the fashions in the court of England?
    Is this the government of Britain's isle,
    And this the royalty of Albion's king?
    What, shall King Henry be a pupil still
    Under the surly Gloucester's governance?
    Am I a queen in title and in style,
    And must be made a subject to a duke?
    I tell thee, Pole, when in the city Tours
    Thou rannest a tilt in honour of my love
    And stolest away the ladies' hearts of France,   50
    I thought King Henry had resembled thee
    In courage, courtship, and proportion.
    But all his mind is bent to holiness,
    To number Ave-Maries on his beads;
    His champions are the prophets and apostles,
    His weapons holy saws of sacred writ;

His study is his tilt-yard, and his loves
Are brazen images of canonized saints.
I would the College of the Cardinals
60 Would choose him Pope, and carry him to Rome,
And set the triple crown upon his head –
That were a state fit for his holiness.

SUFFOLK

Madam, be patient. As I was cause
Your highness came to England, so will I
In England work your grace's full content.

QUEEN

Beside the haughty Protector have we Beaufort
The imperious churchman, Somerset, Buckingham,
And grumbling York; and not the least of these
But can do more in England than the King.

SUFFOLK

70 And he of these that can do most of all
Cannot do more in England than the Nevils;
Salisbury and Warwick are no simple peers.

QUEEN

Not all these lords do vex me half so much
As that proud dame, the Lord Protector's wife;
She sweeps it through the court with troops of ladies,
More like an empress than Duke Humphrey's wife.
Strangers in court do take her for the queen.
She bears a duke's revenues on her back,
And in her heart she scorns our poverty.
80 Shall I not live to be avenged on her?
Contemptuous base-born callet as she is,
She vaunted 'mongst her minions t'other day
The very train of her worst wearing gown
Was better worth than all my father's lands,
Till Suffolk gave two dukedoms for his daughter.

SUFFOLK

Madam, myself have limed a bush for her,
And placed a choir of such enticing birds
That she will light to listen to the lays,
And never mount to trouble you again.
So let her rest; and, madam, list to me,   90
For I am bold to counsel you in this:
Although we fancy not the Cardinal,
Yet must we join with him and with the lords
Till we have brought Duke Humphrey in disgrace.
As for the Duke of York, this late complaint
Will make but little for his benefit.
So one by one we'll weed them all at last,
And you yourself shall steer the happy helm.

Sound a sennet. Enter the King, Gloucester, the
Cardinal, Buckingham, York, Salisbury, Warwick,
Somerset, and the Duchess of Gloucester

KING

For my part, noble lords, I care not which;
Or Somerset or York, all's one to me.   100

YORK

If York have ill demeaned himself in France,
Then let him be denayed the Regentship.

SOMERSET

If Somerset be unworthy of the place,
Let York be Regent. I will yield to him.

WARWICK

Whether your grace be worthy, yea or no,
Dispute not that; York is the worthier.

CARDINAL

Ambitious Warwick, let thy betters speak.

WARWICK

The Cardinal's not my better in the field.

BUCKINGHAM

   All in this presence are thy betters, Warwick.

WARWICK

110   Warwick may live to be the best of all.

SALISBURY

   Peace, son; and show some reason, Buckingham,

   Why Somerset should be preferred in this.

QUEEN

   Because the King, forsooth, will have it so.

GLOUCESTER

   Madam, the King is old enough himself

   To give his censure. These are no women's matters.

QUEEN

   If he be old enough, what needs your grace

   To be Protector of his excellence?

GLOUCESTER

   Madam, I am Protector of the realm,

   And at his pleasure will resign my place.

SUFFOLK

120   Resign it then, and leave thine insolence.

   Since thou wert king – as who is king but thou? –

   The commonwealth hath daily run to wrack,

   The Dauphin hath prevailed beyond the seas,

   And all the peers and nobles of the realm

   Have been as bondmen to thy sovereignty.

CARDINAL

   The commons hast thou racked; the clergy's bags

   Are lank and lean with thy extortions.

SOMERSET

   Thy sumptuous buildings and thy wife's attire

   Have cost a mass of public treasury.

BUCKINGHAM

130   Thy cruelty in execution

   Upon offenders hath exceeded law,

And left thee to the mercy of the law.

QUEEN

Thy sale of offices and towns in France,
If they were known, as the suspect is great,
Would make thee quickly hop without thy head.

Exit Gloucester

The Queen lets fall her fan
Give me my fan. What, minion, can ye not?
She gives the Duchess of Gloucester a box on the ear
I cry you mercy, madam; was it you?

DUCHESS

Was't I? Yea, I it was, proud Frenchwoman.
Could I come near your beauty with my nails,
I could set my ten commandments on your face.   140

KING

Sweet aunt, be quiet; 'twas against her will.

DUCHESS

Against her will, good King? Look to't in time.
She'll hamper thee, and dandle thee like a baby.
Though in this place most master wear no breeches,
She shall not strike Dame Eleanor unrevenged.   *Exit*

BUCKINGHAM

Lord Cardinal, I will follow Eleanor,
And listen after Humphrey, how he proceeds.
She's tickled now; her fume needs no spurs,
She'll gallop far enough to her destruction.   *Exit*

Enter Gloucester

GLOUCESTER

Now, lords, my choler being overblown   150
With walking once about the quadrangle,
I come to talk of commonwealth affairs.
As for your spiteful false objections,
Prove them, and I lie open to the law;
But God in mercy so deal with my soul

As I in duty love my king and country!
But to the matter that we have in hand:
I say, my sovereign, York is meetest man
To be your Regent in the realm of France.

SUFFOLK

160   Before we make election, give me leave
To show some reason of no little force
That York is most unmeet of any man.

YORK

I'll tell thee, Suffolk, why I am unmeet:
First, for I cannot flatter thee in pride;
Next, if I be appointed for the place,
My lord of Somerset will keep me here,
Without discharge, money, or furniture,
Till France be won into the Dauphin's hands.
Last time I danced attendance on his will
170   Till Paris was besieged, famished, and lost.

WARWICK

That can I witness, and a fouler fact
Did never traitor in the land commit.

SUFFOLK

Peace, headstrong Warwick!

WARWICK

Image of pride, why should I hold my peace?
Enter Horner the armourer and his man Peter, guarded

SUFFOLK

Because here is a man accused of treason.
Pray God the Duke of York excuse himself!

YORK

Doth anyone accuse York for a traitor?

KING

What meanest thou, Suffolk? Tell me, what are these?

SUFFOLK

Please it your majesty, this is the man

That doth accuse his master of high treason.   180
His words were these: that Richard Duke of York
Was rightful heir unto the English crown,
And that your majesty was an usurper.

KING Say, man, were these thy words?

HORNER An't shall please your majesty, I never said nor
thought any such matter. God is my witness, I am falsely
accused by the villain.

PETER By these ten bones, my lords, he did speak them
to me in the garret one night as we were scouring my
lord of York's armour.   190

YORK
Base dunghill villain and mechanical,
I'll have thy head for this thy traitor's speech.
I do beseech your royal majesty,
Let him have all the rigour of the law.

HORNER Alas, my lord, hang me if ever I spake the words.
My accuser is my prentice, and when I did correct him
for his fault the other day, he did vow upon his knees
he would be even with me. I have good witness of this;
therefore I beseech your majesty, do not cast away an
honest man for a villain's accusation.   200

KING
Uncle, what shall we say to this in law?

GLOUCESTER
This doom, my lord, if I may judge:
Let Somerset be Regent o'er the French,
Because in York this breeds suspicion;
And let these have a day appointed them
For single combat in convenient place,
For he hath witness of his servant's malice.
This is the law, and this Duke Humphrey's doom.

SOMERSET
I humbly thank your royal majesty.

HORNER

210   And I accept the combat willingly.

PETER Alas, my lord, I cannot fight; for God's sake,
       pity my case. The spite of man prevaileth against me. O
       Lord, have mercy upon me! I never shall be able to fight
       a blow. O Lord, my heart!

GLOUCESTER

       Sirrah, or you must fight or else be hanged.

KING Away with them to prison; and the day of combat
      shall be the last of the next month. Come, Somerset,
      we'll see thee sent away!   *Flourish. Exeunt*

I.4   *Enter the witch, Margery Jourdain, the two priests,*
           Hume and Southwell, and Bolingbroke

HUME Come, my masters, the Duchess, I tell you, expects
      performance of your promises.

BOLINGBROKE Master Hume, we are therefore provided.
       Will her ladyship behold and hear our exorcisms?

HUME Ay, what else? Fear you not her courage.

BOLINGBROKE I have heard her reported to be a woman of
       an invincible spirit; but it shall be convenient, Master
       Hume, that you be by her aloft, while we be busy below;
       and so I pray you go in God's name, and leave us.

                                              Exit Hume

10   Mother Jourdain, be you prostrate and grovel on the
       earth. John Southwell, read you; and let us to our work.

       Enter the Duchess of Gloucester aloft, Hume following

DUCHESS Well said, my masters, and welcome all. To this
       gear the sooner the better.

BOLINGBROKE

       Patience, good lady; wizards know their times.
       Deep night, dark night, the silent of the night,
       The time of night when Troy was set on fire,

The time when screech-owls cry and ban-dogs howl,
And spirits walk, and ghosts break up their graves,
That time best fits the work we have in hand.
Madam, sit you and fear not. Whom we raise   20
We will make fast within a hallowed verge.

> *Here do the ceremonies belonging, and make the*
> *circle. Bolingbroke or Southwell reads 'Conjuro*
> *te' etc. It thunders and lightens terribly; then the*
> *Spirit riseth*

SPIRIT
Adsum.
JOURDAIN
Asmath!
By the eternal God, whose name and power
Thou tremblest at, answer that I shall ask;
For till thou speak, thou shalt not pass from hence.
SPIRIT
Ask what thou wilt. That I had said and done!
BOLINGBROKE (*reads*)
First, of the King: what shall of him become?
SPIRIT
The duke yet lives that Henry shall depose;
But him outlive, and die a violent death.   30

> *As the Spirit speaks, Bolingbroke writes the answer*

BOLINGBROKE (*reads*)
What fates await the Duke of Suffolk?
SPIRIT
By water shall he die, and take his end.
BOLINGBROKE (*reads*)
What shall befall the Duke of Somerset?
SPIRIT
Let him shun castles;
Safer shall he be upon the sandy plains
Than where castles mounted stand.

Have done, for more I hardly can endure.

BOLINGBROKE

Descend to darkness and the burning lake!
False fiend, avoid!

> *Thunder and lightning. Exit Spirit*
> *Enter the Duke of York and the Duke of Bucking-*
> *ham with their guard, Sir Humphrey Stafford as*
> *captain, and break in*

YORK

40 Lay hands upon these traitors and their trash.
Beldam, I think we watched you at an inch.
What, madam, are you there? The King and common-
   weal
Are deeply indebted for this piece of pains.
My Lord Protector will, I doubt it not,
See you well guerdoned for these good deserts.

DUCHESS

Not half so bad as thine to England's king,
Injurious duke, that threatest where's no cause.

BUCKINGHAM

True, madam, none at all. What call you this?
Away with them, let them be clapped up close,
50 And kept asunder. You, madam, shall with us.
Stafford, take her to thee.

> *Exeunt above the Duchess and Hume, guarded*

We'll see your trinkets here all forthcoming.
All away!   *Exeunt Jourdain, Southwell,*
> *Bolingbroke, escorted by Stafford*
> *and the guard*

YORK

Lord Buckingham, methinks you watched her well.
A pretty plot, well chosen to build upon!
Now pray, my lord, let's see the devil's writ.
What have we here?

(Reads) The duke yet lives that Henry shall depose;
But him outlive and die a violent death.
Why, this is just   60
Aio te, Aeacida, Romanos vincere posse.
Well, to the rest:
Tell me what fate awaits the Duke of Suffolk?
By water shall he die, and take his end.
What shall befall the Duke of Somerset?
Let him shun castles;
Safer shall he be upon the sandy plains
Than where castles mounted stand.
Come, come, my lords, these oracles
Are hardly attained and hardly understood.   70
The King is now in progress towards Saint Albans;
With him the husband of this lovely lady.
Thither goes these news, as fast as horse can carry
      them –
A sorry breakfast for my Lord Protector.

BUCKINGHAM
Your grace shall give me leave, my lord of York,
To be the post, in hope of his reward.

YORK
At your pleasure, my good lord. Who's within there, ho?
      Enter a Servingman
Invite my lords of Salisbury and Warwick
To sup with me tomorrow night. Away!   *Exeunt*

*

Enter the King, Queen, Gloucester, Cardinal, and   II.I
Suffolk, with falconers hallooing

QUEEN
Believe me, lords, for flying at the brook,

I saw not better sport these seven years' day;
Yet, by your leave, the wind was very high,
And, ten to one, old Joan had not gone out.

KING

But what a point, my lord, your falcon made,
And what a pitch she flew above the rest!
To see how God in all his creatures works!
Yea, man and birds are fain of climbing high.

SUFFOLK

No marvel, an it like your majesty,
10   My Lord Protector's hawks do tower so well;
They know their master loves to be aloft,
And bears his thoughts above his falcon's pitch.

GLOUCESTER

My lord, 'tis but a base ignoble mind
That mounts no higher than a bird can soar.

CARDINAL

I thought as much; he would be above the clouds.

GLOUCESTER

Ay, my lord Cardinal, how think you by that?
Were it not good your grace could fly to heaven?

KING

The treasury of everlasting joy.

CARDINAL

Thy heaven is on earth; thine eyes and thoughts
20   Beat on a crown, the treasure of thy heart,
Pernicious Protector, dangerous peer,
That smoothest it so with King and commonweal!

GLOUCESTER

What, Cardinal? Is your priesthood grown peremptory?
Tantaene animis coelestibus irae?
Churchmen so hot? Good uncle, hide such malice;
With such holiness can you do it?

SUFFOLK
  No malice, sir; no more than well becomes
  So good a quarrel and so bad a peer.
GLOUCESTER
  As who, my lord?
SUFFOLK   Why, as you, my lord,
  An't like your lordly Lord's Protectorship.   30
GLOUCESTER
  Why, Suffolk, England knows thine insolence.
QUEEN
  And thy ambition, Gloucester.
KING   I prithee peace,
  Good Queen, and whet not on these furious peers;
  For blessèd are the peace-makers on earth.
CARDINAL
  Let me be blessèd for the peace I make
  Against this proud Protector with my sword!
GLOUCESTER (*aside to Cardinal*)
  Faith, holy uncle, would 'twere come to that!
CARDINAL (*aside to Gloucester*)
  Marry, when thou darest.
GLOUCESTER (*aside to Cardinal*)
  Make up no factious numbers for the matter;
  In thine own person answer thy abuse.   40
CARDINAL (*aside to Gloucester*)
  Ay, where thou darest not peep; an if thou darest,
  This evening on the east side of the grove.
KING
  How now, my lords?
CARDINAL   Believe me, cousin Gloucester,
  Had not your man put up the fowl so suddenly,
  We had had more sport. (*Aside to Gloucester*) Come
with thy two-hand sword.

GLOUCESTER
  True, uncle.
CARDINAL (*aside to Gloucester*)
  Are ye advised? The east side of the grove.
GLOUCESTER (*aside to Cardinal*)
  Cardinal, I am with you.
KING   Why, how now, uncle Gloucester?
GLOUCESTER
  Talking of hawking; nothing else, my lord.
  (*Aside to Cardinal*)
50 Now, by God's mother, priest, I'll shave your crown
        for this,
  Or all my fence shall fail.
CARDINAL (*aside to Gloucester*) *Medice, teipsum* –
  Protector, see to't well; protect yourself.
KING
  The winds grow high; so do your stomachs, lords.
  How irksome is this music to my heart!
  When such strings jar, what hope of harmony?
  I pray, my lords, let me compound this strife.
    Enter a Man crying 'A miracle!'
GLOUCESTER
  What means this noise?
  Fellow, what miracle dost thou proclaim?
MAN
  A miracle! A miracle!
SUFFOLK
60 Come to the King and tell him what miracle.
MAN
  Forsooth, a blind man at Saint Alban's shrine
  Within this half-hour hath received his sight,
  A man that ne'er saw in his life before.
KING
  Now God be praised, that to believing souls

Gives light in darkness, comfort in despair!
> *Enter the Mayor of Saint Albans and his brethren,*
> *with music, bearing the man Simpcox between two*
> *in a chair; Simpcox's Wife and others following*

CARDINAL

Here comes the townsmen, on procession,
To present your highness with the man.

KING

Great is his comfort in this earthly vale,
Although by his sight his sin be multiplied.

GLOUCESTER

Stand by, my masters; bring him near the King.　　　70
His highness' pleasure is to talk with him.

KING

Good fellow, tell us here the circumstance,
That we for thee may glorify the Lord.
What, hast thou been long blind and now restored?

SIMPCOX Born blind, an't please your grace.

WIFE Ay, indeed was he.

SUFFOLK What woman is this?

WIFE His wife, an't like your worship.

GLOUCESTER Hadst thou been his mother, thou couldst
have better told.　　　80

KING Where wert thou born?

SIMPCOX At Berwick in the north, an't like your grace.

KING

Poor soul, God's goodness hath been great to thee.
Let never day nor night unhallowed pass,
But still remember what the Lord hath done.

QUEEN

Tell me, good fellow, camest thou here by chance,
Or of devotion, to this holy shrine?

SIMPCOX

God knows, of pure devotion, being called

A hundred times and oftener, in my sleep,
90 By good Saint Alban, who said 'Simon, come;
Come, offer at my shrine, and I will help thee.'

WIFE

Most true, forsooth; and many time and oft
Myself have heard a voice to call him so.

CARDINAL

What, art thou lame?

SIMPCOX   Ay, God Almighty help me!

SUFFOLK

How camest thou so?

SIMPCOX   A fall off of a tree.

WIFE

A plum-tree, master.

GLOUCESTER   How long hast thou been blind?

SIMPCOX

O, born so, master.

GLOUCESTER   What! And wouldst climb a tree?

SIMPCOX

But that in all my life, when I was a youth.

WIFE

Too true; and bought his climbing very dear.

GLOUCESTER

100 Mass, thou loved'st plums well, that wouldst venture so.

SIMPCOX

Alas, good master, my wife desired some damsons,
And made me climb with danger of my life.

GLOUCESTER

A subtle knave! But yet it shall not serve.
Let me see thine eyes; wink now; now open them.
In my opinion yet thou seest not well.

SIMPCOX Yes, master, clear as day, I thank God and
Saint Alban.

GLOUCESTER
　Sayst thou me so? What colour is this cloak of?
SIMPCOX Red, master, red as blood.

GLOUCESTER
　Why, that's well said. What colour is my gown of?   110
SIMPCOX Black, forsooth, coal-black as jet.

KING
　Why then, thou knowest what colour jet is of?

SUFFOLK
　And yet, I think, jet did he never see.

GLOUCESTER
　But cloaks and gowns before this day a many.

WIFE
　Never, before this day, in all his life.

GLOUCESTER Tell me, sirrah, what's my name?
SIMPCOX Alas, master, I know not.
GLOUCESTER What's his name?
SIMPCOX I know not.
GLOUCESTER Nor his?   120
SIMPCOX No indeed, master.
GLOUCESTER What's thine own name?
SIMPCOX Saunder Simpcox, an if it please you, master.
GLOUCESTER Then, Saunder, sit there, the lyingest knave
　in Christendom. If thou hadst been born blind, thou
　mightst as well have known all our names as thus to
　name the several colours we do wear. Sight may distin-
　guish of colours; but suddenly to nominate them all, it
　is impossible. My lords, Saint Alban here hath done a
　miracle; and would ye not think his cunning to be great,   130
　that could restore this cripple to his legs again?
SIMPCOX O master, that you could!
GLOUCESTER My masters of Saint Albans, have you not
　beadles in your town, and things called whips?
MAYOR Yes, my lord, if it please your grace.

GLOUCESTER Then send for one presently.

MAYOR Sirrah, go fetch the beadle hither straight.

Exit an attendant

GLOUCESTER Now fetch me a stool hither by and by.
Now, sirrah, if you mean to save yourself from whipping,
140 leap me over this stool and run away.

SIMPCOX Alas, master, I am not able to stand alone. You
go about to torture me in vain.

Enter a Beadle with whips

GLOUCESTER Well, sir, we must have you find your legs.
Sirrah beadle, whip him till he leap over that same
stool.

BEADLE I will, my lord. Come on, sirrah, off with your
doublet quickly.

SIMPCOX Alas, master, what shall I do? I am not able
to stand.

*After the Beadle hath hit him once, he leaps over the
stool and runs away; and they follow and cry 'A
miracle!'*

KING

150 O God, seest thou this, and bearest so long?

QUEEN

It made me laugh to see the villain run.

GLOUCESTER

Follow the knave, and take this drab away.

WIFE Alas, sir, we did it for pure need.

GLOUCESTER

Let them be whipped through every market-town
Till they come to Berwick, from whence they came.

*Exeunt Mayor and townspeople,
and the Beadle dragging Simpcox's Wife*

CARDINAL

Duke Humphrey has done a miracle today.

SUFFOLK

    True; made the lame to leap and fly away.

GLOUCESTER

    But you have done more miracles than I;
    You made in a day, my lord, whole towns to fly.

      Enter Buckingham

KING

    What tidings with our cousin Buckingham?   160

BUCKINGHAM

    Such as my heart doth tremble to unfold:
    A sort of naughty persons, lewdly bent,
    Under the countenance and confederacy
    Of Lady Eleanor, the Protector's wife.
    The ringleader and head of all this rout,
    Have practised dangerously against your state,
    Dealing with witches and with conjurers,
    Whom we have apprehended in the fact,
    Raising up wicked spirits from under ground,
    Demanding of King Henry's life and death,   170
    And other of your highness' Privy Council,
    As more at large your grace shall understand.

CARDINAL

    And so, my Lord Protector, by this means
    Your lady is forthcoming yet at London.
    (*Aside to Gloucester*)
    This news, I think, hath turned your weapon's edge;
    'Tis like, my lord, you will not keep your hour.

GLOUCESTER

    Ambitious churchman, leave to afflict my heart.
    Sorrow and grief have vanquished all my powers;
    And, vanquished as I am, I yield to thee
    Or to the meanest groom.   180

KING

    O God, what mischiefs work the wicked ones,

Heaping confusion on their own heads thereby!

QUEEN

Gloucester, see here the tainture of thy nest,
And look thyself be faultless, thou wert best.

GLOUCESTER

Madam, for myself, to heaven I do appeal,
How I have loved my king and commonweal;
And for my wife I know not how it stands.
Sorry I am to hear what I have heard.
Noble she is; but if she have forgot
190 Honour and virtue, and conversed with such
As, like to pitch, defile nobility,
I banish her my bed and company,
And give her as a prey to law and shame.
That hath dishonoured Gloucester's honest name.

KING

Well, for this night we will repose us here;
Tomorrow toward London back again,
To look into this business thoroughly,
And call these foul offenders to their answers,
And poise the cause in Justice' equal scales,
Whose beam stands sure, whose rightful cause prevails.

Flourish. Exeunt

II.2   *Enter York, Salisbury, and Warwick*

YORK

Now, my good lords of Salisbury and Warwick,
Our simple supper ended, give me leave,
In this close walk, to satisfy myself
In craving your opinion of my title,
Which is infallible, to the English crown.

SALISBURY

My lord, I long to hear it at full.

WARWICK

    Sweet York, begin; and if thy claim be good,

    The Nevils are thy subjects to command.

YORK

    Then thus:

    Edward the Third, my lords, had seven sons: 10

    The first, Edward the Black Prince, Prince of Wales;

    The second, William of Hatfield; and the third,

    Lionel Duke of Clarence; next to whom

    Was John of Gaunt, the Duke of Lancaster;

    The fifth was Edmund Langley, Duke of York;

    The sixth was Thomas of Woodstock, Duke of

        Gloucester;

    William of Windsor was the seventh and last.

    Edward the Black Prince died before his father,

    And left behind him Richard, his only son,

    Who, after Edward the Third's death, reigned as king   20

    Till Henry Bolingbroke, Duke of Lancaster,

    The eldest son and heir of John of Gaunt,

    Crowned by the name of Henry the Fourth,

    Seized on the realm, deposed the rightful king,

    Sent his poor queen to France, from whence she came,

    And him to Pomfret; where, as all you know,

    Harmless Richard was murdered traitorously.

WARWICK

    Father, the Duke hath told the truth;

    Thus got the house of Lancaster the crown.

YORK

    Which now they hold by force and not by right;   30

    For Richard, the first son's heir, being dead,

    The issue of the next son should have reigned.

SALISBURY

    But William of Hatfield died without an heir.

YORK

    The third son, Duke of Clarence, from whose line
    I claim the crown, had issue Philippe, a daughter,
    Who married Edmund Mortimer, Earl of March;
    Edmund had issue, Roger Earl of March;
    Roger had issue, Edmund, Anne, and Eleanor.

SALISBURY

    This Edmund, in the reign of Bolingbroke,
40   As I have read, laid claim unto the crown,
    And, but for Owen Glendower, had been king,
    Who kept him in captivity till he died.
    But to the rest.

YORK   His eldest sister, Anne,

    My mother, being heir unto the crown,
    Married Richard Earl of Cambridge, who was
    To Edmund Langley, Edward the Third's fifth son, son.
    By her I claim the kingdom; she was heir
    To Roger Earl of March, who was the son
    Of Edmund Mortimer, who married Philippe,
50   Sole daughter unto Lionel Duke of Clarence;
    So, if the issue of the elder son
    Succeed before the younger, I am king.

WARWICK

    What plain proceedings is more plain than this?
    Henry doth claim the crown from John of Gaunt,
    The fourth son; York claims it from the third.
    Till Lionel's issue fails, his should not reign;
    It fails not yet, but flourishes in thee,
    And in thy sons, fair slips of such a stock.
    Then, father Salisbury, kneel we together,
60   And in this private plot be we the first
    That shall salute our rightful sovereign
    With honour of his birthright to the crown.

WARWICK *and* SALISBURY
> Long live our sovereign Richard, England's king!

YORK
> We thank you, lords; but I am not your king
> Till I be crowned, and that my sword be stained
> With heart-blood of the house of Lancaster;
> And that's not suddenly to be performed
> But with advice and silent secrecy.
> Do you as I do in these dangerous days,
> Wink at the Duke of Suffolk's insolence,   70
> At Beaufort's pride, at Somerset's ambition,
> At Buckingham, and all the crew of them,
> Till they have snared the shepherd of the flock,
> That virtuous prince, the good Duke Humphrey.
> 'Tis that they seek; and they, in seeking that,
> Shall find their deaths, if York can prophesy.

SALISBURY
> My lord, break we off; we know your mind at full.

WARWICK
> My heart assures me that the Earl of Warwick
> Shall one day make the Duke of York a king.

YORK
> And, Neville, this I do assure myself: 80
> Richard shall live to make the Earl of Warwick
> The greatest man in England but the king.   *Exeunt*

> *Sound trumpets. Enter the King, Queen, Gloucester,*   II.3
> *York, Suffolk, and Salisbury; the Duchess of*
> *Gloucester, Margery Jourdain, Southwell, Hume,*
> *and Bolingbroke, guarded*

KING
> Stand forth, Dame Eleanor Cobham, Gloucester's wife.
> In sight of God and us your guilt is great;

Receive the sentence of the law for sins
Such as by God's book are adjudged to death.
You four, from hence to prison back again;
From thence unto the place of execution.
The witch in Smithfield shall be burnt to ashes,
And you three shall be strangled on the gallows.
You, madam, for you are more nobly born,
10 Despoilèd of your honour in your life,
Shall, after three days' open penance done,
Live in your country here in banishment
With Sir John Stanley in the Isle of Man.

DUCHESS

Welcome is banishment; welcome were my death.

GLOUCESTER

Eleanor, the law, thou seest, hath judged thee;
I cannot justify whom the law condemns.
Mine eyes are full of tears, my heart of grief.

Exeunt the Duchess and the other prisoners, guarded
Ah, Humphrey, this dishonour in thine age
Will bring thy head with sorrow to the ground!
20 I beseech your majesty give me leave to go;
Sorrow would solace, and mine age would ease.

KING

Stay, Humphrey Duke of Gloucester. Ere thou go,
Give up thy staff. Henry will to himself
Protector be; and God shall be my hope,
My stay, my guide, and lantern to my feet.
And go in peace, Humphrey, no less beloved
Than when thou wert Protector to thy King.

QUEEN

I see no reason why a king of years
Should be to be protected like a child.
30 God and King Henry govern England's realm!
Give up your staff, sir, and the King his realm.

GLOUCESTER

My staff? Here, noble Henry, is my staff;
As willingly do I the same resign
As ere thy father Henry made it mine;
And even as willingly at thy feet I leave it
As others would ambitiously receive it.
Farewell, good King. When I am dead and gone,
May honourable peace attend thy throne.   *Exit*

QUEEN

Why, now is Henry King and Margaret Queen;
And Humphrey Duke of Gloucester scarce himself,   40
That bears so shrewd a maim; two pulls at once –
His lady banished and a limb lopped off.
This staff of honour raught, there let it stand
Where it best fits to be, in Henry's hand.

SUFFOLK

Thus droops this lofty pine and hangs his sprays;
Thus Eleanor's pride dies in her youngest days.

YORK

Lords, let him go. Please it your majesty,
This is the day appointed for the combat,
And ready are the appellant and defendant,
The armourer and his man, to enter the lists,   50
So please your highness to behold the fight.

QUEEN

Ay, good my lord; for purposely therefore
Left I the court to see this quarrel tried.

KING

A God's name, see the lists and all things fit;
Here let them end it, and God defend the right!

YORK

I never saw a fellow worse bestead,
Or more afraid to fight, than is the appellant,
The servant of this armourer, my lords.

Enter at one door Horner the armourer and his
Neighbours, drinking to him so much that he is
drunk; and he enters with a drum before him and his
staff with a sand-bag fastened to it; and at the other
door Peter his man, with a drum and sand-bag, and
Prentices drinking to him

60 FIRST NEIGHBOUR Here, neighbour Horner, I drink to
you in a cup of sack; and fear not, neighbour, you
shall do well enough.

SECOND NEIGHBOUR And here, neighbour, here's a cup
of charneco.

THIRD NEIGHBOUR And here's a pot of good double beer,
neighbour. Drink, and fear not your man.

HORNER Let it come, i'faith, and I'll pledge you all;
and a fig for Peter!

FIRST PRENTICE Here, Peter, I drink to thee; and be not
afraid.

70 SECOND PRENTICE Be merry, Peter, and fear not thy
master. Fight for the credit of the prentices.

PETER I thank you all. Drink and pray for me, I pray you,
for I think I have taken my last draught in this world.
Here, Robin, an if I die, I give thee my apron; and,
Will, thou shalt have my hammer; and here, Tom,
take all the money that I have. O Lord bless me, I pray
God, for I am never able to deal with my master, he hath
learnt so much fence already.

SALISBURY Come, leave your drinking and fall to blows.
80 Sirrah, what's thy name?

PETER Peter, forsooth.

SALISBURY Peter? What more?

PETER Thump.

SALISBURY Thump? Then see thou thump thy master
well.

HORNER Masters, I am come hither, as it were, upon my

man's instigation, to prove him a knave and myself an
honest man; and touching the Duke of York, I will take
my death I never meant him any ill, nor the King, nor
the Queen; and therefore, Peter, have at thee with a
downright blow.   90

YORK Dispatch; this knave's tongue begins to double.
Sound, trumpets, alarum to the combatants.

Alarum; they fight and Peter strikes Horner down

HORNER Hold, Peter, hold! I confess, I confess treason.

He dies

YORK Take away his weapon. Fellow, thank God and the
good wine in thy master's way.

PETER O God, have I overcome mine enemies in this
presence? O Peter, thou hast prevailed in right!

KING
Go, take hence that traitor from our sight;
For by his death we do perceive his guilt,
And God in justice hath revealed to us   100
The truth and innocence of this poor fellow,
Which he had thought to have murdered wrongfully.
Come, fellow, follow us for thy reward.

Sound a flourish. Exeunt

Enter Gloucester and his men in mourning cloaks   II.4

GLOUCESTER
Thus sometimes hath the brightest day a cloud;
And after summer evermore succeeds
Barren winter, with his wrathful nipping cold;
So cares and joys abound, as seasons fleet.
Sirs, what's o'clock?

SERVANT   Ten, my lord.

GLOUCESTER
Ten is the hour that was appointed me

To watch the coming of my punished duchess;
Uneath may she endure the flinty streets,
To tread them with her tender-feeling feet.
10 Sweet Nell, ill can thy noble mind abrook
The abject people gazing on thy face
With envious looks, laughing at thy shame,
That erst did follow thy proud chariot wheels
When thou didst ride in triumph through the streets.
But soft, I think she comes; and I'll prepare
My tear-stained eyes to see her miseries.

> *Enter the Duchess of Gloucester barefoot, in a white*
> *sheet and verses written on her back and pinned on and*
> *a taper burning in her hand, with Sir John Stanley, the*
> *Sheriff, and officers with bills and halberds*

SERVANT
So please your grace, we'll take her from the Sheriff.
GLOUCESTER
No, stir not for your lives; let her pass by.
DUCHESS
Come you, my lord, to see my open shame?
20 Now thou dost penance too. Look how they gaze!
See how the giddy multitude do point
And nod their heads and throw their eyes on thee.
Ah, Gloucester, hide thee from their hateful looks,
And, in thy closet pent up, rue my shame,
And ban thine enemies, both mine and thine.
GLOUCESTER
Be patient, gentle Nell; forget this grief.
DUCHESS
Ah, Gloucester, teach me to forget myself;
For whilst I think I am thy married wife,
And thou a prince, Protector of this land,
30 Methinks I should not thus be led along,
Mailed up in shame, with papers on my back,

And followed with a rabble that rejoice
To see my tears and hear my deep-fet groans.
The ruthless flint doth cut my tender feet,
And when I start, the envious people laugh
And bid me be advisèd how I tread.
Ah, Humphrey, can I bear this shameful yoke?
Trowest thou that e'er I'll look upon the world,
Or count them happy that enjoys the sun?
No, dark shall be my light, and night my day;   40
To think upon my pomp shall be my hell.
Sometime I'll say I am Duke Humphrey's wife,
And he a prince and ruler of the land;
Yet so he ruled and such a prince he was
As he stood by whilst I, his forlorn duchess,
Was made a wonder and a pointing-stock
To every idle rascal follower.
But be thou mild and blush not at my shame,
Nor stir at nothing till the axe of death
Hang over thee, as sure it shortly will;   50
For Suffolk, he that can do all in all
With her that hateth thee and hates us all,
And York, and impious Beaufort, that false priest,
Have all limed bushes to betray thy wings;
And fly thou how thou canst, they'll tangle thee.
But fear not thou until thy foot be snared,
Nor never seek prevention of thy foes.

GLOUCESTER

Ah, Nell, forbear! Thou aimest all awry;
I must offend before I be attainted;
And had I twenty times so many foes,   60
And each of them had twenty times their power,
All these could not procure me any scathe
So long as I am loyal, true, and crimeless.
Wouldst have me rescue thee from this reproach?

Why, yet thy scandal were not wiped away,
But I in danger for the breach of law.
Thy greatest help is quiet, gentle Nell.
I pray thee sort thy heart to patience;
These few days' wonder will be quickly worn.
   Enter a Herald

HERALD

70   I summon your grace to his majesty's parliament,
Holden at Bury the first of this next month.

GLOUCESTER

And my consent ne'er asked herein before!
This is close dealing. Well, I will be there.
                         Exit Herald
My Nell, I take my leave; and, Master Sheriff,
Let not her penance exceed the King's commission.

SHERIFF

An't please your grace, here my commission stays,
And Sir John Stanley is appointed now
To take her with him to the Isle of Man.

GLOUCESTER

Must you, Sir John, protect my lady here?

STANLEY

80   So am I given in charge, may't please your grace.

GLOUCESTER

Entreat her not the worse in that I pray
You use her well. The world may laugh again;
And I may live to do you kindness if
You do it her. And so, Sir John, farewell.

DUCHESS

What, gone, my lord, and bid me not farewell?

GLOUCESTER

Witness my tears, I cannot stay to speak.
            Exit Gloucester with his men

DUCHESS

    Art thou gone too? All comfort go with thee!
    For none abides with me; my joy is death –
    Death, at whose name I oft have been afeard,
    Because I wished this world's eternity.   90
    Stanley, I prithee, go and take me hence;
    I care not whither, for I beg no favour;
    Only convey me where thou art commanded.

STANLEY

    Why, madam, that is to the Isle of Man,
    There to be used according to your state.

DUCHESS

    That's bad enough, for I am but reproach;
    And shall I then be used reproachfully?

STANLEY

    Like to a duchess and Duke Humphrey's lady,
    According to that state you shall be used.

DUCHESS

    Sheriff, farewell, and better than I fare,   100
    Although thou hast been conduct of my shame.

SHERIFF

    It is my office; and, madam, pardon me.

DUCHESS

    Ay, ay, farewell; thy office is discharged.
    Come, Stanley, shall we go?

STANLEY

    Madam, your penance done, throw off this sheet,
    And go we to attire you for our journey.

DUCHESS

    My shame will not be shifted with my sheet.
    No; it will hang upon my richest robes
    And show itself, attire me how I can.
    Go, lead the way; I long to see my prison.   *Exeunt* 110

*

III.I   *Sound a sennet. Enter the King, Queen, Cardinal,*
              Suffolk, York, Buckingham, Salisbury, and
              Warwick to the parliament

KING

    I muse my lord of Gloucester is not come;
    'Tis not his wont to be the hindmost man,
    Whate'er occasion keeps him from us now.

QUEEN

    Can you not see? Or will ye not observe
    The strangeness of his altered countenance?
    With what a majesty he bears himself,
    How insolent of late he is become,
    How proud, how peremptory, and unlike himself?
    We know the time since he was mild and affable,
10 And if we did but glance a far-off look,
    Immediately he was upon his knee,
    That all the court admired him for submission;
    But meet him now, and be it in the morn,
    When everyone will give the time of day,
    He knits his brow and shows an angry eye,
    And passeth by with stiff unbowèd knee,
    Disdaining duty that to us belongs.
    Small curs are not regarded when they grin,
    But great men tremble when the lion roars;
20 And Humphrey is no little man in England.
    First note that he is near you in descent,
    And should you fall, he is the next will mount.
    Me seemeth then it is no policy,
    Respecting what a rancorous mind he bears
    And his advantage following your decease,
    That he should come about your royal person
    Or be admitted to your highness' Council.
    By flattery hath he won the commons' hearts,
    And when he please to make commotion,

'Tis to be feared they all will follow him.   30
Now 'tis the spring, and weeds are shallow-rooted;
Suffer them now and they'll o'ergrow the garden,
And choke the herbs for want of husbandry.
The reverent care I bear unto my lord
Made me collect these dangers in the Duke.
If it be fond, call it a woman's fear;
Which fear if better reasons can supplant,
I will subscribe and say I wronged the Duke.
My lord of Suffolk, Buckingham, and York,
Reprove my allegation if you can;   40
Or else conclude my words effectual.

SUFFOLK

Well hath your highness seen into this Duke;
And had I first been put to speak my mind,
I think I should have told your grace's tale.
The Duchess by his subornation,
Upon my life, began her devilish practices;
Or if he were not privy to those faults,
Yet by reputing of his high descent,
As next the King he was successive heir,
And such high vaunts of his nobility,   50
Did instigate the bedlam brain-sick Duchess
By wicked means to frame our sovereign's fall.
Smooth runs the water where the brook is deep,
And in his simple show he harbours treason.
The fox barks not when he would steal the lamb.
No, no, my sovereign, Gloucester is a man
Unsounded yet and full of deep deceit.

CARDINAL

Did he not, contrary to form of law,
Devise strange deaths for small offences done?

YORK

And did he not, in his Protectorship,   60

Levy great sums of money through the realm
For soldiers' pay in France, and never sent it?
By means whereof the towns each day revolted.

BUCKINGHAM

Tut, these are petty faults to faults unknown,
Which time will bring to light in smooth Duke
    Humphrey.

KING

My lords, at once; the care you have of us,
To mow down thorns that would annoy our foot,
Is worthy praise; but, shall I speak my conscience,
Our kinsman Gloucester is as innocent

70   From meaning treason to our royal person
As is the sucking lamb or harmless dove.
The Duke is virtuous, mild, and too well given
To dream on evil or to work my downfall.

QUEEN

Ah, what's more dangerous than this fond affiance?
Seems he a dove? His feathers are but borrowed,
For he's disposèd as the hateful raven.
Is he a lamb? His skin is surely lent him,
For he's inclined as is the ravenous wolves.
Who cannot steal a shape that means deceit?

80   Take heed, my lord; the welfare of us all
Hangs on the cutting short that fraudful man.

    Enter Somerset

SOMERSET

All health unto my gracious sovereign!

KING

Welcome, Lord Somerset. What news from France?

SOMERSET

That all your interest in those territories
Is utterly bereft you; all is lost.

KING
 Cold news, Lord Somerset; but God's will be done!
YORK (*aside*)
 Cold news for me; for I had hope of France
 As firmly as I hope for fertile England.
 Thus are my blossoms blasted in the bud,
 And caterpillars eat my leaves away;   90
 But I will remedy this gear ere long,
 Or sell my title for a glorious grave.
  Enter Gloucester
GLOUCESTER
 All happiness unto my lord the King!
 Pardon, my liege, that I have stayed so long.
SUFFOLK
 Nay, Gloucester, know that thou art come too soon,
 Unless thou wert more loyal than thou art.
 I do arrest thee of high treason here.
GLOUCESTER
 Well, Suffolk, thou shalt not see me blush,
 Nor change my countenance for this arrest;
 A heart unspotted is not easily daunted.   100
 The purest spring is not so free from mud
 As I am clear from treason to my sovereign.
 Who can accuse me? Wherein am I guilty?
YORK
 'Tis thought, my lord, that you took bribes of France;
 And, being Protector, stayed the soldiers' pay,
 By means whereof his highness hath lost France.
GLOUCESTER
 Is it but thought so? What are they that think it?
 I never robbed the soldiers of their pay,
 Nor ever had one penny bribe from France.
 So help me God, as I have watched the night,   110
 Ay, night by night, in studying good for England!

That doit that e'er I wrested from the King,
Or any groat I hoarded to my use,
Be brought against me at my trial day!
No, many a pound of mine own proper store,
Because I would not tax the needy commons,
Have I dispursèd to the garrisons,
And never asked for restitution.

CARDINAL
It serves you well, my lord, to say so much.

GLOUCESTER
120 I say no more than truth, so help me God!

YORK
In your Protectorship you did devise
Strange tortures for offenders, never heard of,
That England was defamed by tyranny.

GLOUCESTER
Why, 'tis well known that, whiles I was Protector,
Pity was all the fault that was in me;
For I should melt at an offender's tears,
And lowly words were ransom for their fault.
Unless it were a bloody murderer
Or foul felonious thief that fleeced poor passengers,
130 I never gave them condign punishment;
Murder indeed, that bloody sin, I tortured
Above the felon or what trespass else.

SUFFOLK
My lord, these faults are easy, quickly answered;
But mightier crimes are laid unto your charge,
Whereof you cannot easily purge yourself.
I do arrest you in his highness' name;
And here commit you to my lord Cardinal
To keep until your further time of trial.

KING
My lord of Gloucester, 'tis my special hope

That you will clear yourself from all suspense;   140
My conscience tells me you are innocent.

GLOUCESTER

Ah, gracious lord, these days are dangerous;
Virtue is choked with foul ambition,
And charity chased hence by rancour's hand;
Foul subornation is predominant,
And equity exiled your highness' land.
I know their complot is to have my life;
And if my death might make this island happy,
And prove the period of their tyranny,
I would expend it with all willingness.   150
But mine is made the prologue to their play;
For thousands more, that yet suspect no peril,
Will not conclude their plotted tragedy.
Beaufort's red sparkling eyes blab his heart's malice,
And Suffolk's cloudy brow his stormy hate;
Sharp Buckingham unburdens with his tongue
The envious load that lies upon his heart;
And doggèd York, that reaches at the moon,
Whose overweening arm I have plucked back,
By false accuse doth level at my life.   160
And you, my sovereign lady, with the rest,
Causeless have laid disgraces on my head,
And with your best endeavour have stirred up
My liefest liege to be mine enemy.
Ay, all of you have laid your heads together –
Myself had notice of your conventicles –
And all to make away my guiltless life.
I shall not want false witness to condemn me,
Nor store of treasons to augment my guilt;
The ancient proverb will be well effected: 170
'A staff is quickly found to beat a dog.'

CARDINAL

My liege, his railing is intolerable.
If those that care to keep your royal person
From treason's secret knife and traitor's rage
Be thus upbraided, chid, and rated at,
And the offender granted scope of speech,
'Twill make them cool in zeal unto your grace.

SUFFOLK

Hath he not twit our sovereign lady here
With ignominious words, though clerkly couched,
180   As if she had suborned some to swear
False allegations to o'erthrow his state?

QUEEN

But I can give the loser leave to chide.

GLOUCESTER

Far truer spoke than meant. I lose indeed;
Beshrew the winners, for they played me false!
And well such losers may have leave to speak.

BUCKINGHAM

He'll wrest the sense and hold us here all day.
Lord Cardinal, he is your prisoner.

CARDINAL

Sirs, take away the Duke and guard him sure.

GLOUCESTER

Ah, thus King Henry throws away his crutch
190   Before his legs be firm to bear his body.
Thus is the shepherd beaten from thy side,
And wolves are gnarling who shall gnaw thee first.
Ah, that my fear were false; ah, that it were!
For, good King Henry, thy decay I fear.
            Exit Gloucester, guarded by the Cardinal's men

KING

My lords, what to your wisdoms seemeth best
Do or undo, as if ourself were here.

QUEEN

    What, will your highness leave the parliament?

KING

    Ay, Margaret; my heart is drowned with grief,
    Whose flood begins to flow within mine eyes,
    My body round engirt with misery;   200
    For what's more miserable than discontent?
    Ah, uncle Humphrey, in thy face I see
    The map of honour, truth, and loyalty;
    And yet, good Humphrey, is the hour to come
    That e'er I proved thee false or feared thy faith.
    What lowering star now envies thy estate,
    That these great lords, and Margaret our Queen,
    Do seek subversion of thy harmless life?
    Thou never didst them wrong, nor no man wrong;
    And as the butcher takes away the calf,   210
    And binds the wretch, and beats it when it strays,
    Bearing it to the bloody slaughter-house,
    Even so remorseless have they borne him hence;
    And as the dam runs lowing up and down,
    Looking the way her harmless young one went,
    And can do naught but wail her darling's loss;
    Even so myself bewails good Gloucester's case
    With sad unhelpful tears, and with dimmed eyes
    Look after him, and cannot do him good,
    So mighty are his vowèd enemies.   220
    His fortunes I will weep, and 'twixt each groan
    Say 'Who's a traitor? Gloucester he is none.'

        Exit with Buckingham, Salisbury, and Warwick

QUEEN

    Free lords, cold snow melts with the sun's hot beams:
    Henry my lord is cold in great affairs,
    Too full of foolish pity; and Gloucester's show
    Beguiles him as the mournful crocodile

With sorrow snares relenting passengers;
Or as the snake rolled in a flowering bank,
With shining checkered slough, doth sting a child
230   That for the beauty thinks it excellent.
Believe me, lords, were none more wise than I –
And yet herein I judge mine own wit good –
This Gloucester should be quickly rid the world,
To rid us from the fear we have of him.

CARDINAL
That he should die is worthy policy;
But yet we want a colour for his death.
'Tis meet he be condemned by course of law.

SUFFOLK
But in my mind that were no policy.
The King will labour still to save his life,
240   The commons haply rise to save his life;
And yet we have but trivial argument,
More than mistrust, that shows him worthy death.

YORK
So that, by this, you would not have him die.

SUFFOLK
Ah, York, no man alive so fain as I.

YORK
'Tis York that hath more reason for his death.
But, my lord Cardinal, and you, my lord of Suffolk,
Say as you think, and speak it from your souls:
Were't not all one, an empty eagle were set
To guard the chicken from a hungry kite,
250   As place Duke Humphrey for the King's Protector?

QUEEN
So the poor chicken should be sure of death.

SUFFOLK
Madam, 'tis true; and were't not madness then
To make the fox surveyor of the fold?

Who being accused a crafty murderer,
His guilt should be but idly posted over
Because his purpose is not executed.
No; let him die, in that he is a fox,
By nature proved an enemy to the flock,
Before his chaps be stained with crimson blood,
As Humphrey, proved by reasons, to my liege.   260
And do not stand on quillets how to slay him;
Be it by gins, by snares, by subtlety,
Sleeping or waking, 'tis no matter how,
So he be dead; for that is good deceit
Which mates him first that first intends deceit.

QUEEN

Thrice-noble Suffolk, 'tis resolutely spoke.

SUFFOLK

Not resolute, except so much were done;
For things are often spoke and seldom meant;
But that my heart accordeth with my tongue,
Seeing the deed is meritorious,   270
And to preserve my sovereign from his foe,
Say but the word and I will be his priest.

CARDINAL

But I would have him dead, my lord of Suffolk,
Ere you can take due orders for a priest.
Say you consent and censure well the deed,
And I'll provide his executioner;
I tender so the safety of my liege.

SUFFOLK

Here is my hand; the deed is worthy doing.

QUEEN

And so say I.

YORK

And I; and now we three have spoke it,   280
It skills not greatly who impugns our doom.

Enter a Post

POST

 Great lords, from Ireland am I come amain,
 To signify that rebels there are up
 And put the Englishmen unto the sword.
 Send succours, lords, and stop the rage betime,
 Before the wound do grow uncurable;
 For, being green, there is great hope of help.

CARDINAL

 A breach that craves a quick expedient stop!
 What counsel give you in this weighty cause?

YORK

290 That Somerset be sent as Regent thither.
 'Tis meet that lucky ruler be employed;
 Witness the fortune he hath had in France.

SOMERSET

 If York, with all his far-fet policy,
 Had been the Regent there instead of me,
 He never would have stayed in France so long.

YORK

 No, not to lose it all, as thou hast done.
 I rather would have lost my life betimes
 Than bring a burden of dishonour home,
 By staying there so long till all were lost.
300 Show me one scar charactered on thy skin;
 Men's flesh preserved so whole do seldom win.

QUEEN

 Nay then, this spark will prove a raging fire
 If wind and fuel be brought to feed it with.
 No more, good York; sweet Somerset, be still.
 Thy fortune, York, hadst thou been Regent there,
 Might happily have proved far worse than his.

YORK

 What, worse than naught? Nay, then a shame take all!

SOMERSET

And, in the number, thee that wishest shame!

CARDINAL

My lord of York, try what your fortune is.
Th'uncivil kerns of Ireland are in arms　　　　　　310
And temper clay with blood of Englishmen;
To Ireland will you lead a band of men,
Collected choicely, from each county some,
And try your hap against the Irishmen?

YORK

I will, my lord, so please his majesty.

SUFFOLK

Why, our authority is his consent,
And what we do establish he confirms.
Then, noble York, take thou this task in hand.

YORK

I am content. Provide me soldiers, lords,
Whiles I take order for mine own affairs.　　　　　　320

SUFFOLK

A charge, Lord York, that I will see performed.
But now return we to the false Duke Humphrey.

CARDINAL

No more of him; for I will deal with him
That henceforth he shall trouble us no more.
And so break off, the day is almost spent.
Lord Suffolk, you and I must talk of that event.

YORK

My lord of Suffolk, within fourteen days
At Bristow I expect my soldiers;
For there I'll ship them all for Ireland.

SUFFOLK

I'll see it truly done, my lord of York.　　　　　　330

Exeunt all but York

YORK

Now, York, or never, steel thy fearful thoughts,
And change misdoubt to resolution;
Be that thou hopest to be, or what thou art
Resign to death; it is not worth th'enjoying.
Let pale-faced fear keep with the mean-born man,
And find no harbour in a royal heart.
Faster than spring-time showers comes thought on
          thought,
And not a thought but thinks on dignity.
My brain, more busy than the labouring spider,
340   Weaves tedious snares to trap mine enemies.
Well, nobles, well; 'tis politicly done,
To send me packing with an host of men.
I fear me you but warm the starvèd snake,
Who, cherished in your breasts, will sting your hearts.
'Twas men I lacked, and you will give them me;
I take it kindly; yet be well assured
You put sharp weapons in a madman's hands.
Whiles I in Ireland nourish a mighty band,
I will stir up in England some black storm
350   Shall blow ten thousand souls to heaven or hell;
And this fell tempest shall not cease to rage
Until the golden circuit on my head,
Like to the glorious sun's transparent beams,
Do calm the fury of this mad-bred flaw.
And, for a minister of my intent,
I have seduced a headstrong Kentishman,
John Cade of Ashford,
To make commotion, as full well he can,
Under the title of John Mortimer.
360   In Ireland have I seen this stubborn Cade
Oppose himself against a troop of kerns,
And fought so long till that his thighs with darts

Were almost like a sharp-quilled porpentine;
And, in the end being rescued, I have seen
Him caper upright like a wild Morisco,
Shaking the bloody darts as he his bells.
Full often, like a shag-haired crafty kern,
Hath he conversèd with the enemy,
And undiscovered come to me again
And given me notice of their villainies.   370
This devil here shall be my substitute;
For that John Mortimer, which now is dead,
In face, in gait, in speech he doth resemble;
By this I shall perceive the commons' mind,
How they affect the house and claim of York.
Say he be taken, racked, and torturèd,
I know no pain they can inflict upon him
Will make him say I moved him to those arms.
Say that he thrive, as 'tis great like he will,
Why, then from Ireland come I with my strength,   380
And reap the harvest which that rascal sowed;
For Humphrey being dead, as he shall be,
And Henry put apart, the next for me.   *Exit*

Enter two Murderers running over the stage from   III.2
    the murder of the Duke of Gloucester
FIRST MURDERER
    Run to my lord of Suffolk; let him know
    We have dispatched the Duke as he commanded.
SECOND MURDERER
    O that it were to do! What have we done?
    Didst ever hear a man so penitent?
        Enter Suffolk
FIRST MURDERER Here comes my lord.
SUFFOLK Now, sirs, have you dispatched this thing?

FIRST MURDERER Ay, my good lord, he's dead.

SUFFOLK
Why, that's well said. Go, get you to my house;
I will reward you for this venturous deed.
10 The King and all the peers are here at hand.
Have you laid fair the bed? Is all things well,
According as I gave directions?

FIRST MURDERER 'Tis, my good lord.

SUFFOLK Away, be gone!   *Exeunt Murderers*
    Sound trumpets. Enter the King, Queen, Cardinal,
    and Somerset, with attendants

KING
Go, call our uncle to our presence straight;
Say we intend to try his grace today
If he be guilty, as 'tis publishèd.

SUFFOLK
I'll call him presently, my noble lord.   *Exit*

KING
Lords, take your places; and, I pray you all,
20 Proceed no straiter 'gainst our uncle Gloucester
Than from true evidence, of good esteem,
He be approved in practice culpable.

QUEEN
God forbid any malice should prevail
That faultless may condemn a noble man!
Pray God he may acquit him of suspicion!

KING
I thank thee, Meg; these words content me much.
    Enter Suffolk
How now? Why lookest thou so pale? Why tremblest
    thou?
Where is our uncle? What's the matter, Suffolk?

SUFFOLK
Dead in his bed, my lord. Gloucester is dead.

QUEEN

  Marry, God forfend!   30

CARDINAL

  God's secret judgement; I did dream tonight
  The Duke was dumb and could not speak a word.
    The King swoons

QUEEN

  How fares my lord? Help, lords! The King is dead.

SOMERSET

  Rear up his body; wring him by the nose.

QUEEN

  Run, go, help, help! O Henry, ope thine eyes!

SUFFOLK

  He doth revive again. Madam, be patient.

KING

  O heavenly God!

QUEEN   How fares my gracious lord?

SUFFOLK

  Comfort, my sovereign! Gracious Henry, comfort!

KING

  What, doth my lord of Suffolk comfort me?
  Came he right now to sing a raven's note,   40
  Whose dismal tune bereft my vital powers;
  And thinks he that the chirping of a wren,
  By crying comfort from a hollow breast,
  Can chase away the first-conceivèd sound?
  Hide not thy poison with such sugared words;
  Lay not thy hands on me; forbear, I say;
  Their touch affrights me as a serpent's sting.
  Thou baleful messenger, out of my sight!
  Upon thy eyeballs murderous tyranny
  Sits in grim majesty to fright the world.   50
  Look not upon me, for thine eyes are wounding;
  Yet do not go away; come, basilisk,

And kill the innocent gazer with thy sight;
For in the shade of death I shall find joy,
In life but double death, now Gloucester's dead.

QUEEN

Why do you rate my lord of Suffolk thus?
Although the Duke was enemy to him,
Yet he, most Christian-like, laments his death;
And for myself, foe as he was to me,
60 Might liquid tears or heart-offending groans
Or blood-consuming sighs recall his life,
I would be blind with weeping, sick with groans,
Look pale as primrose with blood-drinking sighs,
And all to have the noble Duke alive.
What know I how the world may deem of me?
For it is known we were but hollow friends;
It may be judged I made the Duke away;
So shall my name with slander's tongue be wounded,
And princes' courts be filled with my reproach.
70 This get I by his death. Ay me, unhappy,
To be a queen and crowned with infamy!

KING

Ah, woe is me for Gloucester, wretched man!

QUEEN

Be woe for me, more wretched than he is.
What, dost thou turn away and hide thy face?
I am no loathsome leper; look on me.
What! Art thou like the adder waxen deaf?
Be poisonous too and kill thy forlorn Queen.
Is all thy comfort shut in Gloucester's tomb?
Why, then Dame Margaret was ne'er thy joy.
80 Erect his statue and worship it,
And make my image but an alehouse sign.
Was I for this nigh wrecked upon the sea,
And twice by awkward wind from England's bank

Drove back again unto my native clime?
What boded this, but well forewarning wind
Did seem to say 'Seek not a scorpion's nest,
Nor set no footing on this unkind shore'?
What did I then, but cursed the gentle gusts
And he that loosed them forth their brazen caves;
And bid them blow towards England's blessèd shore,   90
Or turn our stern upon a dreadful rock.
Yet Aeolus would not be a murderer,
But left that dreadful office unto thee;
The pretty vaulting sea refused to drown me,
Knowing that thou wouldst have me drowned on shore
With tears as salt as sea through thy unkindness.
The splitting rocks cowered in the sinking sands,
And would not dash me with their ragged sides,
Because thy flinty heart, more hard than they,
Might in thy palace perish Margaret.   100
As far as I could ken thy chalky cliffs,
When from thy shore the tempest beat us back,
I stood upon the hatches in the storm,
And when the dusky sky began to rob
My earnest-gaping sight of thy land's view,
I took a costly jewel from my neck –
A heart it was, bound in with diamonds –
And threw it towards thy land. The sea received it,
And so I wished thy body might my heart;
And even with this I lost fair England's view,   110
And bid mine eyes be packing with my heart,
And called them blind and dusky spectacles
For losing ken of Albion's wishèd coast.
How often have I tempted Suffolk's tongue –
The agent of thy foul inconstancy –
To sit and witch me, as Ascanius did
When he to madding Dido would unfold

His father's acts, commenced in burning Troy!
Am I not witched like her? Or thou not false like him?
120   Ay me! I can no more. Die, Margaret!
For Henry weeps that thou dost live so long.
      Noise within. Enter Warwick, Salisbury, and many
      Commons

WARWICK
   It is reported, mighty sovereign,
   That good Duke Humphrey traitorously is murdered
   By Suffolk and the Cardinal Beaufort's means.
   The commons, like an angry hive of bees
   That want their leader, scatter up and down
   And care not who they sting in his revenge.
   Myself have calmed their spleenful mutiny,
   Until they hear the order of his death.

KING
130   That he is dead, good Warwick, 'tis too true;
   But how he died God knows, not Henry.
   Enter his chamber, view his breathless corpse,
   And comment then upon his sudden death.

WARWICK
   That shall I do, my liege. Stay, Salisbury,
   With the rude multitude till I return.
                    Exeunt Warwick, then Salisbury
                              and the Commons

KING
   O Thou that judgest all things, stay my thoughts,
   My thoughts that labour to persuade my soul
   Some violent hands were laid on Humphrey's life.
   If my suspect be false, forgive me, God,
140   For judgement only doth belong to Thee.
   Fain would I go to chafe his paly lips
   With twenty thousand kisses, and to drain
   Upon his face an ocean of salt tears,

To tell my love unto his dumb deaf trunk,
And with my fingers feel his hand unfeeling;
But all in vain are these mean obsequies,
And to survey his dead and earthy image,
What were it but to make my sorrow greater?

Bed put forth with Gloucester's body in it. Enter
Warwick

WARWICK

Come hither, gracious sovereign, view this body.

KING

That is to see how deep my grave is made;   150
For with his soul fled all my worldly solace,
For, seeing him, I see my life in death.

WARWICK

As surely as my soul intends to live
With that dread King that took our state upon Him
To free us from His Father's wrathful curse,
I do believe that violent hands were laid
Upon the life of this thrice-famèd Duke.

SUFFOLK

A dreadful oath, sworn with a solemn tongue!
What instance gives Lord Warwick for his vow?

WARWICK

See how the blood is settled in his face.   160
Oft have I seen a timely-parted ghost
Of ashy semblance, meagre, pale, and bloodless,
Being all descended to the labouring heart;
Who, in the conflict that it holds with death,
Attracts the same for aidance 'gainst the enemy;
Which with the heart there cools, and ne'er returneth
To blush and beautify the cheek again.
But see, his face is black and full of blood,
His eyeballs further out than when he lived,
Staring full ghastly like a strangled man;   170

His hair upreared, his nostrils stretched with struggling;
His hands abroad displayed, as one that grasped
And tugged for life, and was by strength subdued.
Look, on the sheets his hair, you see, is sticking;
His well-proportioned beard made rough and rugged,
Like to the summer's corn by tempest lodged.
It cannot be but he was murdered here;
The least of all these signs were probable.

SUFFOLK

Why, Warwick, who should do the Duke to death?
Myself and Beaufort had him in protection;
And we, I hope, sir, are no murderers.

WARWICK

But both of you were vowed Duke Humphrey's foes,
And you, forsooth, had the good Duke to keep;
'Tis like you would not feast him like a friend,
And 'tis well seen he found an enemy.

QUEEN

Then you belike suspect these noblemen
As guilty of Duke Humphrey's timeless death.

WARWICK

Who finds the heifer dead and bleeding fresh,
And sees fast by a butcher with an axe,
But will suspect 'twas he that made the slaughter?
Who finds the partridge in the puttock's nest,
But may imagine how the bird was dead,
Although the kite soar with unbloodied beak?
Even so suspicious is this tragedy.

QUEEN

Are you the butcher, Suffolk? Where's your knife?
Is Beaufort termed a kite? Where are his talons?

SUFFOLK

I wear no knife to slaughter sleeping men;
But here's a vengeful sword, rusted with ease,

That shall be scourèd in his rancorous heart
That slanders me with murder's crimson badge.   200
Say, if thou darest, proud Lord of Warwickshire,
That I am faulty in Duke Humphrey's death.

Exit Cardinal

WARWICK

What dares not Warwick, if false Suffolk dare him?

QUEEN

He dares not calm his contumelious spirit,
Nor cease to be an arrogant controller,
Though Suffolk dare him twenty thousand times.

WARWICK

Madam, be still, with reverence may I say,
For every word you speak in his behalf
Is slander to your royal dignity.

SUFFOLK

Blunt-witted lord, ignoble in demeanour!   210
If ever lady wronged her lord so much,
Thy mother took into her blameful bed
Some stern untutored churl, and noble stock
Was graft with crabtree slip, whose fruit thou art,
And never of the Nevils' noble race.

WARWICK

But that the guilt of murder bucklers thee
And I should rob the deathsman of his fee,
Quitting thee thereby of ten thousand shames,
And that my sovereign's presence makes me mild,
I would, false murderous coward, on thy knee   220
Make thee beg pardon for thy passèd speech,
And say it was thy mother that thou meantest;
That thou thyself was born in bastardy;
And, after all this fearful homage done,
Give thee thy hire and send thy soul to hell,
Pernicious blood-sucker of sleeping men!

SUFFOLK

Thou shalt be waking while I shed thy blood,
If from this presence thou darest go with me.

WARWICK

Away even now, or I will drag thee hence.
230   Unworthy though thou art, I'll cope with thee,
And do some service to Duke Humphrey's ghost.

Exeunt Suffolk and Warwick

KING

What stronger breastplate than a heart untainted!
Thrice is he armed that hath his quarrel just;
And he but naked, though locked up in steel,
Whose conscience with injustice is corrupted.

A noise within

QUEEN

What noise is this?

*Enter Suffolk and Warwick with their weapons
drawn*

KING

Why, how now, lords! Your wrathful weapons drawn
Here in our presence? Dare you be so bold?
Why, what tumultuous clamour have we here?

SUFFOLK

240   The traitorous Warwick, with the men of Bury,
Set all upon me, mighty sovereign.

Enter Salisbury

SALISBURY (*to the Commons within*)

Sirs, stand apart; the King shall know your mind.
Dread lord, the commons send you word by me,
Unless Lord Suffolk straight be done to death,
Or banishèd fair England's territories,
They will by violence tear him from your palace
And torture him with grievous lingering death.
They say by him the good Duke Humphrey died;

They say in him they fear your highness' death;
And mere instinct of love and loyalty,   250
Free from a stubborn opposite intent,
As being thought to contradict your liking,
Makes them thus forward in his banishment.
They say, in care of your most royal person,
That if your highness should intend to sleep,
And charge that no man should disturb your rest
In pain of your dislike, or pain of death,
Yet, notwithstanding such a strait edict,
Were there a serpent seen, with forkèd tongue,
That slily glided towards your majesty,   260
It were but necessary you were waked,
Lest, being suffered in that harmful slumber,
The mortal worm might make the sleep eternal;
And therefore do they cry, though you forbid,
That they will guard you, whe'er you will or no,
From such fell serpents as false Suffolk is;
With whose envenomèd and fatal sting,
Your loving uncle, twenty times his worth,
They say is shamefully bereft of life.

COMMONS (*within*)

An answer from the King, my lord of Salisbury!   270

SUFFOLK

'Tis like the commons, rude unpolished hinds,
Could send such message to their sovereign.
But you, my lord, were glad to be employed,
To show how quaint an orator you are;
But all the honour Salisbury hath won
Is that he was the lord ambassador
Sent from a sort of tinkers to the King.

COMMONS (*within*)

An answer from the King, or we will all break in!

KING

Go, Salisbury, and tell them all from me

280   I thank them for their tender loving care;

And had I not been cited so by them,

Yet did I purpose as they do entreat;

For sure my thoughts do hourly prophesy

Mischance unto my state by Suffolk's means.

And therefore by His majesty I swear

Whose far unworthy deputy I am,

He shall not breathe infection in this air

But three days longer, on the pain of death.

Exit Salisbury

QUEEN

O Henry, let me plead for gentle Suffolk!

KING

290   Ungentle Queen, to call him gentle Suffolk!

No more, I say; if thou dost plead for him,

Thou wilt but add increase unto my wrath.

Had I but said, I would have kept my word;

But when I swear, it is irrevocable.

(*To Suffolk*)

If after three days' space thou here beest found

On any ground that I am ruler of,

The world shall not be ransom for thy life.

Come, Warwick, come, good Warwick, go with me;

I have great matters to impart to thee.

Exeunt all but the Queen and Suffolk

QUEEN

300   Mischance and sorrow go along with you!

Heart's discontent and sour affliction

Be playfellows to keep you company!

There's two of you, the devil make a third,

And threefold vengeance tend upon your steps!

SUFFOLK

Cease, gentle Queen, these execrations,
And let thy Suffolk take his heavy leave.

QUEEN

Fie, coward woman and soft-hearted wretch!
Hast thou not spirit to curse thine enemy?

SUFFOLK

A plague upon them! Wherefore should I curse them?
Would curses kill, as doth the mandrake's groan,   310
I would invent as bitter searching terms,
As curst, as harsh, and horrible to hear,
Delivered strongly through my fixèd teeth,
With full as many signs of deadly hate,
As lean-faced Envy in her loathsome cave.
My tongue should stumble in mine earnest words,
Mine eyes should sparkle like the beaten flint,
Mine hair be fixed on end, as one distract;
Ay, every joint should seem to curse and ban;
And even now my burdened heart would break,   320
Should I not curse them. Poison be their drink!
Gall, worse than gall, the daintiest that they taste!
Their sweetest shade, a grove of cypress trees!
Their chiefest prospect, murdering basilisks!
Their softest touch as smart as lizards' stings!
Their music frightful as the serpent's hiss,
And boding screech-owls make the consort full!
And the foul terrors in dark-seated hell –

QUEEN

Enough, sweet Suffolk; thou tormentest thyself,
And these dread curses, like the sun 'gainst glass,   330
Or like an overchargèd gun, recoil
And turns the force of them upon thyself.

SUFFOLK

You bade me ban, and will you bid me leave?

Now, by the ground that I am banished from,
Well could I curse away a winter's night,
Though standing naked on a mountain top,
Where biting cold would never let grass grow,
And think it but a minute spent in sport.

QUEEN

O, let me entreat thee cease. Give me thy hand
340   That I may dew it with my mournful tears;
Nor let the rain of heaven wet this place
To wash away my woeful monuments.
O, could this kiss be printed in thy hand,
That thou mightst think upon these by the seal,
Through whom a thousand sighs are breathed for thee.
So get thee gone, that I may know my grief;
'Tis but surmised whiles thou art standing by,
As one that surfeits thinking on a want.
I will repeal thee, or, be well assured,
350   Adventure to be banishèd myself;
And banishèd I am, if but from thee.
Go, speak not to me; even now be gone.
O, go not yet. Even thus two friends condemned
Embrace and kiss and take ten thousand leaves,
Loather a hundred times to part than die.
Yet now farewell, and farewell life with thee.

SUFFOLK

Thus is poor Suffolk ten times banishèd,
Once by the King and three times thrice by thee.
'Tis not the land I care for, wert thou thence;
360   A wilderness is populous enough,
So Suffolk had thy heavenly company;
For where thou art, there is the world itself,
With every several pleasure in the world;
And where thou art not, desolation.
I can no more. Live thou to joy thy life;

Myself no joy in naught but that thou livest.
  Enter Vaux

QUEEN

Whither goes Vaux so fast? What news, I prithee?

VAUX

To signify unto his majesty
That Cardinal Beaufort is at point of death;
For suddenly a grievous sickness took him,   370
That makes him gasp, and stare, and catch the air,
Blaspheming God, and cursing men on earth.
Sometime he talks as if Duke Humphrey's ghost
Were by his side; sometime he calls the King,
And whispers to his pillow, as to him,
The secrets of his overchargèd soul;
And I am sent to tell his majesty
That even now he cries aloud for him.

QUEEN

Go tell this heavy message to the King.
                              Exit Vaux
Ay me! What is this world! What news are these!   380
But wherefore grieve I at an hour's poor loss,
Omitting Suffolk's exile, my soul's treasure?
Why only, Suffolk, mourn I not for thee,
And with the southern clouds contend in tears,
Theirs for the earth's increase, mine for my sorrows?
Now get thee hence; the King, thou knowest, is coming;
If thou be found by me thou art but dead.

SUFFOLK

If I depart from thee I cannot live,
And in thy sight to die, what were it else
But like a pleasant slumber in thy lap?   390
Here could I breathe my soul into the air,
As mild and gentle as the cradle-babe
Dying with mother's dug between its lips;

Where, from thy sight, I should be raging mad,
And cry out for thee to close up mine eyes,
To have thee with thy lips to stop my mouth;
So shouldst thou either turn my flying soul,
Or I should breathe it so into thy body,
And then it lived in sweet Elysium.
400   To die by thee were but to die in jest;
From thee to die were torture more than death.
O, let me stay, befall what may befall!

QUEEN
Away! Though parting be a fretful corrosive,
It is applièd to a deathful wound.
To France, sweet Suffolk! Let me hear from thee;
For wheresoe'er thou art in this world's globe,
I'll have an Iris that shall find thee out.

SUFFOLK
I go.

QUEEN   And take my heart with thee.
      She kisseth him

SUFFOLK
A jewel, locked into the woefullest cask
410   That ever did contain a thing of worth.
Even as a splitted bark so sunder we;
This way fall I to death.

QUEEN   This way for me.
                  Exeunt in opposite directions

III.3   *Enter the King, Salisbury, and Warwick, to the*
           Cardinal in bed

KING
How fares my lord? Speak, Beaufort, to thy sovereign.

CARDINAL
If thou beest Death, I'll give thee England's treasure,

Enough to purchase such another island,
So thou wilt let me live, and feel no pain.

KING

Ah, what a sign it is of evil life
Where death's approach is seen so terrible!

WARWICK

Beaufort, it is thy sovereign speaks to thee.

CARDINAL

Bring me unto my trial when you will.
Died he not in his bed? Where should he die?
Can I make men live whe'er they will or no?   10
O, torture me no more! I will confess.
Alive again? Then show me where he is;
I'll give a thousand pound to look upon him.
He hath no eyes; the dust hath blinded them.
Comb down his hair; look, look, it stands upright,
Like lime-twigs set to catch my wingèd soul.
Give me some drink; and bid the apothecary
Bring the strong poison that I bought of him.

KING

O Thou eternal mover of the heavens,
Look with a gentle eye upon this wretch;   20
O, beat away the busy meddling fiend
That lays strong siege unto this wretch's soul,
And from his bosom purge this black despair.

WARWICK

See how the pangs of death do make him grin!

SALISBURY

Disturb him not; let him pass peaceably.

KING

Peace to his soul, if God's good pleasure be!
Lord Cardinal, if thou thinkest on heaven's bliss,
Hold up thy hand, make signal of thy hope.

                              The Cardinal dies

He dies and makes no sign. O God, forgive him!

WARWICK

30   So bad a death argues a monstrous life.

KING

Forbear to judge, for we are sinners all.
Close up his eyes, and draw the curtain close;
And let us all to meditation.   *Exeunt*

*

IV.I   *Alarum. Fight at sea. Ordnance goes off. Enter a*
       Lieutenant, a Master, a Master's Mate, Walter
       Whitmore, Suffolk, disguised, two Gentlemen
       prisoners, and soldiers

LIEUTENANT

The gaudy, blabbing, and remorseful day
Is crept into the bosom of the sea;
And now loud howling wolves arouse the jades
That drag the tragic melancholy night;
Who with their drowsy, slow, and flagging wings
Clip dead men's graves, and from their misty jaws
Breathe foul contagious darkness in the air.
Therefore bring forth the soldiers of our prize,
For whilst our pinnace anchors in the Downs
10   Here shall they make their ransom on the sand,
Or with their blood stain this discoloured shore.
Master, this prisoner freely give I thee;
And thou that art his mate make boot of this;
The other, Walter Whitmore, is thy share.

FIRST GENTLEMAN

What is my ransom, master? Let me know.

MASTER

A thousand crowns, or else lay down your head.

MATE

> And so much shall you give, or off goes yours.

LIEUTENANT

> What, think you much to pay two thousand crowns,
> And bear the name and port of gentleman?
> Cut both the villains' throats; for die you shall.   20
> The lives of those which we have lost in fight
> Be counterpoised with such a petty sum!

FIRST GENTLEMAN

> I'll give it, sir; and therefore spare my life.

SECOND GENTLEMAN

> And so will I, and write home for it straight.

WHITMORE

> I lost mine eye in laying the prize aboard,
> (*To Suffolk*) And therefore to revenge it shalt thou die;
> And so should these, if I might have my will.

LIEUTENANT

> Be not so rash. Take ransom; let him live.

SUFFOLK

> Look on my George; I am a gentleman.
> Rate me at what thou wilt, thou shalt be paid.   30

WHITMORE

> And so am I; my name is Walter Whitmore.
> How now! Why starts thou? What, doth death affright?

SUFFOLK

> Thy name affrights me, in whose sound is death.
> A cunning man did calculate my birth,
> And told me that by water I should die.
> Yet let not this make thee be bloody-minded;
> Thy name is Gualtier, being rightly sounded.

WHITMORE

> Gualtier or Walter, which it is I care not.
> Never yet did base dishonour blur our name
> But with our sword we wiped away the blot.   40

Therefore, when merchant-like I sell revenge,
Broke be my sword, my arms torn and defaced,
And I proclaimed a coward through the world.

SUFFOLK
Stay, Whitmore, for thy prisoner is a prince,
The Duke of Suffolk, William de la Pole.

WHITMORE
The Duke of Suffolk, muffled up in rags!

SUFFOLK
Ay, but these rags are no part of the Duke;
Jove sometime went disguised, and why not I?

LIEUTENANT
But Jove was never slain, as thou shalt be.

SUFFOLK
50   Obscure and lousy swain, King Henry's blood,
The honourable blood of Lancaster,
Must not be shed by such a jaded groom.
Hast thou not kissed thy hand and held my stirrup?
Bare-headed plodded by my foot-cloth mule,
And thought thee happy when I shook my head?
How often hast thou waited at my cup,
Fed from my trencher, kneeled down at the board,
When I have feasted with Queen Margaret?
Remember it and let it make thee crest-fallen,
60   Ay, and allay this thy abortive pride,
How in our voiding lobby hast thou stood
And duly waited for my coming forth.
This hand of mine hath writ in thy behalf,
And therefore shall it charm thy riotous tongue.

WHITMORE
Speak, captain, shall I stab the forlorn swain?

LIEUTENANT
First let my words stab him, as he hath me.

SUFFOLK
  Base slave, thy words are blunt and so art thou.
LIEUTENANT
  Convey him hence, and on our longboat's side
  Strike off his head.
SUFFOLK   Thou darest not, for thy own.
LIEUTENANT
  Yes, Poole.
SUFFOLK   Poole?
LIEUTENANT   Poole! Sir Poole! Lord!   70
  Ay, kennel, puddle, sink, whose filth and dirt
  Troubles the silver spring where England drinks;
  Now will I dam up this thy yawning mouth
  For swallowing the treasure of the realm.
  Thy lips that kissed the Queen shall sweep the ground;
  And thou that smiled'st at good Duke Humphrey's
       death
  Against the senseless winds shalt grin in vain,
  Who in contempt shall hiss at thee again;
  And wedded be thou to the hags of hell,
  For daring to affy a mighty lord   80
  Unto the daughter of a worthless king,
  Having neither subject, wealth, nor diadem.
  By devilish policy art thou grown great,
  And, like ambitious Sylla, overgorged
  With gobbets of thy mother's bleeding heart.
  By thee Anjou and Maine were sold to France,
  The false revolting Normans thorough thee
  Disdain to call us lord, and Picardy
  Hath slain their governors, surprised our forts,
  And sent the ragged soldiers wounded home.   90
  The princely Warwick, and the Nevils all,
  Whose dreadful swords were never drawn in vain,
  As hating thee, are rising up in arms;

And now the house of York, thrust from the crown
By shameful murder of a guiltless king
And lofty, proud, encroaching tyranny,
Burns with revenging fire, whose hopeful colours
Advance our half-faced sun, striving to shine,
Under the which is writ '*Invitis nubibus*'.

100   The commons here in Kent are up in arms;
And to conclude, reproach and beggary
Is crept into the palace of our King,
And all by thee. Away! Convey him hence.

SUFFOLK
O that I were a god, to shoot forth thunder
Upon these paltry, servile, abject drudges.
Small things make base men proud. This villain here,
Being captain of a pinnace, threatens more
Than Bargulus, the strong Illyrian pirate.
Drones suck not eagles' blood, but rob beehives.

110   It is impossible that I should die
By such a lowly vassal as thyself.
Thy words move rage and not remorse in me.

LIEUTENANT
Ay, but my deeds shall stay thy fury soon.

SUFFOLK
I go of message from the Queen to France;
I charge thee, waft me safely 'cross the Channel.

LIEUTENANT
Walter!

WHITMORE
Come, Suffolk, I must waft thee to thy death.

SUFFOLK
Pene gelidus timor occupat artus;
It is thee I fear.

WHITMORE
120   Thou shalt have cause to fear before I leave thee.

What, are ye daunted now? Now will ye stoop?

FIRST GENTLEMAN

My gracious lord, entreat him, speak him fair.

SUFFOLK

Suffolk's imperial tongue is stern and rough,
Used to command, untaught to plead for favour.
Far be it we should honour such as these
With humble suit. No, rather let my head
Stoop to the block than these knees bow to any
Save to the God of heaven, and to my king;
And sooner dance upon a bloody pole
Than stand uncovered to the vulgar groom.   130
True nobility is exempt from fear;
More can I bear than you dare execute.

LIEUTENANT

Hale him away, and let him talk no more.

SUFFOLK

Come, soldiers, show what cruelty ye can,
That this my death may never be forgot.
Great men oft die by vile Besonians:
A Roman sworder and banditto slave
Murdered sweet Tully; Brutus' bastard hand
Stabbed Julius Caesar; savage islanders
Pompey the Great; and Suffolk dies by pirates.   140

Exeunt Whitmore and soldiers
with Suffolk

LIEUTENANT

And as for these whose ransom we have set,
It is our pleasure one of them depart;
Therefore come you with us, and let him go.

Exeunt all but the First Gentleman
Enter Walter Whitmore with the body of Suffolk

WHITMORE

There let his head and lifeless body lie,

Until the Queen his mistress bury it.   *Exit*

FIRST GENTLEMAN

O, barbarous and bloody spectacle!

His body will I bear unto the King;

If he revenge it not, yet will his friends;

So will the Queen, that living held him dear.

Exit with the body

IV.2   *Enter George Bevis and John Holland*

BEVIS Come, and get thee a sword, though made of a lath;
they have been up these two days.

HOLLAND They have the more need to sleep now then.

BEVIS I tell thee, Jack Cade the clothier means to dress
the commonwealth, and turn it, and set a new nap upon it.

HOLLAND So he had need, for 'tis threadbare. Well, I
say it was never merry world in England since gentlemen came up.

10 BEVIS O miserable age! Virtue is not regarded in handi-
craftsmen.

HOLLAND The nobility think scorn to go in leather aprons.

BEVIS Nay, more; the King's Council are no good workmen.

HOLLAND True; and yet it is said 'Labour in thy
vocation'; which is as much to say as 'Let the magistrates be labouring men'; and therefore should we
be magistrates.

BEVIS Thou hast hit it; for there's no better sign of a
20 brave mind than a hard hand.

HOLLAND I see them, I see them! There's Best's son,
the tanner of Wingham.

BEVIS He shall have the skins of our enemies to make
dog's leather of.

HOLLAND And Dick the butcher.

BEVIS Then is sin struck down like an ox, and iniquity's
  throat cut like a calf.

HOLLAND And Smith the weaver.

BEVIS Argo, their thread of life is spun.

HOLLAND Come, come, let's fall in with them.   30

  *Drums. Enter Jack Cade, Dick the butcher, Smith
  the weaver, and a sawyer, with infinite numbers*

CADE We John Cade, so termed of our supposed father –

DICK (*aside*) Or rather of stealing a cade of herrings.

CADE For our enemies shall fall before us, inspired with
  the spirit of putting down kings and princes. Command
  silence.

DICK Silence!

CADE My father was a Mortimer –

DICK (*aside*) He was an honest man and a good bricklayer.

CADE My mother a Plantagenet –

DICK (*aside*) I knew her well; she was a midwife.   40

CADE My wife descended of the Lacys –

DICK (*aside*) She was indeed a pedlar's daughter, and
  sold many laces.

SMITH (*aside*) But now of late, not able to travel with her
  furred pack, she washes bucks here at home.

CADE Therefore am I of an honourable house.

DICK (*aside*) Ay, by my faith, the field is honourable,
  and there was he born, under a hedge; for his father had
  never a house but the cage.

CADE Valiant I am.   50

SMITH (*aside*) 'A must needs, for beggary is valiant.

CADE I am able to endure much.

DICK (*aside*) No question of that; for I have seen him
  whipped three market days together.

CADE I fear neither sword nor fire.

SMITH (*aside*) He need not fear the sword, for his coat is of
  proof.

DICK (*aside*) But methinks he should stand in fear of fire,
   being burnt i'th'hand for stealing of sheep.

60 CADE Be brave then; for your captain is brave, and vows
   reformation. There shall be in England seven halfpenny
   loaves sold for a penny; the three-hooped pot shall have
   ten hoops; and I will make it felony to drink small beer.
   All the realm shall be in common, and in Cheapside shall
   my palfrey go to grass. And when I am king, as king I
   will be –

ALL God save your majesty!

CADE I thank you, good people. There shall be no money;
   all shall eat and drink on my score; and I will apparel
70 them all in one livery, that they may agree like brothers,
   and worship me their lord.

DICK The first thing we do, let's kill all the lawyers.

CADE Nay, that I mean to do. Is not this a lamentable thing,
   that the skin of an innocent lamb should be
   made parchment? That parchment, being scribbled
   o'er, should undo a man? Some say the bee stings, but I
   say 'tis the bee's wax, for I did but seal once to a thing,
   and I was never mine own man since. How now? Who's
   there?

Enter some rebels with the Clerk of Chartham

80 SMITH The clerk of Chartham; he can write and read and
   cast accompt.

CADE O, monstrous!

SMITH We took him setting of boys' copies.

CADE Here's a villain!

SMITH H'as a book in his pocket with red letters in't.

CADE Nay, then he is a conjurer.

DICK Nay, he can make obligations, and write court-hand.

CADE I am sorry for't. The man is a proper man, of mine
   honour; unless I find him guilty, he shall not die. Come
90 hither, sirrah, I must examine thee. What is thy name?

CLERK Emmanuel.

DICK They use to write it on the top of letters. 'Twill go
hard with you.

CADE Let me alone. Dost thou use to write thy name?
Or hast thou a mark to thyself, like a honest plain-deal-
ing man?

CLERK Sir, I thank God I have been so well brought up
that I can write my name.

ALL He hath confessed; away with him! He's a villain   100
and a traitor.

CADE Away with him, I say; hang him with his pen and
inkhorn about his neck.

Exit one with the Clerk

Enter Michael

MICHAEL Where's our general?

CADE Here I am, thou particular fellow.

MICHAEL Fly, fly, fly! Sir Humphrey Stafford and his
brother are hard by, with the King's forces.

CADE Stand, villain, stand, or I'll fell thee down. He shall
be encountered with a man as good as himself. He is
but a knight, is 'a?

MICHAEL No.   110

CADE To equal him I will make myself a knight presently.
(*He kneels*) Rise up, Sir John Mortimer. (*He rises*) Now
have at him!

*Enter Sir Humphrey Stafford and his brother, with
drum and soldiers*

STAFFORD
Rebellious hinds, the filth and scum of Kent,
Marked for the gallows, lay your weapons down;
Home to your cottages, forsake this groom.
The King is merciful, if you revolt.

BROTHER
But angry, wrathful, and inclined to blood,

If you go forward; therefore yield, or die.

CADE

120   As for these silken-coated slaves, I pass not;
It is to you, good people, that I speak,
Over whom, in time to come, I hope to reign;
For I am rightful heir unto the crown.

STAFFORD

Villain, thy father was a plasterer;
And thou thyself a shearman, art thou not?

CADE

And Adam was a gardener.

BROTHER   And what of that?

CADE

Marry, this: Edmund Mortimer, Earl of March,
Married the Duke of Clarence' daughter, did he not?

STAFFORD

Ay, sir.

CADE

130   By her he had two children at one birth.

BROTHER

That's false.

CADE

Ay, there's the question; but I say 'tis true:
The elder of them, being put to nurse,
Was by a beggar-woman stolen away;
And, ignorant of his birth and parentage,
Became a bricklayer when he came to age.
His son am I; deny it if you can.

DICK

Nay, 'tis too true; therefore he shall be king.

SMITH Sir, he made a chimney in my father's house, and
140   the bricks are alive at this day to testify it; therefore deny
it not.

STAFFORD

> And will you credit this base drudge's words,
> That speaks he knows not what?

ALL

> Ay, marry, will we; therefore get ye gone.

BROTHER

> Jack Cade, the Duke of York hath taught you this.

CADE (*aside*) He lies, for I invented it myself. (*To Stafford*)
Go to, sirrah, tell the King from me that for his father's
sake, Henry the Fifth, in whose time boys went to span-
counter for French crowns, I am content he shall
reign; but I'll be Protector over him.   150

DICK And furthermore, we'll have the Lord Say's head
for selling the dukedom of Maine.

CADE And good reason; for thereby is England mained and
fain to go with a staff, but that my puissance holds it up.
Fellow kings, I tell you that that Lord Say hath gelded
the commonwealth and made it an eunuch; and more
than that, he can speak French; and therefore he is a
traitor.

STAFFORD O gross and miserable ignorance!

CADE Nay, answer if you can; the Frenchmen are our   160
enemies; go to, then, I ask but this: can he that speaks
with the tongue of an enemy be a good counsellor, or
no?

ALL No, no; and therefore we'll have his head.

BROTHER

> Well, seeing gentle words will not prevail,
> Assail them with the army of the King.

STAFFORD

> Herald, away! And throughout every town
> Proclaim them traitors that are up with Cade;
> That those which fly before the battle ends
> May, even in their wives' and children's sight,

170   Be hanged up for example at their doors.
        And you that be the King's friends, follow me.

                            Exit with his brother and soldiers

CADE
        And you that love the commons, follow me.
        Now show yourselves men; 'tis for liberty.
        We will not leave one lord, one gentleman;
        Spare none but such as go in clouted shoon,
        For they are thrifty honest men, and such
        As would, but that they dare not, take our parts.
DICK   They are all in order, and march toward us.
CADE   But then are we in order when we are most out
180   of order. Come, march forward.   *Exeunt*

IV.3   *Alarums to the fight, wherein both the Staffords
                are slain. Enter Cade and the rest*

CADE   Where's Dick, the butcher of Ashford?
DICK   Here, sir.
CADE   They fell before thee like sheep and oxen, and thou
        behaved'st thyself as if thou hadst been in thine own
        slaughter-house. Therefore thus will I reward thee:
        the Lent shall be as long again as it is; and thou shalt have
        a licence to kill for a hundred lacking one.
DICK   I desire no more.
CADE   And to speak truth, thou deservest no less.
                He puts on Sir Humphrey Stafford's coat of mail
10   This monument of the victory will I bear; and the
        bodies shall be dragged at my horse heels till I do
        come to London, where we will have the Mayor's sword
        borne before us.
DICK   If we mean to thrive and do good, break open the
        gaols and let out the prisoners.

CADE Fear not that, I warrant thee. Come, let's march
    towards London.   *Exeunt*

    Enter the King with a supplication, and the Queen   IV.4
    with Suffolk's head, the Duke of Buckingham, and
    the Lord Say

QUEEN (*aside*)
    Oft have I heard that grief softens the mind,
    And makes it fearful and degenerate;
    Think therefore on revenge and cease to weep.
    But who can cease to weep and look on this?
    Here may his head lie on my throbbing breast;
    But where's the body that I should embrace?

BUCKINGHAM What answer makes your grace to the
    rebels' supplication?

KING
    I'll send some holy bishop to entreat;
    For God forbid so many simple souls   10
    Should perish by the sword! And I myself,
    Rather than bloody war shall cut them short,
    Will parley with Jack Cade their general.
    But stay, I'll read it over once again.

QUEEN (*aside*)
    Ah, barbarous villains! Hath this lovely face
    Ruled like a wandering planet over me,
    And could it not enforce them to relent,
    That were unworthy to behold the same?

KING
    Lord Say, Jack Cade hath sworn to have thy head.

SAY
    Ay, but I hope your highness shall have his.   20

KING
    How now, madam?

Still lamenting and mourning for Suffolk's death?
I fear me, love, if that I had been dead,
Thou wouldst not have mourned so much for me.

QUEEN

No, my love; I should not mourn, but die for thee.
Enter First Messenger

KING

How now? What news? Why comest thou in such
haste?

FIRST MESSENGER

The rebels are in Southwark; fly, my lord!
Jack Cade proclaims himself Lord Mortimer,
Descended from the Duke of Clarence' house,
30   And calls your grace usurper, openly,
And vows to crown himself in Westminster.
His army is a ragged multitude
Of hinds and peasants, rude and merciless;
Sir Humphrey Stafford and his brother's death
Hath given them heart and courage to proceed.
All scholars, lawyers, courtiers, gentlemen,
They call false caterpillars and intend their death.

KING

O, graceless men, they know not what they do.

BUCKINGHAM

My gracious lord, retire to Killingworth,
40   Until a power be raised to put them down.

QUEEN

Ah, were the Duke of Suffolk now alive,
These Kentish rebels would be soon appeased!

KING

Lord Say, the traitors hateth thee;
Therefore away with us to Killingworth.

SAY

So might your grace's person be in danger.

The sight of me is odious in their eyes;
And therefore in this city will I stay,
And live alone as secret as I may.
   Enter Second Messenger

SECOND MESSENGER
Jack Cade hath gotten London Bridge;
The citizens fly and forsake their houses;   50
The rascal people, thirsting after prey,
Join with the traitor; and they jointly swear
To spoil the city and your royal court.

BUCKINGHAM
Then linger not, my lord. Away! Take horse!

KING
Come, Margaret. God, our hope, will succour us.

QUEEN
My hope is gone, now Suffolk is deceased.

KING (*to Lord Say*)
Farewell, my lord. Trust not the Kentish rebels.

BUCKINGHAM
Trust nobody, for fear you be betrayed.

SAY
The trust I have is in mine innocence,
And therefore am I bold and resolute.   *Exeunt* 60

   Enter Lord Scales upon the Tower, walking. Then   IV.5
   enter three Citizens below

SCALES How now? Is Jack Cade slain?

FIRST CITIZEN No, my lord, nor likely to be slain; for
they have won the bridge, killing all those that withstand them. The Lord Mayor craves aid of your honour
from the Tower to defend the city from the rebels.

SCALES
Such aid as I can spare you shall command,

But I am troubled here with them myself;
The rebels have assayed to win the Tower.
But get you to Smithfield and gather head,
10   And thither I will send you Matthew Gough.
Fight for your king, your country, and your lives;
And so farewell, for I must hence again.   *Exeunt*

IV.6   *Enter Jack Cade and the rest, and strikes his staff
              on London Stone*

CADE Now is Mortimer lord of this city. And here, sitting upon London Stone, I charge and command that,
of the city's cost, the Pissing Conduit run nothing
but claret wine this first year of our reign. And now
henceforward it shall be treason for any that calls me
other than Lord Mortimer.

              Enter a Soldier, running

SOLDIER Jack Cade! Jack Cade!
CADE Knock him down there.

              They kill him

SMITH If this fellow be wise, he'll never call ye Jack Cade
10   more; I think he hath a very fair warning.
DICK My lord, there's an army gathered together in
Smithfield.
CADE Come then, let's go fight with them. But first,
go and set London Bridge on fire, and, if you can, burn
down the Tower too. Come, let's away.   *Exeunt*

IV.7   *Alarums. Matthew Gough is slain, and all the rest.
              Then enter Jack Cade with his company*

CADE So, sirs. Now go some and pull down the Savoy;
others to th'Inns of Court; down with them all.
DICK I have a suit unto your lordship.

CADE Be it a lordship, thou shalt have it for that word.

DICK Only that the laws of England may come out of your mouth.

HOLLAND (*aside*) Mass, 'twill be sore law then, for he was thrust in the mouth with a spear, and 'tis not whole yet.

SMITH (*aside to Holland*) Nay, John, it will be stinking law, for his breath stinks with eating toasted cheese.   10

CADE I have thought upon it; it shall be so. Away! Burn all the records of the realm; my mouth shall be the parliament of England.

HOLLAND (*aside*) Then we are like to have biting statutes, unless his teeth be pulled out.

CADE And henceforward all things shall be in common.

Enter a Messenger

MESSENGER My lord, a prize, a prize! Here's the Lord Say, which sold the towns in France; he that made us pay one-and-twenty fifteens, and one shilling to the pound, the last subsidy.   20

Enter George Bevis with the Lord Say

CADE Well, he shall be beheaded for it ten times. Ah, thou say, thou serge, nay, thou buckram lord! Now art thou within point-blank of our jurisdiction regal. What canst thou answer to my majesty for giving up of Normandy unto Mounsieur Basimecu, the Dolphin of France? Be it known unto thee by these presence, even the presence of Lord Mortimer, that I am the besom that must sweep the court clean of such filth as thou art. Thou hast most traitorously corrupted the youth of the realm in erecting a grammar school; and   30 whereas, before, our forefathers had no other books but the score and the tally, thou hast caused printing to be used; and, contrary to the King his crown and dignity, thou hast built a paper-mill. It will be proved to thy face that thou hast men about thee that usually

talk of a noun and a verb, and such abominable words as
no Christian ear can endure to hear. Thou hast appointed
justices of the peace, to call poor men before them
about matters they were not able to answer. Moreover,
40   thou hast put them in prison; and because they could not
read, thou hast hanged them; when, indeed, only
for that cause they have been most worthy to live.
Thou dost ride in a foot-cloth, dost thou not?

SAY What of that?

CADE Marry, thou oughtest not to let thy horse wear a
cloak, when honester men than thou go in their hose and
doublets.

DICK And work in their shirt too; as myself, for example,
that am a butcher.

50   SAY You men of Kent —

DICK What say you of Kent?

SAY Nothing but this: 'tis *bona terra, mala gens*.

CADE Away with him! Away with him! He speaks Latin.

SAY

    Hear me but speak, and bear me where you will.
    Kent, in the *Commentaries* Caesar writ,
    Is termed the civilest place of all this isle;
    Sweet is the country, because full of riches,
    To people liberal, valiant, active, wealthy;
    Which makes me hope you are not void of pity.
60   I sold not Maine, I lost not Normandy;
    Yet to recover them would lose my life.
    Justice with favour have I always done;
    Prayers and tears have moved me, gifts could never.
    When have I aught exacted at your hands,
    But to maintain the King, the realm, and you?
    Large gifts have I bestowed on learnèd clerks,
    Because my book preferred me to the King,
    And seeing ignorance is the curse of God,

Knowledge the wing wherewith we fly to heaven,
Unless you be possessed with devilish spirits,   70
You cannot but forbear to murder me.
This tongue hath parleyed unto foreign kings
For your behoof —

CADE Tut, when struckest thou one blow in the field?

SAY

Great men have reaching hands; oft have I struck
Those that I never saw, and struck them dead.

BEVIS O monstrous coward! What, to come behind folks?

SAY

These cheeks are pale for watching for your good.

CADE Give him a box o'th'ear, and that will make 'em red
again.   80

SAY

Long sitting to determine poor men's causes
Hath made me full of sickness and diseases.

CADE Ye shall have a hempen caudle then, and the help of
hatchet.

DICK Why dost thou quiver, man?

SAY

The palsy and not fear provokes me.

CADE Nay, he nods at us as who should say 'I'll be even
with you'; I'll see if his head will stand steadier on a
pole or no. Take him away and behead him.

SAY

Tell me: wherein have I offended most?   90
Have I affected wealth or honour? Speak.
Are my chests filled up with extorted gold?
Is my apparel sumptuous to behold?
Whom have I injured, that ye seek my death?
These hands are free from guiltless bloodshedding,
This breast from harbouring foul deceitful thoughts.
O, let me live!

CADE (*aside*) I feel remorse in myself with his words; but
 I'll bridle it. He shall die, an it be but for pleading so
100 well for his life. Away with him! He has a familiar
 under his tongue; he speaks not a God's name. Go,
 take him away, I say; and strike off his head presently,
 and then break into his son-in-law's house, Sir James
 Cromer, and strike off his head, and bring them both
 upon two poles hither.

ALL It shall be done.

SAY
 Ah, countrymen, if, when you make your prayers,
 God should be so obdurate as yourselves,
 How would it fare with your departed souls?
110 And therefore yet relent and save my life.

CADE Away with him! And do as I command ye.
                                  Exeunt some rebels with Lord Say
 The proudest peer in the realm shall not wear a head
 on his shoulders, unless he pay me tribute; there shall
 not a maid be married, but she shall pay to me her
 maidenhead, ere they have it. Men shall hold of me
 in capite; and we charge and command that their
 wives be as free as heart can wish or tongue can tell.

DICK My lord, when shall we go to Cheapside and take up
 commodities upon our bills?

120 CADE Marry, presently.

ALL O, brave!
                Enter one with the heads of Say and Cromer upon
                two poles

CADE But is not this braver? Let them kiss one another;
 for they loved well when they were alive. Now part
 them again, lest they consult about the giving up of
 some more towns in France. Soldiers, defer the spoil
 of the city until night; for with these borne before us,
 instead of maces, will we ride through the streets, and
 at every corner have them kiss. Away!   *Exeunt*

Alarum and retreat. Enter again Cade and all his   IV.8
rabblement

CADE Up Fish Street! Down Saint Magnus' Corner!
    Kill and knock down! Throw them into Thames!
    Sound a parley
    What noise is this I hear? Dare any be so bold to
    sound retreat or parley, when I command them kill?
    Enter Buckingham and Old Clifford, attended

BUCKINGHAM
    Ay, here they be that dare and will disturb thee;
    Know, Cade, we come ambassadors from the King
    Unto the commons, whom thou hast misled;
    And here pronounce free pardon to them all
    That will forsake thee and go home in peace.

CLIFFORD
    What say ye, countrymen, will ye relent   10
    And yield to mercy, whilst 'tis offered you,
    Or let a rebel lead you to your deaths?
    Who loves the King and will embrace his pardon,
    Fling up his cap and say 'God save his majesty!'
    Who hateth him, and honours not his father,
    Henry the Fifth, that made all France to quake,
    Shake he his weapon at us and pass by.

ALL God save the King! God save the King!

CADE What, Buckingham and Clifford, are ye so brave?
    And you, base peasants, do ye believe him? Will   20
    you needs be hanged with your pardons about your
    necks? Hath my sword therefore broke through London
    gates, that you should leave me at the White Hart
    in Southwark? I thought ye would never have given out
    these arms till you had recovered your ancient freedom.
    But you are all recreants and dastards, and delight to live
    in slavery to the nobility. Let them break your backs with
    burdens, take your houses over your heads, ravish your

wives and daughters before your faces. For me, I will
30 make shift for one, and so God's curse light upon you
all!

ALL We'll follow Cade! We'll follow Cade!

CLIFFORD
Is Cade the son of Henry the Fifth,
That thus you do exclaim you'll go with him?
Will he conduct you through the heart of France,
And make the meanest of you earls and dukes?
Alas, he hath no home, no place to fly to;
Nor knows he how to live but by the spoil,
Unless by robbing of your friends and us.
40 Were't not a shame, that whilst you live at jar,
The fearful French, whom you late vanquishèd,
Should make a start o'er seas and vanquish you?
Methinks already in this civil broil
I see them lording it in London streets,
Crying 'Villiago!' unto all they meet.
Better ten thousand base-born Cades miscarry
Than you should stoop unto a Frenchman's mercy.
To France! To France! And get what you have lost;
Spare England, for it is your native coast.
50 Henry hath money; you are strong and manly;
God on our side, doubt not of victory.

ALL À Clifford! À Clifford! We'll follow the King and
Clifford.

CADE (aside) Was ever feather so lightly blown to and fro
as this multitude? The name of Henry the Fifth hales
them to an hundred mischiefs and makes them leave me
desolate. I see them lay their heads together to surprise me. My sword make way for me, for here is
no staying. – In despite of the devils and hell, have
60 through the very midst of you! And heavens and
honour be witness that no want of resolution in me, but

only my followers' base and ignominious treasons, makes
me betake me to my heels.   *Exit*

BUCKINGHAM

What, is he fled? Go some and follow him;
And he that brings his head unto the King
Shall have a thousand crowns for his reward.

Exeunt some of them

Follow me, soldiers; we'll devise a mean
To reconcile you all unto the King.   *Exeunt*

Sound trumpets. Enter the King, Queen, and   IV.9
Somerset, on the terrace

KING

Was ever king that joyed an earthly throne,
And could command no more content than I?
No sooner was I crept out of my cradle
But I was made a king at nine months old;
Was never subject longed to be a king
As I do long and wish to be a subject.

Enter Buckingham and Clifford

BUCKINGHAM

Health and glad tidings to your majesty!

KING

Why, Buckingham, is the traitor Cade surprised?
Or is he but retired to make him strong?

Enter multitudes, with halters about their necks

CLIFFORD

He is fled, my lord, and all his powers do yield,   10
And humbly thus with halters on their necks,
Expect your highness' doom of life or death.

KING

Then, heaven, set ope thy everlasting gates
To entertain my vows of thanks and praise!

Soldiers, this day have you redeemed your lives,
And showed how well you love your prince and country;
Continue still in this so good a mind,
And, Henry, though he be infortunate,
Assure yourselves, will never be unkind.
20   And so, with thanks and pardon to you all,
I do dismiss you to your several countries.
ALL God save the King! God save the King!

Enter a Messenger

MESSENGER
Please it your grace to be advertisèd
The Duke of York is newly come from Ireland,
And with a puissant and a mighty power
Of gallowglasses and stout kerns
Is marching hitherward in proud array;
And still proclaimeth, as he comes along,
His arms are only to remove from thee
30   The Duke of Somerset, whom he terms a traitor.

KING
Thus stands my state, 'twixt Cade and York distressed;
Like to a ship that, having 'scaped a tempest,
Is straightway calmed and boarded with a pirate.
But now is Cade driven back, his men dispersed,
And now is York in arms to second him.
I pray thee, Buckingham, go and meet him,
And ask him what's the reason of these arms.
Tell him I'll send Duke Edmund to the Tower;
And, Somerset, we will commit thee thither,
40   Until his army be dismissed from him.

SOMERSET
My lord,
I'll yield myself to prison willingly,
Or unto death, to do my country good.

KING

    In any case, be not too rough in terms,
    For he is fierce and cannot brook hard language.

BUCKINGHAM

    I will, my lord, and doubt not so to deal
    As all things shall redound unto your good.

KING

    Come, wife, let's in and learn to govern better;
    For yet may England curse my wretched reign.

Flourish. Exeunt

    Enter Cade   IV.10

CADE Fie on ambitions! Fie on myself, that have a sword
    and yet am ready to famish! These five days have I
    hid me in these woods, and durst not peep out, for all
    the country is laid for me; but now am I so hungry that,
    if I might have a lease of my life for a thousand years,
    I could stay no longer. Wherefore, on a brick wall have
    I climbed into this garden, to see if I can eat grass or pick
    a sallet another while, which is not amiss to cool a man's
    stomach this hot weather. And I think this word 'sallet'
    was born to do me good; for many a time, but for a sallet,   10
    my brain-pan had been cleft with a brown bill; and
    many a time, when I have been dry and bravely march-
    ing, it hath served me instead of a quart pot to drink in;
    and now the word 'sallet' must serve me to feed on.

    Enter Alexander Iden

IDEN

    Lord, who would live turmoilèd in the court,
    And may enjoy such quiet walks as these?
    This small inheritance my father left me
    Contenteth me, and worth a monarchy.
    I seek not to wax great by others' waning,

20 Or gather wealth I care not with what envy;
   Sufficeth that I have maintains my state,
   And sends the poor well pleasèd from my gate.

CADE (*aside*) Here's the lord of the soil come to seize me
   for a stray, for entering his fee-simple without leave.
   (*To Iden*) Ah, villain, thou wilt betray me, and get a
   thousand crowns of the King by carrying my head to
   him; but I'll make thee eat iron like an ostrich, and
   swallow my sword like a great pin, ere thou and I part.

IDEN
   Why, rude companion, whatsoe'er thou be,
30 I know thee not; why then should I betray thee?
   Is't not enough to break into my garden,
   And like a thief to come to rob my grounds,
   Climbing my walls in spite of me the owner,
   But thou wilt brave me with these saucy terms?

CADE Brave thee? Ay, by the best blood that ever was
   broached, and beard thee too. Look on me well; I have
   eat no meat these five days, yet come thou and thy five
   men, and if I do not leave you all as dead as a door-nail, I
   pray God I may never eat grass more.

IDEN
40 Nay, it shall ne'er be said, while England stands,
   That Alexander Iden, an esquire of Kent,
   Took odds to combat a poor famished man.
   Oppose thy steadfast gazing eyes to mine,
   See if thou canst outface me with thy looks;
   Set limb to limb, and thou art far the lesser;
   Thy hand is but a finger to my fist;
   Thy leg a stick comparèd with this truncheon;
   My foot shall fight with all the strength thou hast;
   And if mine arm be heavèd in the air,
50 Thy grave is digged already in the earth.
   As for words, whose greatness answers words,
   Let this my sword report what speech forbears.

CADE By my valour, the most complete champion that
ever I heard! Steel, if thou turn the edge, or cut not
out the burly-boned clown in chines of beef ere thou
sleep in thy sheath, I beseech God on my knees thou
mayst be turned to hobnails.

Here they fight and Cade falls down

O, I am slain! Famine and no other hath slain me; let
ten thousand devils come against me, and give me but
the ten meals I have lost, and I'd defy them all. Wither,   60
garden, and be henceforth a burying-place to all that do
dwell in this house, because the unconquered soul of
Cade is fled.

IDEN

Is't Cade that I have slain, that monstrous traitor?
Sword, I will hallow thee for this thy deed,
And hang thee o'er my tomb when I am dead;
Ne'er shall this blood be wipèd from thy point,
But thou shalt wear it as a herald's coat,
To emblaze the honour that thy master got.

CADE Iden, farewell; and be proud of thy victory. Tell   70
Kent from me she hath lost her best man, and exhort
all the world to be cowards; for I, that never feared any,
am vanquished by famine, not by valour.   *He dies*

IDEN

How much thou wrongest me, heaven be my judge.
Die, damnèd wretch, the curse of her that bare thee;
And as I thrust thy body in with my sword,
So wish I I might thrust thy soul to hell.
Hence will I drag thee headlong by the heels
Unto a dunghill, which shall be thy grave,
And there cut off thy most ungracious head;   80
Which I will bear in triumph to the King,
Leaving thy trunk for crows to feed upon.   *Exit*

*

V.I   *Enter York and his army of Irish, with drum and*
           colours

YORK

From Ireland thus comes York to claim his right,
And pluck the crown from feeble Henry's head.
Ring, bells, aloud; burn bonfires clear and bright,
To entertain great England's lawful king.
Ah, *sancta majestas!* Who would not buy thee dear?
Let them obey that knows not how to rule;
This hand was made to handle naught but gold.
I cannot give due action to my words,
Except a sword or sceptre balance it.
A sceptre shall it have, have I a soul,
On which I'll toss the flower-de-luce of France.

        Enter Buckingham

Whom have we here? Buckingham to disturb me?
The King hath sent him, sure; I must dissemble.

BUCKINGHAM

York, if thou meanest well, I greet thee well.

YORK

Humphrey of Buckingham, I accept thy greeting.
Art thou a messenger, or come of pleasure?

BUCKINGHAM

A messenger from Henry, our dread liege,
To know the reason of these arms in peace;
Or why thou, being a subject as I am,
Against thy oath and true allegiance sworn,
Should raise so great a power without his leave,
Or dare to bring thy force so near the court?

YORK (*aside*)

Scarce can I speak, my choler is so great.
O, I could hew up rocks and fight with flint,
I am so angry at these abject terms;
And now, like Ajax Telamonius,

On sheep or oxen could I spend my fury.
I am far better born than is the King,
More like a king, more kingly in my thoughts;
But I must make fair weather yet awhile,   30
Till Henry be more weak, and I more strong. –
Buckingham, I prithee pardon me,
That I have given no answer all this while;
My mind was troubled with deep melancholy.
The cause why I have brought this army hither
Is to remove proud Somerset from the King,
Seditious to his grace and to the state.

BUCKINGHAM
That is too much presumption on thy part;
But if thy arms be to no other end,
The King hath yielded unto thy demand: 40
The Duke of Somerset is in the Tower.

YORK
Upon thine honour, is he prisoner?

BUCKINGHAM
Upon mine honour, he is prisoner.

YORK
Then, Buckingham, I do dismiss my powers.
Soldiers, I thank you all; disperse yourselves;
Meet me tomorrow in Saint George's Field,
You shall have pay and everything you wish.

                                        Exeunt soldiers

And let my sovereign, virtuous Henry,
Command my eldest son – nay, all my sons –
As pledges of my fealty and love;   50
I'll send them all as willing as I live.
Lands, goods, horse, armour, anything I have,
Is his to use, so Somerset may die.

BUCKINGHAM
York, I commend this kind submission;

We twain will go into his highness' tent.
Enter the King and attendants

KING

Buckingham, doth York intend no harm to us,
That thus he marcheth with thee arm in arm?

YORK

In all submission and humility
York doth present himself unto your highness.

KING

60 Then what intends these forces thou dost bring?

YORK

To heave the traitor Somerset from hence,
And fight against that monstrous rebel Cade,
Who since I heard to be discomfited.
Enter Iden, with Cade's head

IDEN

If one so rude and of so mean condition
May pass into the presence of a king,
Lo, I present your grace a traitor's head,
The head of Cade, whom I in combat slew.

KING

The head of Cade? Great God, how just art Thou!
O, let me view his visage, being dead,
70 That living wrought me such exceeding trouble.
Tell me, my friend, art thou the man that slew him?

IDEN

I was, an't like your majesty.

KING

How art thou called? And what is thy degree?

IDEN

Alexander Iden, that's my name,
A poor esquire of Kent, that loves his king.

BUCKINGHAM

So please it you, my lord, 'twere not amiss

He were created knight for his good service.

KING

Iden, kneel down.
Iden kneels
Rise up a knight.
We give thee for reward a thousand marks,
And will that thou henceforth attend on us.   80

IDEN

May Iden live to merit such a bounty,
And never live but true unto his liege.
Enter the Queen and Somerset

KING

See, Buckingham, Somerset comes with th' Queen;
Go, bid her hide him quickly from the Duke.

QUEEN

For thousand Yorks he shall not hide his head,
But boldly stand and front him to his face.

YORK

How now? Is Somerset at liberty?
Then, York, unloose thy long-imprisoned thoughts
And let thy tongue be equal with thy heart.
Shall I endure the sight of Somerset?   90
False King! Why hast thou broken faith with me,
Knowing how hardly I can brook abuse?
'King' did I call thee? No, thou art not king;
Not fit to govern and rule multitudes,
Which darest not – no, nor canst not – rule a traitor.
That head of thine doth not become a crown;
Thy hand is made to grasp a palmer's staff,
And not to grace an awful princely sceptre.
That gold must round engirt these brows of mine,
Whose smile and frown, like to Achilles' spear,   100
Is able with the change to kill and cure.
Here is a hand to hold a sceptre up,

And with the same to act controlling laws.
Give place; by heaven, thou shalt rule no more
O'er him whom heaven created for thy ruler.

SOMERSET

O monstrous traitor! I arrest thee, York,
Of capital treason 'gainst the King and crown.
Obey, audacious traitor; kneel for grace.

YORK

Wouldst have me kneel? First let me ask of these
110   If they can brook I bow a knee to man.
Sirrah, call in my sons to be my bail;

Exit an attendant

I know, ere they will have me go to ward,
They'll pawn their swords of my enfranchisement.

QUEEN

Call hither Clifford; bid him come amain,
To say if that the bastard boys of York
Shall be the surety for their traitor father.

Exit an attendant

YORK

O blood-bespotted Neapolitan,
Outcast of Naples, England's bloody scourge!
The sons of York, thy betters in their birth,
120   Shall be their father's bail, and bane to those
That for my surety will refuse the boys.

Enter at one door Edward and Richard with their army

See where they come; I'll warrant they'll make it good.

*Enter at another door Clifford and Young Clifford
with an army*

QUEEN

And here comes Clifford to deny their bail.

CLIFFORD

Health and all happiness to my lord the King!

He kneels

YORK

I thank thee, Clifford; say, what news with thee?
Nay, do not fright us with an angry look.
We are thy sovereign, Clifford; kneel again.
For thy mistaking so, we pardon thee.

CLIFFORD

This is my king, York; I do not mistake;
But thou mistakes me much to think I do.   130
To Bedlam with him! Is the man grown mad?

KING

Ay, Clifford; a bedlam and ambitious humour
Makes him oppose himself against his king.

CLIFFORD

He is a traitor; let him to the Tower,
And chop away that factious pate of his.

QUEEN

He is arrested, but will not obey;
His sons, he says, shall give their words for him.

YORK

Will you not, sons?

EDWARD

Ay, noble father, if our words will serve.

RICHARD

And if words will not, then our weapons shall.   140

CLIFFORD

Why, what a brood of traitors have we here!

YORK

Look in a glass and call thy image so;
I am thy king, and thou a false-heart traitor.
Call hither to the stake my two brave bears,
That with the very shaking of their chains
They may astonish these fell-lurking curs;
Bid Salisbury and Warwick come to me.

Enter the Earls of Warwick and Salisbury with an army

CLIFFORD

    Are these thy bears? We'll bait thy bears to death,
    And manacle the bearard in their chains,
150   If thou darest bring them to the baiting-place.

RICHARD

    Oft have I seen a hot o'erweening cur
    Run back and bite, because he was withheld;
    Who, being suffered with the bear's fell paw,
    Hath clapped his tail between his legs and cried;
    And such a piece of service will you do,
    If you oppose yourselves to match Lord Warwick.

CLIFFORD

    Hence, heap of wrath, foul indigested lump,
    As crookèd in thy manners as thy shape!

YORK

    Nay, we shall heat you thoroughly anon.

CLIFFORD

160   Take heed, lest by your heat you burn yourselves.

KING

    Why, Warwick, hath thy knee forgot to bow?
    Old Salisbury, shame to thy silver hair,
    Thou mad misleader of thy brain-sick son!
    What, wilt thou on thy deathbed play the ruffian,
    And seek for sorrow with thy spectacles?
    O, where is faith? O, where is loyalty?
    If it be banished from the frosty head,
    Where shall it find a harbour in the earth?
    Wilt thou go dig a grave to find out war,
170   And shame thine honourable age with blood?
    Why art thou old and wantest experience?
    Or wherefore dost abuse it, if thou hast it?
    For shame! In duty bend thy knee to me,
    That bows unto the grave with mickle age.

SALISBURY

    My lord, I have considered with myself
    The title of this most renownèd Duke;
    And in my conscience do repute his grace
    The rightful heir to England's royal seat.

KING

    Hast thou not sworn allegiance unto me?

SALISBURY

    I have.   180

KING

    Canst thou dispense with heaven for such an oath?

SALISBURY

    It is great sin to swear unto a sin,
    But greater sin to keep a sinful oath.
    Who can be bound by any solemn vow
    To do a murderous deed, to rob a man,
    To force a spotless virgin's chastity,
    To reave the orphan of his patrimony,
    To wring the widow from her customed right,
    And have no other reason for this wrong
    But that he was bound by a solemn oath?   190

QUEEN

    A subtle traitor needs no sophister.

KING

    Call Buckingham, and bid him arm himself.

YORK

    Call Buckingham and all the friends thou hast,
    I am resolved for death or dignity.

CLIFFORD

    The first I warrant thee, if dreams prove true.

WARWICK

    You were best to go to bed and dream again,
    To keep thee from the tempest of the field.

CLIFFORD

> I am resolved to bear a greater storm
> Than any thou canst conjure up today;
> And that I'll write upon thy burgonet,
> Might I but know thee by thy house's badge.

200

WARWICK

> Now by my father's badge, old Nevil's crest,
> The rampant bear chained to the raggèd staff,
> This day I'll wear aloft my burgonet,
> As on a mountain top the cedar shows,
> That keeps his leaves in spite of any storm,
> Even to affright thee with the view thereof.

CLIFFORD

> And from thy burgonet I'll rend thy bear
> And tread it under foot with all contempt,
> Despite the bearard that protects the bear.

210

YOUNG CLIFFORD

> And so to arms, victorious father,
> To quell the rebels and their complices.

RICHARD

> Fie, charity, for shame! Speak not in spite,
> For you shall sup with Jesu Christ tonight.

YOUNG CLIFFORD

> Foul stigmatic, that's more than thou canst tell.

RICHARD

> If not in heaven, you'll surely sup in hell.   *Exeunt*

V.2   *Alarums to the battle. Enter Warwick*

WARWICK

> Clifford of Cumberland, 'tis Warwick calls;
> And if thou dost not hide thee from the bear,
> Now when the angry trumpet sounds alarum,

And dead men's cries do fill the empty air,
Clifford, I say, come forth and fight with me.
Proud northern lord, Clifford of Cumberland,
Warwick is hoarse with calling thee to arms.
　　Enter York
How now, my noble lord? What, all afoot?

YORK

The deadly-handed Clifford slew my steed;
But match to match I have encountered him,　　　10
And made a prey for carrion kites and crows
Even of the bonny beast he loved so well.
　　Enter Clifford

WARWICK

Of one or both of us the time is come.

YORK

Hold, Warwick! Seek thee out some other chase,
For I myself must hunt this deer to death.

WARWICK

Then nobly, York; 'tis for a crown thou fightest.
As I intend, Clifford, to thrive today,
It grieves my soul to leave thee unassailed.　　*Exit*

CLIFFORD

What seest thou in me, York? Why dost thou pause?

YORK

With thy brave bearing should I be in love,　　　20
But that thou art so fast mine enemy.

CLIFFORD

Nor should thy prowess want praise and esteem,
But that 'tis shown ignobly and in treason.

YORK

So let it help me now against thy sword,
As I in justice and true right express it.

CLIFFORD
My soul and body on the action both!

YORK
A dreadful lay! Address thee instantly!
They fight and York kills Clifford

CLIFFORD
La fin couronne les œuvres.   *He dies*

YORK
Thus war hath given thee peace, for thou art still.
30 Peace with his soul, heaven, if it be thy will!   *Exit*
Enter Young Clifford

YOUNG CLIFFORD
Shame and confusion! All is on the rout;
Fear frames disorder, and disorder wounds
Where it should guard. O war, thou son of hell,
Whom angry heavens do make their minister,
Throw in the frozen bosoms of our part
Hot coals of vengeance! Let no soldier fly.
He that is truly dedicate to war
Hath no self-love; nor he that loves himself
Hath not essentially, but by circumstance,
40 The name of valour.
He sees his dead father
                    O, let the vile world end,
And the premised flames of the last day
Knit earth and heaven together.
Now let the general trumpet blow his blast,
Particularities and petty sounds
To cease! Wast thou ordained, dear father,
To lose thy youth in peace, and to achieve
The silver livery of advisèd age,
And, in thy reverence and thy chair-days, thus
To die in ruffian battle? Even at this sight
50 My heart is turned to stone, and while 'tis mine

It shall be stony. York not our old men spares;
No more will I their babes; tears virginal
Shall be to me even as the dew to fire;
And beauty, that the tyrant oft reclaims,
Shall to my flaming wrath be oil and flax.
Henceforth, I will not have to do with pity:
Meet I an infant of the house of York,
Into as many gobbets will I cut it
As wild Medea young Absyrtus did;
In cruelty will I seek out my fame.   60
Come, thou new ruin of old Clifford's house;
As did Aeneas old Anchises bear,
So bear I thee upon my manly shoulders;
But then Aeneas bare a living load,
Nothing so heavy as these woes of mine.

> *Exit with his father on his back*
> *Enter Richard and Somerset to fight. Somerset is*
> *killed*

RICHARD

So, lie thou there;
For underneath an alehouse' paltry sign,
The Castle in Saint Albans, Somerset
Hath made the wizard famous in his death.
Sword, hold thy temper; heart, be wrathful still;   70
Priests pray for enemies, but princes kill.   *Exit*

> *Fight. Excursions. Enter the King, Queen, and soldiers*

QUEEN

Away, my lord! You are slow. For shame, away!

KING

Can we outrun the heavens? Good Margaret, stay.

QUEEN

What are you made of? You'll nor fight nor fly.
Now is it manhood, wisdom, and defence,
To give the enemy way, and to secure us

By what we can, which can no more but fly.
   Alarum afar off
If you be ta'en, we then should see the bottom
Of all our fortunes; but if we haply 'scape –
80 As well we may if not through your neglect –
We shall to London get, where you are loved,
And where this breach now in our fortunes made
May readily be stopped.
   Enter Young Clifford

YOUNG CLIFFORD
But that my heart's on future mischief set,
I would speak blasphemy ere bid you fly;
But fly you must; uncurable discomfit
Reigns in the hearts of all our present parts.
Away, for your relief! And we will live
To see their day and them our fortune give.
90 Away, my lord, away!   *Exeunt*

V.3   *Alarum. Retreat. Enter York, Richard, Warwick,*
       and soldiers with drum and colours

YORK
Of Salisbury, who can report of him,
That winter lion, who in rage forgets
Agèd contusions and all brush of time;
And, like a gallant in the brow of youth,
Repairs him with occasion? This happy day
Is not itself, nor have we won one foot,
If Salisbury be lost.

RICHARD   My noble father,
Three times today I holp him to his horse,
Three times bestrid him; thrice I led him off,
10 Persuaded him from any further act;
But still where danger was, still there I met him,

And like rich hangings in a homely house,
So was his will in his old feeble body.
But, noble as he is, look where he comes.
      Enter Salisbury

SALISBURY
      Now, by my sword, well hast thou fought today;
      By th'mass, so did we all. I thank you, Richard.
      God knows how long it is I have to live,
      And it hath pleased Him that three times today
      You have defended me from imminent death.
      Well, lords, we have not got that which we have;   20
      'Tis not enough our foes are this time fled,
      Being opposites of such repairing nature.

YORK
      I know our safety is to follow them;
      For, as I hear, the King is fled to London,
      To call a present court of parliament.
      Let us pursue him ere the writs go forth.
      What says Lord Warwick? Shall we after them?

WARWICK
      After them! Nay, before them, if we can.
      Now by my hand, lords, 'twas a glorious day.
      Saint Albans battle, won by famous York,   30
      Shall be eternized in all age to come.
      Sound drum and trumpets, and to London all,
      And more such days as these to us befall!   *Exeunt*

An Account of the Text

Henry VI, Part II exists in two versions. The first of these was published by Thomas Millington in quarto format in 1594 (Q1) under the title *The First part of the Contention betwixt the two famous Houses of York and Lancaster*, which was reprinted by the same publisher in 1600 (Q2) and in 1619 by Thomas Pavier, who combined it with a version of *Henry VI, Part III* and called them together *The Whole Contention betweene the two Famous Houses, Lancaster and Yorke* (Q3). The second version appears in the first Folio edition of the collected plays of 1623 (F), where it is the seventh play in the Histories section and is called *The second Part of Henry the Sixt, with the death of the Good Duke Humfrey*. It is obvious that there is a close relationship between these two texts; but its exact nature is still a matter of scholarly debate.

F is clearly the superior text and is about one third longer than Q (Q refers to the text as represented collectively by the three Quartos, but primarily by the first). It seems likely that the two main compositors of the Folio volume, who divided the type-setting of the play between them, worked from a manuscript of theatrical origin. This manuscript may have been Shakespeare's own, because F reproduces features which are normally associated with the author's habits of composition. For example, it is unlikely that anyone but the writer would have been guilty of the slip of memory that caused Queen Margaret to be referred to as Eleanor (Duchess of Gloucester) four times in III.2 (26, 79, 100 and 120). Certain stage directions appear to be authorial rather than theatrical (for example, *Enter multitudes, with halters about their necks* at IV.9.9, where *multitudes* is obviously impractical in the theatre); there is some uncertainty in the designation of characters (for example, Dick's speeches are indicated sometimes by *Dicke.*, sometimes by *But.*); important speaking parts are sometimes covered by a block entry term (for example, at the opening of IV.1, where *others* stands for the Master, the Master's Mate, Walter Whitmore, and the two Gentlemen prisoners); and there is occasional indefiniteness in stage directions which would have been impractical in a theatre prompt book (such as at I.4.21, where either Bolingbroke or Southwell can perform the incantation to raise the Spirit). It has also been suggested that Shakespeare's autograph may have carried theatrical annotations made with a view to the preparation of the prompt book. Some of the stage directions, particularly those specifying sound effects, strike one as being phrased with theatrical production in mind; and the names of Bevis and Holland, who appear among Jack Cade's rebels in IV.2, are almost certainly those of the contemporary actors who first played the roles. However, features like these may well be the result of an actor-playwright composing with a knowledge of the resources of his company in mind.

Q is a much inferior text. In some sections its wording is very close to that of F; but at others material seems to have been transposed or appears to be a poor paraphrase of what is found in F. Q drops some minor characters, includes lines clearly recollected from other plays, and in general is poetically inferior to F. Q's stage directions often read like descriptions of what took place in a particular production rather than instructions of what should be performed.

Various theories have been elaborated to account for the features of these two texts and to explain the relationship between them and its origin:

1. Some scholars argue that Q is an original play which Shakespeare rewrote as *Henry VI, Part II*. Passages where F and Q agree are viewed as having been taken over verbatim by Shakespeare from his source-play; passages in F which are superior to Q are seen as indicating rewriting; and those in F which have no parallel in Q are taken to be Shakespeare's additions.

2. A more generally accepted theory claims that Q is a memorially reconstructed acting version of the play F prints. The fact that some of the roles in Q are more full and accurate than others suggests that the actors who originally played the parts of

Warwick, Suffolk and Lord Clifford may have helped in creating from memory the shortened and faulty version of the text that Millington published.

3. The pattern of agreement and non-agreement in variants between F and Q has been explained as being of printing-house origin. Instead of working from Shakespeare's manuscript, the F compositors are seen to have set type from a copy of Q3 (and possibly Q2) which had been corrected and added to by reference to such a manuscript, following the amended printed text whenever they could and consulting the handwritten copy only when it provided substantial additional material.

4. Many scholars believe that features of F and Q, whatever their relationship, can be explained only by the play's being of multiple authorship. Using mainly stylistic and some external evidence, they argue that the play was originally the work of Robert Greene, Thomas Nashe and George Peele, and Shakespeare working with them and/or revising the original play to make it fit into a three-part sequence.

The purely textual features of Q and F versions are often analysed in connection with various pieces of external historical evidence, which are themselves susceptible to very different interpretations. For example, the first reference we have to Shakespeare as a dramatist occurs in Robert Greene's pamphlet *Groatsworth of Wit* (1592), where the dying writer appears to be warning his fellow dramatists against Shakespeare, whom he characterizes as 'an upstart crow, beautified with our feathers, that with his *Tiger's heart wrapped in a player's hide* supposes he is as well able to bombast out a blank verse as the best of you; and, being an absolute *Johannes fac totum*, is in his own conceit the only Shake-scene in a country'.

Clearly this allusion connects Shakespeare with the authorship of the *Henry VI* plays; but scholars differ as to the exact nature of the charge Greene is making. Obviously he is angered by Shakespeare's theatrical success; but is he implying that Shakespeare plagiarized his and other men's work? Or is he irate at the spectacle of a mere actor competing with university-trained playwrights? Or is he being scornful of Shakespeare's literary imitation of his contemporaries? And what exactly is the point of the misquotation from *Part III* (I.4.137)? With widely different interpretations of Greene's tirade possible, it can easily be seen that it may be used to support a variety of theories about the origins and relationship of the Q and F versions.

It is almost certain that the play belonged to the Earl of Pembroke's Men, a theatrical company which was forced to tour the provinces owing to the closure of the London theatres occasioned by the plague in parts of 1592 and 1593. Apparently these players went bankrupt as a result of this experience and were forced to sell up their effects. Some of their plays ultimately found their way into the repertoire of the Lord Chamberlain's Men, a company of which Shakespeare was to become the chief playwright and a leading shareholder. Like the Greene allusion, this tantalizingly incomplete theatrical history – involving as it does Shakespeare, Greene, Peele, Nashe and Marlowe as playwrights, a company being disbanded and plays changing hands – can be used in support of very different textual theories about *Henry VI, Part II*.

Thus at the moment there is no theory concerning the genesis and early history of the play which has won general acceptance; nor is there agreement about its date of composition (between 1588 and 1592), any estimate of which must obviously take into account much of the same evidence.

As F is the better version of the play it is this that the present edition follows. Only where F presents genuine difficulties has Q been used to make emendations. In the Commentary and in the first and third collations lists Q's readings are recorded when they seem to throw light on possible meaning or stage practice, even where no emendation has been made in F. The fourth list quotes the more substantial passages in Q which are noticeably different from those in F or constitute an addition to what is found there.

COLLATIONS

The following lists are selective. The Quartos are abbreviated as Q1 (1594), Q2 (1600), Q3 (1619), and the editions of the Folio as F1 (1623), F2 (1632), F3 (1663–4), F4 (1685). In lists 1–3 quotations from the early editions are unmodernized, except that 'long s' (ſ) is replaced by 's'.

1 Emendations

Below are listed the more important departures from the text of
F1, with the readings of this edition printed to the left of the
square bracket. Those readings adopted from or based on Q1 are
identified, as are readings taken from the reprints of F. Most
of the other emendations were first made by eighteenth- and
nineteenth-century editors. Corrections of obvious misprints and
demonstrable mislineation, the straightforward regularization of
F's speech-prefixes, the variant spelling of proper names, and
punctuation changes where the sense is not significantly affected
are not recorded.

The Characters in the Play] *not in* F
I.1

49 *it is further agreed between them*] (Q1); *not in* F
51 *over*] (Q1); *not in* F
57 *duchy*] Duches (Q1); *Dutchesse*
   the county of Maine] of *Mayne* (Q1); *Maine*
91 had] hath
166 all together] altogether
176 Protector] (Q1); *Protectors*
205 And so . . . cause] And so . . . Yorke, | For . . . cause
206 Then . . . main] Then . . . away, | And . . . maine
207 Unto . . . lost!] Vnto . . . maine? | Oh . . . lost,

I.3

29 master was] Mistresse was
49 a tilt] at Tilt (Q1); a-tilt

I.4

23–6 Asmath! | By the . . . power | Thou . . . ask; | For
     till . . . hence] *Asmath* . . . God, | Whose . . . trem-
     blest at, | Answere . . . speake, | Thou shalt . . . hence
61 te] *not in* F
65 *befall*] betide
69–70 Come . . . oracles | Are hardly . . . understood]
      Come . . . Lords, | These . . . attain'd, | And . . .
      vnderstood
73 Thither . . . them –] Thither . . . Newes, | As . . . them
77 At your . . . ho] At your . . . Lord. | Who's . . . hoe

II.1

23–5   What . . . peremptory? | *Tantaene . . . irae?* |
       Churchmen . . . malice;] What, Cardinall? | Is . . .
       peremptorie? | *Tantæne . . . hot?* | Good Unckle . . .
       mallice:

32–3   I prithee peace, | Good . . . peers;] I prythee . . .
       Queene, | And whet . . . Peeres,

41–2   Ay, where . . . darest, | This . . . grove] I, where
       peepe: | And if . . . Euening, | On the . . . Groue

46–8   uncle. | CARDINAL . . . Are . . . grove. |
       GLOUCESTER . . . Cardinal] Vnckle, are . . . aduis'd? |
       The . . . Groue: | Cardinall

50–53 Now, by . . . for this, | Or all . . . *teipsum* – |
       Protector . . . yourself. | . . . The winds . . . lords.]
       Now . . . Priest, | Ile . . . this, | Or all . . . fayle. |
       . . . *Medice* . . . your selfe. | . . . The Windes . . .
       high, | So doe . . . Lords:

83   Poor . . . thee.] Poore Soule, | Gods . . . thee:

86–7   Tell . . . chance, | Or . . . shrine] Tell . . . good-
       fellow, | Cam'st . . . Deuotion, | To . . . Shrine

88–91 God knows . . . called | A hundred . . . sleep, | By
       good . . . come; | Come . . . thee.'] God knowes . . .
       Deuotion, | Being . . . oftner, | In my . . . *Albon*: |
       Who . . . Shrine, | And . . . thee.

92–3   Most . . . oft | Myself . . . so] Most . . . forsooth: |
       And . . . Voyce, | To . . . so

101–2 Alas . . . my life] (*prose in* F)

130   his] (Q1); it,

133–4 My masters . . . whips] My Masters . . . *Albones*, |
       Haue . . . Towne | And . . . Whippes

146–7 I will . . . quickly] I will . . . Lord. | Come . . .
       quickly

II.2

34–5   The third . . . line | I claim . . . daughter] The third
       . . . Clarence, | From . . . Crowne, | Had . . .
       Daughter

35, 49 Philippe] *Phillip*

45–50 Married . . . was | To . . . son. | By . . . heir | To
       . . . son | Of . . . Philippe, | Sole . . . Clarence;]

Marryed . . . Cambridge, | Who . . . *Langley*, |
Edward . . . Sonne; | By . . . Kingdome: | She . . .
March, | Who . . . *Mortimer*, | Who . . . Daughter |
Vnto . . . Clarence.

46 son, son] Sonnes Sonne
64–5 We . . . king | Till . . . stained] We . . . Lords: | But
. . . Crown'd, | And . . . stayn'd

II.3

1 Stand . . . wife] Stand . . . *Cobham*, | *Glosters* Wife:
3 sins] sinne
22–5 Stay . . . go, | Give . . . himself | Protector . . . hope, |
My . . . feet.] Stay . . . Gloster, | Ere . . . Staffe, |
Henry . . . be, | And . . . guide, | And . . . feete:

II.4

83–4 And I . . . if | You . . . farewell] And I . . . her. |
And . . . farewell
105 Madam . . . sheet] Madame . . . done, | Throw . . .
Sheet

III.1

104 'Tis . . . France;] 'Tis . . . Lord, | That . . . France,
107 Is . . . it] Is . . . so? | What . . . it
218 eyes] eyes;
223 Free . . . beams] Free Lords: | Cold . . . Beames
333 art] art;
365 caper] (F2); capre

III.2

26 Meg] *Nell*
75 leper] (F3); Leaper
79, 100 Margaret] *Elianor*
116 witch] watch
120 Margaret] *Elinor*
174 Look,] Looke
237 Why . . . drawn] Why . . . Lords? | Your . . .
drawne,
265 whe'er] where
318 on] (Qr); an
359 thence;] thence,
410 worth.] worth,

III.3

    10 whe'er] where

IV.1

    48 Jove . . . I?] (Q1); *not in* F
    50 Obscure . . . blood,] (F *gives this line to Lieutenant*)
  70–71 LIEUTENANT Yes, Poole. | SUFFOLK Poole? | LIEU-
      TENANT Poole! Sir Poole! Lord! | Ay, kennel,
      puddle] *Cap.* Yes Poull. | *Suffolke.* Poull. | *Cap.* I
      Poull, puddle (Q1); *Lieu. Poole*, Sir *Poole*? Lord, | I
      kennell, puddle
    85 mother's bleeding] Mother-bleeding
    93 are] and
  113 LIEUTENANT Ay . . . soon] (Q1); *not in* F
  114 SUFFOLK] (Q1); *not in* F
 116–17 LIEUTENANT Walter! | WHITMORE Come, Suffolk]
      Lieu. Water: W. Come Suffolke
  118 *Pene*] *Pine*
  134 Come, soldiers . . . can,] (F *gives this line to*
      Lieutenant)

IV.2

    33 fall] (F4); faile
 127–8 Marry . . . not?] (*prose in* F)
  127 this:] this
 142–3 And . . . what?] (*prose in* F)

IV.4

    58 be] (F2); *not in* F1

IV.5

   2–5 No . . . rebels] No. . . . slaine: | For . . . Bridge, |
      Killing . . . them: | The . . . Tower | To . . .
      Rebels

IV.6

   1–6 Now . . . Mortimer] Now . . . City, | And . . . Stone, |
      I . . . cost | The . . . Wine | This . . . raigne. | And
      . . . any, | That . . . *Mortimer*
    9 SMITH] *But.* (*i.e. 'Butcher'*)
 13–15 Come . . . away] Come . . . them: | But . . . fire, |
      And . . . too. | Come . . . away

IV.7

 14–15 Then . . . out] Then . . . Statues | Vnlesse . . . out

    64–5 hands, | But to maintain] hands? | Kent to
          maintaine,
       83 caudle] (F4); Candle
   122–8 But . . . Away!] But . . . brauer: | Let . . . well |
          When . . . againe, | Least . . . vp | Of . . . Soldiers, |
          Deferre . . . night: | For . . . Maces, | Will . . .
          Corner | Haue . . . Away.

IV.8
     3–4 What . . . kill] What . . . heare? | Dare . . . Parley |
          When . . . kill
      12 rebel] Traitor (Q1); rabble

IV.9
      33 calmed] (F4); calme

IV.10
      19 waning] warning
      56 God] (Q1); Ioue

V.1
      11 flower-de-luce] (F3); Fleure-de-Luce
     109 these] thee
     111 sons] (Q1); sonne
     194 or] and
     201 house's] housed

V.2
      19 What . . . pause] What . . . Yorke? | Why . . . pause
      28 *couronne les œuvres*] (F2); *Corrone les eumenes*

2 Rejected Emendations

The following list records a selection of emendations and conjectures which have not been adopted in this edition, but which have
been made with some plausibility by other editors. Many of these
emendations are readings adopted from one of the Quartos
or from the reprints of F. To the left of the square brackets are
the readings of the present text; to the right of them are F1's
readings where they differ from this edition, then readings adopted
from the Quartos and the F reprints, and other suggested emendations. When more than one emendation is listed, they are
separated by semi-colons. All emendations made to achieve

metrical regularity have been ignored in this list; and substantial
passages from Q introduced by some editors at various points in
the play, in accordance with their theories of the relationship
between F and Q, are quoted in list 4 below.

I.I

      249 Henry, surfeiting in] Henry surfeit in the

I.2

      19 thought] hour
      38 were] are (Q1)
      75 witch] witch of Ely (Q1–2); witch of Rye (Q3);
          witch of Eie

I.3

      3 in the quill] in sequel
      6 PETER] FIRST PETITIONER (F4)
      20 Melford] Long Melford (Q1)
      66 haughty] haught (F2–4)
      88 the] their
     140 I could] I'd (Q1)
     148 fume] fury
     149 far] fast
     208 This] KING This

I.4

      15 silent] silence (Q1)
      33 *befall*] betide (Q1)

II.1

      48 GLOUCESTER . . . Cardinal, I] CARDINAL I
      90 Simon] (F *Symon*); Simpcox; Saunder

II.2

   35, 49 Philippe] (F *Phillip*); Philippa

II.3

      19 ground] grave
      30 realm] helm
      46 youngest] haughtiest; highest

III.1

     140 suspense] suspect; suspects
     211 strays] strives; strains
     260 reasons] treasons

III.2

393 its] his (Q1)

IV.1

6 Clip] (F Cleape); Clap; Clepe
32 What, doth death] What doth thee
50 lousy] lowly
118 *Pene*; (F *Pine*); *Poenae*; *Perii!*

IV.2

80 Chartham] (F Chartam); Chattam (Q1); Chatham
153 mained] maimed (Q1)

IV.3

7 one] one a week (Q1)

IV.7

57 because] beauteous; bounteous; pleasant; plenteous
58 wealthy] worthy
83 the help of] pap with a

IV.10

37 five] fine

V.1

10 soul] sword
201 house's] (F housed); household (Q1)

V.2

87 parts] part; party

V.3

1 Of] Old (Q1)
29 hand] faith (Q1)

3 Stage Directions

The stage directions of this edition are based on those in F. The more important changes and additions to the F directions are listed below. The normalization of characters' names, minor adjustments in the order in which characters are listed, and the provision of exits and entrances clearly demanded by the action but omitted in F are not recorded. Asides and indications of characters addressed are all editorial, as are the corrections of *Exit* to *Exeunt*. The readings of this edition appear to the left of the square brackets; to the right of the brackets are stage directions

from Q1 wherever they have been adopted as or form the basis
for those of the present edition, and the F readings. Quarto stage
directions which have not been adopted in the present text, but
which clarify the action or provide evidence of possible Elizabethan staging, are quoted and discussed in the Commentary.

I.1

    10 *he kneels*] *not in* F
    51 *Gloucester lets the contract fall*] Duke *Humphrey* lets it
        fall (Q1); *not in* F
    56 *reads*] *not in* F
    72 *Gloucester stays all the rest*] and Duke Humphrey
        staies all the rest (Q1); *Manet the rest*

I.2

    60 *Exeunt Gloucester and Messenger*] *Ex. Hum* (*after line*
        59 *in* F)

I.3

    0 *four*] *three or foure*
  13, 19 *reads*] *not in* F
    24 *offering his petition*] *not in* F
    34 *Servant with Peter*] with the Armourers man (Q1);
        not in F
    98 *Somerset*] (Q1); *not in* F
   135 *The Queen lets fall her fan*] The Queene lets fall her
        gloue (Q1); *not in* F
  174 *guarded*] *not in* F

I.4

    11 *Hume following*] *not in* F
28, 31, 33 *reads*] *not in* F
    30 *As the Spirit speaks, Bolingbroke writes the answer*] *not*
        in F
    39 *Sir Humphrey Stafford as captain*] *not in* F
    51 *Exeunt above the Duchess and Hume, guarded*] *Exet*
        Elnor aboue (Q1); *not in* F
    53 *Exeunt Jourdain, Southwell, Bolingbroke, escorted by*
        Stafford and the guard] *Exet* with them (Q1); *Exit*

II.1

    65 *with music*] (Q1); *not in* F
      Simpcox's Wife and others following] *not in* F

137 *an attendant*] one (Q1); *not in* F

155 *Exeunt Mayor and townspeople, and the Beadle dragging Simpcox's Wife*] *Exet* Mayor (Q1); *Exit*

II.3

   0 *Enter the King, Queen, Gloucester, York, Suffolk, and
     Salisbury; the Duchess of Gloucester, Margery
     Jourdain, Southwell, Hume, and Bolingbroke, guarded*]
     Enter King *Henry*, and the Queene, Duke *Humphrey*,
     the Duke of *Suffolke*, and the Duke of *Buckingham*,
     the *Cardinall*, and Dame *Elnor Cobham*, led with the
     Officers, and then enter to them the Duke of *Yorke*,
     and the Earles of *Salsbury* and *Warwicke* (Q1); *Enter
     the King and State, with Guard, to banish the Duchesse*

  17 *Exeunt the Duchess and the other prisoners, guarded*]
     Exet some with *Elnor* (Q1); *not in* F

  92 *Alarum*] *Alarmes* (Q1); *not in* F
     Horner] him

  93 *He dies*] (Q1); *not in* F

II.4

  16 *Enter the Duchess of Gloucester barefoot, in a white
     sheet and verses written on her back and pinned on and
     a taper burning in her hand, with Sir John Stanley, the
     Sheriff, and officers with bills and halberds*] Enter
     Dame *Elnor Cobham* bare-foote, and a white sheete
     about her, with a waxe candle in her hand, and
     verses written on her backe and pind on, and accom-
     panied with the Sheriffes of London, and Sir *Iohn
     Standly*, and Officers, with billes and holbards (Q1);
     *Enter the Duchesse in a white Sheet, and a Taper
     burning in her hand, with the Sherife and Officers*

  73 *Exit Herald*] (Q1); *not in* F

  86 *with his men*] and his men (Q1); *not in* F

III.1

 194 *Exit Gloucester, guarded by the Cardinal's men*] *Exet
     Humphrey*, with the *Cardinals* men (Q1); *Exit Gloster*

 222 *Exit with Buckingham, Salisbury, and Warwick*] *Exet
     King*, *Salsbury*, and *Warwicke* (Q1); *Exit*

III.2

   0 *two Murderers*] two or three

14 *Exeunt Murderers*] *Exet* murtherers (Q1); *Exeunt*
    Sound trumpets. Enter the King, Queen, Cardinal, and
    Somerset, with attendants] Then enter the King and
    Queene, the Duke of *Buckingham*, and the Duke of
    Somerset, and the Cardinall (Q1); *Sound Trumpets.*
    Enter the King, the Queene, Cardinall, Suffolke,
    Somerset, with Attendants

121 *Salisbury*] (Q1); *not in* F

135 *Exeunt Warwick, then Salisbury and the Commons*]
    Exet Salsbury (Q1); *not in* F

148 *with Gloucester's body in it. Enter Warwick*] *not in* F,
    where '*Bed put forth*' follows line 146

202 *Exit Cardinal*] (Q1); *not in* F

231 *Exeunt Suffolk and Warwick*] (Q1); *Exeunt*

288 *Exit Salisbury*] (Q1); *not in* F

299 *Exeunt all but the Queen and Suffolk*] *Exet* King and
    Warwicke, Manet Queene and *Suffolke* (Q1); *Exit*

379 *Exit Vaux*] *Exet Vawse* (Q1); *Exit*

408 *She kisseth him*] (Q1); *not in* F

412 *in opposite directions*] *not in* F

III.3

28 *The Cardinal dies*] (Q1); *not in* F

IV.1

0 *Alarum. Fight at sea. Ordnance goes off. Enter a*
   Lieutenant, a Master, a Master's Mate, Walter
   Whitmore, Suffolk, disguised, two Gentlemen prisoners,
   and soldiers] Alarmes within, and the chambers be
   discharged, like as it were a fight at sea. And then
   enter the Captaine of the ship and the Maister, and
   the Maisters Mate, & the Duke of Suffolke disguised,
   and others with him, and Water Whickmore (Q1);
   Alarum. Fight at Sea. Ordnance goes off. Enter
   Lieutenant, Suffolke, and others

140 *and soldiers*] *not in* F

143 *Exeunt all but the First Gentleman. Enter Walter*
    Whitmore with the body of Suffolk] Exit Lieutenant, and
    the rest. Manet the first Gent. Enter Walter with the body

IV.2

30 *Jack*] *Iacke* (Q1); *not in* F

79 *Enter some rebels with the Clerk of Chartham*] Enter
   Will with the Clarke of *Chattam* (Q1); *Enter a Clearke*

112 *He kneels*] not in F
   He rises] not in F

171 *Exit with his brother and soldiers*] Exet Stafford and
   his men (Q1); *Exit*

IV.3

9 *He puts on Sir Humphrey Stafford's coat of mail*] *not
   in* F

IV.5

0 *three*] two or three

IV.7

111 *Exeunt some rebels with Lord Say*] Exet one or two,
   with the Lord *Say* (Q1); *not in* F

121 *Enter one with the heads of Say and Cromer upon two
   poles*] Enter two with the Lord *Sayes* head, and sir
   Iames Cromers, vpon two poles (Q1); *Enter one with
   the heads*

IV.8

4 *attended*] not in F

IV.10

57 *and Cade falls down*] (Q1); *not in* F

V.1

47 *Exeunt soldiers*] (Q2); *not in* F

78 *Iden kneels*] not in F

111, 116 *Exit an attendant*] not in F

121, 122 *Enter at one door Edward and Richard with their army
   . . . Enter at another door Clifford and Young Clifford
   with an army*] Enter the Duke of *Yorkes* sonnes,
   Edward the Earle of *March*, and crook-backe *Richard*,
   at the one doore, with Drumme and soldiers, and at
   the other doore, enter *Clifford* and his sonne, with
   Drumme and souldiers, and *Clifford* kneels to *Henry*,
   and speakes (Q1, *after line* 122); *Enter Edward and
   Richard . . . Enter Clifford*

124 *He kneels*] (Q1); *not in* F

147 *Enter the Earls of Warwick and Salisbury with an
   army*] Enter at one doore, the Earles of *Salsbury* and
   Warwicke, with Drumme and souldiers (Q1); *Enter
   the Earles of Warwick, and Salisbury*

V.2

    0 *Alarums to the battle*] (Q1); *not in* F

  27 *They fight and York kills Clifford*] (Q1); *not in* F

  28 *He dies*] *not in* F

  30 *Exit*] *Exet Yorke* (Q1); *not in* F

  40 *He sees his dead father*] *not in* F

  65 *Exit with his father on his back*] He takes him vp on
     his backe. . . . *Exet* yoong *Clifford* with his father
     (Q1); *not in* F

     Somerset is killed] *Richard* kils him vnder the signe of
     the Castle in saint *Albones* (Q1); *not in* F

  71 *Exit*] (Q1); *not in* F

     soldiers] *others*

4 Variant and Additional Passages in Q1

In general Q1 offers an inferior and truncated version of the
text in F; but at certain points there occur passages in Q1 which
either are noticeably different in content and expression from their
counterparts in F or constitute genuine additions to what is found
in F. Below are quoted, in modernized form, the more substantial of such passages, each printed below a reference to the appropriate point in the text of this edition.

I.1.24–31 Great King . . . doth minister:

    Th'excessive love I bear unto your grace
    Forbids me to be lavish of my tongue,
    Lest I should speak more than beseems a woman.
    Let this suffice: my bliss is in your liking,
    And nothing can make poor Margaret miserable
    Unless the frown of mighty England's King.

I.1.135–6 My lord of Gloucester . . . the King:

    Why, how now, cousin Gloucester? What needs this?
    As if our King were bound unto your will
    And might not do his will without your leave!

Proud Protector, envy in thine eyes I see,
The big swollen venom of thy hateful heart
That dares presume 'gainst that thy sovereign likes.

After I.3.5:

For but for him a many were undone
That cannot get no succour in the court.

After I.3.206:

KING
Then be it so, my lord of Somerset.
We make your grace Regent over the French,
And to defend our rights 'gainst foreign foes,
And so do good unto the realm of France.
Make haste, my lord, 'tis time that you were gone;
The time of truce I think is full expired.

I.4.0–21 *Enter the witch . . . the Spirit riseth*:

> *Enter Eleanor with Sir John Hum, Roger Bolingbroke, a*
> *conjurer, and Margery Jourdain, a witch*

ELEANOR
Here, Sir John, take this scroll of paper here,
Wherein is writ the questions you shall ask,
And I will stand upon this tower here
And hear the spirit what it says to you;
And to my questions write the answers down.
    She goes up to the tower

SIR JOHN
Now, sirs, begin and cast your spells about,
And charm the fiends for to obey your wills,
And tell Dame Eleanor of the thing she asks.

WITCH
Then, Roger Bolingbroke, about thy task
And frame a circle here upon the earth;
Whilst I thereon all prostrate on my face
Do talk and whisper with the devils below

And conjure them for to obey my will.
> *She lies down upon her face. Bolingbroke makes a circle*

BOLINGBROKE
Dark night, dread night, the silence of the night,
Wherein the furies mask in hellish troops,
Send up, I charge you, from Sosetus lake
The spirit Ascalon to come to me,
To pierce the bowels of this centric earth
And hither come in twinkling of an eye;
Ascalon, *ascenda, ascenda*.
> *It thunders and lightens, and then the Spirit riseth up*

I.4.38–9 Descend to darkness . . . avoid:

Then down, I say, unto the damnèd pool
Where Pluto in his fiery waggon sits,
Riding amidst the singed and parchèd smokes,
The road of Dytas by the River Styx;
There howl and burn for ever in those flames.
Rise, Jourdain, rise, and stay thy charming spells.
Sons, we are betrayed.

II.2.69–76 Do you . . . can prophesy:

WARWICK
Then, York, advise thyself and take thy time;
Claim thou the crown and set thy standard up,
And in the same advance the milk-white rose;
And then to guard it will I rouse the bear,
Environed with ten thousand raggèd staves,
To aid and help thee for to win thy right
Maugre the proudest lord of Henry's blood
That dares deny the right and claim of York.

III.1.281–7 *Enter a Post* . . . hope of help:

> *Enter a Messenger*

QUEEN
How now, sirrah, what news?

MESSENGER
    Madam, I bring you news from Ireland.
    The wild O'Neil, my lords, is up in arms
    With troops of Irish kerns that, uncontrolled,
    Doth plant themselves within the English pale . . .
    And burns and spoils the country as they go. . . .
QUEEN . . . Good York, be patient,
    And do thou take in hand to cross the seas
    With troops of armèd men to quell the pride
    Of those ambitious Irish that rebel.
YORK
    Well, madam, sith your grace is so content,
    Let me have some bands of chosen soldiers
    And York shall try his fortune 'gainst those kerns.
QUEEN
    York, thou shalt. My lord of Buckingham,
    Let it be your charge to muster up such soldiers
    As shall suffice him in these needful wars.
BUCKINGHAM
    Madam, I will, and levy such a band
    As soon shall overcome those Irish rebels.

III.1.322–6 But now . . . that event:

QUEEN
    Suffolk, remember what you have to do,
    And you, Lord Cardinal, concerning Duke Humphrey.
    'Twere good that you did see to it in time.
    Come, let us go, that it may be performed.

IV.2.21–30 HOLLAND I see . . . with them:

NICK But, sirrah, who comes more beside Jack Cade?
GEORGE Why, there's Dick the butcher, and Robin the saddler,
    and Will that came a-wooing to our Nan last Sunday, and Harry,
    and Tom, and Gregory that should have your Parnhill, and a
    great sort more is come from Rochester and from Maidstone
    and Canterbury and all the towns hereabouts; and we must all
    be lords or squires as soon as Jack Cade is king.

IV.2.111–13 To equal . . . have at him:

> Kneel down, John Mortimer;
> Rise up, Sir John Mortimer.
> Is there any more of them that be knights?

TOM Ay, his brother.
>> *He knights Dick Butcher*

CADE
> Then kneel down, Dick Butcher;
> Rise up, Sir Dick Butcher.
>> *Now sound up the drum*

IV.2.163–5 ALL No, no . . . the King:

STAFFORD Well, sirrah, wilt thou yield thyself unto the King's mercy an he will pardon thee and these their outrages and rebellious deeds?

CADE Nay, bid the King come to me an he will; and then I'll pardon him, or otherways I'll have his crown, tell him, ere it be long.

After IV.3.17:

> . . . London, for tomorrow I mean to sit in the King's seat at Westminster.

After IV.7.117:

>> *Enter Robin*

ROBIN O captain, London Bridge is afire.

CADE Run to Billingsgate and fetch pitch and flax and squench it.
>> *Enter Dick and a Sergeant*

SERGEANT Justice! Justice! I pray you, sir, let me have justice of this fellow here.

CADE Why, what has he done?

SERGEANT Alas, sir, he has ravished my wife.

DICK
> Why, my lord, he would have 'rested me,
> And I went and entered my action in his wife's paper house.

CADE
> Dick, follow thy suit in her common place.
> You whoreson villain, you are a sergeant! You'll
> Take any man by the throat for twelve pence
> And 'rest a man when he's at dinner,
> And have him to prison ere the meat be out of his mouth.
> Go, Dick, take him hence; cut out his tongue for cogging,
> Hough him from running, and, to conclude,
> Brave him with his own mace.
> > *Exit Dick with the Sergeant*

IV.7.120 Marry, presently:

> Marry, he that will lustily stand to it
> Shall go with me to take up these commodities following:
> Item, a gown, a kirtle, a petticoat, and a smock.

IV.8.5–53 BUCKINGHAM Ay . . . and Clifford:

CLIFFORD
> Why, countrymen and warlike friends of Kent,
> What means this mutinous rebellions,
> That you in troops do muster thus yourselves
> Under the conduct of this traitor Cade,
> To rise against your sovereign lord and king,
> Who mildly hath his pardon sent to you
> If you forsake this monstrous rebel here?
> If honour be the mark whereat you aim,
> Then haste to France that our forefathers won
> And win again that thing which now is lost
> And leave to seek your country's overthrow.

ALL
> À Clifford! À Clifford!
> > *They forsake Cade*

CADE
> Why, how now? Will you forsake your general
> And ancient freedom which you have possessed?
> To bend your necks under their servile yokes,
> Who, if you stir, will straightways hang you up?

But follow me and you shall pull them down
And make them yield their livings to your hands.

ALL

À Cade! À Cade!

They run to Cade again

CLIFFORD

Brave warlike friends, hear me but speak a word.
Refuse not good whilst it is offered you.
The King is merciful; then yield to him;
And I myself will go along with you
To Windsor Castle, whereas the King abides:
And on mine honour you shall have no hurt.

IV.9.1–21 KING Was ever . . . several countries:

KING

Lord Somerset, what news hear you of the rebel Cade?

SOMERSET

This, my gracious lord, that Lord Say is done to death,
And the city is almost sacked.

KING

God's will be done, for as He hath decreed, so must it be;
And be it as He please to stop the pride of those rebellious men.

QUEEN

Had the noble Duke of Suffolk been alive,
The rebel Cade had been suppressed ere this
And all the rest that do take part with him.

*Enter the Duke of Buckingham and Clifford, with the rebels
with halters about their necks*

CLIFFORD

Long live King Henry, England's lawful king!
Lo, here, my lord, these rebels are subdued
And offer their lives before your highness' feet.

KING

But tell me, Clifford, is their captain here?

CLIFFORD No, my gracious lord, he is fled away; but proclamations are sent forth that he that can but bring his head shall have
a thousand crowns. But may it please your majesty to pardon
these their faults that by that traitor's means were thus misled.

KING

> Stand up, you simple men, and give God praise;
> For you did take in hand you know not what;
> And go in peace, obedient to your king,
> And live as subjects, and you shall not want,
> Whilst Henry lives and wears the English crown.

IV.9.48–9 Come, wife . . . wretched reign:

> Come, let us haste to London now with speed,
> That solemn processions may be sung
> In laud and honour of the God of heaven,
> And triumphs of this happy victory.

IV.10.1–22 CADE Fie . . . my gate:

IDEN

> Good Lord, how pleasant is this country life;
> This little land my father left me here,
> With my contented mind, serves me as well
> As all the pleasures in the court can yield;
> Nor would I change this pleasure for the court.

V.2.15–30 For I . . . thy will! *Exit*:

YORK

> Now, Clifford, since we are singled here alone,
> Be this the day of doom to one of us;
> For now my heart hath sworn immortal hate
> To thee and all the house of Lancaster.

CLIFFORD

> And here I stand and pitch my foot to thine,
> Vowing never to stir till thou or I be slain;
> For never shall my heart be safe at rest
> Till I have spoiled the hateful house of York.
> > *Alarums, and they fight, and York kills Clifford*

YORK

> Now, Lancaster, sit sure; thy sinews shrink.
> Come, fearful Henry, grovelling on thy face;

Yield up thy crown unto the prince of York.

Exit York

V.2.30–65 *Enter Young Clifford . . . his back*:

> *Alarums, then enter Young Clifford alone*
> YOUNG CLIFFORD
>   Father of Cumberland,
>   Where may I seek my agèd father forth?
>   O, dismal sight! See where he breathless lies,
>   All smeared and weltered in his lukewarm blood!
>   Ah, agèd pillar of all Cumberland's true house!
>   Sweet father, to thy murdered ghost I swear
>   Immortal hate unto the house of York.
>   Nor never shall I sleep secure one night
>   Till I have furiously revenged thy death
>   And left not one of them to breathe on earth.
>   *He takes him up on his back*
>   And thus as old Anchises' son did bear

Genealogical Tables

Table 1: The House of Lancaster

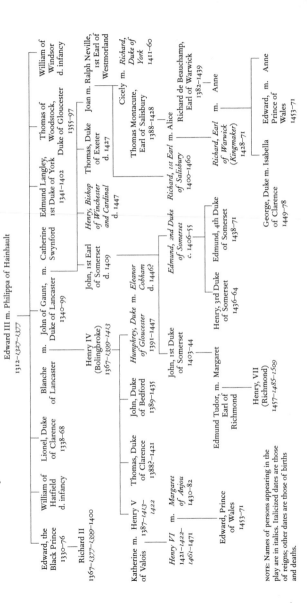

NOTE: Names of persons appearing in the play are in italics. Italicized dates are those of reigns; other dates are those of births and deaths.

Table 2: The House of York and the
line of the Mortimers

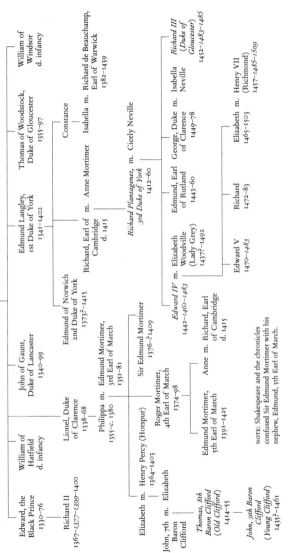

Commentary

The chief sources of the play are the chronicles of Edward Hall, Raphael Holinshed, Robert Fabyan, and perhaps Richard Grafton. In this Commentary Hall is quoted where all the chroniclers agree, Holinshed, Fabyan and Grafton only where special use seems to have been made of them. References are to the following editions: Hall's *The Union of the Two Noble and Illustre Families of Lancaster and York* (1548–50), the reprint of 1809; Holinshed's *The Chronicles of England, Scotland, and Ireland* (2nd edn, 1587), the reprint of 1808; Fabyan's *The New Chronicles of England and France* (1516), the reprint of 1811; Grafton's *A Chronicle at Large* (1569), the reprint of 1809. Quotations from John Foxe's *Acts and Monuments* (1563) are from the edition of 1844, and biblical quotations are from the Bishops' Bible (1568, etc.), the official English translation of Elizabeth's reign. Quotations are normally given in modernized spelling and punctuation, with the exception of those from Q1 or F.

The Characters in the Play: For the family relationships between the principal characters, see the Genealogical Tables; and for the regularization of names in this edition, see Emendations in An Account of the Text. Biographical facts about each character are given in the Commentary at his or her first appearance in the play or mention in the text.

I.1

The scene is located in the royal palace in London. *Henry VI, Part I* ended with Suffolk receiving from Henry VI his commission to depart for France to secure

Margaret as Queen of England and swearing to rule
the kingdom through his influence over Margaret.
Historically Suffolk left England in November 1444
and returned with Margaret in April 1445. According
to Hall, they landed at Portsmouth, from whence 'she
was conveyed to . . . Southwick in Hampshire, where
she . . . was coupled in matrimony to King Henry VI.
After which marriage she was . . . conveyed to London
and so to Westminster, where upon the thirtieth day of
May she . . . was crowned queen.'

o *Flourish*: A fanfare of trumpets
hautboys: Oboes
the King: Born in 1421, Henry VI succeeded his father,
Henry V, in 1422 under the Protectorship of the Duke
of Bedford. He married Margaret of Anjou by proxy
in 1445 at the instigation of the Earl of Suffolk and
against the wishes of the Duke of Gloucester.
Gloucester: Humphrey of Lancaster (1391–1447),
youngest son of Henry IV, was created duke in 1414
and fought at Agincourt. He claimed the Regency at
the death of Henry V, but was allowed only to act as
the Duke of Bedford's deputy. He was in constant
strife with his uncle Henry Beaufort, Bishop of
Winchester; he was Protector in 1427–9, and his influence over the King was strong until 1441. He had vainly
advocated marriage between Henry VI and the
daughter of the Duke of Armagnac.
Salisbury: Richard Neville (1400–1460), first Earl
of Salisbury and son of Ralph Neville, first Earl of
Westmorland, had as his second wife Joan Beaufort
(the mother of Warwick), who was the daughter of
John of Gaunt and the sister of Henry Beaufort. He
joined Henry VI in France in 1431 and was one of the
officers who arrested the Duke of Gloucester in 1447.
Warwick: Richard Neville (1428–71), 'The Kingmaker',
was the son of the first Earl of Salisbury. He succeeded
to the Earldom of Warwick in 1449 by the right of his
wife, Anne Beauchamp. He sided with the Duke of
York when he claimed the Regency in 1453.

Cardinal Beaufort: Henry Beaufort (d. 1447) was the second illegitimate son of John of Gaunt and Catherine Swynford. He was created Bishop of Winchester in 1404 and was Chancellor on the accession of Henry V, who named him guardian to Henry VI; he was nominated Cardinal-Priest in 1426, and he crowned Henry VI in Paris in 1431. He was constantly at loggerheads with the Duke of Gloucester, whose efforts to deprive him of his see he defeated in 1432.

the Queen: Margaret (1430–82) was the daughter of René, Duke of Anjou and Count of Maine and titular King of Naples, Sicily and Jerusalem. She married Henry VI in 1445 and as queen identified herself with the Beaufort–Suffolk party at the English court.

Suffolk: William de la Pole (1396–1450), fourth Earl and first Duke of Suffolk, served in the French wars under Henry V. At the death of the fourth Earl of Salisbury in 1428, he assumed command of the English forces in France. Inclined by his marriage to the widowed Countess of Salisbury to support the Beauforts, he emerged as the chief opponent of the Duke of Gloucester and was one of the instigators of Henry VI's marriage to Margaret of Anjou.

York: Richard Plantagenet (1411–60) was the only son of Richard, Earl of Cambridge, and thus the grandson of Edmund Langley, the fifth son of Edward III. He became the third Duke of York in 1415 and was Henry VI's lieutenant in France from 1440 to 1445. He enjoyed the support of Warwick and was a strong opponent of Somerset.

Somerset: Edmund Beaufort (c. 1406–55) was the second Duke of Somerset, succeeding his older brother John in 1444. He was son-in-law of Richard de Beauchamp, the Earl of Warwick, and was a bitter enemy of the Duke of York. It was during his Regency that most of the English possessions in France were lost.

Buckingham: Humphrey Stafford (1402–60), first Duke of Buckingham, was the grandson of Thomas of Woodstock, the sixth son of Edward III. He accompanied Henry VI abroad in 1430 and was Captain

of Calais in 1442 and Warden of the Cinque Ports in
1450. He was an opponent of the Duke of York.

1 *imperial*: Henry VI was ruler of the empire of England,
Ireland and France.

2 *had in charge*: Was commissioned.
depart: Departure.

3–8 *As procurator . . . bishops*: This is based on Hall:

> This noble company came to the city of Tours in Touraine,
> where they were honourably received both of the French
> King and of the King of Sicily; where the Marquess of
> Suffolk, as procurator to King Henry, espoused the said lady
> in the church of Saint Martin's. At which marriage were
> present the father and mother of the bride, the French King
> himself, which was uncle to the husband, and the French
> Queen also, which was aunt to the wife. There were also the
> Dukes of Orleans, of Calabria, of Alençon, and of Brittany,
> seven earls, twelve barons, twenty bishops, beside knights
> and gentlemen.

3 *procurator to*: Deputy for.

4 *marry*: On Henry's behalf.

6 *France*: Charles VII (1403–61), who had succeeded his
father in 1422.
Sicil: Margaret's father, René I (Reignier; 1409–80)
Duke of Anjou, Count of Maine, King of Naples, Sicily
and Jerusalem.

7 *Orleans*: Charles of Orleans (1391–1465), half-brother
of John, Count of Dunois, 'The Bastard'.
Calaber: Calabria (in the southern extremity of Italy).
Bretagne: Francis I, who succeeded John V as Duke of
Brittany in 1442.
Alençon: John, second Duke (1409–76), ally of Charles
VII in the wars against the English.

9 *espoused*: Married (in Henry's name).

11 *England*: Henry VI as representative of the nation.

12 *title in*: Rights to (a legal term).

13–14 *the substance | Of that great shadow I did represent*: The
real power behind the image I acted for. This is a

common Shakespearian idea also used for dramatic
effect in *Part I*, II.3.35–65.

15 *happiest*: Most fortunate.

18 *kinder*: More according to nature.

19 *kind*: Loving (with a pun on *kinder*).

19–22 *O Lord . . . my soul*: Even while Henry is initially
intoxicated with Margaret, his religious cast of mind is
stressed by Shakespeare.

19 *lends*: Grants.

21–2 *in this beauteous face | A world of earthly blessings*: Henry
is elaborating the proverb 'Beauty is a blessing'.

23 *sympathy*: Mutual feeling.

25 *mutual*: Intimate.
    conference: Communication (here by dwelling men-
    tally).

27 *In courtly company*: Among courtiers.
    at my beads: Saying my prayers (with the help of a
    rosary).

28 *alderliefest*: Most beloved (an archaic word in Shake-
    speare's day).

29 *salute*: Greet.

30 *ruder*: More unpolished.
    wit: Intelligence.

31 *overjoy*: Excess of happiness.
    minister: Supply.

32 *Her sight*: The sight of her.

33 *y-clad*: Decked (an archaic form in Shakespeare's day).

34 *Makes*: The singular verb form with a group of subjects
    was common in Elizabethan English.
    wondering: Admiring.

39 *Protector*: Historically Gloucester had ceased to be
    Protector when Henry VI was crowned in 1429 in
    London.

40–42 *Here are . . . by consent*: Cf. Hall: 'But in conclusion,
    for many doubts and great ambiguities which rose on
    both parties, a final concord could not be agreed; but,
    in hope to come to a peace, a certain truce as well by
    sea as by land was concluded by the commissioners for
    eighteen months.'

43–60 *Imprimis, it is agreed . . . any dowry*: These articles are based on Hall:

> The Earl of Suffolk . . . either corrupted with bribes or too much affectionate to this unprofitable marriage, condescended and agreed . . . that the duchy of Anjou and the county of Maine should be released and delivered to the King her father, demanding for her marriage neither penny nor farthing.

43 *Imprimis*: In the first place (the normal opening of an official document initiating a series of items).

49 *Item*: Also (a legal formula).
   it is further agreed between them: F omits this clause here, although it has it in the Cardinal's speech at 56. Q1 has it in both Gloucester's and the Cardinal's quotations.

51 *released*: No longer controlled (by England).
   Gloucester lets the contract fall: This direction is found only in Q1 and probably reflects contemporary stage practice.

53 *qualm*: Attack of faintness.

54 *that*: So that.

55 *Uncle*: The Cardinal was actually Henry IV's half-brother and hence great-uncle of the King.

59–60 *own proper cost and charges*: This was a legal formula, indicating that Henry would bear all Margaret's expenses.

61 *They*: The terms of the agreement.

62 *first Duke of Suffolk*: Historically Suffolk was created duke in 1448, three years after his return from France; see Hall: 'This Marquess, thus gotten up into Fortune's throne, not content with his degree, by the means of the Queen was shortly erected to the estate and degree of a duke and ruled the King at his pleasure.' However, when the marriage contract was agreed, among the other celebratory elevations 'the Earl of Suffolk [was] made Marquess of Suffolk'.

63 *girt*: Gird.

63–5 *Cousin of York . . . France*: Historically York was replaced as Regent the year after the King's marriage; see

Hall: 'the Duke of Somerset was appointed Regent of Normandy and the Duke of York thereof discharged'.

63 *Cousin*: The monarch's form of address to a duke of the realm.

65 *parts*: Territories.

66 *full*: Fully.

70 *entertainment*: Welcoming reception.

72 *her coronation*: See the quotation from Hall in the head-note to this scene.

73 *peers*: The pun is with 'piers' meaning *pillars*.

76 *my brother Henry*: Henry V.

78 *lodge*: Sleep.

79 *In winter's cold and summer's parching heat*: Cf. Hall: 'No cold made him slothful nor heat caused him to loiter.'

80 *his true inheritance*: Through Edward III's marriage with Isabella, daughter of Philip IV of France, England claimed the French throne. Henry V had secured the title with the Treaty of Troyes in 1420, although his father-in-law, Charles VI, actually wore the crown.

81 *Bedford*: John of Lancaster (1389–1435), third son of Henry IV, was Regent of France and Protector of England. He raised the siege of Orleans in 1429 and effected the death of Joan of Arc in 1431.

toil his wits: Exercise his intelligence. As Regent of France after Henry V's death, Bedford had negotiated an alliance with Burgundy and Brittany against Charles VII and attempted to secure English rule in France by the establishment of trading relations and sound administration. Cf. Hall: 'the Duke of Bedford, Regent of France, no less studied than took pain . . . to keep and order the countries and regions by King Henry late conquered and gained'.

82 *policy*: Skilful political action (with overtones of craftiness).

86–90 *Or hath mine uncle . . . in awe*: In Hall, Gloucester assumed the Protectorship 'as a man remembering others and forgetting himself, called to him wise and grave coun-sellors by whose advice he provided and ordained for all things which either redounded to the honour of the realm or seemed profitable to the public wealth of the same'.

86 *Beaufort*: The Cardinal.

87 *Council*: The King's Privy Council.

89 *debating to and fro*: Discussing the arguments for and against.

90 *awe*: Subjection. Hall's phrase is 'brought to due obeisance'.

92 *Crownèd in Paris*: See *Part I*, IV.1. Henry was crowned in Paris in 1431 when he was ten years old (Hall).
    despite: Spite.

96–101 *O peers of England . . . had never been*: The full explanation for Gloucester's opposition is found in *Part I*, V.5, and in Hall:

Humphrey Duke of Gloucester, Protector of the realm, repugned and resisted as much as in him lay this new alliance and contrived matrimony, alleging that it was neither consonant to the law of God nor man, nor honourable to a prince, to infringe and break a promise or contract by him made and concluded for the utility and profit of his realm and people; declaring that the King by his ambassadors, sufficiently instructed and authorized, had concluded and contracted a marriage between his highness and the daughter of the Earl of Armagnac upon conditions both to him and his realm as much profitable as honourable.

96 *league*: Agreement.

98 *books of memory*: Chronicles. Cf. Hall's phrase 'book of fame' and *Part I*, II.4.101.

99 *Razing the characters*: Erasing the written records.

100 *monuments*: In two senses: (1) memory; (2) stone memorials.

101 *as*: As though.

102 *passionate*: Excessively emotional.

103 *peroration with such circumstance*: Rhetorical speech with so many illustrative details.

104 *For*: As for.
    still: For ever.

107 *rules the roast*: Proverbial.

109–10 *Reignier, whose large style* | *Agrees not with the leanness of his purse*: Cf. Hall: 'King Reignier her father, for all his long style, had too short a purse to send his daughter honourably to the King her spouse.'

109 *large style*: Impressive-sounding titles; see note to 6 above.

110 *Agrees*: Accords.

111 *the death of Him that died for all*: A reference to 2 Corinthians 5:15.

112 *the keys of Normandy*: Shakespeare seems to have taken this phrase from Fabyan; Hall calls Maine and Anjou 'the very stays and backstands to the Duchy of Normandy'.

117 *Myself did win them both*: Richard Neville, who became the Earl of Warwick in 1449, is here credited with the military achievements of his father-in-law, Richard de Beauchamp (1382–1439), who appears in *Part I*.

120 *Delivered up*: Surrendered.

121 *Mort Dieu*: A common French oath, literally 'by the death of God'.

122 *suffocate*: The pun is with *Suffolk*.

125 *yielded*: Consented.

126–29 *I never read . . . no vantages*: This seems to have been suggested by Hall: 'This marriage seemed to many both infortunate and unprofitable to the realm of England . . . the King with her had not one penny.'

128 *own*: Own money and possessions.

129 *match with*: Marry.
    vantages: Profits; benefits.

131–2 *Suffolk should demand . . . her*: Cf. Hall: 'for the fetching of her the Marquess of Suffolk demanded a whole fifteen in open parliament'.

131 *fifteenth*: A tax of one fifteenth on all personal property. In *Part I*, V.5.92–3, Henry promises Suffolk a 10 per cent tax levy for expenses.

133 *starved*: Died.

135 *hot*: Choleric.

140 *proud prelate*: This phrase is twice used in the section

on Humphrey of Gloucester in *A Mirror for Magistrates* (1559).

142 *ancient bickerings*: Gloucester's and Winchester's quarrels are dramatized in *Part I*, III.1. They are also stressed by the chroniclers; cf. Hall: 'the Duke of Gloucester sore grudged at the proud doings of the Cardinal of Winchester, and . . . the Cardinal likewise sore envied and disdained at the rule of the Duke of Gloucester'.

143 *Lordings*: A form of address meaning 'my lords'.

149 *next of blood*: As Henry V's only surviving brother and in the absence of a child of Henry VI, Gloucester at this time is next in line to the throne; see Genealogical Table 1.

150 *heir apparent*: Technically 'heir presumptive'.

152 *the wealthy kingdoms of the west*: The reference is, anachronistically, to the Spanish possessions in America.

153 *he*: Gloucester.

154 *Look to it*: Beware.
    smoothing: Flattering.

156 *What*: Even.

156–7 *the common people favour him, | Calling him 'Humphrey, the good Duke of Gloucester'*: Hall and Holinshed both give idealized portraits of Gloucester; but for the phrasing here Shakespeare seems to be indebted to John Foxe's *Acts and Monuments*: 'for the noble prowess and virtues . . . he was both loved of the poor commons and well spoken of of all men, and no less deserving the same, being called the "good" Duke of Gloucester'.

161 *flattering gloss*: Attractive appearance.

162 *found*: Revealed to be.

164 *He*: Henry VI.
    of age: Historically Henry was twenty-four at this time.

167 *hoise*: Remove by violence.

168 *brook*: Allow.

169 *I'll*: I'll go.
    presently: Immediately.

171 *place*: Position in the government.
    grief: Irritation.

173 *insolence*: Overbearing pride.

174 *the princes' in the land beside*: That of all the other noblemen of the realm.

175 *displaced*: Removed from the Protectorship.
    he: The Cardinal.

176 *Or . . . or*: Either . . . or.

178 *Pride went before; Ambition follows him*: Salisbury is adapting the proverb 'Pride goes before and ambition comes after'. *Pride* stands for the Cardinal, *Ambition* for Somerset and Buckingham.

179 *preferment*: Advancement.

182 *bear him*: Conduct himself.

185 *stout*: Proud.
    as he: As if he.

186 *demean himself*: Act.

187 *commonweal*: State.

188–90 *Warwick, my son . . . the commons*: Cf. Hall:

> This Richard was . . . a man of marvellous qualities . . . but also from his youth . . . so set them forward with witty and gentle demeanour . . . that among all sorts of people he obtained great love, much favour, and more credence; which things daily more increased by his abundant liberality and plentiful house-keeping than by his riches, authority, or high parentage; by reason of which doings he was in such favour and estimation amongst the common people that they judged him able to do all things and that without him nothing to be well done.

189 *house-keeping*: Hospitality.

191 *Excepting none but*: Except that which they have shown to.

192–3 *brother York . . . discipline*: York is erroneously given credit for having suppressed a rebellion in Ireland before 1445. He actually did this in 1449, and his appointment as English general in Ireland is dramatized in III.1; see the note to III.1.282–329, and cf. Hall: '[York's] politic governance, his gentle behaviour to all the Irish nation . . . had brought that rude and savage nation to civil fashion and English urbanity.'

192 *brother*: York was Salisbury's brother-in-law, having married Cecily Neville, Salisbury's sister; see Genealogical Table I.

193 *them*: The Irish rebels.

194 *late exploits*: Recent military actions.

201 *cherish*: Give support to.

202 *tend the profit*: Serve the welfare.

206 *look unto the main*: Have an eye to the main chance (proverbial).

207 *main*: (1) Main chance; (2) most important business.

208 *main force*: Overpowering strength.

213–14 *the state of Normandy | Stands on a tickle point now they are gone*: See the note to 112 above.

214 *Stands on a tickle point*: Is in a precarious position.

215–17 *Suffolk concluded . . . fair daughter*: This is an echo of Hall: 'that godly affinity which he had concluded, omitting nothing . . . of the nobility of her kin . . . that she was of such an excellent beauty and of so high a parentage . . . This marriage pleased well the King and divers of his Council.'

215 *concluded on the articles*: Negotiated the final details of the marriage contract.

219 *thine*: York's.

220 *make cheap pennyworths*: Squander.

222 *Still*: Continually.

223 *While as*: While.
    silly: Pitiful.

224 *hapless*: Unfortunate.

225 *stands aloof*: Remains at a distance.

228 *bite his tongue*: In order to hold his peace.

231 *proportion*: Relation.

232–3 *the fatal brand Althaea burnt | Unto the Prince's heart of Calydon*: Ovid in the *Metamorphoses* relates how the Fates decreed that Meleager, Prince of Calydon, should live only as long as a specified brand on the hearth should continue to burn. His mother Althaea snatched the brand from the fire and kept it alight for many years until in a fit of anger she tossed it into a heap of blazing wood.

233 *the Prince's heart of Calydon*: The heart of the Prince of Calydon.

235 *Cold*: Unwelcome.

hope of France: Expectations of possessing the French crown.

238 *And therefore I will take the Nevils' parts*: Cf. Hall: 'When the Duke saw men's appetites and felt well their minds, he chiefly entertained two Richards, and both Nevilles, the one of Salisbury, the other of Warwick, being earl, the first the father, the second the son.'

239 *make a show*: Give the appearance.

240 *advantage*: Opportunity.

241 *mark*: Target. The image is from archery.

242 *Lancaster*: Henry VI.

244 *diadem*: Crown.

245 *Whose church-like humours fits not for a crown*: Cf. Hall: 'King Henry . . . was a man of a meek spirit, and . . . preferring . . . quietness before labour . . . He . . . studied only for the health of his soul.'

245 *church-like humours*: Pious nature.

246 *be still*: Remain politically inactive.

247 *Watch*: Remain alert.

248 *pry into the secrets of the state*: Probe governmental intrigues.

249 *surfeiting*: Having become satiated through over-indulgence.

251 *at jars*: Into dissension.

252 *the milk-white rose*: The symbol of the house of York; see *Part I*, II.4.

254 *standard*: Battle ensign.
arms: Coat of arms.

255 *grapple*: The word takes up the second sense of *arms* in 254.

256 *force perforce*: By violent compulsion (a tautology for emphasis).

257 *bookish*: Scholarly, interested only in religious books (hence 'ineffectual').
bookish rule: This perhaps is an echo of Hall's depicting Henry 'like a young scholar or innocent pupil'.

I.2

This scene, which presumably takes place in Gloucester's house, is based upon an event recorded in the chronicles which took place historically in 1441, four years before the arrival of Margaret in England. Cf. Hall: 'For first this year Dame Eleanor Cobham, wife to the said Duke, was accused of treason for that she by sorcery and enchantment intended to destroy the King, to the intent to advance and to promote her husband to the crown.' See also the headnote to I.4.

0 *the Duchess*: Eleanor Cobham (d. 1446?) was originally Gloucester's mistress; she became his wife at some time before 1431.

2 *Ceres*: Roman goddess of agriculture.
  plenteous load: Rich harvest.

5 *sullen*: Dark; dull.

8 *Enchased*: Decorated.

9 *grovel on thy face*: There may be a trace of Eleanor's interest in witchcraft in this phrase; cf. I.4.10–11.

12 *is't*: Is your arm.

13 *heaved*: Raised.

15 *abase*: Lower.

18 *canker*: Spreading sore (here eating away at the mind).

19 *imagine ill*: Conceive evil intentions.

21 *last breathing*: Final breath of life.

22 *this night*: Last night.

23 *requite it*: Repay you for it.

24 *rehearsal*: Recital; telling.
  morning's dream: Dream which will come true. (In folklore a morning dream was considered a favourable prophecy.)

25 *mine office-badge*: The symbol of my Protectorship.

29 *Edmund Duke of Somerset*: The duke at this time historically was John Beaufort (1403–44), the first Duke; but Shakespeare confuses him with his younger brother Edmund (c. 1406–55), the second Duke; see Genealogical Table 1.

31 *bode*: Presage.

32 *argument*: Proof.

34 *presumption*: Pronounced quadrisyllabically.

35 *list*: Listen.

38 *chair*: The coronation throne.

42 *Ill-nurtured*: Poorly educated; badly bred.

43 *second woman in the realm*: As the wife of Gloucester, who is heir presumptive.

46 *compass*: Range.

47 *hammering*: Designing; shaping.

49 *From top of honour*: This phrase appears to come from *A Mirror for Magistrates*.

54 *checked*: Rebuked; scolded.

56–8 *'tis his highness'* . . . *mean to hawk*: Cf. Hall: 'Queen Margaret . . . caused the King to make a progress into Warwickshire for his health and recreation, and so with hawking and hunting came to the city of Coventry.'

56 *pleasure*: Wish.

57 *Saint Albans*: The town in Hertfordshire, twenty miles north of London, was the scene of two major battles of the Wars of the Roses.

58 *Where as*: Where.
hawk: Hunt with hawks.

60 *presently*: Immediately.

61 *Follow I must; I cannot go before*: Proverbial.
go before: Take precedence over Queen Margaret.

67 *pageant*: Play; spectacle.

68 *Sir John*: John is Hume's christian name in the chronicles; but 'Sir John' was also used as a type-name for a clerk of the Church.

69 *Hume*: This spelling is found only in the account given in Foxe's *Acts and Monuments*; all the chronicles have the form 'Hum'.

71 *Majesty*: The term is an anachronism; as a form of address for the monarch it was first used for the Tudors.
but 'grace': Only a duchess.

73 *Your grace's title shall be multiplied*: The pun is with *the grace of God*, and the allusion is to 1 Peter 1:2: 'Grace and peace be multiplied unto you.'

75–6 *Margery Jourdain, the cunning witch . . . Roger Bolingbroke, the conjurer*: Cf. Hall: 'counsellors to the said Duchess

. . . Roger Bolingbroke, a cunning necromancer, and
Margery Jourdain, surnamed the Witch of Eye'.

75 *cunning*: Skilful.

77 *do me good*: Cause me to prosper.

88 *Marry*: A mild oath, originally meaning 'by the Virgin
Mary'.

88–9 *Hume . . . mum*: There may be a vestigial rhyme here
originating in the chronicles' spelling of the name, 'Hum'.

89 *no words but mum*: Proverbial.

90 *asketh*: Demands.

93 *flies from another coast*: Which comes from another
quarter.

97–106 *They, knowing Dame Eleanor's . . . Humphrey's fall*:
There is no historical evidence for this suborning of
Hume by the Cardinal and Suffolk. The chronicles
record only that Hume alone among the Duchess's
confederates received a pardon.

97 *aspiring humour*: Ambitious character.

98 *undermine*: This was still a military term in Shakespeare's
day, meaning 'place explosives beneath a citadel's walls'.

99 *buzz*: Implant by means of whispers.
   conjurations: Incantations.

100 *A crafty knave does need no broker*: Proverbial.
   broker: Agent; go-between.

102–3 *go near | To call*: Come close to naming.

105 *wrack*: Ruin.

106 *attainture*: Conviction (and fall from grace).

107 *Sort how it will*: Let it turn out how it likes.

1.3

The scene is located in the royal palace in London. The
developing sexual intimacy between the Queen and
Suffolk has no basis in the chronicles, but is dramatized in the Duke's capture of Margaret in *Part I*, V.3.
The court rivalries and personal animosities are all
historically based. For the chronicles' account of the
episode of the armourer and his apprentice, see the
notes to 24–6 below and to II.3.59–103.

1 *close*: All together in a body.

3 *supplications*: Petitions.

in the quill: In a group.

4 *the Lord protect*: The pun is with Gloucester's title.

6–12 *Here 'a comes . . . for my Lord Protector*: The stage direction in Q1 makes the action clear: *Enter the Duke of Suffolke with the Queene, and they take him for Duke Humphrey, and giues him their writings.*

6–7 *Here 'a comes . . . sure*: The reprint of F in 1685 gives this speech to the First Petitioner and is followed by some modern editors. While there are arguments for making the change, the action as it appears in the first three editions of the Folio is understandable. As Suffolk and the Queen enter, the petitioners surge forward, with Peter aggressively trying to be first (6–7). He is set right about Suffolk's identity by the Second Petitioner (8–9) and Suffolk stops and addresses the First Petitioner, who is in the front of the group and from whom the Queen takes the petition.

6 *'a*: A common Elizabethan colloquial form of 'he'.

10 *fellow*: A contemptuous, condescending form of address.

15 *an't*: If it.

16 *against John Goodman, my lord Cardinal's man*: This complaint indicates how the conflict at court between Gloucester and the Cardinal has seeped down to the lower levels of society. A similar point is made in *Part I*, III.1. *man* agent

18 *Thy wife too! That's some wrong indeed*: In view of Suffolk's relations with the Queen, he says this ironically, and probably with a knowing look at Margaret.

19–20 *Against the Duke of Suffolk . . . Melford*: Cf. Hall:

> . . . the forenamed Duke of Suffolk, only for lucre of money, vexed, oppressed and molested the poor people; so that men's minds were not intentive, nor given to outward affairs and foreign conquests, but all their study was how to drive back and defend domestical injuries and daily wrongs done at home.

20 *enclosing the commons*: This practice of landowners, fencing in common land and making it their own property, was a bitter social issue in sixteenth-century

England. In 1614 Shakespeare himself was involved in
a dispute over the enclosure of land he owned in Old
Stratford and Welcombe.

20 *Melford*: Long Melford in Suffolk.

21 *sir knave*: Suffolk is being sarcastic in adding a commonly
used courtesy title to the term of abuse *knave*.

23 *of*: On behalf of.

24–6 *Against my master . . . the crown*: Although the episode
of the armourer and his apprentice appears in the
chronicles, it is Shakespeare's invention that the Duke
of York is the subject of the treasonous remarks.

32–3 *pursuivant*: Messenger serving the royal herald.

33 *presently*: Immediately.

35 *protected*: Another pun on Gloucester's title.

38 *base*: Of low birth.
cullions: Wretches (from the Italian '*coglioni*', meaning
'testicles').

40 *guise*: Custom; habit.

43 *Albion*: England.

44–5 *shall King Henry be a pupil still* | *Under the surly
Gloucester's governance*: Cf. Hall: 'she had neither
wit nor stomach which would permit and suffer her
husband, being of perfect age and man's estate, like a
young scholar or innocent pupil to be governed by the
disposition of another man'. Margaret was advised by
her father, King Reignier, that 'she and her husband
should take upon them the rule and governance of the
realm and not to be kept under like young wards'.

44 *still*: For ever.

46 *style*: The way I am addressed.

48–50 *when in the city Tours . . . of France*: This is an echo of
Christopher Marlowe's *Edward II*, V.5.67–9: 'Tell
Isabel, the queen, I looked not thus | When for her
sake I ran at tilt in France.' Hall reports that at Margaret's
marriage in Tours 'There were triumphant jousts'.

49 *rannest a tilt*: Competed in a jousting tournament.

52 *courtship*: (1) Courtly manner; (2) wooing ability.
proportion: Bodily shape.

53–8 *But all his mind . . . canonized saints*: Hall notes about

Henry 'there could be none more chaste, more meek, more holy, nor a better creature'. His pious nature is touched upon in *Part I*, III.1 and IV.1.

53 *bent to*: Directed towards.

54 *To number Ave-Maries on his beads*: Cf. *Part III*, II.1.161: 'Numbering our Ave-Maries with our beads'.
   beads: Rosary beads.

55 *champions*: The image is of the Christian as God's champion, which is developed at length in Ephesians 6. Margaret is also referring to the King's Champion, a warrior chosen to represent the king in single combat.

56 *saws*: Sayings.

57 *tilt-yard*: Arena in which knights jousted.

58 *brazen images*: Bronze statues.
   canonized: Accented on the second syllable.

59 *the College of the Cardinals*: The highest council of the Church of Rome, which is responsible for electing the Pope from among its members.

61 *the triple crown*: The diadem of the papacy.

62 *state*: Status.
   his holiness: (1) Henry's piety; (2) the title used to designate the pope.

65 *work*: Bring about.

68 *grumbling*: Discontented.

72 *simple*: Ordinary. The allusion is to their relationship to the royal family. See the note on Salisbury at the beginning of I.1.

73–85 *Not all these lords . . . his daughter*: Historically the Duchess of Gloucester had been accused of witchcraft and disgraced in 1441, some four years before Margaret became Queen of England.

75 *sweeps it*: Struts proudly.

77 *Strangers*: Visiting foreigners.

78 *on her back*: In the clothes she wears.

81 *Contemptuous*: Contemptible.
   base-born: Of low birth.
   callet: Drab.

82 *vaunted*: Boasted.
   minions: (1) Followers; (2) saucy women.

83 *worst wearing*: Most unfashionable.

84 *better worth*: Worth more.

85 *Suffolk gave two dukedoms for his daughter*: Cf. I.1.215–17.

86 *limed a bush*: Set a trap. The metaphor is from the practice of smearing twigs with birdlime to catch young birds.

87 *enticing birds*: Decoys.

88 *light*: Perch.
   lays: Songs.

90 *let her rest*: Bother yourself no more about her.
   list: Listen.

91 *am bold*: Presume, take it upon myself.

92 *fancy*: Love.

95 *late*: Recent. The complaint referred to is Peter's against the armourer (24–30 above).

96 *make but little for his benefit*: Do him little good.

98 *steer the happy helm*: Be in charge of the successful government. The metaphor is derived from the idea of the ship of state; cf. *Part I*, I.1.177.
   sennet: A flourish of trumpets indicating a ceremonial entrance or exit.

100–104 *Or Somerset or York . . . yield to him*: Shakespeare makes use of this rivalry in *Part I*, as well as here and later in III.1 and V.1. The chronicles refer to the animosity between the two peers and their competition for the Regency on several occasions.

100 *Or . . . or*: Either . . . or.

101 *ill demeaned himself*: Behaved improperly.

102 *denayed*: Denied.

108 *field*: Of combat.

109 *presence*: Royal receiving chamber.
   betters: Superiors in rank.

115 *censure*: Judgement.

116–17 *If he be . . . excellence*: Hall discusses the Queen's attitude which lies behind these lines:

   This woman, perceiving that her husband did not frankly rule as he would but did all thing by the advice and counsel of Humphrey Duke of Gloucester, and that he passed not much

on the authority and governance of the realm, determined
with herself to take upon her the rule and regiment both of
the King and his kingdom and to deprive and evict out of all
rule and authority the said duke, then called the Lord Protector
of the realm, lest men should say and report that she had
neither wit nor stomach.

121–35 *Since thou wert king . . . hop without thy head*: The
combined attack on Gloucester by the nobles following
the Queen's rebuke is based upon Hall's account of
Gloucester's fall:

. . . by her permission and favour divers noblemen conspired
against him, of the which divers writers affirm the Marquess
of Suffolk and the Duke of Buckingham to be the chief, not
unprocured by the Cardinal of Winchester and the Archbishop of York. Divers articles both heinous and odious were
laid to his charge in open council.

121–5 *Since thou wert king . . . sovereignty*: These charges are
based upon those brought against Suffolk himself in
1449 (Hall).

121 *Since thou wert king – as who is king but thou*: See note
to 116–17.

122 *The commonwealth hath daily run to wrack*: Cf. Hall on
Suffolk: 'the expeller from the King of all good and
virtuous counsellors and the bringer in and advancer
of vicious persons, common enemies and apparent
adversaries to the public wealth'.

123 *The Dauphin hath prevailed beyond the seas*: Cf. Hall on
Suffolk's 'negligent provision and improvident policy
of . . . the affairs and business in the parts beyond the
sea. . . . the most swallower up and consumer of the
King's treasure, by reason whereof the wars in France
were not maintained'.
Dauphin: This was the title of the heir apparent to the
French throne, but it is used here to describe Charles VI,
whose title the English did not recognize. The F spelling,
Dolphin, reflects Elizabethan pronunciation and clarifies
the quibble in the phrase *prevailed beyond the seas*.

125 *bondmen*: Slaves.

126 *commons*: Ordinary people.

   racked: Reduced to poverty by extorting money from them.

   bags: Purses.

128 *Thy sumptuous buildings*: The reference is to the Duke of Gloucester's residence, Greenwich Palace, which he had enlarged and embellished to satisfy his taste for Italian Renaissance architecture. Cf. Hall: 'the Duke of Gloucester had not so much advanced and preferred the common wealth and public utility as his own private things and peculiar estate'.

129 *treasury*: Wealth.

130–31 *Thy cruelty in execution | Upon offenders hath exceeded law*: Among the charges brought against Gloucester, Hall singles out 'in especial one that he had caused men adjudged to die to be put to other execution than the law of the land had ordered or assigned'.

133 *Thy sale of offices and towns in France*: Among the charges brought against Suffolk in 1449 were that he was 'corrupted by rewards of the French King' and that he purveyed 'his arms, furniture of his towns, and all other ordnances whereby the King's enemies . . . have gotten towns and fortresses and the King by that mean deprived of his inheritance' (Hall).

134 *suspect*: Suspicion (accented on the second syllable).

135 *hop without thy head*: Be beheaded (proverbial).

136 *minion*: Hussy.

137 *cry you mercy*: Beg your pardon.

140 *my ten commandments*: The marks of my ten fingernails (a proverbial expression thought to be derived from the legend that God scratched the commandments on the tablets with his nail).

141 *quiet*: Calm.

   against her will: Unintentional.

143 *hamper*: (1) Bind; (2) encradle.

   dandle: Pet.

144 *most master wear no breeches*: A proverbial saying indicating that the wife is master of the house.

147 *listen after*: Enquire about.
   proceeds: Behaves.
148 *tickled*: (1) Irritated, provoked; (2) almost caught (like
   a trout which has been 'tickled').
   fume: Smoking rage. Some editors read 'fury', which
   is defensible on the grounds of both sense and metre.
149 *She'll gallop far enough to her destruction*: The Duchess
   is viewed metaphorically as a maddened mare.
150 *overblown*: Dispersed.
153 *objections*: Accusations.
156 *duty*: Reverence.
158 *meetest*: The most suitable.
160 *election*: The choice.
162 *unmeet*: Unfitting.
164 *for*: Because.
165–70 *if I be appointed . . . and lost*: Hall reports that in 1435

   Although the Duke of York, both for birth and courage, was
   worthy of this honour and preferment, yet he was so disdained
   of Edmund Duke of Somerset, being cousin to the King, that
   he was promoted to so high an office (which he in very deed
   gaped and looked for) that by all ways and means possible
   he both hindered and detracted him, glad of his loss and
   sorry of his well-doing, causing him to linger in England,
   without dispatch, till Paris and the flower of France were
   gotten by the French King.

   But there also seems to be some reliance on Holinshed's
   account of the events of 1446:

   But the Duke of Somerset, still maligning the Duke of
   York's advancement, as he had sought to hinder his dispatch
   at the first when he was sent over to be Regent, as before
   ye have heard, he likewise now wrought so that the King
   revoked his grant made to the Duke of York for enjoying
   of that office the term of other five years, and with help
   of William Marquess of Suffolk obtained that grant for
   himself.

167 *discharge*: Making a proper financial settlement with me.
    furniture: Military supplies.

169 *danced attendance on his will*: A proverbial phrase.

171 *fact*: Crime; deed.

174 *Image*: Model; embodiment.

177 *for*: Of being.

178 *what*: Who.

186 *God is my witness*: Romans 1:9.
    falsely: Treacherously.

188 *these ten bones*: My fingers.

191 *mechanical*: Menial (literally, 'engaged in manual labour').

194 *have all the rigour*: Experience the fullest severity.

196 *prentice*: Apprentice.
    correct: Punish.

197 *fault*: Mistake.

199 *cast away*: Destroy.

200 *for*: On account of.

202 *doom*: judgment; sentence.

203 *Let Somerset be Regent o'er the French*: Cf. Hall: 'the
    Duke of Somerset was appointed Regent of Normandy
    and the Duke of York thereof discharged'.

204 *in York this breeds suspicion*: This accusation arouses
    doubt about York's loyalty to the Crown.

205 *these*: Horner and Peter.

206 *single combat*: A duel. Q1 specifies *with Eben staues and
    Sandbags combatting in Smithfield before your royal
    Majesty*.
    convenient: Appropriate.

208 *This is the law, and this Duke Humphrey's doom*: Some
    editors give this line to the King, on the grounds that
    Somerset and Horner both appear to reply to Henry;
    others insert two lines spoken by the King in Q1: *Then
    be it so my Lord of Somerset.* | *We make your grace
    Regent ouer the French*. But F's version may be implying
    that Gloucester's influence over the King is total, which
    illuminates the enmity of the Queen and the other
    peers. On stage the action would be clear if Henry
    were to nod in agreement at the end of Gloucester's
    speech.

215 *Sirrah*: The customary form of address for a social inferior.

I.4

The scene takes place in Gloucester's house. All of the accomplices of the Duchess are taken from the chronicles:

At the same season were arrested, as aiders and counsellors to the said Duchess, Thomas Southwell, priest and canon of Saint Stephen's in Westminster, John Hum, priest, Roger Bolingbroke, a cunning necromancer, and Margery Jourdain, surnamed the Witch of Eye, to whose charge it was laid that they, at the request of the Duchess, had devised an image of wax representing the King, which by their sorcery a little and little consumed, intending thereby in conclusion to waste and destroy the King's person and so to bring him death.

3 *therefore provided*: Equipped for that purpose.

4 *exorcisms*: Technically these are rituals performed by the Church for expelling evil spirits; but here the word is used to mean ceremonies for conjuring up spirits.

5 *what else*: Most certainly.
  Fear you not: Do not doubt.

8 *aloft*: See note to 11.
  below: That is, on the main stage, though there may be a pun on 'below' meaning 'underworld'.

10–11 *be you prostrate and grovel on the earth*: In Q1 Jourdain gives the reason for this: *frame a Cirkle here vpon the earth,* | *Whilst I thereon all prostrate on my face,* | *Do talk and whisper with the diuels below.*

11 *aloft*: In Q1 the Duchess at this point *goes vp to the Tower*, presumably a raised area above the stage similar to that used in *Part I*, I.4.22.

12 *Well said*: The Duchess enters in time to catch Bolingbroke's words *let us to our work*. The phrase could also mean 'Well done'.

12–13 *To this gear the sooner*: The quicker we get on with this business.

14 *wizards*: Practisers of black magic.

15 *silent*: In phrases like this the adjectival form was often used; cf. 'the sweet o'th'night' (*Henry IV, Part II*, V.3.49–50).

16 *when Troy was set on fire*: The reference is to the *Aeneid*, Book II, in which Virgil describes the sacking of Troy by the Greeks.

17 *screech-owls*: Birds of ill-omen whose cry was thought to herald death.

   ban-dogs: Watch-dogs chained up because of their excessive fierceness.

18 *break up*: Rise out of.

20 *Whom*: Whichever spirit.

21 *hallowed verge*: Magic circle.

   Here do the ceremonies belonging: Here perform the ritual proper to the raising of spirits. In popular plays of the period, such as Christopher Marlowe's *Doctor Faustus* and Robert Greene's *Friar Bacon and Friar Bungay*, similar supernatural rituals are used.

   Conjuro te: I conjure you.

22 *Adsum*: I am here.

23 *Asmath*: This is not the name of any known spirit in magic. It resembles 'Asmenoth' and 'Asmodeus'.

24–5 *By the eternal God . . . tremblest at*: The allusion is to James 2:19: 'the devils also believe and tremble'.

25 *that*: That which.

27 *That*: Would that. The tradition was that spirits were reluctant to answer human questions. Cf. *Macbeth*, IV.1.71: 'Dismiss me. Enough.'

29–30 *The duke yet lives that Henry shall depose;* | *But him outlive, and die a violent death*: Presumably the reference is to the Duke of York, whose death at the Battle of Wakefield is dramatized in *Part III*, I.4. In the manner of infernal prophecies, the form of the utterance is quibbling: *shall depose* and *die a violent death* can apply to York or Henry.

30 *Bolingbroke*: Some editors have Southwell copying down the Spirit's answers as Bolingbroke asks the questions.

34 *Let him shun castles*: Hall notes, though not in connection with the Duchess's magic practices, that at the first
   battle of St Albans 'there died under the sign of the
   Castle Edmund Duke of Somerset, who long before
   was warned to eschew all castles'. See the treatment of
   this at V.2.67–9.

36 *mounted*: On mountains.

37 *Have done*: Finish quickly. See the note to 27.

38 *the burning lake*: Cf. Revelation 19:20: 'a pond of fire,
   burning with brimstone'.

39 *False*: Treacherous.
   avoid: Be gone.
   Sir Humphrey Stafford as captain: This phrase is not in
   F. In view of line 51, I think Sir Humphrey Stafford,
   who appears in the play later (IV.2), is intended to
   be captain of the guard to whom the Duchess is
   committed.
   break in: Burst on to the stage (through one of the entry
   doors).

40 *trash*: Conjuring paraphernalia.

41 *Beldam*: Hag.
   watched you at an inch: Kept you under the closest obser-
   vation. The phrase 'at an inch' is proverbial.

43 *this piece of pains*: All this trouble you have gone to
   (ironical).

45 *guerdoned*: Rewarded.
   these good deserts: What you have well deserved.

47 *Injurious*: Insulting.

49 *clapped up close*: Securely imprisoned.

50 *asunder*: Apart from one another.

51 *Stafford*: See note to 39. Some editors claim that here
   Buckingham (whose family name is Stafford) is
   addressing himself, and so do not include Sir Humphrey
   Stafford in this scene.

52 *trinkets*: Conjuring apparatus.
   all forthcoming: A legal term meaning that the goods
   are properly confiscated and will be produced later as
   evidence.

54 *you watched her well*: Your surveillance of the Duchess was very successful.

55 *plot*: (1) Trick; (2) piece of ground.
   build upon: (1) Pursue to our advantage; (2) erect a structure.

60 *just*: Precisely; exactly.

61 *Aio te, Aeacida, Romanos vincere posse*: This was a classic example of the ambiguous statement. In *De Divinatione*, II.56, Cicero cites Ennius' *Annals* which records this answer given by the Pythian Apollo to the Greek Pyrrhus, who wished to know whether he would conquer Rome. Its two interpretations are (1) I proclaim that you, the descendant of Aeacus, can conquer the Romans; (2) I proclaim that the Romans can conquer you, the descendant of Aeacus.

65 *befall*: F has *betide*, but the emendation seems necessary in view of 33.

70 *hardly attained and hardly understood*: Obtained with difficulty and not comprehended at all.

71 *in progress*: On a royal journey.

73 *these news*: 'News' was often treated as plural in sixteenth-century English.

76 *post*: Messenger.

II.1

The idea of a hawking expedition as the scene for a conflict between Gloucester and the nobles was probably suggested by a passage in Hall where Margaret persuades her husband to make a progress to Warwickshire

for his health and recreation, and so with hawking and hunting came to the city of Coventry, where were divers ways studied privily to bring the Queen to her heart's ease and long expectate desire, which was the death and destruction of the Duke of York, the Earls of Salisbury and Warwick.

The location of the scene is the city of St Albans.

0 *Enter the King . . . hallooing*: In Q1 the stage direction is more explicit: the Queen has *her Hawke on her fist*

and the whole royal party is to act *as if they came from hawking*.

1 *flying at the brook*: Hawking water-fowl. This was a sport favoured by the nobility.

2 *these seven years' day*: For the past seven years.

4 *old Joan had not gone out*: Presumably the meaning is that this particular hawk would not have flown on account of its age.

5 *point*: Position, usually to windward, from which to swoop on the prey.

6 *pitch*: The maximum height to which the hawk flies before swooping.

8 *fain*: Fond.

9 *an*: If.
   like: Please.

10 *My Lord Protector's hawks do tower so well*: Gloucester's family crest was a falcon with a maiden's head, which fact lies behind Suffolk's and the Cardinal's gibes in 9–15.
   tower: Fly in mounting circular spirals until the 'pitch' is reached.

11 *aloft*: (1) High in the sky; (2) in a high position in the state.

18–20 *The treasury of everlasting joy . . . thy heart*: From Matthew 6:19–21: 'Hoard not up for yourselves treasures upon earth . . . but lay up for you treasures in heaven . . . For where your treasure is, there will your heart be also.'

20 *Beat*: Dwell.

21–56 *Pernicious Protector . . . this strife*: This seems to have been suggested by Hall's account of the year 1442–3:

You have heard before how the Duke of Gloucester sore grudged at the proud doings of the Cardinal of Winchester, and how the Cardinal likewise sore envied and disdained at the rule of the Duke of Gloucester, and how . . . each was reconciled to other in perfect love and amity to all men's outward judgements . . . But venom will once break out and inward grudge will soon appear . . . for divers secret attempts

were advanced forward this season against the noble Duke
Humphrey of Gloucester afar off, which in conclusion came
so near that they bereft him both of life and land . . . For
first this year Dame Eleanor Cobham, wife to the said Duke,
was accused of treason.

21 *Pernicious*: Dangerous.
   dangerous: Threatening.
22 *smoothest it so*: Adopt such a flattering manner.
23 *peremptory*: Overbearing.
24 *Tantaene animis coelestibus irae*: The quotation is from
   Virgil's *Aeneid* and means 'Is it possible for there to be
   so much wrath in the minds of heavenly creatures?'
27 *well becomes*: Is very appropriate to.
28 *good*: Just.
30 *An't like*: If it please.
31 *insolence*: Pride.
33 *whet not on*: Do not encourage.
34 *blessèd are the peace-makers on earth*: from Matthew 5:9.
35-6 *Let me be blessèd for the peace I make | Against this proud
   Protector with my sword*: Cf. Matthew 10:34: 'I came not
   to send peace, but a sword.'
37 *that*: A single combat between us.
39 *Make up no factious numbers for the matter*: Do not bring
   supporters of your faction into the quarrel.
40 *In thine own person*: Alone on your own behalf.
   abuse: Insult, offence.
41 *peep*: Even appear.
44 *man*: Falconer.
   put up the fowl: Raised the water-fowl.
45 *two-hand sword*: It is not certain what effect Shakespeare
   was aiming at in specifying this weapon. The long
   two-handed sword was archaic by the time of Elizabeth,
   so it may be an anachronism intended to underline the
   fact that it is two old men who are proposing to fight
   with antiquated weapons; or Shakespeare may be
   naming a weapon appropriate to the date of the events
   he is dramatizing.
47 *Are . . . grove*: F gives this line to Gloucester (see

(Emendations in An Account of the Text), but some
emendation is necessary, as the King's words (48)
indicate that it is Gloucester who has spoken last.

Are ye advised: Is it agreed.

50 *shave your crown*: The allusion is to the Cardinal's
tonsure.

51 *fence shall fail*: Expertise at sword-play shall prove
inadequate.

Medice, teipsum: This was proverbial: 'Physician, heal
thyself', based upon the Vulgate: Luke 4:23: '*Medice,
cura te ipsum.*'

52 *protect*: Another pun on Gloucester's title.

53 *stomachs*: Angry passions.

55 *such strings jar*: (1) Such strings of a musical instrument sound in discord; (2) such high noblemen fall into
dispute.

harmony: (1) Musical concord; (2) peace at court.

56 *compound this strife*: Settle this dispute.

Enter a man crying 'A miracle!': The episode that this
direction introduces is found in the chronicles only in
Grafton, from which Shakespeare may have derived
his material; but some details suggest that he actually
used the account found in Foxe's *Acts and Monuments*.
See the notes below for quotations from this source.

61–80 *Forsooth, a blind man . . . have better told*: There are
echoes throughout this exchange of the account of
Jesus's restoration of the beggar's sight in John 9.

61–3 *a blind man . . . life before*: Cf. Foxe:

> . . . there came to St Albans a certain beggar with his wife
> . . . saying that he was born blind, and never saw in his life
> . . . suddenly this blind man, at St Alban's shrine, had his
> sight again, and a miracle solemnly rung, and *Te Deum* sung;
> so that nothing was talked of in all the town but this miracle.

61 *Saint Alban*: Alban was reputed to be the first British
Christian martyr. He was executed by the Romans in
AD 304 in Verulam (St Albans) for harbouring Christian
converts.

64 *Now God be praised*: In Foxe it is Gloucester who is delighted at the report of the miracle, 'showing himself joyous of God's glory'.

64–5 *to believing souls | Gives light in darkness*: Cf. Luke 1:79: 'To give light to them that sit in darkness'; also Isaiah 42:16 and Psalm 112:4.

65 *the Mayor of Saint Albans*: St Albans was not incorporated until the reign of Edward IV. In Henry VI's time the town's chief officer was the bailiff.

66 *on*: In.

68 *this earthly vale*: Cf. Psalm 84:6: 'the vale of tears'; and *Homily against Wilful Rebellion*, 490: 'this wretched earth and vale of all misery'.

69 *by his sight his sin be multiplied*: Cf. John 9:41: 'If ye were blind, ye should have no sin, but now ye say "We see": therefore your sin remaineth.'

72 *circumstance*: Detail.

73 *glorify the Lord*: From Matthew 5:16: 'and glorify your Father which is in heaven'.

76 *Ay, indeed was he*: See the note to 96–102.

78 *like*: Please.

82 *Berwick*: A Scottish border fortress town at the mouth of the Tweed. See the note to 88–9.

83–5 *Poor soul . . . hath done*: In Foxe it is Gloucester who tutors the beggar about God's gifts, 'exhorting him to meekness, and to no ascribing of any part of the worship to himself, nor to be proud of the people's praise, who would call him a good and godly man thereby'.

84 *unhallowed*: Without saying prayers.

85 *still*: Always.

87 *of*: For.

88–9 *being called . . . in my sleep*: Cf. Foxe: 'he . . . was warned in his dream that he should come out of Berwick, where he said he had ever dwelled, to seek St Alban'.

90 *Simon*: The name of which 'Simpcox' is a derivative.

91 *offer*: Submit an offering of money.

94 *lame*: Simpcox's lameness is Shakespeare's addition to his source.

96 *plum-tree*: A slang term for the female genitals.

96–102 *How long hast thou . . . of my life*: Cf. Foxe: '[Gloucester] looked well upon his eyes, and asked whether he could see nothing at all in all his life before. And . . . his wife, as well as himself, affirmed falsely "no".'

97–9 *What! And wouldst . . . very dear*: The proverb 'He that never climbed never fell' lies behind this exchange.

98 *But that*: Only on that occasion.

100 *Mass*: By the Mass.

101 *damsons*: A slang term for testicles.

103 *subtle*: Clever, crafty.
shall not serve: Is not good enough for him to get away with it.

104 *wink*: Close your eyes.

105–29 *In my opinion . . . impossible*: Cf. Foxe:

[Gloucester] said 'I believe you very well, for me thinketh ye cannot see well yet.' 'Yea, sir,' quoth he; 'I thank God and his holy martyr, I can see now as well as any man.' 'You can,' quoth the Duke; 'what colour is my gown?' Then anon the beggar told him. 'What colour,' quoth he, 'is *this* man's gown?' He told him also, and so forth; without any sticking he told him the names of all the colours that could be showed him. And when the Duke saw that, he bade him 'walk, traitor', and made him to be set openly in the stocks; for though he could have seen suddenly, by miracle, the difference between diverse colours; yet could he not, by the sight, so suddenly tell the names of all these colours except he had known them before, no more than the names of all the men that he should suddenly see.

106 *clear as day*: Proverbial phrase.

108 *Sayst thou me so*: That's what you are telling me, is it?

109 *red as blood*: Proverbial phrase.

111 *black as jet*: Proverbial phrase.

114 *many*: Multitude.

124 *sit there*: There you are.

125–9 *If thou hadst . . . impossible*: Cf. the proverb: 'A blind man can judge no colours.'

128 *nominate*: Identify by name.

130 *cunning*: Skill.

134 *beadles*: Minor Church officials appointed originally to keep order in church and to deal with petty offenders, often by inflicting corporal punishment.

   things called whips: This phrase gained some notoriety after it was used by Ben Jonson in his additions to Thomas Kyd's *The Spanish Tragedy*, III.11: 'And there is Nemesis and Furies, | And things called whips . . .' Robert Armin in *A Nest of Ninnies* (1608) wrongly associates its popularity with *Hamlet*.

136 *presently*: Immediately.

137 *straight*: At once.

138 *by and by*: Immediately.

140 *me*: For me, at my command.

142 *go about*: Are trying.

150 *bearest*: Endurest (the sins of the world).

152 *drab*: Slut.

153 *pure need*: Sheer economic necessity.

157 *the lame to leap*: Cf. Isaiah 35:6: 'Then shall the lame man leap as an hart.'

159 *fly*: Be lost. The allusion is to Suffolk's bargaining away French towns as part of Margaret's marriage settlement.

161 *unfold*: Reveal.

162 *A sort of naughty persons, lewdly bent*: A gang of disreputable people disposed to evil.

163 *Under the countenance and confederacy*: With the patronage and complicity.

165 *head*: Leader.

   rout: Disorderly mob.

166 *practised*: Conspired.

168 *in the fact*: Red-handed; in the act.

170 *Demanding of*: Asking questions about.

171 *other*: Other members.

172 *at large*: In detail.

174 *forthcoming*: In custody waiting to be tried. Cf. I.4.52.

175 *turned*: Blunted.

176 *like*: Likely.

your hour: The appointment you have made (for the
duel; see 40–48)

177 *leave to afflict*: Desist from afflicting.

180 *meanest*: Most socially inferior.

181–2 *what mischiefs work the wicked ones, | Heaping confusion
on their own heads*: Cf. Psalm 7:16: 'For his travail shall
come upon his own head; and his wickedness shall fall
upon his own pate' (Prayer Book).

182 *confusion*: Destruction.

183 *tainture of thy nest*: Defilement of your own house. Cf.
the proverb: 'It is a foul bird that defiles his own nest.'

184 *look thyself be faultless, thou wert best*: You had better
make sure you yourself are free from connection with
the crime.

185 *for myself*: So far as I am concerned.

187 *how it stands*: What the circumstances are.

190 *conversed*: Been associated.

191 *like to pitch, defile nobility*: Cf. the proverb: 'He that
touches pitch shall be defiled'; also the Apocrypha of
the Geneva Bible, Ecclesiastes 13:1.

195 *repose us here*: Stay in St Albans.

198 *answers*: Defence in court.

199 *poise the cause in Justice' equal scales*: Weigh the case in
the fair scales of Justice.

200 *Whose beam stands sure*: Whose cross-bar (from which
the scale-pans are suspended) is perfectly level (to
ensure impartiality of judgement).

II.2

The scene takes place in a secluded part of the Duke
of York's garden and is based on Hall's account of his
activities in 1448–9:

Richard Duke of York . . . perceiving the King to be a ruler
not ruling and the whole burden of the realm to depend in
the ordinances of the Queen and the Duke of Suffolk, began
secretly to allure to his friends of the nobility and privately
declared to them his title and right to the crown.

2 *supper*: York issued the invitation at I.4.78–9.

3 *close walk*: Secluded garden path.

9–52 *Then thus . . . I am king*: This is a fuller version of York's justification for his claim to the throne than that which appears in *Part I*, II.4 and 5. It is based on various passages found in Hall – the first is from the Introduction to the reign of Henry IV:

Edward III . . . had issue Edward, his first begotten son, Prince of Wales; William of Hatfield, the second begotten son; Lionel Duke of Clarence, the third begotten son; John of Gaunt, Duke of Lancaster, the fourth begotten son; Edmund of Langley, Duke of York, the fifth begotten son; Thomas of Woodstock, Duke of Gloucester, the sixth begotten son; and William of Windsor, the seventh begotten son. The said Prince Edward died in the life of his father, King Edward III, and had issue Richard, born at Bordeaux, which after the death of King Edward III, as cousin and heir to him . . . succeeded him . . . and died without issue. Lionel Duke of Clarence . . . had issue Philippe, his only daughter, which was married to Edmund Mortimer, Earl of March, and had issue Roger Mortimer, Earl of March; which Roger had issue Edmund Mortimer, Earl of March, Anne, and Eleanor, which Edmund and Eleanor died without issue. And the said Anne was married to Richard Earl of Cambridge, son to Edmund of Langley, Duke of York, the fifth begotten son of the said King Edward III, which Richard had issue the famous prince Richard Plantagenet, Duke of York.

The second passage is from the account of the first year of the reign of Henry IV:

Owen Glendower . . . made war . . . on . . . Lord Grey of Ruthen and took him prisoner, promising him liberty and discharging his ransom if he would espouse and marry his daughter . . . The Lord Grey . . . assented . . . But this false father-in-law . . . kept him with his wife still in captivity till he died. And not content with this heinous offence, made war on Lord Edmund Mortimer, Earl of March, and . . . took him prisoner.

The third passage comes from York's oration to the parliament in 1460:

Which King Richard, of that name the second, was lawfully and justly possessed of the crown and diadem of this realm and region till Henry of Derby, Duke of Lancaster and Hereford, son to John Duke of Lancaster . . . wrongfully usurped and intruded upon the royal power and high estate of this realm and region, taking on him the name, style, and authority of king and governor of the same . . . After whose piteous death . . . the right and title of the crown . . . was lawfully . . . returned to Roger Mortimer, Earl of March, son and heir to Lady Philippe, the only child of the above rehearsed Lionel Duke of Clarence, to which Roger's daughter, called Anne, my . . . mother, I am the very true and lineal heir . . . Edmund Earl of March, my most well-beloved uncle, in the time of the first usurper, in deed but not by right called King Henry IV . . . he being then in captivity with Owen Glendower, the rebel in Wales, made his title and righteous claim to the destruction of both the noble persons.

See also Genealogical Table 2.

10 *Edward the Third*: 1312–77, Eldest son of Edward II; he reigned 1327–77.

11 *Edward the Black Prince*: 1330–76, Eldest son of Edward III, so named because of the colour of his armour at the battle of Crécy.

12 *William of Hatfield*: Second son of Edward III; he died in infancy.

13 *Lionel Duke of Clarence*: 1338–68, Third son of Edward III, from whom the Mortimers were descended.

14 *John of Gaunt*: 1340–99, Fourth son of Edward III; father of Henry IV by his first wife Blanche and of the Beauforts (including the Cardinal) by his mistress Catherine Swynford.

15 *Edmund Langley, Duke of York*: 1341–1402, Fifth son of Edward III, progenitor of the house of York.

16 *Thomas of Woodstock, Duke of Gloucester*: 1355–97,

Sixth son of Edward III, probably murdered on the orders of his nephew, Richard II.

17 *William of Windsor*: Seventh son of Edward III; he died in infancy.

19 *Richard*: Richard II, 1367–1400, younger son of Edward, the Black Prince; he reigned 1377–99, and was deposed and murdered by his cousin Henry Bolingbroke.

21 *Henry Bolingbroke*: 1367–1413; He reigned as Henry IV 1399–1413.

25 *his poor queen*: Richard II married Isabella of France (*c.* 1389–1409) in 1396.

26 *Pomfret*: Pontefract Castle, twenty-one miles from York, where Richard II was murdered.
all you know: This way of addressing only two listeners may be due to the fact that the material Shakespeare is working from is Hall's account of York's oration to parliament in 1460, in which the same phrase occurs; but 'all' is used to refer to two people in *Henry IV, Part II*, III.1.35, and in *The Faerie Queene*, II.1.61.

35 *issue*: A child.
Philippe: Philippa, 1355–*c.* 1380, the daughter of Lionel, Duke of Clarence, third son of Edward III; she married Edmund Mortimer, third Earl of March, and transmitted the claim of Lionel through her granddaughter, Anne, to the house of York.

36 *Edmund Mortimer*: 1351–81, Third Earl of March.

37 *Roger*: 1374–98, Fourth Earl of March.

38 *Edmund*: 1391–1425, Fifth Earl of March; declared heir presumptive by Richard II in 1398.
Anne: 1388–*c.* 1412; Married Richard Earl of Cambridge, becoming mother of Richard Duke of York.

39–42 *This Edmund . . . till he died*: Following Hall, Shakespeare confuses Edmund Mortimer, the fifth Earl of March (see note to 38), with Sir Edmund Mortimer (1376?–1409), the brother of Roger Mortimer, the fourth Earl of March, who married Owen Glendower's daughter while in captivity.

41 *Owen Glendower*: Welsh rebel, born *c.* 1359, who refused Henry V's general pardon and is thought to have died

of starvation in the mountains of North Wales *c.* 1416.

42 *Who*: Glendower.

45 *Richard Earl of Cambridge*: d. 1415, Second son of Edmund Langley, Duke of York; he was executed for treason on the vote of his peers.

53 *proceedings*: Line of descent.

56 *his*: John of Gaunt's.

57 *fails not*: Has not died out.

58 *slips*: Cuttings. *Fails, flourishes, slips* and *stock* are all terms suggested by the idea of the family tree.
   stock: Tree trunk.

60 *private plot*: Secluded area. *Plot* continues the gardening metaphor of 57–8.

62 *birthright*: Rightful claim according to the law of primogeniture.

64 *We*: Notice York's immediate adoption of the royal plural.

65 *that*: Until the time that.

67 *suddenly*: Quickly.

68 *advice*: Careful consideration.

70 *Wink at*: Close your eyes to.

71 *Beaufort's pride . . . Somerset's ambition*: Cf. I.1.178.

73 *the shepherd of the flock*: This is a phrase used by Hall in praise of Henry V.

77 *break we off*: Let us finish talking.

82 *but*: Except for.

II.3

Most editors locate this scene in a hall of justice, though this seems inappropriate for the Horner–Peter duel, which historically took place at Smithfield. F's stage direction, *Enter the King and State, with Guard, to banish the Duchesse*, and the Queen's lines 52–3 suggest an open public place.

3–4 *for sins | Such as by God's book are adjudged to death*: Cf. Deuteronomy 18:10–12; Leviticus 20:6; Exodus 22:18: 'Thou shalt not suffer a witch to live.'

5–8 *You four . . . the gallows*: Contrast the punishments detailed in Hall's account:

... for the which treason they were adjudged to die; and so
Margery Jourdain was burnt in Smithfield, and Roger
Bolingbroke was drawn and quartered at Tyburn, taking
upon his death that there was never no such thing by them
imagined; John Hum had his pardon, and Southwell died in
the Tower before execution.

7 *Smithfield*: A favoured London spot for the burning of
heretics.

9 *for*: Because.

10 *Despoilèd of your honour in your life*: Deprived of your
good name for the rest of your life.

11–13 *after three days' . . . Isle of Man*: Cf. Hall:

Dame Eleanor Cobham . . . was examined in Saint Stephen's
Chapel before the Bishop of Canterbury and there by examination convict and judged to do open penance in three open
places within the City of London, and after that adjudged to
perpetual prison in the Isle of Man, under the keeping of Sir
John Stanley, Knight.

13 *With*: In the custody of.
Sir John Stanley: Historically it was Sir Thomas Stanley
who was custodian of the Duchess of Gloucester.
Among the chroniclers, Fabyan and Stowe (*The Annals
of England*, 1592) have the name correctly. Sir Thomas's
brother appears in *Part III*, IV.5.

14 *were*: Would be.

15–21 *Eleanor, the law . . . would ease*: In Hall, Gloucester at
his wife's sentence 'took all these things patiently and
said little'.

16 *justify*: Exonerate; excuse.

19 *Will bring thy head with sorrow to the ground*: Cf. Genesis
42:38: 'ye shall bring my grey head with sorrow unto
the grave'.

21 *would*: Requires; would have.

22–3 *Ere thou go, | Give up thy staff*: There is no historical
evidence that Gloucester's loss of his Protectorship

followed from his wife's conviction; but Hall does
deal with the two topics in a single paragraph (see the
quotation in the note to II.1.21–56).

23 *staff*: Symbol of the Protectorship; cf. I.2.25.

25 *lantern to my feet*: Cf. Psalm 119:105: 'thy word is a
lantern unto my feet' (Geneva Bible).

28–31 *I see no reason . . . his realm*: See the quotations from
Hall in the notes to I.3.121.

28 *of years*: No longer a minor; of age.

29 *be to be*: Need to be.

30 *govern*: Guide; control.
realm: There is a possibility that this is a misprint due
to the F compositor's eye catching the word *realm* in
the next line. The manuscript copy may have read
'helm'; cf. I.3.98.

31 *King his*: King's.

34 *Henry*: Henry V.

41 *That bears so shrewd a maim*: Who has suffered so severe
a mutilation.
two pulls at once: Two things torn from him in a single
moment (his wife and his office).

43 *raught*: Snatched; seized.

45 *this lofty pine*: This is probably an allusion to the heraldic
device of a pine tree adopted by Henry IV, Gloucester's
father, from Thomas of Woodstock, Edward III's sixth
son. The destruction of a lofty pine is compared with
those who 'are often snared with wiles, | And from aloft
do headlong fall to ground' in one of Geoffrey Whitney's
Emblems (1586), a book that Shakespeare knew.

45 *sprays*: Branches.

46 *her youngest days*: When her pride was at its height.
Eleanor is being viewed as one of Gloucester's *sprays*
which is cut off at her sprouting stage.

47 *let him go*: Bother your heads no more about him.
Please it: If it please.

49 *appellant and defendant*: These were terms used in a
trial by single combat to describe the challenger and
the challenged.

50 *the lists*: Literally the arena within which knightly

combatants had to fight; here it merely means 'the place designated for the fight'.

52 *therefore*: For that reason.

53 *quarrel*: Dispute; difference.
    tried: Resolved by combat.

54 *A*: In.
    fit: Properly arranged.

55 *end it*: Settle the matter.

56 *worse bestead*: In such a bad state of preparedness.

58 *drum*: Drummer.
    staff with a sand-bag fastened to it: Usually a mock weapon used in sporting contests.

59–103 *Here, neighbour Horner . . . for thy reward*: This episode is based on Hall:

> . . . an armourer's servant of London appealed his master of treason, which offered to be tried by battle. At the day assigned, the friends of the master brought him malmsey and *aqua vitae* to comfort him withal; but it was the cause of his and their discomfort, for he poured in so much that when he came into the place in Smithfield where he should fight, both his wit and strength failed him; and so he being a tall and a hardy personage, overloaded with hot drinks, was vanquished of his servant, being but a coward and a wretch, [and his] body was drawn to Tyburn and there hanged and beheaded.

Shakespeare's making the armourer confess to treason is part of the dramatic build-up to York's rebellion.

60 *sack*: A general term used for sweet Spanish and Canary wine.

63 *charneco*: A sweet wine, possibly from Portugal.

64 *double*: Extra strong.

66 *Let it come*: Pass the tankard round for the toast.
    pledge you: Drink your health.

67 *a fig for*: A proverbial saying related to an obscene gesture made by pushing the thumb between the first and second fingers.

71 *credit*: Honour and reputation.

78 *fence*: Skill in fencing.

87–8 *take my death*: Take my oath on pain of death, stake my life on it.

89 *have at*: Let me get at.

90 *downright*: Administered vertically (and thus with one's full force).

91 *Dispatch*: Let us get on with it.

double: Grow thick and slurred (with drink).

92 *alarum*: The call to arms, signal to begin fighting.

95 *in thy master's way*: Which hindered your master's ability to fight.

96–7 *in this presence*: In this place before the King.

102 *Which*: Whom.

II.4

The scene is located in a London street; Holinshed specifies Cheapside. For Hall's account of the Duchess of Gloucester's sentence and punishment, see the note to II.3.11–13.

0 *mourning cloaks*: Long black cloaks with hoods.

1 *Thus sometimes hath the brightest day a cloud*: Proverbial: 'No day so clear but has a dark cloud.'

4 *fleet*: Pass by rapidly.

8 *Uneath*: With difficulty.

10 *abrook*: Endure.

11 *abject*: Low; common.

12, 35 *envious*: Spiteful; malicious.

13 *erst*: Formerly.

15 *soft*: Stay; hold.

16 *barefoot . . . verses written on her back and pinned on*: These details from Q1 are not in F's stage direction but are justified in its text; see 31, 34 and 105–7.

taper: This detail is not found in Hall; Holinshed has a note that 'Polychronicon saith she was enjoined to go through Cheapside with a taper in her hand', and Foxe has it also. The account in *A Mirror for Magistrates* specifies the bare feet, the taper and the sheet.

bills: Weapons consisting of a staff terminating in a hook-shaped blade.

16 *halberds*: Weapons consisting of a battleaxe and a pike
    mounted on a six-foot pole.

17 *take her*: Rescue her by force.

19 *open shame*: The same phrase occurs twice in the
    portrait of Eleanor in *A Mirror for Magistrates*.

21 *giddy*: Fickle.

23 *hateful*: Full of hate.

24 *closet*: Private room; study.
    pent up: Barricaded in; locked in.
    rue: Grieve for.

25 *ban*: Curse.

31 *Mailed up*: Enveloped.
    papers on my back: See the stage direction at 16: *verses
    written on her back*, describing the nature of her crimes.

32 *with*: By.

33 *deep-fet*: Brought from deep within my being.

34 *ruthless*: Unpitying.

35 *start*: Flinch with the pain.

36 *be advisèd*: Take care.

38 *Trowest thou*: Do you believe.

45 *As*: That.
    forlorn: Ruined; disgraced.

46 *wonder*: Object to be looked at with amazement.
    pointing-stock: Object to be pointed at with scorn.

47 *rascal*: Worthless; good-for-nothing.

52 *her*: Queen Margaret.

54 *limed*: Smeared with birdlime. See the note to I.3.86.

55 *fly thou how thou canst*: No matter how you try to fly.
    tangle: Ensnare.

56 *fear not . . . snared*: The Duchess is being sarcastic about
    her husband's unsuspecting nature.

57 *seek prevention of*: Take action to forestall.

58–63 *Ah, Nell, forbear . . . and crimeless*: This is based on
    Hall's depiction of one aspect of Gloucester's char-
    acter at this time: 'he thought neither of death nor of
    condemnation to die, such affiance had he in his strong
    truth and such confidence had he in indifferent justice'.

58 *Thou aimest all awry*: Your conjectures are quite wide
    of the mark.

59 *attainted*: Condemned for treason.

62 *procure me*: Bring about for me.
   scathe: Harm.

65 *were not*: Would not be.

67 *quiet*: To endure uncomplainingly.

68 *sort*: Frame; adapt.

69 *These few days' wonder will be quickly worn*: Proverbial:
   'A wonder lasts but nine days.'
   worn: Worn out (and thus forgotten).

70–73 *I summon your grace ... will be there*: Cf. Hall: 'So, for the
   furtherance of their purpose, a parliament was summoned
   to be kept at Bury, whither resorted all the peers of the
   realm, and amongst them the Duke of Gloucester.'
   Historically the parliament at Bury did not meet until 1447,
   some six years after the Duchess's conviction.

71 *Holden*: To be held.
   Bury: Bury St Edmunds in Suffolk.

73 *close dealing*: Secret plotting.

75 *the King's commission*: The royal warrant (specifying
   the punishment).

76 *stays*: Is ended.

77 *Sir John Stanley*: See the note to II.3.13.

79 *protect*: Act as custodian of.

80 *given in charge*: Ordered.

81 *Entreat*: Treat.
   in that: Just because.

82 *The world may laugh again*: Proverbial expression
   meaning better days may come again.

90 *this world's eternity*: To enjoy this world for ever.

95 *state*: Status; rank.

96 *but reproach*: Someone deserving only censure. Eleanor
   is quibbling on *state* meaning 'condition'.

100 *better than I fare*: May you prosper better than I.

101 *conduct*: Conductor; guide.

102 *office*: Duty; function.

103 *is discharged*: Has been carried out.

107 *shifted*: Altered; removed (with a pun on *shifted* meaning
   'changed like an undergarment').

109 *attire me how I can*: No matter what clothes I wear.

The scene is located in the Abbey at Bury St Edmunds. The plotting of the downfall and death of Gloucester is based upon Hall's account of the events in 1447–8, as he details the Queen's resentment against the Protectorship and her plot to deprive the Duke of his office:

This . . . invention . . . was furthered and set forward by such as of long time had borne malice to the Duke . . . Which venomous serpents and malicious tigers persuaded, incensed, and exhorted the Queen to look well upon the expenses and revenues of the realm and thereof to call an account, affirming plainly that she should evidently perceive that the Duke of Gloucester had not so much advanced and preferred the common wealth and public utility as his own private things and peculiar estate. . . And although she joined her husband with her in name . . . yet she did all, she said all, and she bore the whole swing . . . and first of all she excluded the Duke of Gloucester from all rule and governance, not prohibiting such as she knew to be his mortal enemies to invent and imagine causes and griefs against him and his; so that by her permission and favour divers noblemen conspired against him, of the which . . . the Marquess of Suffolk and the Duke of Buckingham [were] the chief, not unprocured by the Cardinal of Winchester and the Archbishop of York. Divers articles both heinous and odious were laid to his charge in open council, and in especial one that he had caused men adjudged to die to be put to other execution than the law of the land had ordered or assigned . . . But his capital enemies and mortal foes, fearing that some tumult or commotion might arise if a prince so well beloved of the people should be openly executed and put to death, determined to trap and undo him . . . So, for the furtherance of their purpose, a parliament was summoned to be kept at Bury, whither resorted all the peers of the realm, and amongst them the Duke of Gloucester, which on the second day of the session was by the Lord Beaumond, then High Constable of England, accompanied by the Duke of Buckingham and other, arrested, apprehended, and put in ward, and all his servants sequestered from him.

Shakespeare also allows the peers to accuse Gloucester of irregularities in his handling of the French wars, which were historically attributed to Suffolk and Somerset.

1 *muse*: Wonder why.

5–17 *The strangeness of his altered countenance . . . to us belongs*: In John Hardyng's *Chronicles of England* (1543) the change in Gloucester's demeanour is attributed to his sorrow at his wife's disgrace: 'He waxed then strange each day unto the King, | For cause she was forejudged for sorcery . . . | And to the King had great heaviness . . .'

5 *strangeness*: Aloofness.

7 *insolent*: Proudly overbearing.

9 *since*: When.

12 *That*: So that.
   admired: Was amazed at.

14 *give the time of day*: Extend a greeting.

17 *Disdaining duty*: Refusing to show respect.
   to us belongs: Is proper to us.

18 *grin*: Bare their teeth.

19 *the lion*: The heraldic symbol of England.

21 *near*: Closely related to. See the note to I.1.149.

22 *mount*: Ascend (the throne of England).

23 *Me seemeth*: It appears to me.
   no policy: Not prudent political tactics.

24 *Respecting*: Considering.

25 *his advantage*: The good that will come to him.

26 *come about*: Be in regular contact with.

28–30 *By flattery . . . will follow him*: For the nobles' fears of Gloucester's popularity, see the quotation from Hall in the headnote to this scene.

29 *make commotion*: Cause a rebellion.

31–3 *Now 'tis the spring . . . husbandry*: Imagery derived from the idea of the garden of state was extensively used by Shakespeare, his fullest treatment being in *Richard II*, III.4.

32 *Suffer*: Allow them to flourish.

35 *collect*: Perceive; infer.

36 *fond*: Foolish.

38 *subscribe*: Agree (from the sense of signing a legal document).

40 *Reprove*: Refute.

41 *effectual*: Decisive.

45 *subornation*: Instigation.

46 *practices*: Plottings.

47 *privy to*: Aware of; informed about.
   faults: Crimes.

48 *reputing of*: Setting great store by.

50 *vaunts*: Boasts.

51–2 *Did instigate . . . fall*: Shakespeare has been careful to show the audience in I.2.1–60 that this is not the case. Suffolk is politic enough to allow that there is the possibility of no direct involvement by Gloucester (47) and to suggest that it was the Duchess's consciousness of Gloucester's royal birth which encouraged her to plot against the King – which is true.

51 *bedlam*: Crazy (like an inhabitant of Bedlam, the London hospital for the insane).

52 *frame*: Plot.

53 *Smooth runs the water where the brook is deep*: Proverbial.

54 *simple show*: Innocent outward appearance.

57 *Unsounded*: With unrevealed depths.

59 *Devise strange deaths for small offences done*: See the note to I.3.130–31.

60–63 *And did he not . . . each day revolted*: See the note to I.3.133. There may also be an echo here of Hall's suggestion that 'the Duke of Somerset, for his own peculiar profit, kept not half his number of soldiers, and put their wages in his purse'.

63 *By means whereof*: Because of which.

64 *to*: Compared with.

65 *smooth*: Plausible.

66 *at once*: There are three possible meanings: (1) answering you all together; (2) without further discussion; (3) once and for all.

67 *annoy*: Injure; wound.

68 *shall I speak*: If I am to speak according to.

71 *sucking lamb*: 1 Samuel 7:9.

      harmless dove: Proverbial; cf. Matthew 10:16.

72 *well given*: Kindly disposed.

74 *fond affiance*: Foolish confidence.

76 *he's disposèd as*: He has a disposition like that of.

77–8 *Is he a lamb . . . wolves*: Proverbial: 'a wolf in lamb's skin'.

77 *lent him*: Borrowed by him.

79 *Who cannot steal a shape that means deceit*: What man who is intent on deception is unable to assume a false outward appearance.

81 *Hangs*: Depends.

      cutting short: (1) Beheading; (2) forestalling.

      fraudful: Treacherous.

84–5 *That all your interest . . . lost*: Somerset is referring here to events that took place historically in 1448–9, some two years after the parliament at Bury St Edmunds. Hall blames Somerset for the losses and corruption that Gloucester is accused of in 104–6 below:

> The Duke of Somerset . . . made an agreement with the French King that he would render the town so that he and all his might depart in safeguard with all their goods and substance, which offer the French King gladly accepted and allowed, knowing that by force he might longer have longed for the strong town than to have possessed the same so soon . . . The other towns of Normandy, being persuaded, voluntarily rendered themselves vassals and subjects to the French nation. Now rested English only the town of Cherbourg, whereof was captain Thomas Gonville, which surely valiantly defended the town as long as victual and munition served; but when those two hands were spent and consumed, he, destitute of all comfort and aid, upon a reasonable composition, yielded the town and went to Calais, where the Duke of Somerset and many Englishmen then sojourned, lamenting their loss and desperate of all recovery.

85 *utterly bereft*: Completely seized from.

      all is lost: In Holinshed's account of the French wars at this time (1448) there is a marginal gloss, 'The English lose all in France.'

87–92 *Cold news for me . . . glorious grave*: On Somerset's loss
of the French territories, Hall reports:

Sir Davy Hall, with divers other of his trusty friends, departed
to Cherbourg and from thence sailed into Ireland to the Duke
of York, making relation to him of all these doings, which
thing kindled so great a rancour in his heart and stomach that
he never left persecuting of the Duke of Somerset.

87–8 *Cold news . . . England*: Cf. I.1.235–6.
  89 *Thus are my blossoms blasted in the bud*: Proverbial.
  91 *gear*: Business.
  92 *sell*: Exchange.
  94 *stayed*: Stayed away.
  99 *for*: On account of.
 100 *unspotted*: Innocent.
 104 *of*: From.
105–6 *stayed the soldiers' pay . . . lost France*: The same accusation is made at 60–63. See also the notes to 84–5 and
to I.3.133 and 165–70.
 105 *stayed*: Retained; kept back.
 107 *What*: Who.
 110 *watched the night*: Stayed up all night.
 112 *doit*: Small Dutch coin worth about half an English
farthing.
 113 *groat*: Coin worth 4d.
    to my: For my personal.
 115 *proper store*: Personal fortune.
 117 *dispursèd*: Paid out.
 119 *serves you well*: Is to your advantage.
121–3 *In your Protectorship . . . by tyranny*: Cf. 59 and see the
note to I.3.130–31.
 123 *That England was defamed by*: With the result that
England became infamous for.
 124 *whiles*: During the time.
 126 *should*: Was wont to.
 127 *lowly*: Humble.
    fault: Offence.
 129 *felonious*: Wicked.

fleeced: Stripped by robbing; plundered.

passengers: Travellers.

130 *condign*: Justly deserve.

132 *Above the felon or what trespass else*: More than the man convicted of a felony or any other kind of crime.

133 *easy*: Insignificant.

answered: Explained away.

138 *keep*: Be guarded.

further: Future.

140 *suspense*: Suspicion.

145 *subornation*: Instigation to commit crime.

predominant: In the ascendant; ruling (an astrological term).

146 *equity*: Justice.

exiled: Is exiled from (accented on the second syllable).

147 *complot*: Scheme; plot (accented on the first syllable).

149 *prove the period*: Mark the end.

150 *expend it*: Pay the price (of my death).

151 *mine*: My death.

153 *conclude their plotted tragedy*: Bring an end to the tragedy they have planned.

155 *cloudy*: Frowning.

156 *unburdens*: Unloads; releases.

157 *envious*: Malicious.

158 *doggèd*: (1) Determined; (2) like a cur.

reaches at the moon: Proverbial.

159 *overweening*: Overreaching.

160 *accuse*: Accusation.

level: Aim (as with a weapon).

162 *Causeless*: Without reason.

164 *liefest*: Dearest.

165 *laid your heads together*: Plotted; contrived.

166 *conventicles*: Secret meetings. This is the only occurrence of the word in Shakespeare. He probably used it under the influence of Hall: 'The Earls of March and Warwick and other, being at Calais, had knowledge of all these doings and secret conventicles.'

167 *make away*: Destroy.

168 *want*: Lack.

169 *store*: Numerous accusations.

170 *effected*: Shown to be true.

173 *care*: Exercise care.

       keep: Protect.

175 *rated at*: Berated.

176 *scope*: Full freedom.

178 *twit*: Taunted.

179 *clerkly couched*: Phrased in an educated way.

180–81 *subornèd some to swear | False allegations*: Procured some people to bear false witness. Cf. Acts 6:11–13.

181 *o'erthrow his state*: Bring him down from his high position.

182 *I can give the loser leave to chide*: Proverbial.

184 *Beshrew*: Curse.

       played me false: Deceived me.

186 *wrest the sense*: Distort the meaning.

188 *sure*: Securely.

191–2 *Thus is the shepherd . . . first*: Cf. Matthew 26:31 and Ezekiel 34:8.

192 *gnarling*: snarling over.

194 *decay*: Downfall; ruin.

200 *engirt*: Encircled.

203 *map*: Image.

206 *lowering*: Ominous.

       envies thy estate: Shows malice towards your position.

208 *subversion*: Destruction.

211 *strays*: There are some arguments for the emendation 'strains' here; but *binds* may mean 'pens in' rather than 'ties up'.

214 *dam*: Mother.

219 *do him good*: Give him any assistance.

223 *Free*: Magnanimous; honourable.

224 *cold*: Uninterested.

225 *show*: Display of innocence.

226 *the mournful crocodile*: The allusion is to 'crocodile tears'. Hakluyt's account of Sir John Hawkins's second voyage (1565) includes a description of the crocodile's propensity for trickery: 'His nature is ever, when he would have his prey, to cry and sob like a Christian

body, to provoke them to come to him; and then he
snatcheth at them.'

227 *relenting passengers*: Sympathetic travellers (taken in by
the crocodile's signs of sorrow).

228–9 *as the snake . . . child*: Proverbial.

228 *rolled*: Curled up.

229 *checkered slough*: Patterned skin.

233 *rid*: Removed from.

235 *is worthy policy*: Deserves shrewd planning.

236 *colour*: pretext; justification.

237 *meet*: Fitting.

238 *were*: Would be.

239 *still*: Continually.

240 *The commons haply rise to save his life*: Cf. 28–30, and
see the quotation from Hall in the headnote to this
scene.
   haply: Perhaps.
   rise: In rebellion.

241 *but trivial argument*: Only insubstantial evidence.

242 *mistrust*: Suspicion.

247 *Say as you think, and speak it from your souls*: Proverbial.

248 *all one*: Just the same as if.
   empty: Hungry.

249 *kite*: Scavenging hawk, frequently seen in Elizabethan
London.

251 *So*: If so.

252–3 *were't not madness . . . the fold*: Proverbial: 'Give not
the fox the sheep to keep.'

253 *surveyor*: Guardian.

254–6 *Who being . . . executed*: The guilt of someone who has
been charged as a cunning killer would be foolishly
disregarded by a too rapid examination based on the
fact that he has not carried out his plans.

255 *idly posted over*: Foolishly disregarded (due to being
hurried over).

256 *executed*: Accomplished.

259 *chaps*: Jaws.

260 *reasons*: Arguments. Some editors emend this to
'treasons', but the whole point is that Gloucester cannot

be proved to have committed treason and so the peers have to resort to giving the weak King trivial arguments as justification for their animosity.

261 *stand on quillets*: Insist upon subtle legal arguments.

262 *gins*: Traps.

264 *So*: So long as.

264–5 *that is good . . . deceit*: Proverbial: 'To deceive the deceiver is no deceit.'

265 *mates*: Checkmates; finishes off.

267 *except*: Unless.

269 *that*: To show that.

272 *be his priest*: Kill him (literally 'perform the last offices for him'; a proverbial phrase).

274 *take due orders for*: (1) Make arrangements to procure; (2) prepare yourself to be.

275 *censure well*: Give your approval of.

276 *And I'll provide his executioner*: Some editors see a contradiction between this line and the First Murderer's words at III.2.1–2: *Run to my lord of Suffolk; let him know | We have dispatched the Duke as he commanded.* However, all the Cardinal is saying in 273–7 is that he wants the murder carried out more quickly than Suffolk's metaphorical way of speaking implies. Suffolk (277) agrees that expedition is necessary and so accepts the Cardinal's offer to supply him immediately with an assassin to do the deed. This is also the sense of Q1's version: *Suffol. Let that be my Lord Cardinals charge & mine. | Car. Agreed, for hee's already kept within my house.* Later, at 326, the Cardinal underlines his working together with Suffolk on the murder.

277 *tender so*: Am so solicitous over.

281 *It skills not greatly who impugns our doom*: It does not matter much who questions our decision.
     Post: Messenger.

282–329 *Great lords . . . for Ireland*: Cf. Hall:

It was not enough the realm of England this season thus to be vexed and unquieted with the business of Normandy, but also a new rebellion began in Ireland, to the great

displeasure of the King and his Council; for repressing
whereof Richard Duke of York, with a convenient number
of men, was sent thither as lieutenant to the King, which
not only appeased the fury of the wild and savage people
there, but also got him such love and favour of the country
and the inhabitants that their sincere love and friendly
affection could never be separated from him and his lineage.

282 *amain*: At full speed.
283 *signify*: Report.
     up: In arms.
285 *rage*: Outrage.
     betime: Promptly.
287 *being green, there is great hope of help*: Proverbial: 'A
     green wound is soon healed.'
     green: Fresh; new.
288 *breach*: Outbreak.
     craves: Requires.
     expedient: Speedy.
291 *meet*: Appropriate; proper.
     lucky ruler: Successful governor. York is being ironical
     because of Somerset's lack of success in France; see
     the quotation in the note to 87–92.
293 *far-fet*: Far-fetched; deeply evolved.
297 *betimes*: Sooner.
299 *staying there so long*: Temporizing.
300 *charactered*: Inscribed (accented on the second syllable).
301 *Men's flesh preserved so whole*: Unwounded men.
302–3 *this spark will prove . . . feed it with*: Proverbial.
304 *still*: Quiet.
306 *happily*: Perhaps.
308 *And, in the number, thee that wishest shame*: Cf. 'Evil be
     to him that evil thinks', the motto of the Order of the
     Garter.
     in the number: Among them.
310 *uncivil kerns*: Uncivilized, primitively armed Irish infantry.
311 *temper clay*: Moisten the ground.
314 *hap*: Fortune.
320 *take order for*: Arrange.

321 *charge*: Duty.

322 *return we to*: Let us get back to the subject of.

325 *break off*: Let us conclude.

326 *event*: Business.

328 *Bristow*: Bristol.

331 *Now . . . or never*: Proverbial.
     steel: Harden.
     fearful: Timid.

332 *misdoubt*: Suspicion; mistrust.

333 *that*: That which.

335 *keep*: Live.
     mean-born: Of lowly birth.

338 *dignity*: The position of kingship.

340 *tedious*: Laboriously intricate.

342 *packing*: On a journey.

343–4 *you but warm the starvèd snake . . . hearts*: The allusion
     is to the Aesop fable in which a man is stung by a snake
     which he had placed next to his chest to protect it from
     the cold; cf. the proverb 'to nourish a viper in one's
     bosom'.

343 *starvèd*: Stiff with cold.

347 *You put sharp weapons in a madman's hands*: Proverbial.

349–54 *I will stir up . . . mad-bred flaw*: Cf. Hall: 'to set open the
     flood-gates of these devices it was thought necessary
     to cause some great commotion and rising of people
     to be made against the King; so that, if they prevailed,
     then had the Duke of York and his complices their
     appetite and desire'.

350 *Shall*: Which shall.

351 *fell*: Ferocious.

352 *circuit*: Crown.

354 *mad-bred*: Produced by madness.
     flaw: Squall.

355–9 *And, for a minister . . . Mortimer*: Cf. Hall:

     . . . because the Kentishmen be impatient in wrongs, dis-
     daining of too much oppression and ever desirous of new
     change and new-fangleness, the overture of this matter was
     put first forth in Kent; and to the intent that it should not be

known that the Duke of York or his friends were the cause
of the sudden rising, a certain young man of a goodly stature
and pregnant wit was enticed to take upon him the name of
John Mortimer, although his name were John Cade, and not
for a small policy, thinking that by that surname the line and
lineage of the assistant house of the Earl of March, which
were no small number, should be to him both adherent and
favourable.

355 *minister*: Agent.

358 *commotion*: Uprising.

359 *Under the title of John Mortimer*: For Mortimer's con-
    nection with the Crown, see Genealogical Table 2 and
    II.2.34–52. For Jack Cade's fictional descent, see
    IV.2.127–37.

360 *In Ireland . . . Cade*: The connection between Cade and
    the Irish wars may have been suggested by Holinshed's
    note: 'John Cade . . . an Irishman, as Polychronicon
    saith.'

362 *till that*: Until. ('That' was often added after words
    such as 'if', 'after', 'when'.)
    darts: Arrows. A contemporary account of the Irish
    kerns notes that they were armed with 'darts and short
    bows'.

363 *porpentine*: Porcupine.

365 *Morisco*: Morris dancer. The morris dance in Elizabethan
    England was apparently a good deal wilder than its
    modern counterpart, often involving play with weapons.

366 *as he his bells*: As the morris dancer shakes the bells
    attached to his shins.

367 *shag-haired*: Rough-haired.

372 *For that John Mortimer, which now is dead*: Sir John
    Mortimer died by execution in 1424, after several years
    in prison, for urging his cousin Edmund Mortimer's
    claim to the throne on the grounds that Richard II had
    recognized him as heir presumptive in 1398. He has a
    long conversation with the Duke of York about his
    lineage and claim in *Part I*, II.5.

372 *For that*: Because.

375 *affect*: Favour; are inclined to.

376 *taken*: Captured.

378 *moved him to those arms*: Incited him to take up arms against the King.

379 *great like*: Most likely.

380 *strength*: Troops.

381 *reap the harvest which that rascal sowed*: Proverbial: 'One sows, another reaps.'

III.2

The scene is located in a room in the Cardinal's house in Bury St Edmunds. The chief source is Hall:

The Duke [of Gloucester] the night after his imprisonment was found dead in his bed and his body showed to the lords and commons, as though he had died of a palsy or imposthume; but all indifferent persons well knew that he died of no natural death but of some violent force. Some judged him to be strangled; some affirm that a hot spit was put in at his fundament; other write that he was stifled or smouldered between two feather beds. After whose death, none of his servants . . . were put to death: for the Marquess of Suffolk, when they should have been executed, showed openly their pardon, but this doing appeased not the grudge of the people, which said that the pardon of the servants was no amends for murdering of their master.

0 *Enter two Murderers . . . Gloucester*: In Q1 Gloucester is killed onstage: *Then the Curtaines being drawne, Duke Humphrey is discouered in his bed, and two men lying on his brest, and smothering him in his bed. And then enter the Duke of Suffolke to them.*

2 *dispatched*: Done away with; killed.
 as he commanded: See the note to III.1.276.

3 *to do*: To do again (so that we might refrain from doing it).

6 *dispatched this thing*: Taken care of this business.

8 *well said*: Well done.

9 *venturous*: Bold; daring.

11 *laid fair*: Rearranged (so as to look normal after being upset in the struggle; see note to 0).

14 *Exeunt Murderers*: In F Suffolk enters with the royal
   party after exiting with the murderers after 14. It is
   obviously more sensible for him to remain on stage
   after the murderers leave, as in Q1; see the list of stage
   directions in An Account of the Text.

15 *straight*: Immediately.

17 *If*: Whether.
   publishèd: Publicly proclaimed.

18 *presently*: At once.

20 *straiter*: More severely.

21 *of good esteem*: Worthy to be believed.

22 *approved in*: Proved guilty of.
   practice: Conspiracy; plotting.

24 *faultless may condemn a noble man*: May condemn a good
   and innocent man. In view of the King's attitude to
   Gloucester the reading *noble man* should be retained as
   in F rather than changed to 'nobleman' as in most editions.

25 *acquit him*: Exonerate himself.

26 *Meg*: F has *Nell*; cf. similar variations at 79, 100 and
   120, for which see Emendations in An Account of the
   Text. Referring to Margaret as Eleanor must have been
   Shakespeare's oversight in his manuscript, as such as
   error could not have survived in a theatre prompt book.

30 *forfend*: Forbid.

31 *tonight*: Last night.

34 *Rear up*: Raise; support.
   wring him by the nose: To restore him to consciousness.

40 *right now*: A moment ago.
   raven's note: The cry of the raven was reputed to herald
   death; cf. the proverb 'The croaking raven bodes death'
   and *Macbeth*, I.5.36–8.

41 *bereft*: Robbed me of.
   vital powers: Human faculties (believed to be necessary
   to sustain life).

43 *hollow*: Deceitful.

44 *first-conceivèd*: Previously perceived.

48 *baleful*: Deadly.

49 *murderous tyranny*: The tyranny of murder.

52 *basilisk*: A fabulous monster which killed with a glance,

thought to be hatched by a serpent or toad from the egg of a cock.

54 *shade*: Shadow.

56 *rate*: Berate.

59 *for*: As for.

60 *heart-offending*: Doing injury to the heart.

61 *blood-consuming sighs*: It was believed that every sigh drew a drop of blood from the heart.

63 *with*: Because of.

65 *deem*: Judge.

66 *hollow*: False.

67 *judged*: Believed that.

69 *my reproach*: Blame of me.

72 *woe*: Sorry.

76 *like the adder waxen deaf*: A proverbial saying referring to the belief that the adder resisted the snake charmer by stopping one ear with its tail and pressing the other to the ground; cf. Psalm 58:4–5.
   waxen: Grown.

80 *statue*: Pronounced trisyllabically.

82 *wrecked*: Shipwrecked.

83 *awkward*: Adverse.
   bank: Shore.

84 *clime*: Country.

85 *well forewarning*: Truthfully predicting.

87 *unkind*: Cruel.

89 *he*: Aeolus, god of the winds.
   loosed them forth: Released them from.
   brazen: Powerful. The allusion is to the bronze walls surrounding the isle of Aeolus in Homer's *Odyssey*.

94 *pretty vaulting*: Attractively rising and falling.

97 *splitting*: Capable of splitting ships.
   sinking sands: Sands which cause ships to sink.

99 *Because*: In order that.
   thy flinty heart, more hard than they: Proverbial.

100 *perish*: Destroy.

101 *ken*: Make out (a nautical term).

105 *earnest-gaping*: Eagerly peering.

110 *fair England's view*: The view of fair England.

111 *be packing*: Be gone.
    heart: The heart-shaped ornament.
112 *spectacles*: Instruments of vision.
113 *Albion*: England.
    wishèd: Longed-for.
114 *tempted*: Induced.
115 *The agent of thy foul inconstancy*: The allusion is to
    Suffolk's acting as Henry's proxy in the marriage
    contract arrangements.
116 *witch*: Bewitch. F's reading, *watch*, makes no sense in
    the context.
116–18 *as Ascanius did . . . burning Troy*: In Virgil's *Aeneid* Venus
    transforms Cupid into the shape of Aeneas's son,
    Ascanius, so that he can bewitch Dido, Queen of
    Carthage, with stories of his father's exploits at the
    siege of Troy.
117 *madding*: Becoming mad.
    unfold: Disclose; relate.
119 *witched*: Bewitched.
    him: Aeneas, who deserted Dido and caused her
    suicide.
120 *I can no more*: My strength fails me; I am capable of no
    more.
122–9 *It is reported . . . of his death*: Cf. Hall: 'When the rumour
    of the Duke's death was blown through the realm,
    many men were suddenly appalled and amazed for
    fear; many abhorred and detested the fact, but all
    men reputed it an abominable cruelty and a shameful
    tyranny.'
126 *want*: Lack.
127 *his revenge*: Revenge for his death.
128 *spleenful mutiny*: Angry uprising.
129 *order*: details; manner.
132 *breathless*: Lifeless.
133 *comment then upon*: Then explain.
135 *rude*: Uncivilized.
136 *Thou that judgest all things*: Cf. Genesis 18:25: 'the
    judge of all the world'.
    stay: Restrain.

139 *suspect*: Suspicion.

141 *Fain*: Gladly.

     chafe: Warm.

     paly: Bloodless; colourless.

145 *unfeeling*: Incapable of feeling.

146 *mean obsequies*: Insignificant funeral rites.

147 *earthy image*: Reflection of what he was, now only dead earth.

152 *my life in death*: What my own corpse will be like when I am dead.

154 *King*: Christ.

     took our state upon Him: Became human. Cf. the Collect for Christmas Day: 'to take our nature upon him'.

155 *To free us from His Father's wrathful curse*: Cf. Galatians 3:13: 'Christ hath redeemed us from the curse of the law . . .'

157 *thrice-famèd*: Very famous.

159 *instance*: Evidence; proof.

160–78 *See how the blood . . . were probable*: Like Q1's opening stage direction for this scene (see note to 0), this passage is clear about the manner of Gloucester's death. Contrast the variety of possibilities suggested by Hall in the passage quoted in the headnote.

160 *settled*: Congealed.

161 *a timely-parted ghost*: The body of a person who has died naturally.

162 *meagre*: Emaciated.

163 *Being all descended to*: (The blood) having all drained into.

164 *Who*: The heart.

165 *the same*: The blood.

     aidance: Assistance.

166 *Which*: The blood.

171 *upreared*: Standing on end.

172 *abroad displayed*: Spread wide apart.

175 *rugged*: Shaggy; bristling.

176 *lodged*: Beaten flat; levelled.

178 *were probable*: Would be sufficient proof.

183 *keep*: Protect; guard.

184 *'Tis like*: It is likely.

185 *well seen*: Easily perceived.

186 *belike*: Perhaps.

187 *timeless*: Untimely.

189 *fast*: Close.

191 *puttock*: Kite.

192 *was dead*: Came to be killed.

198 *with ease*: As a result of disuse.

199 *scourèd*: Washed clean.

202 *faulty in*: Guilty of.
     Exit Cardinal: F has no exit for the Cardinal and so the
     direction of Q1 has been adopted. It is appropriate that
     the Cardinal should leave the stage earlier than the
     general exit at 299, perhaps after displaying signs of
     incipient sickness and guilt after seeing Gloucester's
     corpse.

204 *contumelious*: Slanderous.

205 *controller*: Critic; detractor.

212 *blameful*: Guilty.

213 *stern*: Rough.
     churl: Peasant.
     stock: Tree trunk.

214 *graft*: Grafted.
     slip: Cutting (with possibly a pun on *slip* meaning 'moral
     lapse').

216 *bucklers*: Shields; protects.

217 *deathsman*: Executioner.

218 *Quitting thee*: Getting rid for you.

219 *that*: Except for the fact that.

221 *passèd*: Just uttered.

224 *fearful homage*: Cowardly submission.

225 *hire*: Payment (that is, death).

226 *Pernicious*: Destructive.

227 *waking*: Awake.

228 *presence*: Royal presence.

230 *cope with thee*: Meet you in combat.

232-3 *What stronger breastplate ... just*: Proverbial: 'Innocence
     bears its defence with it.' Cf. also Ephesians 6:14: 'the
     breastplate of righteousness'.

234 *naked*: Unprotected.
     locked up in steel: Buckled in his armour.
237–8 *Your wrathful weapons drawn | Here in our presence*:
     Drawing a sword in the king's presence was a serious
     political offence; cf. *Part I*, I.3.46.
243–7 *the commons . . . lingering death*: Cf. Hall:

> They . . . began to make exclamation against the Duke of
> Suffolk, affirming him to be the only cause of the delivery
> of Anjou and Maine, the chief procurer of the death of the
> good Duke of Gloucester, the very occasion of the loss of
> Normandy, the most swallower up and consumer of the
> King's treasure . . . So that the Duke was called in every
> man's mouth a traitor, a murderer, a robber of the King's
> treasure, and worthy to be put to most cruel punishment.

At the parliament at Leicester later in the same year

> the commons of the lower house, not forgetting their old
> grudge, beseeched the King that such persons as assented to
> the release of Anjou and deliverance of Maine might be
> extremely punished and tormented; and to be privy to this
> fact, they accused as principal the Duke of Suffolk.

244 *straight*: Immediately.
250 *mere instinct of*: Pure impulse toward. *instinct* is accented
     on the second syllable.
251 *opposite intent*: Antagonistic purpose.
252 *contradict your liking*: Oppose your wishes.
253 *forward in*: Insistent upon.
256 *charge*: Give orders that.
257 *In pain*: Under penalty.
     dislike: Displeasure.
258 *strait*: Strict.
259 *Were there a serpent seen, with forkèd tongue*: This was
     probably suggested by Hall's description of Suffolk as
     'the abhorred toad . . . of the realm'.
262 *suffered*: Allowed to remain.
     harmful: Dangerous.

263 *mortal worm*: Deadly snake.

265 *whe'er*: Whether.

266 *fell*: Cruel; fierce.

268 *his worth*: More worthy than he.

269 *bereft*: Deprived.

271 *like*: Probable (ironical).

    hinds: Boors; peasants.

274 *quaint*: Skilful.

277 *sort*: Gang; crew.

    tinkers: A general term for vagabonds.

281 *cited*: Urged.

284 *Mischance*: Disaster.

285–97 *And therefore by His majesty . . . for thy life*: Cf. Hall:

> When King Henry perceived that the commons were thus
> stomached and bent against the Queen's darling, William
> Duke of Suffolk, he plainly saw that neither glozing would
> serve nor dissimulation could appease the continual clamour
> of the importunate commons. Wherefore to begin a short
> pacification in so long a broil . . . he . . . banished and put
> in exile the Duke of Suffolk, as the abhorred toad and
> common nuisance of the realm of England, for the term of
> five years, meaning by this exile to appease the furious rage
> of the outrageous people; and, that pacified, to revocate him
> into his old estate as the Queen's chief friend and counsellor.

287 *breathe infection in this air*: Pollute the air of England
    with his breath.

289 *gentle*: Noble.

290 *Ungentle*: Unkind.

293 *said*: Pronounced it.

299 *great*: Important.

    Exeunt all but the Queen and Suffolk: Neither F nor Q1
    contains any direction for getting Gloucester's body
    off the stage. Presumably at this point the bed would
    be carried offstage by attendants or perhaps curtains
    would be drawn round it. The same bed would be
    needed for the Cardinal's death in the next scene.

303 *There's two of you, the devil make a third*: Proverbial:

'There cannot lightly come a worse except the devil come himself.'

304 *tend upon*: Follow; dog.

306 *heavy*: Mournful.

310 *the mandrake's groan*: Numerous superstitions attached themselves to this plant with the root shaped like a human body, including the belief that it shrieked when pulled out of the ground, which caused the hearer to die or go mad.

311 *searching*: Cutting.

312 *curst*: Malignant; savage.

313 *fixèd*: Gritted.

315 *lean-faced Envy in her loathsome cave*: Envy was conventionally depicted as thin; cf. Arthur Golding's translation of Ovid's *Metamorphoses* (1567):

> She goes me straight to Envy's house, a foul and
>   irksome cave,
> Replete with black and loathly filth and stinking like
>   a grave . . .
> There saw she Envy sit within, fast gnawing on the
>   flesh . . .
> Her lips were pale, her cheeks were wan, and all her
>   face was swart;
> Her body lean as any rake.

318 *distract*: Mad.

319 *curse and ban*: Excommunicate.

322 *daintiest*: Most delicious drink.

323 *cypress trees*: Trees associated with death; cf. *Twelfth Night*, II.4.50–51: 'Come away, come away, death, | And in sad cypress let me be laid.'

324 *prospect*: Sight; view.
    basilisks: See the note to 52.

325 *smart*: Painful.
    lizards' stings: The lizard was confused with the snake and thus thought to be poisonous.

326 *frightful*: Terrifying.

327 *boding*: Presaging death.

screech-owls: See the note to I.4.17.

make the consort full: Complete the group of musicians.

331 *overchargèd*: Overloaded.

333 *ban*: Curse.

leave: Stop.

342 *woeful monuments*: Memorials of grief (that is, tears).

344–5 *thou mightst think upon these by the seal, | Through whom a thousand sighs are breathed for thee*: You might think about my lips, which left their imprint on your hand and between which a thousand sighs pass for you.

346 *know my grief*: Feel the full weight of my sorrow.

347 *but surmised*: Only guessed at.

348 *surfeits*: Overeats.

want: Lack of food.

349 *repeal thee*: Get you recalled from exile. See the quotation from Hall in the note to 285–97.

350 *Adventure*: Risk.

363 *several*: Separate; distinct.

365 *joy*: Enjoy.

366 *Vaux*: Sir William Vaux was a zealous Lancastrian who died at the battle of Tewkesbury in 1471.

368 *signify*: Report.

371 *That makes him gasp, and stare, and catch the air*: Note the similarity to Warwick's description of Gloucester's death in 160–76.

373 *Sometime*: From time to time.

375–6 *whispers to his pillow . . . soul*: Proverbial: 'Take counsel of your pillow.'

376 *overchargèd*: Overburdened (with guilt).

379 *heavy*: Sorrowful.

381 *an hour's poor loss*: The loss of a few hours of life (since the Cardinal, at his age, did not have long to live anyway).

382 *Omitting*: Forgetting about.

384 *southern clouds*: Commonly considered to be carriers of rain and fog.

contend: Rival; compete.

385 *earth's increase*: Growth of crops.

387 *by me*: At my side.

393 *dug*: Nipple; breast.
394 *Where*: Whereas.
   from: Out of.
399 *lived*: Would live.
   Elysium: In Virgil, the region of Hades which housed
   the souls of the blessed after death; in Greek mythology,
   an island in the western ocean where the souls of the
   virtuous lived in perfect happiness.
400 *but to die in jest*: Not to die at all.
401 *From*: Absent from.
402 *befall what may befall*: Proverbial: 'Come hap what hap
   may.'
403 *fretful corrosive*: Gnawing painful remedy.
404 *deathful*: Deathly; mortal.
407 *Iris*: The messenger of Juno, queen of the gods.
   find thee out: Locate you.
409 *into*: In.
   cask: Casket; jewel-box.
411 *splitted bark*: Ship split in two.
   sunder we: Do we separate.

III.3

The scene is located in a bedchamber in the Cardinal's
house. His death occurred historically in 1447, a year
after Gloucester's murder. Hall's account differs
radically from Shakespeare's. Instead of the play's
picture of a guilty villain making a dreadful end, the
chronicle stresses the regrets of a very worldly prelate
for a life dedicated to power and material possessions:

During these doings Henry Beaufort, Bishop of Winchester
and called the rich Cardinal, departed out of this world and
was buried at Winchester. This man was son to John of Gaunt,
Duke of Lancaster, descended of an honourable lineage but
born in baste [bastardy], more noble of blood than notable
in learning, haught in stomach . . . rich above measure of all
men and to few liberal, disdainful to his kin, and dreadful to
his lovers, preferring money before friendship, many things
beginning and nothing performing. His covertise insatiable
and hope of long life made him both to forget God, his

prince, and himself in his latter days. For Dr John Baker, his privy counsellor and his chaplain, wrote that he, lying on his death bed, said these words: 'Why should I die, having so much riches? If the whole realm would save my life, I am able either by policy to get it or by riches to buy it. Fie, will not death be hired, nor will money do nothing? When my nephew of Bedford died, I thought myself half up the wheel; but when I saw my other nephew of Gloucester deceased, then I thought myself able to be equal with kings, and so thought to increase my treasure in hope to have worn a triple crown. But I see now the world faileth me, and so I am deceived, praying you all to pray for me.'

0 *Enter the King . . . in bed*: The Q1 stage direction gives an indication of how the scene was staged by means of the use of a curtained area: *Enter King and Salsbury, and then the Curtaines be drawne, and the Cardinall is discouered in his bed, rauing and staring as if he were madde.*

4 *So*: If.

10 *whe'er*: Whether.

15 *Comb down his hair . . . it stands upright*: Cf. III.2.171.

16 *lime-twigs*: See the note to I.3.86.

18 *of*: From.

19 *eternal mover*: God.

21 *meddling*: Interfering in the lives of men.

24 *the pangs of death*: Cf. 2 Samuel 22:5 and Psalm 18:3.
    grin: Bare his teeth (in pain).

25 *pass*: Die; pass on.

28 *make signal*: Make a gesture; give a sign.

30 *argues*: Gives evidence of.

31 *Forbear to judge*: Cf. Matthew 7:1.
    we are sinners all: Cf. Romans 3:23.

32 *Close up his eyes*: The traditional last office for the dead.
    curtain: Of the bed; see the Q1 opening stage direction for this scene, quoted in the note to 0.

33 *meditation*: Prayer.

IV.1

The scene takes place on the coast of Kent. It is developed from Hall's account of Suffolk's death:

But fortune would not that this flagitious person should so escape; for when he shipped in Suffolk, intending to be transported into France, he was encountered with a ship of war appertaining to the Duke of Exeter, the Constable of the Tower of London, called the *Nicholas of the Tower*. The captain of the same bark with small fight entered into the Duke's ship, and perceiving his person present brought him to Dover road, and there on the one side of a cock boat caused his head to be stricken off, and left his body with the head upon the sands of Dover, which corpse was there found by a chaplain of his and conveyed to Wingfield College in Suffolk and there buried. This end had William de la Pole, first Duke of Suffolk, as men judge by God's punishment; for above all things he was noted to be the very organ, engine, and deviser of the destruction of Humphrey, the good Duke of Gloucester, and so the blood of the innocent man was with his dolorous death recompensed and punished.

0 *Alarum. Fight at sea. Ordnance goes off*: The Q1 stage direction gives an indication of how the sound effects were managed in the Elizabethan theatre: *Alarmes within, and the chambers be discharged, like as it were a fight at sea.*

1 *blabbing*: Revealing secrets; tell-tale.
  remorseful: Conscience-stricken.

2 *crept into the bosom*: Proverbial.

3 *jades*: Wretched horses (but here referring to the dragons that drew the chariot of the night, driven by Hecate).

5 *flagging*: Drooping.

6 *Clip*: Embrace; drape over. The sense is not altogether satisfactory and there is some case to be made for the emendations 'Clepe' ('summon') and 'Clap' ('bang on').
  their: The graves'.

7 *contagious*: The night was considered unhealthy.

8 *of our prize*: From the vessel we have captured.

9 *pinnace*: Small, single-masted boat.
  the Downs: An anchorage off the Kent coast, sheltered by the Goodwin Sands; see the quotation from Hall in the headnote to this scene.

10 *make*: Agree to.

11 *discoloured*: Thus to be discoloured (with their blood).

13 *make boot of*: Make a profit out of.

   this: The Second Gentleman.

16 *lay down*: Lose.

18 *think you much*: Do you consider it a heavy burden.

19 *port*: Demeanour; standard of living.

22 *counterpoised*: Set against; balanced.

24 *straight*: At once.

25 *laying the prize aboard*: Boarding the captured ship.

28 *rash*: Precipitate in your decision.

29 *George*: A badge depicting St George on horseback slaying the dragon, the insignia of the Order of the Garter which Suffolk had received in Henry V's reign.

30 *Rate me*: Set my ransom; value me.

33 *Thy name*: Walter, pronounced 'Water'.

34 *cunning man*: Astrologer. The reference is to the prophecy at I.4.31–2.

   calculate my birth: Cast my horoscope.

36 *bloody-minded*: Bloodthirsty.

37 *Gualtier*: The French equivalent of 'Walter'.

   sounded: Pronounced.

41 *sell revenge*: For ransom.

42 *arms*: Coat of arms.

   torn and defaced: Obliterated (the heraldic witness to disgrace).

48 *Jove sometime went disguised, and why not I*: This line, not in F, is adopted from Q1; it is obviously necessary in view of 49.

50 *Obscure and lousy swain, King Henry's blood*: In F this line is assigned to the Lieutenant, which is obviously an error due to the misplacement of the speech-prefix for Suffolk.

   lousy: Scurvy; contemptible. Some editors emend to 'lowly'; but the word was probably adopted from Hall's account of Cade's slaughter of his old acquaintances lest 'they should blaze and declare his base birth and lousy lineage'.

   King Henry's blood: This claim is false; Suffolk's mother

was a remote cousin of Henry VI.

52 *jaded*: Base; ignoble.

54 *Bare-headed*: Hatless (as a sign of respect).

foot-cloth mule: Mule carrying the ceremonial hangings used to drape a horse.

55 *happy*: Fortunate.

shook my head: Gave you a signal of approval.

57 *trencher*: Dinner plate.

board: Dining table.

59 *crest-fallen*: Humble.

60 *abortive*: Untimely and outrageous.

61 *voiding lobby*: Antechamber where petitioners waited for entrance to a lord's presence.

62 *duly*: Dutifully.

63 *writ in thy behalf*: Provided you with letters of recommendation.

64 *charm*: Silence.

riotous: Unrestrained.

65 *forlorn swain*: Wretched fellow.

67 *blunt*: Unable to inflict harm.

69 *for thy own*: Because of the risk of losing your own head.

70–71 *Poole! Sir Poole! Lord!* | *Ay, kennel*: The punning is on (1) Pole; (2) pool; (3) Sir Pol (parrot); (4) poll. Various attempts have been made to explain the unsatisfactory nature of the speeches in both F and Q1 at this point. Q1 indicates that the point of the exchange lies in the punning possibilities of Suffolk's name, which F appears to exploit more fully. Therefore both texts have been conflated for the reading of this edition.

71 *kennel*: Open gutter in a street for drainage.

sink: Sewer.

74 *For swallowing*: Lest it swallow. This was one of the accusations against Suffolk; cf. Hall: 'the . . . swallower up and consumer of the King's treasure'.

77 *Against*: Faced with.

senseless: Unfeeling.

grin: Grimace.

78 *again*: In return.

79 *the hags of hell*: The Furies.

80 *to affy*: To affiance; to wed.

81 *worthless king*: Reignier, Margaret's father; see the note
to I.1.109–10.

83 *policy*: Political trickery (which the Elizabethans
associated with Machiavelli).

84 *Sylla*: Lucius Cornelius Sulla (138–78 BC) was notorious
for his ruthless persecution of his enemies when he was
dictator of Rome.
overgorged: Overfed.

85 *gobbets*: Chunks of raw flesh.
thy mother: (1) Rome (in Sulla's case); (2) England (in
Suffolk's case).

87 *revolting*: Rebellious.
thorough: Because of.

88 *Picardy*: There is no record in the chronicles of a
rebellion in Picardy.

95 *a guiltless king*: Richard II, whose usurpation and
murder by Bolingbroke began the Lancastrian dynasty.

98 *Advance*: Raise high.
half-faced sun: Both Edward III and Richard II sported
the device of a sun's rays emerging from the tops of
clouds.

99 *Invitis nubibus*: In spite of clouds.

100 *The commons here in Kent are up in arms*: This is a link
between York's plans at III.1.348–59 and IV.2.

105 *drudges*: Slaves.

108 *Bargulus*: A Balkan pirate referred to by Cicero in
De Officiis, which was used as an Elizabethan school
textbook.

109 *Drones suck not eagles' blood, but rob beehives*: Two pieces
of popular Elizabethan imaginative natural history are
alluded to here: (1) a drone or beetle that was reputed
to lodge under the eagle's wing and suck its blood; (2)
the drone bee was believed to devour the honey of the
hive.

111 *By*: By the hand of.

112 *remorse*: Compunction.

113 *Ay, but my deeds shall stay thy fury soon*: This line is

adopted from Q1, where it is the reply to the equivalent of line 112 here. Suffolk clearly continues to act high-handedly until the Lieutenant assures him he is about to act, at which Suffolk introduces his mission for the Queen as a new argument against his death. The Lieutenant's reply is to give the order to Whitmore in the form that recalls the prophecy mentioned by Suffolk in 33–5. The arrangement of the type in F suggests that a complete line may have dropped out during imposition.

113 *stay*: Prevent; stop.

114 *of message*: As messenger.
France: The French King.

115 *waft*: Transport by water.

118 *Pene gelidus timor occupat artus*: Cold fear almost completely seizes my limbs. This is not a classical quotation; it appears to be made up of a recollection of two passages: '*subitus tremor occupat artus*' (Virgil, *Aeneid*, VII.446); '*gelidos pavor occupat artus*' (Lucan, *Pharsalia*, I.246).
Pene: Latin for 'almost'. F's *Pine* makes no sense. The suggestion '*Perii*' ('I am lost') is attractive, but it is difficult to see how it could have produced *Pine* palaeographically or typographically.

122 *fair*: Politely; courteously.

126 *suit*: Pleading.

129 *sooner dance upon a bloody pole*: Rather be displayed upon a bloodstained staff. The heads of traitors were so displayed on the gatehouse ramparts of London Bridge. There is also a pun on 'Pole'.

130 *uncovered*: With hat in hand (as a sign of respect).
vulgar groom: Low-born servant.

133 *Hale*: Drag.

136 *Besonians*: Scoundrels (from the Italian '*bisogno*', meaning 'need').

137–8 *A Roman . . . Tully*: Cicero (*Tully*; 106–43 BC) was actually killed on the orders of Mark Antony 'by Herennius, a centurion, and Popilius Laena, tribune of the soldiers' (Thomas North's translation (1579) of Plutarch's *Life of Cicero*).

137 *sworder*: Gladiator.

    banditto: Bandit.

138–9 *Brutus' bastard hand* | *Stabbed Julius Caesar*: According to Suetonius, Brutus was Caesar's illegitimate son, an erroneous belief based on the fact that Brutus's mother became Caesar's mistress after her husband's death.

139–40 *savage islanders* | *Pompey the Great*: Pompey was killed in Egypt in 48 BC by a group of his own former centurions who had gone into the service of King Ptolemy. The idea that he was murdered by *islanders* may have come from the belief that he was slain on Lesbos or from Plutarch's reference to the Egyptians being incited to the murder by 'Theodotus, that was born in the Isle of Chios'.

140 *by*: At the hands of.

142 *pleasure*: Desire that.

147 *body*: As well as the severed head; see IV.4.

149 *living*: While he was living.

IV.2

The location of the scene is Blackheath. In the chronicles Cade inflames his mob with the possibility of seizing the government and abolishing taxes, and leads them to Blackheath to present their supplications to the King, who sends an army against them, as Hall describes:

This captain . . . promising them that if, either by force or policy, they might once take the King, the Queen, and other their counsellors into their hands and governance that they would honourably entreat the King and so sharply handle his counsellors that neither fifteens should hereafter be demanded nor once any impositions or tax should be spoken of. These persuasions, with many other fair promises of liberty (which the common people more affect and desire, rather than reasonable obedience and due conformity), so animated the Kentish people that they, with their captain above named, in good order of battle (not in great number) came to the plain of Blackheath, between Eltham and Greenwich. . . . Whereupon the King assembled a great army and marched toward them, which had lain on Blackheath by the space of seven days.

Shakespeare combines these events with those which
happened after Cade had retired to Sevenoaks and
defeated the Staffords (for which see note to 105–13).
Some details of the scene are taken from Grafton's
account of the Peasants' Revolt led by Wat Tyler against
Richard II in 1381.

0 *George Bevis and John Holland*: There is some evidence
that these may be the names of the contemporary actors
who played these roles originally.

1 *lath*: Piece of wood. A 'dagger of lath' was one of the
stock properties of the Vice character in the Tudor
morality plays.

2 *up*: In arms.

3 *They have the more need to sleep now then*: Holland takes
the meaning of *up* to be 'out of bed'.

4 *dress*: (1) Put on clothes; (2) put in good order.

5 *turn it*: (1) Renew it (by turning the material inside
out, as in repairing an old coat); (2) turn it upside down
socially.

5–6 *set a new nap upon it*: (1) Improve the surface texture
of its cloth; (2) reform it.

7 *threadbare*: (1) Worn out; (2) decadent; bankrupt.

8–18 *it was never . . . we be magistrates*: Cf. Grafton's account
of the words of John Ball (whom Grafton calls Wall)
in the 1381 revolt: 'that there be no villains nor
gentlemen, but that we be all as one and that the lords
be no greater than we be'.

8 *merry world*: Good times.

9 *came up*: Became fashionable.

10 *regarded*: Valued; highly estimated.

12 *think scorn*: Think it beneath their dignity; disdain.
go in: Wear.
leather aprons: Worn by workmen.

15–16 *Labour in thy vocation*: Proverbial: 'Everyone must
labour in his own vocation.'

18 *magistrates*: Rulers.

19 *hit it*: Made a good point; hit the nail on the head.

20 *brave*: Noble.
hard: Calloused (with manual work).

22 *Wingham*: A village near Canterbury.

24 *dog's leather*: Inferior leather, used for making gloves.

29 *Argo*: Therefore (a corrupted form of the Latin *ergo*).
    their thread of life is spun: A proverbial phrase alluding
    to the Fate in Greek mythology who spun the threads
    of human existence.

31 *so termed of*: Thus named after.

32 *of*: On account of (with a quibble on *of* in 31).
    cade of: Cask containing five hundred.

33 *For*: Because.
    fall: A pun with the Latin '*cadere*', meaning 'to fall'.

37 *a Mortimer*: See the note to III.1.355–9.

38 *bricklayer*: The quibble is on 'mortar' / *Mortimer*.

41 *Lacys*: Lacy was the family name of the Earls of Lincoln.

43 *laces*: A pun with *Lacys*.

44 *travel*: (1) Journey as a pedlar; (2) work ('travail').

45 *furred pack*: (1) Backpack made from animal skins with
    the fur on the outside; (2) female genitals.
    washes bucks: (1) Takes in laundry; (2) frees men from
    their cuckoldry (by giving them the opportunity to be
    even with their wives).

46 *honourable*: Noble.

47 *field*: The quibble is on the heraldic term for the
    background against which the devices are set in a coat
    of arms.

48 *under a hedge*: The phrase 'hedge-born' was a collo-
    quialism for the lowest kind of lineage.

49 *cage*: A small prison in the marketplace where vagrants
    and minor criminals were exhibited.

51 *'A must needs*: He must be.
    valiant: The allusion is to the term 'valiant beggar',
    meaning one capable of work to whom it was illegal
    to give alms.

54 *whipped*: The punishment for vagabonds and minor
    criminals.

56–7 *of proof*: (1) Badly worn; (2) impenetrable (like good
    armour).

59 *burnt i'th'hand*: Branded with a 'T' on the hand (a
    common punishment for a thief).

61 *reformation*: Change of government.

62–3 *the three-hooped pot shall have ten hoops*: A wooden drinking-cup holding a quart was bound by three equidistantly placed hoops; so that Cade's reform will make it three-and-a-half times as large as it is.

63 *small*: Weak.

64 *All the realm shall be in common*: This detail seems to have been taken from Grafton, where John Wall (Ball) says 'Ah, good people, matters go not well to pass in England in these days, nor shall not do until everything be common.'

in common: Community land.

Cheapside: The chief market area of Elizabethan London, just east of St Paul's Churchyard; under Cade's rule it will be empty and deserted.

65 *palfrey*: Riding horse.

go to grass: Graze.

69 *on my score*: At my expense (literally 'on my tavern bill').

70 *livery*: Uniform indicating the household in which a servant is employed.

72 *let's kill all the lawyers*: Cf. Grafton: 'and so kept on their way toward London . . . spoiling and burning as they went all the houses that belonged to any man of law'; and Holinshed's account of the 1381 revolt: 'destroy first the great lords of the realm and after the judges and lawyers'.

76 *undo*: Bring about the ruin of.

77 *the bee's wax*: The sealing wax used on legal documents.

did but seal once to a thing: Put my name only once to a bond.

79 *Clerk*: Town clerk.

80–102 *The clerk of Chartham . . . his neck*: Cf. Holinshed's account of the 1381 revolt:

The rage of the commons was universally such as it might seem they had generally conspired together to do what mischief they could devise. As, among sundry other, what wickedness was it to compel teachers of children in grammar schools to swear never to instruct any in their art? Again,

could they have a more mischievous meaning than to burn
and destroy all old and ancient monuments and to murder
and dispatch out of the way all such as were able to commit
to memory either any new or old records? For it was
dangerous among them to be known for one that was learned
and more dangerous if any man were found with a penner
and inkhorn at his side; for such seldom or never escaped
from them with life.

80 *Chartham*: A village near Canterbury; but it is possible
   that 'Chatham' was intended.

81 *cast accompt*: Do arithmetic.

83 *setting of boys' copies*: Giving schoolboys passages to
   copy out. A village clerk often doubled as the schoolmaster.

85 *H'as*: He has.
   a book . . . with red letters: A book, perhaps a textbook
   or almanac, with certain capitals printed in red.

86 *conjurer*: Necromancer.

87 *make obligations*: Draw up legal bonds.
   court-hand: The handwriting used in legal documents,
   as opposed to the secretary-hand used for ordinary
   business purposes.

88 *proper*: Handsome.
   of: On.

91 *Emmanuel*: That is, 'God with us'; often written at the
   opening of letters and legal documents.

95 *a mark*: A personal mark, used by illiterates in place of
   a signature.

104 *particular*: Private (a quibble on *general* in 103).

105–13 *Fly, fly, fly . . . have at him*: In the chronicles the events
   of this scene take place in Kent:

The subtle captain, named Jack Cade, intending to bring the
King farther within the compass of his net, broke up his camp
and retired backward to the town of Sevenoaks in Kent . . .
and made his abode. The Queen, which bare the rule, being
of his retreat well advertised, sent Sir Humphrey Stafford,
Knight, and William, his brother, with many other gentlemen,

to follow the chase of the Kentishmen, thinking that they had fled; but verily they were deceived, for at the first skirmish both the Staffords were slain and all their company shamefully discomfited.

105 *Sir Humphrey Stafford*: The Staffords were descendants of one of William the Conqueror's favourite captains.

105–6 *his brother*: William Stafford.

109 *'a*: He.

110 *No*: An answer to the negative implied in *but a*.

111 *presently*: Immediately.

113 *have at*: Let me get at.

114 *hinds*: Peasants.

115 *Marked*: Destined.

116 *groom*: Low fellow.

117 *revolt*: Turn again to your previous condition.

120–26 *As for these ... gardener*: Cf. John Wall (Ball) in Grafton:

> What have we deserved or why should we be thus kept in servitude and bondage? We be all come from one father and one mother, Adam and Eve. Wherefore can they say ... that they are greater lords than we be? ... They are clothed in velvet and chamlet furred richly, and we be clad with the poorest sort of cloth. They have their wines, spices, and fine bread, and we have the drawing out of the chaff and drink water.

120 *pass*: Care.

125 *a shearman*: A member of the cloth trade, the man who sheared the excess nap from cloth during its manufacture.

126 *Adam was a gardener*: This is a reflection of John Wall's theme in his sermon, which included (in Holinshed's account) the couplet 'When Adam delved and Eve span, who was then the gentleman?'

132 *question*: Problem.

142 *credit*: Believe.
    drudge: Mean fellow.

145 *Jack Cade, the Duke of York hath taught you this*: Hall's remarks about Cade's preparation for the rebellion

may lie behind this line: 'This captain [was] not only suborned by teachers but also enforced by privy schoolmasters', with 'the intent that it should not be known that the Duke of York or his friends were the cause of the sudden rising'.

148–9 *Henry the Fifth . . . French crowns*: The reference is to Henry V's success in the French wars.

    went to span-counter: Played at the game of span-counters (a pastime in which the players used metal discs, normally employed for counting money, to see who could toss his 'counter' so that it fell within a 'span' of his competitors').

149 *French crowns*: (1) French gold coins, *écus*; (2) bald heads (caused by venereal disease); (3) the French King's coronet.

151 *Lord Say*: James Fynes (d. 1450) was one of Henry V's captains in France. He was made Sheriff of Kent in 1437 and Warden of the Cinque Ports in 1447. At the time of his death at Cade's hands he had recently been dismissed as Treasurer of England; see the note to IV.4.19.

153 *mained*: Crippled (with a pun on *Maine*).

154 *fain to go*: Obliged to walk.

    puissance: Power.

155–6 *gelded the commonwealth*: The phrase is from Cicero's *De Oratore*: '*Nolo dici morte Africani castratam esse rem publicam.*'

167 *up*: In arms.

170 *for*: To serve as an.

173–4 *'tis for liberty.* | *We will not leave one lord, one gentleman*: Cf. Holinshed, where John Ball urges the rebels to destroy lords so that 'there should be an equality in liberty, no difference in degree of nobility, but a like dignity and equal authority in all things brought among them'.

175 *clouted shoon*: Patched-up shoes.

179 *in order*: Lined up in formation.

179–80 *out of order*: Disorderly; rebellious.

IV.3

The scene is located in Blackheath. See the note to IV.2.105–13.

6–7   *the Lent shall . . . lacking one*: Cade clearly intends to reward Dick for his services by giving him a special slaughtering privilege during an extended Lent. Under Elizabeth's statute of 1563, slaughtering of animals was forbidden during the Lenten period so that more fish might be sold. It is not so clear what Dick's licence will amount to. F's phrase *for a hundred lacking one*, resembling as it does the usual legal formula for a lease, may mean that Dick's tenure of his right will be for ninety-nine years; or it may mean that Dick may provide meat for up to ninety-nine people who had dispensation from the Lenten statute; or it may be the number of beasts he will be allowed to slaughter. Q1 has . . . *licence to kil for foure score and one a week*, which suggests that perhaps the number of the butcher's customers is meant.

9   *Sir Humphrey Stafford's coat of mail*: The phrase *This monument of the victory will I bear* requires this direction, which is based on information found in the chronicles. Hall has 'When the Kentish captain, or the covetous Cade, had thus obtained victory and slain the two valiant Staffords, he apparelled himself in their rich armour'; but Holinshed and Fabyan have additional details of Cade's prize: 'Sir Humphrey's brigandine, set full of gilt nails' (Holinshed); and 'the knight's apparel . . . his briganders, set with gilt nail, and his salade and his gilt spurs' (Fabyan).

10   *monument*: Memorial; testimony to success (Sir Humphrey Stafford's armour).

12–13   *we will have the Mayor's sword borne before us*: There is no evidence in the chronicles for this; but in Grafton's account of Wat Tyler, the rebel is killed with the Mayor's sword.

14–15   *If we mean . . . the prisoners*: Cf. Hall: 'the lusty Kentish captain, hoping on more friends, brake up the gaols of the King's Bench and Marshalsea and set at liberty a swarm of gallants both meet for his service and apt for his enterprise'. Another source is Grafton's account of the 1381 rebellion, in which the mob 'set all the prisoners of Newgate and the Counters at large'.

14 *do good*: Prosper; succeed.

16 *Fear not that*: Do not worry about our not doing that.

IV.4

The location of the scene is the royal palace in London. Historically Cade's supplication was submitted to the King before the Staffords were sent against the rebels; otherwise the material for this scene is derived from Hall.

2 *fearful*: Full of terror.

5 *throbbing*: Grief-stricken.

7–8 *the rebels' supplication*: See the headnote to IV.2.

9 *I'll send some holy bishop to entreat*: Although this is not dramatized in the play, it is exactly the step Henry takes in the chronicles: 'to whom [Cade] were sent by the King the Archbishop of Canterbury and Humphrey Duke of Buckingham' (Hall).

entreat: Enter into negotiations.

11–13 *I myself . . . Will parley with Jack Cade*: This is what Cade demands in the chronicles: 'These lords found him sober in communication, wise in disputing, arrogant in heart, and stiff in his opinion, and by no ways possible to be persuaded to dissolve his army except the King in person would come to him' (Hall). Richard II faced the Peasants' Revolt personally in 1381.

12 *cut them short*: Destroy them; cut short their lives.

16 *wandering planet*: Influential star (an astrological term).

17 *enforce*: Force.

them: Suffolk's murderers.

18 *That*: Who.

19 *Lord Say, Jack Cade hath sworn to have thy head*: In the chronicles, although Lord Say is not specified in Cade's supplication to the King, he is one of the 'traitors' that surrendered Maine, whose punishment Cade demands; and so the King agrees, 'to the intent to appease the furious rage of the inconstant multitude, to commit the

Lord Say, Treasurer of England, to the Tower of London' (Hall).

27 *Southwark*: At this time Southwark was a suburb of the city.

32–3 *His army is a ragged multitude | Of hinds and peasants*: Cf. Hall: 'a multitude of evil, rude, and rustical persons'.

37 *false caterpillars*: Treacherous parasites (in the garden of the state).

38 *graceless*: Deprived of divine grace.
they know not what they do: Cf. Luke 23:34.

39 *retire to Killingworth*: Cf. Hall:

The King, somewhat hearing and more marking the sayings of this outrageous losel, and having daily report of the concourse and access of people which continually resorted to him, doubting as much his familiar servants as his unknown subjects . . . departed in all haste to the castle of Killingworth in Warwickshire.

Killingworth: Kenilworth.

40 *power*: Army.

42 *appeased*: Rendered peaceful.

51 *rascal people*: This is a phrase from Hall.

53 *spoil*: Despoil; loot.

59–60 *The trust I have . . . resolute*: Proverbial: 'Innocence is bold.'

IV.5

The scene is based upon the chronicles' account of the events during Cade's capture of London immediately after the King's departure for Kenilworth Castle.

0 *Lord Scales*: Thomas de Scales, seventh Baron (1399?–1460), was a staunch Lancastrian; he was hated by Londoners and was murdered by boatmen and his body cast ashore at Southwark. Cf. Hall: 'The King . . . departed in all haste . . . leaving only behind him the Lord Scales to keep the Tower of London.'
the Tower: The Tower of London. The upper acting area used here would probably have been the same as that employed for I.4.

3–4 *they have won the bridge, killing all those that withstand them*: In Hall, Cade, 'being advertised of the King's absence, came first into Southwark, and there lodged at the White Hart . . . But after that he entered into London and cut the ropes of the drawbridge.' After Matthew Gough had been sent against the rebels, his troops attempted to 'keep the bridge'; but the rebels 'ran with great haste to open their passage where between both parts was a fierce and cruel encounter . . . for the multitude of the rebels drove the citizens from the stoops at the bridge foot . . . and got the drawbridge'.

4–6 *The Lord Mayor . . . you shall command*: This is based on an event in the chronicles after Cade had already entered London:

The wise Mayor and sage magistrates of the city of London, perceiving themselves neither to be sure of goods nor of life well warranted, determined with fear to repel and expulse this mischievous head and his ungracious company. And because the Lord Scales was ordained keeper of the Tower of London with Matthew Gough . . . they purposed to make them privy both of their intent and enterprise. The Lord Scales promised them his aid, with shooting of ordnance, and Matthew Gough was by him appointed to assist the Mayor and the Londoners, because he was both of manhood and experience greatly renowned and noised.

8 *assayed*: Tried.

9 *Smithfield*: This was an open area outside the city wall, north-west of St Paul's Church. It is not associated with Cade in the chronicles, but was the site of Richard II's meeting with the peasants and of Wat Tyler's death in 1381.

gather head: Raise forces.

IV.6

The location of the scene is Cannon Street, London; see note to 2.

0 *and strikes his staff on London Stone*: Cf. Hall: 'he

entered into London and cut the ropes of the drawbridge, striking his sword on London Stone, saying
"Now is Mortimer lord of this city", and rode in every
street like a lordly captain.'

2 *London Stone*: This city landmark is a block of ancient
stone, thought to be of Roman origin, still to be
found in Cannon (then Canwick) Street.

3 *of the city's cost*: At the expense of the city.

the Pissing Conduit: This was a small conduit in
Cheapside near the junction of Threadneedle Street
and Cornhill.

5–6 *henceforward it shall be . . . Mortimer*: Cf. Hall:

He also put to execution in Southwark divers persons, some
for infringing his rules and precepts because he would be
seen indifferent, other he tormented of his old acquaintance
lest they should blaze and declare his base birth and lousy
lineage, disparaging him from his usurped surname of
Mortimer.

14 *set London Bridge on fire*: During the fight between
Matthew Gough's troops and Cade's at London Bridge,
'the multitude of the rebels drove the citizens from the
stoops at the bridge foot to the drawbridge and began
to set fire in divers houses' (Hall).

14–15 *burn down the Tower too*: In the chronicles there is no
attack by the rebels on the Tower; but see IV.5.8.

IV.7

The scene is located in Smithfield and is based upon
Hall's account of the deaths of Lord Say and Sir James
Cromer:

And upon the third day of July [Cade] caused Sir James
Fynes, Lord Say and Treasurer of England, to be brought
to the Guildhall of London and there to be arraigned, which,
being before the King's Justices put to answer, desired to be
tried by his peers for the longer delay of his life. The captain,
perceiving his dilatory plea, by force took him from the
officers and brought him to the Standard in Cheapside, and

there, before his confession ended, caused his head to be cut off and pitched it on a high pole, which was openly borne before him through the streets. And this cruel tyrant, not content with the murder of the Lord Say, went to Mile End and there apprehended Sir James Cromer, then Shrieve of Kent and son-in-law to the said Lord Say, and him, without confession or excuse heard, caused there likewise to be beheaded and his head to be fixed on a pole; and with these two heads this bloody butcher entered into the city again and in despite caused them in every street to kiss together, to the great detestation of all the beholders.

o *Matthew Gough is slain*: Cf. Hall's account of the fight for London Bridge:

Yet the captains . . . fought on the drawbridge all the night valiantly; but in conclusion the rebels got the drawbridge and drowned many and slew John Sutton, Alderman; and Robert Heysand, a hardy citizen; with many other, beside Matthew Gough, a man of great wit, much experience in feats of chivalry, the which in continual wars had valiantly served the King and his father in the parts beyond the sea.

all the rest: The royal forces.

1–2 *Now go some . . . them all*: These details probably come from Fabyan's account of the 1381 Peasants' Revolt:

They . . . came unto the Duke of Lancaster's palace standing without the Temple Bar, called Savoy, and spoiled it was therein, and after set it upon fire and burnt it . . . Then they entered the city and searched the Temple and other Inns of Court and spoiled their places and burnt their books of law.

1 *the Savoy*: This house was the London residence of the Duke of Lancaster and was destroyed in the Wat Tyler rebellion of 1381. It was rebuilt in 1505.

2 *th'Inns of Court*: Centres of the London legal profession.

4 *lordship*: Lord's domain.

5–6 *the laws of England may come out of your mouth*: Wat Tyler made a similar pronouncement, 'putting his hand to his lips, that within four days all the laws of England should come forth of his mouth' (Holinshed).

11–12 *Burn all the records of the realm*: See note to 1–2.

14 *biting*: Severe (with a quibble on *teeth*).

16 *all things shall be in common*: See note to IV.2.64.

17–18 *the Lord Say, which sold the towns in France*: See the note to IV.4.19.

19 *one-and-twenty fifteens*: This was an enormously exaggerated rate of taxation (see the note to I.1.131). In Hall one of Cade's promises to the mob is that 'neither fifteens should hereafter be demanded nor once any impositions or tax should be spoken of'.

20 *subsidy*: A special tax assessment.

22 *thou say, thou serge . . . thou buckram lord*: *say* was a kind of silk cloth resembling serge; and *buckram* was a coarse linen fabric stiffened with glue, used for making crude cloth articles for the stage. A *buckram lord* was a 'stuffed lord'.

23 *point-blank*: Easy range.

25 *Basimecu*: Anglicizing of the French '*baise mon cul*', meaning 'kiss my arse'.

26 *Be it known unto thee by these presence*: The standard formula in legal documents and proclamations; but Cade confuses 'presents' (meaning 'documents') with 'presence' (meaning 'in the company of the King').

27–8 *the besom that . . . filth*: Proverbial.

28 *besom*: Broom; sweeping-brush.

29–30 *corrupted the youth*: See note to IV.2.80–102.

32 *the score and the tally*: This was a method of keeping account of debts among the common people. A slat of wood was notched to indicate the sums of money owed, then split down the centre, one half being given to the debtor and the other half to the creditor.

printing: This is anachronistic; the first printing press was not operated in England until William Caxton's in 1474, twenty-four years after Cade's rebellion.

33 *used*: Practised.

33–4 *the King his crown and dignity*: Cade is again using a standard legal formula.

34 *paper-mill*: Paper was available in England from the beginning of the fourteenth century; but the first English paper-mill on record is John Tate's at Hereford in 1495–6.

35 *usually*: Habitually.

39 *answer*: Acquit themselves of; explain away.

40–41 *because they could not read, thou hast hanged them*: The allusion is to the practice of excusing criminals from hanging if they claimed 'the benefit of the clergy', which right was proved by their demonstrating that they could read Latin.

41–2 *only for*: This could mean 'were it not for'; but considering Cade's view of learning, the phrase probably means 'for that reason alone'.

43 *foot-cloth*: See the second note to IV.1.54. As it is a sign of wealth to use a foot-cloth, Cade finds it an especially blameworthy practice.

46–7 *hose and doublets*: Breeches and short-coats (with no top covering, such as a cloak).

52 *bona terra, mala gens*: Latin for 'a good country, an evil people'. This was apparently applied by Italians to England.

55–6 *Kent, in the Commentaries Caesar writ,* | *Is termed the civilest place of all this isle*: Arthur Golding in his 1564 translation of Caesar's *De Bello Gallico* has 'Of all the inhabitants of this isle the civilest are the Kentish folk'.

56 *civilest*: Most civilized.

58 *liberal*: Refined; polished.

59 *void of*: Without.

62 *favour*: Leniency.

64 *exacted at your hands*: Taken from you in taxes.

66 *clerks*: Men of learning; scholars.

67 *my book preferred me to the King*: My own learning enabled me to rise in the King's service.

72 *parleyed unto*: Spoken with; negotiated with.

73 *behoof*: Welfare.

74 *in the field*: During battle.

75 *Great men have reaching hands*: Proverbial: 'Kings have long arms.'

   reaching: Far-reaching.

78 *for watching*: With staying awake (to work).

81 *sitting*: On the judicial bench.

   determine: Decide.

   causes: Law-suits.

83 *hempen caudle*: This was a cant term for the hangman's rope.

   caudle: A potion for an invalid, composed of sweet warm gruel and wine. F's reading, *Candle*, is probably due to the fact that 'u' and 'n' were almost indistinguishable in Elizabethan handwriting.

83–4 *the help of hatchet*: The assistance of the executioner's axe. The emendation 'pap with a hatchet' (a proverbial term describing the physical punishment of children for their own good) is attractive, as it balances *hempen caudle* metaphorically.

86 *provokes me*: Makes me tremble.

87 *as who*: Like one who.

91 *affected*: Loved.

95 *guiltless bloodshedding*: Spilling the blood of innocent people.

98 *remorse*: Pity.

99 *an it be but*: If only.

100 *a familiar*: A personal devil he can call on to serve him, because he has sold his soul to Satan.

101 *a*: In.

102 *presently*: At once.

103–4 *Sir James Cromer*: Son-in-law to Lord Say.

109 *it fare with your departed souls*: Your souls be treated after you are dead.

114–15 *pay to me her maidenhead*: The allusion is to the *droit de seigneur*, the feudal right of the lord of the manor to spend the first night with the bride of any of his vassals.

115–16 *hold of me in capite*: Own the property that has been granted to them directly by me as their head (with possibly a pun on *maidenhead*).

117 *free*: Liberal (with their sexual favours).

as heart can wish: Cf. Psalm 73:7.

118–19 *take up commodities upon our bills*: Obtain goods on credit (with possibly a pun on *bills* meaning 'weapons').

121 *brave*: Splendid.

125 *spoil*: Pillage.

127 *maces*: Public dignitaries' symbols of office.

IV.8

The location of the scene is Southwark. It is based upon the final stages of Cade's rebellion in the chronicles, where two prelates perform the task Shakespeare gives to Buckingham and Clifford in the play. According to Hall,

The Archbishop of Canterbury, being then Chancellor of England, and for his surety lying in the Tower of London, called to him the Bishop of Winchester, which also for fear lurked at Holywell. These two prelates, seeing the fury of the Kentish people, by reason of their beating back, to be mitigate and minished, passed the river of Thames from the Tower into Southwark, bringing with them under the King's Great Seal a general pardon unto all the offenders, which they caused to be openly proclaimed and published. Lord, how glad the poor people were of this pardon . . . and how they accepted the same, in so much that the whole multitude, without bidding farewell to their captain, retired the same night, every man to his own home, as men amazed and stricken with fear . . . a proclamation [was] made that whosoever could apprehend the said Jack Cade should have for his pain a thousand marks.

0 *retreat*: Signal for the recall of forces.

1 *Fish Street . . . Saint Magnus' Corner*: In Hall, during the final battle for London 'for some time the Londoners were beat back to the stoops at St Magnus' Corner; and suddenly again the rebels were repulsed and driven back to the stoops in Southwark'. Fish Street is on the north side of the Thames, across London Bridge from Southwark; and at the end of the street nearest the bridge stands St Magnus' Church.

2 *parley*: Signal to request a conference.

4 *Old Clifford*: Thomas de Clifford (1414–55) was the eighth Baron Clifford and Baron of Westmorland. He fought with the Duke of Bedford in France in 1435 and went to the relief of Calais in 1452 and 1454. He was slain at the first battle of St Albans.

8 *pronounce*: Make proclamation of.
free: Generous.

12 *rebel*: The F reading, *rabble*, may have been due to the compositor misreading 'rebbel' in the manuscript.

13 *embrace*: Welcome; accept.

17 *Shake he his weapon*: Make a sign of martial defiance.

19 *brave*: Arrogant; audacious.

22–3 *therefore . . . that*: To that end; for that purpose.

23 *the White Hart*: After the King's flight to Kenilworth, Cade, 'being advertised of the King's absence, came first into Southwark, and there lodged at the White Hart' (Hall).

24 *given out*: Surrendered; given up.

25 *ancient*: Former; historically sanctioned.

26 *recreants*: Traitors.
dastards: Cowards.

29–30 *For me, I will make shift for one*: Proverbial: 'Every man for himself.'

30 *make shift*: Manage; look out.

36 *meanest of*: Lowest in birth among.

38 *the spoil*: Looting.

40 *at jar*: At odds with one another.

41 *fearful*: Frightened.

42 *make a start*: Suddenly rouse themselves to action (a hunting term).

43 *broil*: Conflict.

45 *Villiago*: Villain (from the Italian '*vigliocco*', meaning 'coward').

46 *base-born*: Of low origin.
miscarry: Encounter disaster; die.

47 *stoop unto*: Humble yourselves to beg for.

51 *God*: With God.

52 *À Clifford*: (Rally) to Clifford (a cry like 'À Talbot',

which was made famous during the French campaigns;
see *Part I*, I.1.128).

55 *hales*: Draws; drags.

57 *lay their heads together*: Conspire; plot (a proverbial
phrase).

57–8 *surprise me*: Capture me.

59 *despite*: Spite.

60 *have through the very midst of you*: I'll get through the
centre of your party.

63 *Exit*: The Q1 direction makes the action explicit: *He
runs through them with his staffe, and flies away.*

66 *a thousand crowns*: A very large sum of money in gold.
The chronicles' 'thousand marks' is more realistic.

67 *mean*: Method; means.

IV.9

The scene is located in Kenilworth Castle, whence the
King retired at the end of IV.4. It is based upon scattered events spread over two years in the chronicles
following Cade's death.

0 *on the terrace*: Of Kenilworth Castle; the upper acting
area was probably that used in I.4 and IV.5.

1 *joyed*: Enjoyed.

4 *made a king at nine months old*: Henry was born at
Windsor on 6 December 1421; Henry V died at
Vincennes on 31 August 1422.

8 *surprised*: Taken prisoner.

9 *him*: Himself.
with halters about their necks: This display is thought to
have been based upon the anonymous play *Edward III*,
where the citizens of Calais surrender in the same way
in 1346.

10–22 *He is fled . . . the King*: In the chronicles the King hears
of Cade's death when he has left Kenilworth – cf. Hall:

After this commotion the King himself came into Kent and
there sat in judgement upon the offenders, and if he had not
mitigated his justice with mercy and compassion more than five
hundred by the rigour of his law had been justly put to execution; but he considered both their fragility and innocency and

how they with perverse people were seduced and deceived, and
so punished the stubborn heads and delivered the ignorant and
miserable people, to the great rejoicing of all his subjects.

10 *powers*: Soldiers.

12 *Expect*: Await.

doom: Judgement; sentence.

13 *set ope thy everlasting gates*: Cf. Psalm 7:9.

14 *entertain*: Receive favourably.

17 *still*: Always.

18 *infortunate*: Unfortunate.

19 *unkind*: Cruel.

21 *several*: Separate; different.

countries: Localities; districts.

23–7 *Please it . . . in proud array*: In 1451 York 'returned out
of Ireland and came to London in the parliament time,
where he deliberately consulted with his especial
friends, as John Duke of Norfolk, Richard Earl of
Salisbury, and Lord Richard, his son, which after was
Earl of Warwick' (Hall).

23 *advertisèd*: Informed (accented on the second syllable).

25–6 *with a puissant . . . kerns*: In Hall, York, 'with help of
his friends, assembled a great army in the Marches of
Wales'.

25 *power*: Army.

26 *gallowglasses*: Irish soldiers who were armed with axes
and usually fought on horseback.

stout: Strong; valiant.

kerns: See the note to III.1.310.

28–30 *And still proclaimeth . . . a traitor*: In the chronicles York
uses his enmity towards Somerset as a cover for his
aspirations to the Crown: 'After long consultation it
was thought expedient first to seek some occasion and
pick some quarrel to the Duke of Somerset, which ruled
the King, ordered the realm, and most might do with
the Queen' (Hall).

28 *still*: Continually.

comes along: Advances.

29 *arms*: Armed men.

30 *whom he terms a traitor*: Cf. Hall, who has the Yorkists
    'protesting and declaring . . . that their intent was for
    the revenging of great injuries done to the public
    wealth'.

31–5 *Thus stands my state . . . second him*: Cf. Hall: 'The
    King, much astonished with this sudden commotion'.

31 *state*: Situation.

33 *calmed*: Becalmed. The F reading, *calme*, was probably
    due to 'd' being misread as 'e' by the compositor; the
    two letters were very similar in Elizabethan hand-
    writing.
    with: By.

34 *But now*: Just now.

35 *second*: Support.

37 *of*: For.

38–40 *Tell him I'll send . . . from him*: In the chronicles Henry
    leads an army to Blackheath and, once the two forces
    are drawn up against each other, the King sends the
    Bishops of Winchester and Ely to negotiate with York,
    who (according to Hall), informs the prelates that

> his intent was to remove from him [the King] certain evil-
> disposed persons of his Council . . . amongst whom he chiefly
> named Edmund Duke of Somerset, whom if the King would
> commit to ward to answer to such articles as against him
> should in open parliament be both proponed and proved, he
> promised not only to dissolve his army and dispatch his people
> but also offered himself like an obedient subject to come to
> the King's presence . . . The King . . . granted their requests,
> caused the Duke of Somerset to be committed to ward . . . till
> the fury of the people were somewhat assuaged and pacified.

38 *Duke Edmund*: Edmund Beaufort, Duke of Somerset.

44 *be not too rough in terms*: Do not use violent language.

45 *brook*: Endure.

46 *deal*: Negotiate.

47 *redound unto*: Turn out for.

49 *yet*: Up till now.

IV.10
The location of the scene is the garden of Iden's house.
It is Shakespeare's invention that Cade dies on the
property of the ideal English country gentleman. The
scene is based on a brief passage in Hall, which describes
Cade's death:

John Cade, desperate of succours which by the friends of the
Duke of York were to him promised, and seeing his company
thus without his knowledge suddenly depart, mistrusting the
sequel of the matter, departed secretly in habit disguised into
Sussex; but all his metamorphosis or transfiguration little
prevailed. For, after a proclamation made that whosoever
could apprehend the said Jack Cade should have for his pain
a thousand marks, many sought for him, but few espied him,
till one Alexander Iden, Esquire of Kent, found him in a
garden, and there in his defence manfully slew the caitiff
Cade, and brought his dead body to London, whose head
was set on London Bridge.

0 *Enter Cade*: Q1 makes the action explicit but gives Iden
   an accompanying band of men: *Enter Iacke Cade at one
   doore, and at the other maister Alexander Eyden and his
   men, and Iacke Cade lies downe picking of hearbes and
   eating them.* See note to 37–8.
2 *famish*: Starve.
4 *is laid for me*: Is circulated with orders for my arrest.
5–6 *if I might have . . . longer*: Proverbial: 'No man has a
   lease of his life.'
6 *stay*: Remain in hiding.
8 *sallet*: Salad.
8–9 *cool a man's stomach*: (1) Satisfy a man's hunger; (2)
   pacify a man's anger.
10 *sallet*: A light circular helmet.
11 *brown bill*: Bronzed pike, usually carried by constables.
14 *Alexander Iden*: A Kentish gentleman, Iden came
   from a very ancient Sussex family and married Lord
   Say's daughter when she was widow of Sir James
   Cromer.

15 *turmoilèd*: harassed; worried.

18 *and*: And is.

20 *envy*: Malice.

21 *Sufficeth that*: It is enough for me that what.
   maintains my state: Supports my way of life.

22 *well pleasèd*: With the alms they have received.

23 *lord of the soil*: Landowner (a legal term).

24 *stray*: Stray animal (which a landowner had the right
   to impound should he capture it on his land).
   fee-simple: An estate belonging to a *lord of the soil* and
   his heirs for ever.

27 *eat iron like an ostrich*: A proverbial saying, based on
   the popular belief that ostriches ate iron for the sake
   of their digestion. Cade means 'be killed with my sword
   in your stomach'.

29 *rude companion*: Rough fellow.
   whatsoe'er: Whoever.

34 *brave*: Defy; insult.
   saucy terms: Insolent language.

35 *best*: Most noble.

36 *broached*: Let flow (like wine out of a cask).
   beard thee: Defy you to your face.

37 *eat*: Eaten.

37–8 *and thy five men*: This may be a sneering reference to
   the small size of Iden's estate and his few retainers.
   However, some editors take it literally and cause Iden
   to enter, as he does in Q1, with a group of men. In F
   Iden is clearly alone, the function of the scene being
   to show Cade the anarchist overcome by a single representative of a stable society.

38 *as dead as a door-nail*: Proverbial.

42 *odds*: Advantage.

44 *outface me with thy looks*: Stare me down.

45 *Set*: Compare.

47 *truncheon*: Stout club (Iden's leg).

49 *heavèd*: Raised up.

51 *answers words*: Matches your words.

52 *report what speech forbears*: Perform what words refuse
   to utter.

53 *complete*: Accomplished.

55 *burly-boned*: Hulking.

    chines: Roasts.

56 *God*: This is Q1's reading. The F reading, *Ioue* (that is, 'Jove'), was probably due to a change made in accordance with the law of 1606 against blasphemy in plays.

64 *monstrous*: Unnatural (in rebelling against his king).

65 *hallow*: Bless.

66 *hang thee*: Have you hung.

    o'er my tomb when I am dead: The arms of a warrior were sometimes used to decorate his tomb.

69 *emblaze*: Publicly proclaim (as the device on a herald's coat announces the quality of a nobleman).

75 *her that bare thee*: Your mother.

78 *headlong*: Unceremoniously.

V.1

Historically the scene is located in the fields between Dartford and Blackheath. Shakespeare uses events some of which the chronicles place in 1452–3 on York's return from Ireland and some in 1455 immediately prior to the first battle of St Albans.

0 *colours*: Flag-bearers.

1–11 *From Ireland thus . . . France*: Cf. Hall: 'the Duke of York, which sore gaped and more thirsted for the superiority and pre-eminence, studied, devised, and practised all ways and means by the which he might attain to his pretensed purpose and long-hoped desire'.

4 *entertain*: Welcome; receive favourably.

5 *sancta majestas*: Sacred majesty. The phrase is from Ovid's *Ars Amatoria*: '*Sanctaque maiestas et erat vener- abile nomen | Vatibus et largae saepe dabantur opes*' ('Sacred was the majesty and venerable the name of the poet; and often lavish wealth was given them').

7 *gold*: The golden royal regalia.

8 *give due action to my words*: Accompany my words with the appropriate action.

9 *Except*: Unless.

    balance: Give due weight to.

it: Action.

10 *have I*: As I have.

11 *toss*: Impale and bear aloft.

   flower-de-luce: Fleur-de-lis, the heraldic three-leafed lily of the French royal coat of arms.

12–47 *Whom have we . . . you wish*: In the chronicles it is two bishops who negotiate with York in 1452–3 rather than Buckingham. However, after hearing the King's promise to commit Somerset 'to ward', York 'dissolved his army, and broke up his camp, and came to the King's tent' (Hall).

13 *sure*: For certain.

18 *of these arms*: For these armed men.

21 *power*: Army.

23 *choler*: Wrath.

25 *abject terms*: Despicable words.

26–7 *like Ajax Telamonius . . . fury*: During the Trojan War the Greek hero Ajax, son of Telamon, became angry when Achilles' armour was awarded to Ulysses. As a result he was afflicted with a fit of insanity during which he attacked a flock of sheep before committing suicide.

27 *spend*: Vent.

30 *make fair weather*: Accommodate myself to the circumstances by pretending to be pleasant (proverbial).

32 *prithee*: Beg you to.

36–7 *to remove proud Somerset . . . state*: See the note to IV.9.28–30.

41–4 *The Duke of Somerset . . . my powers*: See the note to IV.9.38–40.

46 *Saint George's Field*: This open area, named after the church of St George the Martyr, which was nearby, lay between Southwark and Lambeth on the south side of the Thames and was used as an assembly ground for the London militia.

49 *Command*: Demand.

50 *pledges*: Hostages; guarantees.

   fealty: Loyalty to the Crown.

53 *use*: Call on for his use.

   so: Provided.

54 *kind*: Natural; correct.

55 *We twain will go into his highness' tent*: See note to 12–47.
   twain: Two.

62, 106 *monstrous*: Unnatural.

63 *discomfited*: Defeated.

64 *rude*: Uncivilized; unpolished.
   mean condition: Low rank.

72 *an't like*: If it please.

73 *degree*: Rank in society.

78–80 *Iden, kneel down . . . on us*: This episode may be
   based on the knighting of William Walworth, who
   slew Wat Tyler in 1381, as it is reported in Holinshed,
   or on a scene in the anonymous play *Jack Straw*, in
   which Walworth is knighted in a similarly abrupt
   manner.

79 *marks*: These were worth each about two thirds of a
   pound, although there were no specific coins of this
   denomination. A thousand marks is the amount
   mentioned as a reward for Cade's death in the chronicles, but *crowns* are specified at IV.8.66 and IV.10.26.

80 *will*: Command.

86 *front*: Confront.

87–92 *How now? . . . brook abuse*: Cf. Hall, where York visits
   the King after the dismissal of his army but, 'beside his
   expectation and contrary to the promise made by the
   King, he found the Duke of Somerset set at large and
   at liberty, whom the Duke of York boldly accused of
   treason, of bribery, oppression, and many other crimes'.

89 *be equal with*: Express exactly what is in.

92 *how hardly*: With what great difficulty.
   brook abuse: Endure deception.

95 *Which*: Who.

96 *doth not become*: Is not fit to wear.

97 *palmer's staff*: Carried by religious pilgrims and thus a
   sign of great piety.

98 *awful*: Awe-inspiring.

99 *gold*: Golden crown.

100 *Achilles' spear*: Proverbial. According to post-Homeric
   legend, the spear of Achilles was used to wound

Telephus, who was later cured by the application to the wound of rust from the spear itself.

101 *the change*: From *frown* to *smile* and vice versa.

103 *act*: Enact; enforce.

106–8 *O monstrous traitor . . . for grace*: Cf. Hall: 'The Duke of Somerset not only made answer to the Duke's objections but also accused him of high treason toward the King his sovereign lord, affirming that he with his fautors and complices had consulted together how to obtain the crown and sceptre of the realm.'

109 *Wouldst have me kneel*: In the chronicles at this point York is arrested only to be released and march again on London three years later in 1455, which event leads to the first battle of St Albans. Shakespeare here conflates the events of 1452–3 and 1455.

these: As York has already dismissed his troops (45–7), and his sons are not yet present with their forces, he probably gestures in the direction of the door where his sons are to enter.

110 *brook I bow a knee to man*: Bear that I should humble myself to anyone.

111 *sons*: Historically York's sons at the time of the first battle of St Albans were young children, Edward being thirteen and Richard three. See notes to 121.

112 *to ward*: Into custody.

113 *of my enfranchisement*: In the matter of my freedom.

114 *amain*: Quickly.

117 *Neapolitan*: The reference is to Margaret's being the daughter of Reignier, titular King of Naples.

118 *Outcast of Naples*: Reignier had never managed to take possession of the throne his father had held.

120 *bane*: Destruction.

121, 122 *Enter at one door . . . with an army*: The direction in Q1 parallel with these conveys the confrontation clearly: *Enter the Duke of Yorkes sonnes, Edward the Earle of March, and crook-backe Richard, at the one doore, with Drumme and soldiers, and at the other doore, enter Clifford and his sonne, with Drumme and souldiers, and Clifford kneeles to Henry, and speakes.*

121 *Enter . . . Edward*: This may have been suggested by the rumour reported by Hall after York had been imprisoned in 1452:

> While the Council treated of saving or losing of this dolorous Duke of York, a rumour sprang throughout London that Edward Earl of March, son and heir apparent to the said Duke, a young prince of great wit and much stomach, accompanied with a strong army of Marchmen, was coming toward London, which tidings sore appalled the Queen and the whole Council . . . The King's Council . . . set the Duke of York at liberty.

> *Edward*: He was born at Rouen in 1442. After defeating the Lancastrians at Towton he proclaimed himself king and was crowned Edward IV in 1461. He died in 1483. *Richard*: He was born at Fotheringay in 1452, and created Duke of Gloucester in 1461. Parliament proclaimed him Richard III in 1483, and he was slain at Bosworth Field in 1485.

122 *Young Clifford*: John de Clifford (1435?–1461), ninth Baron Clifford and Baron of Westmorland, was a strong Lancastrian. He was nicknamed 'The Butcher' after killing in cold blood the Earl of Rutland, the second son of York. He was slain six weeks after the second battle of St Albans.

123 *deny*: Refuse.

131 *Bedlam*: See the note to III.1.51.

132 *bedlam*: Crazy.
humour: Disposition.

135 *factious pate*: Rebellious head.

142 *glass*: Mirror.

143 *false-heart*: Treacherous.

144–7 *Call hither . . . to me*: Cf. Hall's description of York's reliance on the Nevilles: 'the Duke of York had fastened his chain between these two strong and robustious pillars'.

144 *stake*: The post to which the fighting bear was chained in the popular Elizabethan sport of bear-baiting.
two brave bears: The Nevilles, father and son, are so

referred to because the Warwick heraldic device was a
bear chained to a ragged staff, inherited from Warwick's
father-in-law, Richard Beauchamp.

146 *astonish*: Terrify.
    fell-lurking curs: Cruelly waiting dogs (which attacked
    the bear in bear-baiting).

149 *bearard*: Bear handler; bear-ward.

150 *baiting-place*: Bear-baiting pit.

151 *hot*: Angry.
    o'erweening: Overambitious; overreaching.

152 *Run back and bite, because he was withheld*: Proverbial:
    'A man may cause his own dog to bite him.'

153 *suffered*: Injured.
    with: By.

156 *oppose yourselves*: Undertake resistance.

157 *indigested*: Improperly formed. Richard of Gloucester's
    deformities are dwelt on in *Part III* and in *Richard III*.
    Cf. Hall:

    . . . he was small and little of stature, so was he of body
    greatly deformed, the one shoulder higher than the other, his
    face small, but his countenance was cruel and such that a man
    at the first aspect would judge it to savour and smell of malice,
    fraud, and deceit. When he stood musing he would bite and
    chew busily his nether lip, as who said that his fierce nature
    in his cruel body always chafed, stirred, and was ever unquiet.

158 *As crookèd in thy manners as thy shape*: All the chroni-
    clers and Shakespeare saw a symbolic relationship
    between Richard's twisted body and evil nature. See
    note to 157.

159 *heat you*: Make you sweat with fighting.
    anon: Soon.

165 *spectacles*: Eye-glasses (a sign of Salisbury's age).

167 *frosty*: White with age.

172 *abuse it*: Put it to bad use.

174 *That*: That is, *thy knee*.
    mickle: Much; great.

177 *repute*: Consider.

181 *dispense with*: Expect dispensation from.
    for: For breaking.
182 *swear*: Pledge oneself.
183 *greater sin to keep a sinful oath*: Proverbial: 'An unlawful
    oath is better broken than kept.'
187 *reave*: Bereave; rob.
188 *customed right*: The portion of her husband's estate
    which a widow has the right to under law.
191 *sophister*: Skilful arguer.
194 *I am resolved for death or dignity*: Cf. Hall:

> The Duke of York and his adherents, perceiving that neither
> exhortation served nor accusement prevailed against the Duke
> of Somerset, determined to revenge their quarrel and obtain
> their purpose by open war and martial adventure and no
> longer to sleep in so weighty a business.

    resolved for: Determined to possess.
    dignity: High place.
196 *You were best to*: You had better.
200 *burgonet*: A small, light Burgundian helmet.
201 *Might I but know thee by thy house's badge*: If I can
    recognize you by your family crest (during the battle).
202–3 *my father's badge . . . bear*: Actually the crest of his
    father-in-law; see note to 144.
204 *aloft*: On top of.
205 *cedar*: A tree associated with royalty because of its
    great height and strength.
207 *affright*: Terrify.
212 *complices*: Allies.
213 *in spite*: Spitefully.
215 *stigmatic*: Branded (with deformity).

V.2

> The location of the scene is the field of the first battle
> of St Albans (1455), and Shakespeare develops in terms
> of personalities some of the events of the battle. In the
> chronicles, York with Warwick, Salisbury and Lord
> Cobham leads his army towards London. On 20 May
> the King, accompanied by Somerset, Buckingham, Old

Clifford, and the Earls of Stafford and Northumberland, leads his forces from Westminster to St Albans, where they are trapped by York three days later.

0 *Enter Warwick*: In the chronicles the King sends messengers to York at one end of St Albans, commanding his obedience; meanwhile 'the Earl of Warwick with the Marchmen entered at the other gate of the town and fiercely set on the King's forward and them shortly discomfited' (Hall).

1 *of Cumberland*: One of the titles of the Cliffords.

2 *the bear*: See note to V.1.144.

4 *dead*: Dying.

8 *afoot*: On foot (without your horse).

9 *deadly-handed*: Murderous.

10 *match to match*: As opponent to opponent.

11 *carrion kites*: Kites who eat carrion.

12 *bonny beast*: Horse. Q1 expands the allusion as *the boniest gray that ere was bred in North*.

14 *chase*: Prey; game.

20 *bearing*: Deportment; behaviour.

21 *fast*: Firmly; unalterably.

23 *shown ignobly and in treason*: Displayed in an ignoble and treasonous cause.

26 *action*: Outcome of the action.

27 *lay*: Wager.
    Address thee: Prepare to fight.
    York kills Clifford: This event is based upon (1) Hall's report that Clifford was among those slain at St Albans; and (2) his report of Young Clifford's words to York's second son, the Earl of Rutland, before he stabbed him in 1461: 'By God's blood, thy father slew mine, and so will I do thee and all thy kin.'

28 *La fin couronne les œuvres*: The end crowns the works; the proverb 'The end crowns all'.

31 *confusion*: Destruction.
    on the rout: In disorderly flight.

32 *frames*: Creates.

34 *Whom angry heavens do make their minister*: Cf. Ezekiel 14:21.

34 *minister*: Agent.

35 *frozen*: With fear.

   part: Side; faction.

36 *Hot coals of vengeance*: Cf. Psalm 140:10.

37 *dedicate*: Devoted; committed.

39–40 *Hath not . . . valour*: Does not possess true courage, only the external signs of it owing to chance.

41 *premised*: Preordained.

   the last day: Doomsday.

43 *the general trumpet*: The trumpet which summons all men.

44 *Particularities*: Individual affairs.

45 *cease*: Put an end to.

   ordained: Destined; fated.

46 *lose*: Pass away; spend.

47 *silver livery*: White uniform (afforded by white hair).

   advisèd age: Wise and prudent old age.

48 *reverence*: Venerable old age.

   chair-days: Final days (appropriate to sitting in a chair).

51 *stony*: Without pity.

52 *No more will I their babes*: This looks ahead to Young Clifford's notorious murder of the young Duke of Rutland; see *Part III*, I.3.

52 *virginal*: Of young girls.

53 *as the dew to fire*: Water drops sprinkled on to fire were believed to have the effect of making it burn more fiercely.

54 *reclaims*: Subdues.

55 *to my flaming wrath be oil and flax*: A blending of two proverbs: 'Put not fire to flax' and 'To add oil to the fire'.

56–60 *Henceforth, I will not . . . my fame*: See note to 27.

57 *Meet I*: Should I encounter.

58 *gobbets*: Chunks of meat.

59 *wild*: Savage.

   Absyrtus: The younger brother of Medea. In order to escape with her lover Jason from her father's kingdom of Colchos, Medea murdered Absyrtus and strewed the pieces of his corpse behind her so that her father, by

picking them up, would be delayed in his pursuit of
her.

60 *seek out my fame*: Earn my reputation (of 'The Butcher';
see the note to the stage direction at V.1.122).

61 *new ruin of old Clifford's house*: His father's body.

62 *did Aeneas old Anchises bear*: In the *Aeneid* Aeneas
rescues his aged father from burning Troy by carrying
him on his back.

64 *bare*: Carried.

65 *Nothing*: Not at all.
heavy: (1) Weighty; (2) sorrowful.

67–9 *underneath . . . death*: See note to I.4.34. The reference
here is directly to I.4.65–8, where York reads the
prophecies copied down from the Spirit's pronounce-
ments by Roger Bolingbroke, who is thus made *famous*
because Somerset died in the way he foretold.

70 *hold*: Maintain.
still: Always.

71 *Excursions*: Sorties; sallies.

72–83 *Away, my lord! . . . be stopped*: Cf. Hall: 'the Duke of
York sent ever fresh men to succour the weary and put
new men in the places of the hurt persons, by which
only policy the King's army was profligate and
dispersed and all the chieftains of the field almost slain
and brought to confusion'.

73 *outrun the heavens*: Escape from the will of heaven.Cf.
Psalm 139:7–12.

74 *nor . . . nor*: Neither . . . nor.

76 *secure us*: Make ourselves safe.

77 *what*: Whatever means.
which: Who.

78 *bottom*: Lowest ebb.

79 *haply*: By chance.

80 *if not through*: If we do not fail to do so owing to.

81 *We shall to London get, where you are loved*: In Hall it
is York who has 'too many friends about the city of
London'. See note to V.3.24.

86 *uncurable discomfit*: Irrevocable discouragement.

87 *present parts*: Remaining forces.

89 *To see their day and them our fortune give*: To witness a
time when we shall gain a victory as they have now
and when they shall experience our bad luck.

V.3

The location is still St Albans.

2 *winter*: Aged.

3 *Agèd contusions and all brush of time*: The bruises of
old age and the assault of time.

4 *brow*: Peak; height.

5 *Repairs him with occasion*: Takes advantage of the opportunity to renew himself (by fighting).

6 *one foot*: Of ground.

8 *holp*: Helped.

9 *bestrid*: Stood over (while he was on the ground, in
order to protect him from the enemy).
  led him off: From the battlefield.

11 *still*: Always.

PENGUIN SHAKESPEARE

THE TWO GENTLEMEN OF VERONA
WILLIAM SHAKESPEARE

WWW.PENGUINSHAKESPEARE.COM

Leaving behind both home and beloved, a young man travels to Milan to meet his closest friend. Once there, however, he falls in love with his friend's new sweetheart and resolves to seduce her. Love-crazed and desperate, he is soon moved to commit cynical acts of betrayal. And comic scenes involving a servant and his dog enhance the play's exploration of how passion can prove more powerful than even the strongest loyalty owed to a friend.

This book includes a general introduction to Shakespeare's life and the Elizabethan theatre, a separate introduction to *The Two Gentlemen of Verona*, a chronology of his works, suggestions for further reading, an essay discussing performance options on both stage and screen, and a commentary.

Edited by Norman Sanders

With an introduction by Russell Jackson

General Editor: Stanley Wells

Penguin Shakespeare

HENRY IV, PART I
WILLIAM SHAKESPEARE

WWW.PENGUINSHAKESPEARE.COM

Prince Hal, the son of King Henry IV, spends his time in idle pleasure with dissolute friends, among them the roguish Sir John Falstaff. But when the kingdom is threatened by rebellious forces, the prince must abandon his reckless ways. Taking arms against a heroic enemy, he begins a great and compelling transformation – from irresponsible reprobate to noble ruler of men.

This book includes a general introduction to Shakespeare's life and the Elizabethan theatre, a separate introduction to *Henry IV, Part I*, a chronology of his works, suggestions for further reading, an essay discussing performance options on both stage and screen, and a commentary.

Edited by: Peter Davison

With an introduction by Charles Edelman

General Editor: Stanley Wells

Penguin Shakespeare

HENRY IV, PART II
WILLIAM SHAKESPEARE

WWW.PENGUINSHAKESPEARE.COM

Angered by the loss of his son in battle, the Earl of Northumberland supports another rebellion against King Henry IV, bringing the country to the brink of civil war. Sick and weary, the old King sends out his forces, including the unruly Sir John Falstaff, to meet the rebels. But as the conflict grows, he must also confront a more personal problem – how to make his reprobate son Prince Hal aware of the duties he must bear, as heir to the throne.

This book includes a general introduction to Shakespeare's life and the Elizabethan theatre, a separate introduction to *Henry IV, Part II*, a chronology of his works, suggestions for further reading, an essay discussing performance options on both stage and screen, and a commentary.

Edited by Peter Davison

With an introduction by Adrian Poole

General Editor: Stanley Wells

PENGUIN SHAKESPEARE

JULIUS CAESAR
WILLIAM SHAKESPEARE

WWW.PENGUINSHAKESPEARE.COM

When it seems that Julius Caesar may assume supreme power, a plot to destroy him is hatched by those determined to preserve the threatened republic. But the different motives of the conspirators soon become apparent when high principles clash with malice and political realism. As the nation plunges into bloody civil war, this taut drama explores the violent consequences of betrayal and murder.

This book includes a general introduction to Shakespeare's life and the Elizabethan theatre, a separate introduction to *Julius Caesar*, a chronology of his works, suggestions for further reading, an essay discussing performance options on both stage and screen, and a commentary.

Edited by Norman Sanders

With an introduction by Martin Wiggins

General editor: Stanley Wells

PENGUIN SHAKESPEARE

KING JOHN
WILLIAM SHAKESPEARE

WWW.PENGUINSHAKESPEARE.COM

Under the rule of King John, England is forced into war when the French challenge the legitimacy of John's claim to the throne and determine to install his nephew Arthur in his place. But political principles, hypocritically flaunted, are soon forgotten, as the French and English kings form an alliance based on cynical self-interest. And as the desire to cling to power dominates England's paranoid and weak-willed king, his country is threatened with disaster.

This book includes a general introduction to Shakespeare's life and the Elizabethan theatre, a separate introduction to *King John*, a chronology of his works, suggestions for further reading, an essay discussing performance options on both stage and screen, and a commentary.

Edited by R. L. Smallwood

With an introduction by Eugene Giddens

General Editor: Stanley Wells

PENGUIN SHAKESPEARE

RICHARD III
WILLIAM SHAKESPEARE

WWW.PENGUINSHAKESPEARE.COM

The bitter, deformed brother of the King is secretly plotting to seize the throne of England. Charming and duplicitous, powerfully eloquent and viciously cruel, he is prepared to go to any lengths to achieve his goal – and, in his skilful manipulation of events and people, Richard is a chilling incarnation of the lure of evil and the temptation of power.

This book includes a general introduction to Shakespeare's life and the Elizabethan theatre, a separate introduction to *Richard III*, a chronology of his works, suggestions for further reading, an essay discussing performance options on both stage and screen by Gillian Day, and a commentary.

Edited by E. A. J. Honigmann

With an introduction by Michael Taylor

General Editor: Stanley Wells

PENGUIN SHAKESPEARE

MACBETH
WILLIAM SHAKESPEARE

WWW.PENGUINSHAKESPEARE.COM

Promised a golden future as ruler of Scotland by three sinister witches, Macbeth murders the king to ensure his ambitions come true. But he soon learns the meaning of terror – killing once, he must kill again and again, and the dead return to haunt him. A story of war, witchcraft and bloodshed, *Macbeth* also depicts the relationship between husbands and wives, and the risks they are prepared to take to achieve their desires.

This book includes a general introduction to Shakespeare's life and the Elizabethan theatre, a separate introduction to *Macbeth*, a chronology of his works, suggestions for further reading, an essay discussing performance options on both stage and screen, and a commentary.

Edited by George Hunter

With an introduction by Carol Rutter

General Editor: Stanley Wells

PENGUIN SHAKESPEARE

KING LEAR
WILLIAM SHAKESPEARE

WWW.PENGUINSHAKESPEARE.COM

An ageing king makes a capricious decision to divide his realm among his three daughters according to the love they express for him. When the youngest daughter refuses to take part in this charade, she is banished, leaving the king dependent on her manipulative and untrustworthy sisters. In the scheming and recriminations that follow, not only does the king's own sanity crumble, but the stability of the realm itself is also threatened.

This book includes a general introduction to Shakespeare's life and the Elizabethan theatre, a separate introduction to *King Lear*, a chronology of his works, suggestions for further reading, an essay discussing performance options on both stage and screen, and a commentary.

Edited by George Hunter

With an introduction by Kiernan Ryan

General Editor: Stanley Wells

Read more in Penguin

PENGUIN SHAKESPEARE